Riding the Line

Emma Lucy is a romance author based in London who loves writing books that will make you swoon, blush, and hopefully learn to believe in yourself a little more. When she's not writing, she's usually reading, listening to whatever new country music artist she's obsessed with, or trying to convince her boyfriend to go to a bookstore with her.

Live, Ranch, Love was Emma's debut novel.

You can find her on Instagram and TikTok at @emmalucyauthor.

EMMA LUCY

A WILLOW RIDGE NOVEL

Riding the Line

HarperCollins*Publishers*

HarperCollins*Publishers* Ltd
1 London Bridge Street,
London SE1 9GF

www.harpercollins.co.uk

HarperCollins*Publishers*
Macken House, 39/40 Mayor Street Upper
Dublin 1, D01 C9W8, Ireland

First published by HarperCollins*Publishers* Ltd 2025
1

A catalogue record for this book is available from the British Library.

ISBN: 978-0-00-875751-9 (PBO)

This novel is entirely a work of fiction.
The names, characters and incidents portrayed in it are
the work of the author's imagination. Any resemblance to
actual persons, living or dead, events or localities is
entirely coincidental.

Set in Sabon LT Std by HarperCollins*Publishers* India

Printed and bound in the UK using 100%
Renewable Electricity by CPI Group (UK) Ltd

To those struggling to find their strength, remember that even the gentle and the quiet can still move mountains. I believe in you.

And to Martin – I miss you every day. I hope you're proud of me.

Prologue

Cherry

Eight Years Ago

The first things I hear when I wake up are the skidding of tyres, the abrupt cut of an engine, and the distant rumble of his voice.

'What happened to her?'

The words filter through the fading ringing in my ears and the throbbing in my head. Frantic footsteps rush closer, vibrating through the ground that presses into my cheek.

'I don't know—'

'Is she hurt?'

Inch by inch, the nerves in my body awaken, clusters of pain prickling to life. Tingling flows through my side, blooming across my chest and neck. The sun's heat beats down on me, my skin burning under its scrutiny. Sweat pools beneath the fabric of my clothes.

A futile attempt to open my eyes barely makes my lashes flutter.

'She just fell and then started having some sort of fit. She's only just stopped—'

'Here.' Warmth floods my side, the heat of a body suddenly hovering next to me.

Leather scuffles and squeaks, heavy breathing underlying it, before a large hand cradles my head with such care, as if I'm made of glass. He lifts my cheek, then slides something beneath it, and when he lowers me back down, there's something cold and leather-like providing me comfort.

'Did you call an ambulance?'

'No, I—'

That's Jodie's voice – my riding instructor. I recognise it now.

I wonder where the horses are.

'Just do it. Now.'

Nothing comes out when I try to speak. So, I settle for a brief, croaky moan to signal that I'm at least alive and somewhat conscious. That begs for someone to reassure me.

'It's okay, I'm here.' Fingers lightly stroke along my hair as my jaw starts to tremble. A stinging pressure builds behind my eyes. 'It's all gonna be okay.'

Every time I hear his familiar voice, I'm pulled closer to awareness, limbs lightening. Each word is a flashing beacon of hope amongst the dark storm, guiding me back to shelter. Because I know he'd do anything to get me back to my family safely.

A sob crawls up my throat, but withers there. The cool

streak of one escaped tear slides down my cheek, only to be wiped away by the soft pad of a thumb.

'Duke,' I finally manage to whisper, my fingers stretching out to reach him. The warmth of his presence calls me – *urges* me to try to move. When I finally open my eyes, the first things I see are drawings – no, tattoos – roses and trees and barbed wire banded around thick, dark-skinned arms. My heavy eyes trail up each one until I reach his face, deep umber eyes watching over me, his broad frame clothed in his biker leathers. Golden sunlight rains down and lines his silhouette like he's a guardian angel.

I drive my hand into the dirt, trying to push myself up but barely manage to shakily lift myself more than a few inches before Duke's arms come under mine, holding me when my body finally gives up. The movement sends pain sparking through my shoulder, setting it ablaze. I cry out from the fire burning in the joint.

'Woah, don't push yourself, Cherry,' Duke cautions me. He attempts to haul me up to a sitting position, but it just makes it worse.

'My . . . shoulder,' I rasp out, struggling through each breath.

Duke curses, then swiftly manoeuvres us around until he's cradling me and I'm leaning back against his chest. Relief sweeps through me as he takes my weight, his hold on me thorough yet gentle. Once I've fully sunk back into him, his fingers stroking my hair again rhythmically, I let the sob blocking my throat pour out and whimper, 'I wanna go home.'

'I know, I'm gonna get you home soon, I promise.' Duke rocks me softly. 'I've got you, Baby Hensley.'

1

Cherry

Present Day

I never thought something as insignificant and small as a drawing on a napkin could make me smile so much. I can't stop the silly grin that spreads through my cheeks as I admire the rough sketch of me. Black pen strokes follow the curve of my body and my flowing hair as I lean across the table, while the neon light from the sign hanging above the glass shelves of liquor behind me casts a sultry red glow over the drawing. I imagine Duke as he was sketching me – dark eyes roving over every inch of my body, taking note of each line and contour of my figure under the red mood lighting, committing them to memory.

But deep down, I know it's just a product of bartender boredom. He's always scribbling on napkins, even if he doesn't let me see what sketch has distracted him. A girl can only dream that she's so special—

'Earth to Cherry!' Montana – my best friend – shouts, ripping me from my childish daydream.

My attention whips up over the bar to where she's standing amongst the mismatched wooden tables, waving at me with a cloth in her hand. Levi – the other bartender who's also helping us close up Duke's bar tonight – gives me a quick, closed-lip smile from where he's been wiping down the red leather seats in the booths.

'Sorry.' I quickly fold up the napkin and pocket it in my jeans. As I round the dark wooden bar, I swipe up the cloth I was *supposed* to be using and start wiping down the top. 'What's up?'

'It's your turn, girl,' Montana relays, her eyes brightening with anticipation. 'Truth or dare?'

Right, we're still playing this game – Montana's attempt to make closing time feel a little less of a drag tonight. It's a stark difference to the *closing argument* game I usually play with our boss, Duke, to pass the time. I make a mental note that it's my turn to pick the next debate for Monday night.

I sigh, 'Truth.'

Montana and Levi both groan in response, before Montana skips up to the bar, pinning me with her critical stare. I know exactly what's coming when she raises her brows – the exact same look she usually gives me before convincing me to come out to whatever house party or club I'd decided against going to. The same look she's been giving me since we became best friends on the first day of high school.

'Oh, come on, Cherry. You *always* pick truth – it's

getting boring now. There's only so many times I can hear about the *two* guys you've slept with.'

'Hey, that's one more than last year. It's an improvement.' I attempt to deter her with an innocent smile. Montana doesn't need to know that said encounter was a bit too quick and awkward, and just meant I ended up using my vibrator when I got home to finish myself off.

She doesn't budge, just folds her arms.

I can't help but smile at her strong will. The same strong will that had her standing by my side throughout high school, even as my seizures and constant doctor's appointments had me missing too many classes and other friends withdrew, not willing to wait up for me. Even miles apart when I'm at college studying interior design, that friendship holds, and once I'm back working at the bar during school breaks, we pick it right up where we left off.

'Besides, maybe I don't want to make a fool out of myself, like some people.' I wave my hand down her front to emphasise the stain on her dress as a result of Levi daring her to chug a drink in five seconds.

Montana grins, as if somehow proud of the mess. She leans an elbow against the bar to blink her big chestnut eyes at me. 'Okay, but *you're* the one who's been going on and on since you've been back home about wanting to do more *crazy* things before you graduate. I didn't make that bucket list to help you step out of your comfort zone for no reason, girl.'

I chew on my lip, because that bucket list is still sitting in my bag, waiting for me to stop ignoring it and start ticking things off – like getting tattoos together.

Montana settles a hand on my shoulder. 'Choosing truth all the time ain't gonna make you feel more confident, Cherry. I'm just trying to help.'

Neither is always choosing dare, necessarily. It's not my fault that seven minutes in heaven intensified during my teen years and no longer meant giggling awkwardly in a closet together before returning to your friends blushing. Instead, you're running out of the bathroom at your friends' party at seventeen, cheeks flaming, because you froze when one of the guys from the football team tried to stick his tongue in your mouth. And I'd *just* gotten over the humiliation of halting the final football game of the season after my brain decided that would be a great time to have a seizure in front of the whole high school and their families.

Though, I suppose had I been allowed to go to more parties and had those awkward encounters growing up, I might not have freaked out so much when I got dared to make out with Jonny Miller at Montana's party . . . Nor would I have probably knocked over that tray of drinks last summer when one of my friend Sawyer's bull-riding associates tried hitting on me. I don't know if it was his wicked smile or the fact he called me darlin' – either way my limbs were stunned and the drinks went flying. It was that or word vomit and shouting any sports facts I can think of, which is the usual extent of my flirting abilities.

I'm not like Montana, with overflowing confidence and sass built from years of dating through high school. My two older brothers, Wyatt and Hunter, made sure of that too, letting most of the boys at high school know that I was off limits unless they wanted to chance their wrath too. Or perhaps it's because the only guy I've ever found myself wanting basically treats me like a little sister, and makes all other guys seem . . . bland.

Whoever said unrequited feelings were a bitch, hit the nail on the head.

But I'm working on it. And Montana knows my awkwardness around the opposite sex is part of the reason I'm so intent on building my confidence this year before I graduate and get a job at an interior design firm. I want to be able to utter more than a single sentence when I look at a man and have more experiences than the years spent at home fearing my epilepsy. So I'm not forever destined to be the toned-down version of me I relegated myself to as a teen.

It's why I asked her to help make that bucket list.

'Fine!' I shake my head, laughing, and throw the cloth down. Montana grins wildly, clearly satisfied with how easily she's convinced me. 'I pick dare. Do your worst.'

She giggles and pretends to stroke her invisible beard. Her face crumples in deliberation before zapping to light with what I know is going to be the cause of terrible regret for me.

'Ooh, I've got it!' She beams, the fairy lights along the rafters in the bar twinkling in her eager eyes. 'Give Levi a lap dance.'

My eyes immediately snap over to Levi, who freezes midway through rearranging some chairs. His face pales, but I doubt his heart is beating as fast as mine – like hooves pounding against dirt. Levi shoves the chair he's holding under the table. 'Montana, that's just weird. You can't make Cherry do that.'

Montana pouts, moaning, 'You're no fun, Levi!'

He holds up his hands. 'Just trying to be respectful.'

In all honesty, he probably wouldn't be the worst guy to give a lap dance to – he's reasonably attractive, with golden skin and copper hair, and is a good few inches taller than me, which as a girl of five-foot-nine isn't always the easiest to find. But I've never seen him as anything more than a co-worker, and I'd rather not be so embarrassed I can't ever work the same shift as him again.

'Fine,' Montana huffs, twirling her brunette hair in contemplation, before a feline smirk settles on her face. 'You can give *me* a lap dance instead.'

Levi snorts and I shoot him a look. 'Not going to protest against that one, huh?'

He shrugs, failing to hide the smug grin dancing on his lips. 'Wouldn't be the worst thing to watch.'

'Exactly!' Montana squeals and grabs my hands, dragging me over to one of the tables.

As we approach, Levi swivels out a chair, gesturing for us both. I offer him a saccharine smile. Montana plonks herself in the chair, letting go of my hands as she says, 'Choose a good song, something sexy.'

This really was not how I expected my night to go.

I gulp down a calming breath before whipping out my phone from my pocket, the napkin accidentally coming with it. Even though I know it means nothing, I lie to myself that Duke must think I'm captivating enough to ignore his work for, that I'm so distracting he just had to stop and draw me.

Like I'm his muse.

As opposed to just his best friend's little sister.

I shove the drawing back in my pocket and scroll through the playlist I usually save for when I'm alone in bed, eventually choosing 'Worst Way' by Riley Green.

Montana's face lights up when the song starts. 'Make me proud.'

I try to ignore the fact that Levi's watching as I school my features into something more serious, keeping my eyes on Montana. When the lyrics start, I slowly walk towards her, trailing my fingers along her shoulders and neck as I circle the chair.

I've danced with Montana at parties before, our hands roaming each other's bodies, both tipsy and lost in the music, not caring about who was watching. This doesn't have to be any different. I close my eyes and let my mind drift off into the beat of the music, dropping into that primal part of me that wants to feel the heat of another pressed against me.

When I'm back at her front, I bend over, showing off my ass, which Montana responds to with a loud cheer. Flipping my hair over one shoulder, I bring myself back up to a stand, purposefully dragging out the movement for an achingly long time. She pats me on the ass with a giggle and I fail to suppress my smile as I pivot.

Settling my arms over her shoulders, I straddle her lap. Her warmth seeps into me and I try to imagine I'm a few drinks in, letting myself grind against her in time with the music. My chest presses against hers and her hot breath flows across my skin as she laughs. I'm half expecting her to pull out some dollars and shove them down my top with the way she seems to be enjoying it so much. My body loosens even more, and before I know it, I'm flipping around again, ass still in her lap as I lean over, continuing to roll my hips against her.

I'm so lost in the way the music waves through me, dropping deeper into the euphoria of it, almost forgetting that we're in the middle of an empty bar.

I must miss the sound of the locks going and the door swinging open, because when I flick my hair back up, biting my lip, I suddenly lock eyes with the man standing in the doorway.

My boss.

My brother's best friend.

Duke Bennett.

2

Duke

The last thing I need in my life is the knowledge of what Cherry Hensley looks like giving a lap dance. Yet, here I am, frozen in the doorway to my bar as I watch her grind her ass against Montana and then flick her long, silky black hair up as she lifts her gaze to mine.

God, she's even biting her lip.

I don't need to know what that looks like either. She's Wyatt's sister, for God's sake.

Dark eyes latch onto me, the ecstasy and wildness in them immediately extinguishing, replaced with widening alarm. It takes everything to rip my stare from her and glance at Levi and Montana, both wide-eyed and silent, nobody moving an inch.

Including me.

I should say something – I'm the boss here. I should be annoyed that they're playing games as opposed to cleaning up and closing the bar. I just need to remove myself from the situation quickly and pretend this never happened, so I don't give myself enough time to let what I've just seen Cherry doing brand itself on my memory. To avoid going down the road I work so well to avoid.

I clear my throat and throw out, 'It's a bar, not a strip club, kids.' Then, I half-run straight towards my office at the back of the bar, purposefully not looking behind as I add on, 'Put the chairs back and go home, I'll finish up and close.'

I shut my office door once inside, flick on the light, and lean against my desk, my lungs emptying on a sigh.

It's a bar, not a strip club, kids. Jesus, I sound like an old man, as opposed to the twenty-seven-year-old I am.

I run a hand down my face as I wait for them to leave. I really did *not* need this tonight. Behind the door, I hear Cherry squeal with humiliation at the other two. God, I hope she doesn't hate me now, thinking I'm some mean old boss sending them home.

The sounds of chairs scraping, frantic footsteps, and doors swinging echo as they all grab their stuff from the staff room. It's not until I hear the back door closing and the bar empty of hushed voices that I start my search through the piles of random crap on my desk for my laptop which I'd accidentally left in my office – the reason I popped down here tonight from my apartment above the bar. I couldn't sleep knowing I hadn't replied to that email yet. What it could mean for me and my life here.

Though, I doubt I'll be getting any sleep at all now I'm going to have Cherry Hensley playing through my head. *Twerking*.

No – I'm *not* going to think about that.

Grabbing my laptop from my desk, I walk back out into

the bar, only to stop short at the sight of Cherry, bag on her shoulder, leaning against one of the tables. The fairy lights and a couple of still-lit candles on the tables reflect off her black hair, making it look like the starry sky. A teasing slither of tan skin separates the faded jeans hugging her hips and long, slender legs from her tight black tank top.

She nibbles one of her nails, staring at the ground, until she hears me approach and swiftly whips her head up. Her cherry-red lips press together, brows dropping. Silence hovers between us for a few beats. Just like it always does when we first see each other.

'Everything alright, Baby Hensley?' I eventually ask, moving myself to behind the bar to check everything is tidied up, and putting a physical barrier between us.

The flutter of her lashes almost conceals her quick eye roll at the nickname – the same one I've teased her with since she was a kid. The one that reminds me who she is – the baby of the Hensley clan. Memories of Wyatt and me staring down any man that has had the audacity to check her out since she started working at the bar filter into my mind.

'I'm sorry,' she says, teeth tugging on her bottom lip again.

I shrug. 'Don't be, it's cool.'

'I don't normally do things like that, though.' Cherry pushes off the table and shuffles towards the bar, forcing me backwards against the counter.

When she reaches the bar, she swings her bag up onto it and—

The bag goes toppling off, plummeting to the ground in front of me, its contents spilling across the floor. Her phone and purse hit my feet as a notebook and some paper also scatter out.

Cherry curses and rushes around the bar to join me as I drop to the floor to shove everything back in her bag. I assume the paper fell out of her notebook, so I go to file it back inside when I catch the title sprawled across the top, each word a different colour: *Montana's Super-Hot and Crazy Bucket List for Cherry.*

Oh, this looks like some top-tier material to tease her for.

'What the hell is this?' I snort, coming to a stand.

'Oh my God, no!' Cherry lunges towards me to grab the paper, but I lift it up out of her reach. Her hands scramble against me, trying to snatch the paper, forcing me to hold her back with my arm, laughing. She begs, 'Duke, no, please!'

Her nails graze my bicep and forearm as she continues to battle against me, whining. I ignore the slight rush of pleasure that courses through me. It's moments like these when I have to drop into the familiar role of her older brother's friend who enjoys annoying her, as if she was my own little sister.

So that I'm not crossing any lines.

So that I don't end up losing anyone else.

When Cherry wails again, I twist around to block her and hold the paper above my head to start reading through, picking out random ones on the list. 'Learn to roller-skate, get a tattoo, wild swim at night.'

Her hands grapple against my shoulder, trying to tug me around. Her chest presses against me, curves melting against my body. 'Duke, I'm begging you—'

'Break into somewhere,' I wheeze out, unable to imagine Cherry doing anything criminal ever. This is the best thing I've ever read. I wish I could show Wyatt and the others. 'Go speed dating, have a firework kiss, have a guy give me an org—'

The rest of the word comes out strangled.

A sharp gasp sounds behind me and Cherry freezes. I think I can actually *feel* her cringing. I let myself take one more glance down the paper and immediately regret it when I see what follows:

Have a one night stand
Have sex in a car
Have sex in a pool
Have sex in the shower
Have sex in a hot tub
Have sex in a public place
Have sex in a restroom

And I was worried about not being able to get her dancing on Montana out of my head . . . Now, that seems trivial.

Trying to force the memory of what I've just read out of my head, I gently fold the paper up and turn to Cherry. Her brows draw in, dark eyes shining wildly as she watches me turn. She worries her lip again, the dark red so stark against her white teeth. Hesitantly, she takes the paper from my hand as I pass it over. Her fingers only faintly brush mine yet still leave a tingling sensation in their wake.

'Please don't judge me,' Cherry begs.

I rub the back of my neck. 'What? I wouldn't—'

'Um, yes you would!' she barks out in a laugh, slapping me on my upper arm. There's the Cherry I know. 'You and the guys always make fun of me. I put my hair in space buns one time in high school and you all called me Princess Leia for weeks!'

Her sweet giggle instantly goads my own laugh out.

I hold up my hands. 'Okay, you got me there . . . I'm, um, guessing tonight's behaviour has something to do with that?' I nod towards the list she's now stuffing into her back pocket.

'Maybe,' Cherry groans, leaning back against the counter beside me. I shuffle a few inches away. The neon lights give her skin a scarlet glow, the sensuous kind that I'd love to capture with my paints, as opposed to the pen and napkins I usually have to revert to. Speaking of, I wonder what happened to the one I left on the bar earlier...

Her chest deflates on a sigh. 'I . . . I asked Montana to make me a bucket list of things to do before I graduate. To try and make me feel a bit more confident. And that I haven't wasted the best years of my life.'

'*Best* years of your life?' I repeat, crossing my arms. 'Cherry, you're so young. You've got your whole life ahead of you.' One that I'll eventually no longer be a part of.

'Yeah.' Cherry smiles softly, though it barely reaches her cheeks. 'But that's what they say about college. Because after that, you have to be a serious adult and don't have time for as much. I've got one year left before that's my fate and I just . . . I feel like I haven't done any big, cool things yet, you know?'

I think back to summer nights at rodeos and fairs when Cherry would always have to leave before the rest of our group, fear of a seizure from tiredness hanging over her. Or that time when I came back to the Hensleys' house to stay with Wyatt after one of Sawyer's bull-riding competitions, only to find Cherry on the couch in the dark with her prom dress beside her, the seizure she'd had only a couple of days before already decided to be too serious to risk junior prom for her. Everyone had thought almost a year with no seizures meant things were finally looking up for her; if anything, it only made her parents monitor her harder.

'Eh, I think *big, cool things* are a little overrated,' I suggest.

'What?' Cherry's hair tumbles over her shoulders as she shakes her head. 'But that's what everyone always says on their death bed – that they wish they'd done more big, exciting things with their life. That they'd lived it to its fullest.'

'Oh yeah? Did you interview every person who's ever died?' I jest, receiving an expected eye roll in return.

But if anyone knows about needing to make the most of life because it could get cut short at any moment, it's me. When you've spent enough days at the hospital watching your mom's health deteriorate, that reminder sticks with you. And now I have another reason to lie awake in bed tonight, heavy memories suddenly clambering to the surface of my mind. Great.

I shrug, trying to push the thoughts away. 'I don't know, I kind of think life is about the slower, smaller moments. The little things that are easy to pass over but actually add together to make life worthwhile. That's what my grandfather said to me.'

That he wished he'd focused more on the little moments with my mom before she got cancer. Savoured them, as opposed to taking them for granted. Like I try to do whenever I'm with my friends. Including Cherry – especially since Wyatt told me she's got her heart set on finding a job anywhere other than Willow Ridge. It's also why I love working at the bar. Even if I'm not always drinking with the rest of our group, they're still here, with me.

'Okay . . .' Cherry's eyes ignite. Unexpectedly, she pulls herself up onto the bar, letting her long legs swing beneath her. 'I have my topic for our closing argument – life should be about doing as many big, crazy things as possible. For or against?'

'It's almost two in the morning, Cherry,' I groan, rubbing a hand across my face, even though I did miss doing our usual closing time game tonight. 'And *you* still need to drive home.'

I know she's a night owl like me – one of the only reasons the Hensleys don't mind her doing the odd late shift considering her epilepsy – but even I'd like to be in bed soon.

Cherry just presses me with her twinkling stare. If I ever got the privilege of painting her, she'd be a canvas of deep reds and midnight blacks, topped with bright white for all the little moments of light she brings to the world.

'For or against, Duke Bennett?'

Still, there's no point in me trying to fight her, I'll always give her what she wants. 'Fine,' I sigh. 'Against.'

'Perfect.' She grins, biting down on those cherry-red lips again. 'I go first, then. I think you need to do big, meaningful things that push you outside of your comfort zone so that you can feel confident.'

'You've been spending too much time with Rory,' I tease, alluding to Wyatt's wellness influencer girlfriend who he runs a ranch retreat with.

Cherry sneers and I revel in the reaction.

'I know what you're saying, and I do agree, but . . . I think our perceptions of what is fun and meaningful has been warped, that the best things in life are those that look good to other people, or on social media, when your life is more than a few photos or stories. It's thousands of individual days, made up of little moments, and it's not appreciating those that makes life dull and uninspiring. People are so eager to go after bigger and better, but . . . what if you have everything you need right now with you?'

That last bit being more for me than anything else. To convince myself not to give in to that offer from my friend on the new bar. Because it would be giving up too much in Willow Ridge, where I'm already happy. Where all my friends are family are, where they need me – I mean, who's going to lend Wyatt an extra hand on the ranch when cattle needs moving, or fences need fixing? He didn't welcome a grief-stricken ten-year-old me into his family just to be cast aside because an opportunity for a bit more cash came up.

'And you think *I've* been spending too much time with Rory? That sounds like you read it straight from one of her Instagram posts.' Cherry giggles. 'I don't get it, though, what little moments would someone on their deathbed think back to?'

I pick up my laptop that I'd rested on the counter, aware that I could easily stay here for hours with her but let out a fake yawn to signal otherwise. 'Plenty of things – like being able to watch the sunset while having a drink with your friends. Like a rainy afternoon inside painting. Like the sense of freedom you get riding down the backroads on your motorcycle, the wind whipping against your—'

'Ooh!' Cherry jumps down from the bar, landing inches away from me. I have nowhere to run. Her glistening eyes peer up at me with too much hope. 'Ride a motorcycle is on my bucket list.'

'No way,' I declare.

'What do you mean, *no way*?' She inches closer, as if she knows how hard I find it to say no to her.

I swallow before I can reply. 'I'm not letting you ride my bike. I know what that brain of yours is thinking.'

'What if I just sat on the back?'

Can't say it wouldn't be the worst thing in the world, having her arms wrapped around me, holding tight—

I shake my head to rid me of the thought. 'Still no way.'

'Why not?' She pouts.

I bring the laptop between us, making her back up a step. Distance is important.

'Because, Cherry, bikes are dangerous and if anything happened to you, we both know that I'd have to suffer the terrifying wrath of Wyatt. Being his best friend doesn't make a difference when it comes to you.'

A truth that applies to more than just this hypothetical

situation. One I have to remind myself every time Cherry comes back to work for me during college breaks. I've lost enough people to know that sometimes it's better to not rock the boat. Not when the very people at risk are the ones that took you in when life became too stormy. The ones who saved up for an extra space on holidays so you didn't have to miss out when your grandparents didn't have the capacity to provide you with such. The ones who picked you up from school when you got ill and your grandparents were busy working.

At that, the light in her eyes dims, but then she angles her head, and a hint of mischief reappears. 'Wyatt doesn't have to know. We could . . . keep it a secret?'

I'm certain my gulp is audible.

She might just be talking about a motorcycle ride, but the words apply to too many things. If I was a fool, I'd let myself read into the suggestive cadence of her voice. But, to my utmost disappointment, I'm anything but.

I sigh and slip away from Cherry, already heading towards the door. 'I'm never lying to my best friend and you're never getting on my bike. Now, come on, it's time to go home.'

3

Cherry

I hold my phone between my ear and shoulder as I stir my coffee, listening to Montana's endless apologies for bailing on me today. The day we were supposed to kickstart my bucket list for the summer with probably one of the most nerve-racking items – aside from the chaotic second half filled with sexual experiences that I've been trying to forget Duke saw last Friday.

As if him catching me giving Montana a lap dance wasn't embarrassing enough. He looked downright appalled at *that* half of the list.

Either way, today was going to be a great distraction from that humiliation – Montana and I were supposed to get tattoos.

'I just couldn't say no, Cherry,' Montana continues explaining, and even though I can't see her, I bet she's blinking her big doe eyes at the phone. 'Austin turned up out of the blue, with the whole day already planned, and activities booked and paid for, bless him.'

I wish I could be annoyed at her, but this might be the first time Montana's actually found a decent guy who wants her beyond her looks. This Austin guy seems to adore her and the last thing I want is for her to get hurt again. So, if that means allowing her to flake on me today, then I guess I'll just have to suck it up.

I'm sure we'll reschedule the tattoos soon, anyway. I know I could go by myself, bite the bullet and ride it solo. But if I was brave enough to do that, I probably wouldn't need this silly bucket list at all.

'Honestly, it's fine. Don't worry about it,' I say, knowing it's hard to expect anyone else to understand why this list is so important. I sip my coffee quickly, its warmth dissipating through me. 'It'll give me more time to think about what tattoo I'm gonna get, anyway.'

'Okay, as long as you're sure. You're the best.' She makes a kissing noise through the phone.

'I know,' I joke. 'Have a great day together.'

'Thanks, girl. Oh! You're still okay to cover my shift tomorrow, right?'

'Yeah, all good. Just let Duke know.'

'Will do. Have I told you how much I love you?'

'Not enough,' I jest, hearing her giggle in response. 'Now, go get ready for your hot date, and voice note me all about it later.'

'Thank you! Talk later, bye!'

I put my phone down with a sigh, leaning back against the counter to bask in the unfiltered country sunshine pouring through the windows this morning as I reassess my plans for the day. I should probably get to updating my interior design portfolio if I want to start applying for jobs and land myself a position at an interior design firm in the city where I can help to make people's spaces as supportive to their lives and dreams as possible. When you spend enough time in the same rooms, lying on the couch or in bed because you're recovering from a seizure or struck down by bad cramps like I did growing up, you come to realise the influence interior design has on you – how the presence of bright paintings can lift your mood when its sunk to its lowest after a month of multiple seizures when you're fourteen, how less clutter can ease your already overwhelmed mind, how a rose-pink wall can provide the calming warmth and comfort you need. A passion and personal mission that became the one silver lining to many of those days as a teenager.

I've still got a bunch of photos from renovating Wyatt and Rory's ranch retreat, Sunset Ranch, last year that need editing, as well as some possible designs to turn one of their old barns into a wedding venue should they ever be interested in that. Which, I really hope they are because there are plenty of unused buildings on that ranch, and my mind goes wild with renovation ideas whenever it finds a place in need of some care.

Plus, I might as well make the most of this spare time before my period is due in the next day or so, since that means the rest of the week will be a write-off anyway.

Just as I go to close my eyes and relish the quiet warmth of the moment, my mom walks into the kitchen, humming to herself. Her grin lights up when she sees me. 'Morning, sweetheart.'

'Morning,' I respond, raising my mug with a smile.

'Was that Montana you were on the phone to? Where

are you two off to today?' Mom asks, filtering through the rack of jackets by the front door until she finds her bag.

I roll my lips together. I'd rather not start my day with a lecture about how pain can trigger seizures, even if I've already researched it plenty to make sure there's no scientific proof that a tattoo can cause such. So, instead, I answer, 'Um, nowhere anymore. She's busy now.'

Mom brings her bag to the table to rifle through it, not looking up as she asks, 'What were you going to do? Some shopping? I can always come into town with you before my shift starts if you still want to go. Maggie said your meds were in the pharmacy, so we could pick them up.' She looks up once to perk an accusatory brow at me. 'Not leave them for weeks like last time you were back home. Even she said she hopes you're better at remembering to take them at college.'

I close my eyes for a moment, letting a long breath filter from my nose.

Growing up in a place like Willow Ridge means *everyone* knows your business and looks out for you, not just your family. Which is great when you're younger, but not so much when they still act like you're that thirteen year old that had a seizure while horse-riding *eight* years ago. Even if I know everyone's worrying is only a symptom of how much they care about me, it's hard not to feel like a kid when I'm back home. Like I can't take care of myself.

I blow another gentle breath out and force a smile. 'Uh, no it's all good, we weren't going shopping, but thanks anyway, Mom. I'll grab my meds later, once I've done some work on my portfolio for college.'

'Oh, what were your plans, then?' Mom still questions, clearly not sensing my tone, and rummaging through her bag, then pulls out her wallet with an *aha!*

The coffee hasn't given me enough of a buzz yet for my brain to work quick enough.

'Cherry?'

Anyone would laugh – here I am complaining about my family's constant worrying making me feel like a child, when I'm too afraid to tell my parents about a tiny tattoo . . . Not quite the assured version of myself I'm striving for. Maybe this could be a good baby step.

Swallowing, I admit, 'We were going to get tattoos.'

My mom drops her purse back into her bag. 'Oh.'

And with perfect timing, my dad waltzes through the front door, already back from an early morning working on Lucky Star Ranch – Sawyer's family ranch. He takes off his hat and wipes his sweaty forehead with the back of his hand before giving my mom a kiss on the cheek in greeting. 'Mornin'. How are we?'

'Cherry's going to get a tattoo,' is how my mom decides to respond, the words coming out a little exasperated. I, personally, was thinking *we're great, thanks*, would've been a more appropriate response, but apparently Mom's ready to dive straight into it.

I settle my mug down and brace myself for the onslaught of questions.

'Is it safe?' Dad starts, eyebrows pulling together, the wrinkles on his weathered forehead deepening. 'We've been so careful with your epilepsy recently, Cherry. No seizures in two years is a record – do we really want to risk that now? For a little tattoo?'

'Dad, it's fine. There's no links between tattoos and seizures whatsoever.'

'Remember what happened last time we thought your seizures were getting better – a whole year without one, then one late night at your friend's birthday and you missed your junior prom.'

One night of staying up gossiping a little too late and saying no to a sip from the bottle of wine Willa Cole stole from her parents had my whole junior year without seizures coming to a crashing end, only a few days before junior prom. And if having a seizure in Willa's kitchen wasn't humiliating enough, then soiling myself during said fit in front of too many popular girls in my year who made sure everyone knew about such afterwards was the cherry on top.

Because I stupidly thought for a second that my life wouldn't forever be ruled by my epilepsy. That I might be able to live a completely normal life like all the other girls in my year. Instead, I got too cocky, and life proved me wrong. Just like it does every time I think my epilepsy's getting better. I realised then, sitting in the dark in my living room on the night of my junior prom, dress beside me because my parents decided it would be better for my health to stay at home, watching videos of the night on my friends' social media knowing I'd never be making the same memories as them, that my epilepsy would always be with me.

And at sixteen years old that felt like the end of the world, but now I can't help but think, if a whole year of being careful still wasn't enough to stop a seizure, is it really worth holding myself back so much? Is it really worth not going through the rite of passage of getting a tattoo I'll probably regret in a few years' time when something far less threatening could trigger another seizure probably just as easily?

My dad runs his fingers across his thick moustache with a 'hmm', tanned face creasing even more. 'Maybe we should call Dr Wells and ask. Better to wait for his thoughts before we decide.'

Because apparently my life is a group decision. My jaw hangs open, but I don't get a chance to reply.

'Pain and stress can be triggers, sweetheart. You know that well enough from your cramps – I'm certain they were the reason you had your last one since they'd gotten so much worse,' my mom reminds me, the memory of waking up on the ground surrounded by my parents' friends and colleagues after a fit at a summer barbecue two years ago sadly not hazy enough yet. Mom doesn't give me an opportunity to respond before she adds on with finality, 'I'll speak to some of the doctors at work too, check what they think before we move forward with anything. We can't be certain how you'll react since you've never had one before. It could be more painful than you think.'

My shoulders curve over, defeat starting to wash over me. 'It's fine. I've looked into it and—'

Deep, rumbling laughter echoes outside the front door seconds before it opens again, and my older brother, Wyatt, walks in with Duke in tow. I'm instantly aware of the fact that I'm currently dressed in an old, oversized T-shirt with some pyjama shorts that are fraying at the hem of one of the legs, while my long hair is wrapped up into the messiest of messy buns on top of my head. At least now I'm at college he only really sees me at the bar when I'm relatively put together, as opposed to looking like a gangly gremlin that's just crawled out of bed. Which feels even more prominent when Duke looks the way he does right now.

He's clearly been helping Wyatt out at Sunset Ranch like he sometimes does before opening the bar for lunch, as he's sporting dusty Wranglers that hug his thick thighs in all the right places, and a black T-shirt, showing off all the tattoos covering his dark skin. Plus, it's one of the rare occasions when he wears a cowboy hat, and man, does it look good on him – the way the dark felt brings out the deep brown of his eyes.

Not that I really care what he looks like, but . . . well, he's an attractive man. Anyone would notice that.

Sure, Cherry. You're convincing no one.

'Everything alright?' Wyatt asks, eyes darting between my parents and me as he heads into the kitchen and fetches a couple of glasses from a cupboard. Duke follows quietly behind him, offering me a tight-lipped smile before opening the fridge and grabbing the carton of juice, as if he's just another Hensley brother. Which he might as well be given how often he's around.

I shuffle behind one of the kitchen chairs to try to hide my slobby attire and rub the back of my neck as I smile quickly back. The urge to rip my hair out of its messy bun is incredibly strong right now.

'Cherry wants to get a tattoo,' Dad declares, folding his arms, as if by saying *wants to* means it's not definitely going to happen.

31

'Is that safe with your epilepsy? You know pain can be a trigger if it makes you too stressed. What's it been now? Two years since your last seizure. I wouldn't risk that, Cherry.' Wyatt repeats my dad's earlier comments as he takes the juice from Duke and pours them both a drink, making me roll my eyes. They accidentally land on Duke whose brows are drawn in as he watches me. I quickly blink away.

First the lap dancing, then the bucket list, and now he's about to witness me probably be forbidden from getting a tattoo like I'm some rebellious seventeen year old, all while I'm in my pyjamas. Can it really get any worse?

'Apparently so,' Mom responds, and it takes me a second to realise she wasn't responding to my thoughts.

'Hmm.' Wyatt fishes his phone from his pocket and types something into it, the screen lighting up his face as he scrolls through. Everyone watches, waiting for his verdict, clearly more trusting in Google than me. 'To be fair, it does say there isn't any evidence of it causing seizures, just to be careful of the pain being an unexpected trigger.'

'What do you think, Duke?' My mom turns to him, as if he's part of the family too, and should get a say in my life. I suppose, given how many years he's been friends with Wyatt, and the amount of time he's spent at ours growing up, he might as well be a Hensley. I can't remember the last Thanksgiving him and his grandmother didn't spend with us.

Duke's brows shoot up and his eyes dart around the group, eventually landing on me.

'Uh . . .' He pauses, as I widen my own eyes in a silent

32

plea. 'I'm not sure I'm really the right person to ask whether someone should or shouldn't be getting a tattoo.' He then holds out his arms, letting the sunshine highlight every inch of his tattooed skin, the darker lines and grey shading, leaving little of his skin bare, except for a small area on his inner wrists. Wyatt snorts out a laugh beside him.

My gaze cuts from Duke to the floor, and my chest caves in. But then he suddenly clears his throat and adds, 'Though, I'm sure Cherry knows what she's doing. She was always the smartest one out of the Hensley kids, anyway.'

'Hey!' Wyatt yells, jabbing Duke in the ribs with his elbow. And while my parents drop into laughter, and Wyatt reels off all the reasons why he's the smartest, Duke's eyes find mine, shining the reminder that maybe someone is in my corner after all.

4

Cherry

I think I might be dying. I knew I shouldn't have agreed to cover Montana's shift today when I felt that first twinge in my stomach this morning, like my mom suggested.

My black tank top is practically a second skin now, soaked with sweat – the feverish wave hit me while I was carrying someone's order. I just managed to shove their drinks onto their table before I ran to the back of the bar, hurrying into the closest room before I was sick. A bathroom probably would've been the best option, but instead, to my pure lack of luck, it was Duke's office.

The only good news is that the shrill ringing in my ears is gradually calming now that I'm curled up on the floor. Which means I'm no longer going to pass out – ideal, considering that I don't think Duke would appreciate finding me unconscious on his floor. I wait for the stabbing pain in my stomach to begin subsiding before I lift myself to a seated position, using the desk behind to prop myself up.

Somehow I need to get myself from this point to the staffroom, where my bag and painkillers are, without collapsing again. The thought makes me let out a scratchy laugh – because it's funny that I'm considering trying to dose myself up to make it through my shift.

Just ten more seconds and I'll get up—

'Jesus, Cherry!' Duke's deep voice booms as the door swings open, forcing my eyes to shoot over to him. 'What happened?'

The sight of him and the way his tattooed muscles and broad chest are wrapped in a tight black T-shirt, is enough to wake me up a little more, while also unfortunately reminding me that I must look like a sweaty mess right now. A weak, sweaty mess from the way Duke's pitiful gaze sweeps over me.

Just a little girl who needs saving. Again.

I can barely look him in the eye as heat rises into my cheeks.

'I'm fine,' I rasp out. The silver stars are almost gone from my vision, thankfully, no longer threatening to pull me from consciousness.

Duke closes his eyes for a long second, shaking his head. Then he reaches to swipe his black leather biker jacket off the back of his chair and drops to his knees to wrap it around me. I hunch my shoulders as he does.

'Cherry,' he says, voice dropping an octave, a commanding depth lacing it. 'Tell me what's wrong.'

My skin prickles and I don't think it's a result of the fever. 'I'm fine, I just felt faint and needed to sit down. Sorry, your office was the closest—'

Another shooting pain lances through my stomach,

cutting me off. Water wells in my eyes, making me squeeze them shut, because that one was way worse than the last, but I try to breathe through it as best as I can. 'I'm also double sorry because I threw up in your bin.'

It's then that I realise Duke never took his hands away after draping his jacket around me. No, instead he's gently rubbing my arms up and down as I shiver beneath his hands. My heartrate threatens to skyrocket in response to his gentle touch.

When I finally open my eyes again, they immediately marry with his and I'm almost breathless at the intensity behind how he regards me. Duke's the beautiful kind of masculine – angled features with soft edges, high cheekbones, and long lashes that frame deep brown eyes. Ones that could say a thousand words even though he's usually the quietest one in the room.

'You need to go home. You shouldn't be covering for people when it's your time of the month,' he says.

My lips pop open, and I even shake my head a little because . . . 'Excuse me?'

'Do you have any of your special painkillers?'

'What . . .' My words trail off as I try to comprehend what he's attempting to discuss with me. What he's suggesting he knows all about . . . but the last thing I want to do is get into a conversation about my *menstrual cycle* with my boss.

'Cherry?' Duke's fingers pulse against my upper arms. He's stopped rubbing them, but he hasn't let go, still on his knees, leaning over me. Heat radiates off him while his dark, wild eyes flick between mine.

'How . . . how do you know about all that?' I ask, glaring at him.

Duke's fingers abruptly retract from me, his eyes flashing at where he'd been holding me, before he rears back, increasing the space between us. I pull my knees up to my chest, circling my arms around them.

His eyes flare before he clears his throat. 'I, uh, spent a lot of time at your house when you were growing up. You used to have a lot of days off school because of it.'

I rub my eyes, desperately wanting the floor to swallow me up. Too many times he no doubt saw me curled up on the couch, unable to make it to school as I was growing up because my period pain was so severe, let alone the hormonal changes and stress of it all only made me more susceptible to seizures and meant I was safer at home on the worst days. Something I found out the hard way when I first started getting bad cramps at thirteen and laboured through a painful day at school only to end up having a fit in the middle of a science class, knocking equipment everywhere. Sure, the birth control, the doctors eventually gave me help to alleviate some of the symptoms by lengthening the times between my periods, but that feels a little bit like slapping a Band-Aid on a broken bone.

Still, I've always found ways to manage – heat pads, plenty of extra-strength painkillers, long naps, and staying at home. Though, as much as that worked through school and college, I'm aware companies don't tend to give every woman a week off each month, so God knows how I'll manage when I finally have a job. Hopefully, I'll find some strength somewhere.

Duke asks, 'Why do you think I always give you a week off every month?'

I throw my hands up with a sigh. 'I *thought* that was because of my epilepsy. Because Wyatt told you not to overwork me. The usual overprotective family stuff, y'know?' I'd always just been grateful that with the pill I could make sure my cycle coincided with those days off, or at least the worst parts of it. 'Not in a million years did I think it was because my boss was tracking my period.'

That he was taking notes when he'd ask me when I wanted my first shift to be every time I came back for the holidays or summer, and I'd purposefully make that first day overlap with my cycle finishing.

'Well, this is incredibly embarrassing,' I groan, dropping my head into my hands. My hair tumbles down, creating a barrier around me, against the moment I really wish wasn't currently playing out right now.

Duke's fingers briefly graze my shins, as if he went to grasp me but decided against it. 'Cherry, it's natural, don't worry.'

'No, it's not,' I snap, my head shooting up.

Duke's quiet demeanour remains as his unyielding, dark eyes behold me. Tears surge into my eyes again and I try my hardest to blink them away.

'It's not natural to be in so much pain, Duke. It's not natural for your boss to have to give you a week off work every month, so you don't faint in the middle of the bar. It's not natural to have to say no to so many things because you're either too exhausted from your stupid period, or you're worried you'll overexert yourself and risk a seizure. It's not natural to feel so fucking *weak*.'

It's not natural to spend so much time off school.

It's not natural to have fewer friends because you've missed out on socialising and parties growing up.

It's not natural that the whole of Willow Ridge always seems to be watching my every move, and treating me like I'm made of brittle glass.

This time, no matter how hard I blink, the tears don't vanish. Instead, they spill out, along with a quiet sob from my lips. I'm not normally someone who cries easily, but according to my hormones, today I am.

Duke's brows draw together, forehead creasing as his eyes trail over my face. His fingers flex at his sides, then he sighs. 'I . . . I didn't realise you felt like this.'

His eyes dart around the floor, as if he's hoping to find the solution to my unhappiness there. Unfortunately, I think it's actually folded up in a notebook in my bag.

I shrug, brushing away any remaining tears with the back of my hand. 'I guess I've been good at hiding it . . . I just get so frustrated sometimes that I – and everyone else – has to worry. That I can't just say yes to everything without a care in the world. I've missed out on so much and I'm sick of it.'

'Hence the bucket list?' Duke perks a brow, a subtle smile playing at the corners of his mouth. Being in this room with him, down on the floor all vulnerable, really can't go on for much longer. Plus, the smell of vomit is really starting to linger.

'Hence the bucket list.' My own smile blooms and I swear his eyes brighten in response, lingering on my lips. 'I just think it will make me feel better about myself. Feel like I'm experiencing the world. If I actually get around to doing any of it, anyway.'

I just need Montana to find some time for me between Austin and flitting between homes now her parents have divorced.

Duke purses his lips as he muses on a thought, running a hand over his closely shaven head. He's obviously been to the barbers since I last saw him because there's a new subtle pattern shaved into the sides of his head. His bottom lip drops, like he's going to say something, but instead he just holds out his hands, waiting. 'Well, I'm sure it can wait another few days, because you need to rest at home. So, let's go get your stuff and I'll drive you home.'

'I can walk—'

'Cherry, I'm driving you.' Duke pins me with a commanding glare. 'It's only a Wednesday evening; the bar will survive. Jeb can cover me for twenty minutes.'

'Fine,' I groan and reluctantly slip my hands into his, watching how they dwarf mine and tense. I let him lift me to my feet, his leather jacket still slung around my shoulders. He even pulls it around me tighter, the corner of his mouth hooking up faintly.

It doesn't take long for me to grab my bag from the staffroom and then he's ushering me into his old red Silverado, driving me the short way home. Once we pull up outside my house, I reach for the truck door handle, and Duke's fingers graze my forearm briefly.

'Cherry,' he whispers. He watches where he touches me for a beat, where goosebumps have broken out, then flicks his gaze back up to catch mine. 'You've never been weak to me, you know that, right?'

40

5

Duke

The golden evening sunshine filters through the chattering crowd as I shuffle my way along the row of seats with Wyatt and Wolfman – two of my best friends since school. Our arms are piled with drinks and snacks while Big & Rich's 'Save a Horse (Ride a Cowboy)' blasts through the speakers, rallying up the surrounding audience. The rodeo stalls are filled with a sea of faded denim, shining buckles, and shuffling boots, all eager for the next competition to commence.

It's our first time at the Fox Falls rodeo, but it's only a few towns over from Willow Ridge. Sawyer – my other best friend from high school – has always tried to attend small town rodeos even after his bull-riding career kicked off and he became the Professional Bull Riders world champion last year. Something about owing his life to the small town, travelling rodeos that took him in fresh out of high school.

And since Sawyer's never had much in the way of a

supportive family, we always do what we can to come out and cheer him on at as many rodeos we can. That's what friends are for – like family on a soul level. The realisation of such hits you harder when you don't have a lot of family left.

Memories of Wyatt inviting me along to rodeos with his family when we were growing up so I could still partake in family traditions even after mine had a hole torn in it, have mirth bubbling in my chest and prove that you don't have to be blood-related to show up for each other. It was summer days spent at rodeos with the Hensleys, or evening barbecues at theirs, or even just afternoons spent playing football with Wyatt, his brother Hunter, and their dad, Beau, that gave me the space to forget about losing my mom for a moment. The opportunity just to be a normal kid that wasn't carrying the heavy burden of loss every day. Sometimes I don't know where I'd be without them.

So, I carry those reminders with me every day, doing what I can to be there for my friends, just like they were for me.

Once we reach our seats, Cherry, Rory, and Fliss – one of the new employees at Sunset Ranch – are huddled together singing along and giggling, which we could hear from the other side of the arena. I look back to Wyatt, who just shakes his head at the girls, trying to fight off the grin that always appears whenever he's around Rory. The one that tells me he's a goner – because Wyatt Hensley smiling used to be a rare sight, until a British wellness influencer waltzed onto the ranch he ran just over a year ago.

Plus, seeing his girlfriend and little sister get along so well no doubt makes him happy. Cherry's always been a good sport, putting up with and hanging around us guys since she's been young, but there's a glow to her when she's with Rory and Fliss, like she's found people who she's finally comfortable enough with to let her true self shine.

Exactly like right now – she seems relaxed, at ease, so at odds to the puddle of frustration and tears I found her in the other day in my office. I cursed myself after dropping her home for not saying more, for not fighting her on her self-depreciation.

But as always, words failed me. Beyond the confines of a therapist's office, anyway. Because no one teaches you about grief or how to manage your feelings at ten years old. After my mom passed, I always struggled to find the words to describe how I was feeling – it was so new, so alien to me – and I found myself better suited to being there for my grandparents, who'd also lost her. Just listening. It was the same with my mom when she'd tell me bedtime stories about my dad who barely made it to my first birthday before a mistake during a routine surgery took him from us. Seeing the light in her eyes as she recounted her memories made me feel useful, just like it does when Gram talks about my grandfather.

Being the listener, I wasn't a burden or a weight, and people would still need me. I found purpose in a time when my world had been turned upside down and I desperately needed something to cling on to.

Plus, when I have let myself dip into that pool of grief, it's hard not to get pulled under. I don't trust myself not to get lost in my emotions, regardless of what they are, especially when it comes to Cherry. So, I'm glad Cherry's got the rest of the group to lift her up when I can't. To make her happy – which is how she looks right now, with the girls. Her long, slender body fits into a pair of tight, flared Wranglers and a cropped black T-shirt, contrasting with the white cowboy hat she always loves to wear to the rodeos. And that raven black hair flows like a waterfall down her back to—

Oh fuck. To where a black G-string thong peeks out above her jeans as she's leaning over into Rory's arms. It's so thin it could pass as dental floss. My heart stammers at the sight. Jesus, the world is being relentless recently when it comes to Cherry – first the lap dance, now I know what underwear she favours.

I struggle to rip my eyes away, but when I do, I glance up to the row behind us where two guys are staring and whispering, making it pretty damn obvious that they're enjoying the view. The cans in my hands crackle as my fists close tighter around them. I settle my glare on them, raising my eyebrows when they both look at me. Then, I cross my arms, purposefully tensing my muscles like an overly jealous asshole. Being six-foot-three and covered in tattoos does have perks.

I'm just being protective of Cherry, like Wyatt's always asked us to do. That's all.

After clearing my throat, I turn back to the group, trying to fight my smug grin from breaking out at the way the two guys shrank into their seats.

'Ladies,' I say, dropping into the free seat beside Cherry, with Wyatt and Wolfman on my other side. Thankfully, all three of them turn to me eagerly, meaning Cherry's thong disappears back beneath her skin-tight jeans. It doesn't stop me from sliding my arm around the back of her seat after handing her Diet Coke over, though, and throwing one final glance over my shoulder to check the sex pests have stopped gawking.

Even if I did my fair share of the same a second ago…

'Lifesaver!' Rory squeals, leaning over Cherry to slip the remaining two Diet Cokes out of my grasp, and hands one to Fliss who smiles her thanks, mousy-brown hair bobbing as she does. Rory clicks the can open and takes a gulp, letting a dreamy expression cross her freckled features. 'I swear this stuff is better than sex.'

'I heard that!' Wyatt barks, shooting Rory a scolding look. Mine and Cherry's heads volley between them.

'Joking! Love you!' Rory giggles and blows Wyatt a kiss, then tosses her copper waves over her shoulders and turns back to Fliss to continue singing along to the last part of the song.

Smiling, I grab my beer from Wyatt before fully relaxing into the seat.

'What time do you need me again tomorrow to help with that delivery?' Wyatt asks.

'Ten, if that works?' I check, even though there hasn't been a single time he's not turned up to help when I've needed him – even if it meant scheduling his ranch hands to cover him or picking up the extra work later that evening. Especially when I first took over the bar from grandfather, and even more so when he passed, running a business was new territory but Wyatt made sure he was there to support me. I'm not sure there's been a day since I lost my mom that he hasn't been by my side.

'Always, brother.' Wyatt clinks his beer against mine with a grin, the endearment hitting me straight in the heart.

It's then that the music peters out and the announcers' voices ring through the arena. As always, my heart begins to stutter, picking up its pace as we get closer to Sawyer riding into a life-or-death situation. Memories of hospital wards creep into my mind. Of doctors breaking the bad news to a ten-year-old orphan. Of my grandmother's words.

'I'm sorry, Junior. She held on as long as she could. She's at peace now. But it'll be okay – you've got us now, and us Bennetts are strong. We stick together.'

But what if I'm not strong enough to lose anyone else?

With my free hand, I clasp the edge of my seat to ground myself, feeling the hard plastic dig into my palm. I've never been a religious man, but I always send a prayer out at this point, hoping that if there is a higher power, then it might listen to me this time.

My leg bounces as I focus on the arena ahead, searching for Sawyer's golden hair beyond the chute. Suddenly, Cherry's knuckles brush against mine as she also clenches her seat in anticipation. I feel a jolt in her hand, but she doesn't move away. Instead, our knuckles remain connected – barely, but enough that goosebumps spread up my arm.

I feel her lean towards me, though her face remains forward, and she whispers, 'Seeing as we missed out on our closing argument on Wednesday, I have one for tonight.'

Holding back my smile takes more effort than I'd like.

It's just a game to pass time, but it's become such a ritual for us now that it honestly makes my day. And right now, it's distracting me from the roiling in my stomach as I watch Sawyer climb up beside the chute. It's why it always feels a little empty when she's at college and can't make it to as many of Sawyer's rides – sure, Wyatt was my best friend growing up, but Cherry accepted me as part of the family just as much. It's why this summer feels more important than any, knowing once she graduates she'll be packing her bags and saying good riddance to Willow Ridge.

To me.

My heart trips at the thought.

Fuck, how is it only just properly hitting me that this summer might be the last time I get to see Cherry every week? That this time next year I'll be down one more person in my life, watching at the sidelines with the rest of her family as she soars off towards whatever faraway dreams she's planning to chase.

'Go on,' I say, shuffling my hand so that it accidentally knocks against hers again.

'Diet Coke is better than normal Coke. For or against?'

I snort. 'What if I'm neither?'

All of Sawyer's bull-riding achievements are relayed over the loudspeaker, every prize echoing through the now silent crowd.

'How can you be neither?'

Sawyer settles himself onto the bull, readying the rope.

'I'd much rather have a Pepsi.'

Cherry makes a disgusted gasp, pressing a hand to her chest. I'm just about to turn and grin at her but the gates fly open, and she grabs my forearm. Her fingers grip at my tensed muscles, pulsing with every second that ticks on the large screen timer.

Sawyer's body effortlessly rides each buck and jump of the bull, absorbing the beast's frenzied movements with his arm outstretched in the classic L shape. The bull's a hooker for sure, trying its best to throw Sawyer forward. Still, the whole time Sawyer's got a smug grin plastered across his face – visible since he stupidly refuses to wear a helmet – like he feeds off the fear and adrenaline.

The buzzer finally sounds, and we all jump to our feet, cheering louder than anyone else in the arena. The girls scream their hearts out, Cherry's hat falls off, and some of Wolfman's beer goes flying over me and Wyatt as he bounces with pride, throwing a fist in the air.

But I don't care. Sawyer made it.

'Yes, Nash!' Wolfman yells, howling afterwards.

Sawyer leaps off the bull – but it follows him, catching one of his legs with its horn. He tumbles into the dirt, head smashing against the ground before he rolls awkwardly. A couple of bullfighters try to coerce the beast away from him, another running to Sawyer's aid.

Sawyer scrambles to pull himself out of further harm's way, seeming to give up once the bull is taken out of the ring. Then, he just lies there, face down on the ground, head in his arms, as the bullfighters begin to surround him.

The silence as we all watch is deafening.

None of us has let out a breath since he hit the floor.

My heart rattles in my chest.

Cherry's fingers grip my forearm tighter, still having not

let go. She might be the only thing keeping me standing right now.

Several brutally long seconds stretch out before Sawyer suddenly springs to his feet, wolfish grin appearing as he waves to the crowd, enjoying the drama of the moment far too much. He laps up the tsunami of applause that follows as he circles the arena.

Relief crashes through me like a wave.

Cheering and music infiltrates my senses again.

I can finally breathe.

Fliss and Rory are hugging, Wyatt and Wolfman have grabbed each other's shoulders as they bounce. I don't know what comes over me, but there's so much emotion brimming inside me that I suddenly wrap an arm around Cherry, tug her into my side, and plant a kiss against her silky hair.

She instantly freezes, her celebratory squeal coming to a halt, which cuts my own cheer off, realisation of what I just did dawning on me.

Cherry's wide eyes blink up at me, her dark-red lips parted. When my gaze lingers on them for too long – mostly because I'm trying to figure out my next step to save myself from this situation – her teeth bite down on her bottom lip.

I'm out of choices and hate that my next move is to drag Cherry towards Rory with the arm still wrapped around her, pulling Rory into our embrace too. I press a kiss this time to Rory's cheek, laughing as I do, hoping that it stops her from thinking too far into what just happened. That I like to kiss all my friends when I'm happy.

Which everyone here knows I definitely do *not* do.

And I'm not looking to start showering Wyatt and Wolfman with smooches any time soon.

Rory receives the hug with joy and peppers both me and Cherry with kisses on the cheek too, squeezing us tighter together.

'Oh gross, get off me,' Cherry grunts, but she laughs through every word as she squirms to push Rory and I away with plenty of force. She shakes her head at us before falling back into her seat, and I chuckle to veil the breath of relief I want to let out.

'Oh, you love it, really,' Rory jests back, attempting to smack another big kiss against Cherry's cheek when she drops to the seat beside her.

I don't know why I even worried about Cherry's reaction – she gave me the exact same response she would have to Sawyer or Wolfman. Because I'm just another of her brother's annoying friends. Exactly how it should be.

I finally settle back down into my seat ready for the next bull rider, keeping my hands in my lap, away from the edge of my seat where they might brush Cherry's again. When the next rider climbs into the chute, we stay silent, and I send up another prayer. Except this time, it's for me, asking for the strength to survive this last summer with her.

6

Cherry

'Feeling alright?' Duke asks, resting his thick frame against the metal fence beside me after sauntering over. The woody, cypress scent of his cologne swirls around me. My eyes dart to the tattoos covering his arms, the way they shift over his corded muscles as he rests.

But I quickly force my gaze back to the pen ahead of me, where I'm reaching out and stroking the beautiful chestnut filly down the white blaze on the bridge of her velvety nose. I let my fingers filter through her silky, lighter forelock and scratch behind her ears, relishing the way she angles her head further into my hand, as if to say, *more, please.* Just being in the presence of such a sweet creature kneads away any tightness in my body, fishing up golden memories of being free-spirited, riding along the trails around Willow Ridge with the hot sun beating down.

Before everyone started worrying that I'd fall again.

Before I started to believe the same story.

Regardless, right now, it's serving as the best way to

keep me distracted from the reminder of how Duke *kissed* me in celebration merely an hour ago.

I'm sure Sawyer and Wolfman have jokingly kissed me on the head or cheek or whatever countless times celebrating at rodeos or football games, and I've never been bothered then. If anything, I probably would've shoved them or punched them in the arm, which is why I made myself act the same with Duke and Rory, as opposed to standing there dazed, batting my eyelashes like an infatuated teenager who had just met their celebrity crush.

So, here I am, pretending to have gone to the restroom after the show, but instead having run off to get some alone time with the horses while everyone chatted to the rest of the bull riders with Sawyer, hoping it will help me calm down.

'You ready to go?' Duke throws out, finally drawing me from my thoughts and making me realise I never responded to his first question. He must have been sent over here to get me.

'Sorry.' I turn to him, offering a smile and he mirrors it, dark eyes lit up under the arena lights. Not as enlarged as they were earlier after he kissed me. 'I got distracted.'

'You always do here.' He reaches over the fence to brush a hand across the filly's neck.

It's then that I notice a small new horseshoe tattoo on what was once bare skin on his inner wrist. After all the late nights closing up the bar, I've come to learn most of his tattoos, usually asking him their meanings as we clean up – so I'm intrigued as to how he snuck this new one past me in the last week. When he clears his throat, I snap my eyes back up to his.

'What do you mean?'

'Get distracted.' Duke nods to the pen. 'With the horses.'

'Yeah.' I sigh out a small chuckle, though struggle to maintain my smile – a momentary flash of the last time I ever rode forces it down into a frown. 'I just miss riding, I guess.'

It's not a second more before I'm leaning over the fence again, giving the filly a few more tickles under her chin, eliciting a soft nicker from her. Mirth bubbles up into my chest at the sound.

Duke hums. 'That wasn't on the list.'

I furrow my brow at him.

'The bucket list,' he continues, studying me with an angle of his head. 'It wasn't on the bucket list. You don't want to try riding again?'

I nibble on my thumbnail as I consider. If I hadn't fallen all those years ago, I might have been here competing today. Barrel racing was what I'd always had my sights set on, eager to convince my parents to let me start practising.

It's not like I was going to be a bronc rider or anything.

But sometimes life just nudges you onto a different path than you expected. Without my epilepsy and my fall, I wouldn't have found my passion for interior design during all those days off school where I spent probably too much time designing and decorating houses on *The Sims* and learning to draw digitally.

That doesn't mean all the *what-ifs* aren't in the back of my head, though.

It's partly why I love the days we get to watch Sawyer at the rodeos, knowing I can catch a glimpse of the other riding competitions, living my old dreams through the women competing. Wondering how much they're risking each time they settle themselves in the saddle.

'Yeah, maybe one day. When I feel ready,' I eventually respond, shrugging as I'm bombarded with all the reasons I shouldn't be up there, fulfilling the image that I've built of myself for years. 'Though, once I get a job in the city, I doubt I'll be that interested anymore.'

Duke just bobs his head. I'm sure he knows I'm dialling down how much I want to get back in the saddle, but he'd never call me out, he always just listens, like he trusts me to eventually make the best decision for myself. Which, as someone who has grown up with a lot of rules around what I can and can't do, means more to me than he probably realises.

Duke regards me for a beat, then he returns to resting against the fence with me, watching the horses. I guess that's the end of that conversation. I twist to finally head off and find the others—

'I was actually, um . . .' Duke starts but trails off, rubbing his hand along his jaw. A divot appears between his brows as his gaze drops from mine, but it's back after a second, and I swear whenever he looks at me the rest of my surroundings quieten. All the chaos of the world suddenly disappearing. No more whinnies from the horses echoing across the pens or Morgan Wallen songs blasting from the speakers.

Just the two of us.

He tries again. 'Well, I was thinking about what you said the other day and I thought . . . maybe I could help you out with it?'

My bottom lip drops. 'What?'

'The bucket list.'

I stand there in dumbstruck silence, blinking as I try

to comprehend whether he's just offered what I think he has. 'Wait, are you being serious?'

'Yeah, why not?' He releases a breathy chuckle. 'If it means you'll feel better. Unless Montana is helping you—'

'No!' I blurt out, and quickly school my features into something less wildly enthusiastic. 'No, she . . . well, she is, but she's been seeing this guy, Austin, a lot recently so she's been pretty busy.'

A dimple pops in one of his cheeks as he gives me a lopsided grin. 'Right. Obviously, I'm only talking about the, um . . .' Duke rubs harshly at his forehead, clearing his throat. 'The non-sexual stuff. Just want to make that clear, Cherry.'

Wishing the ground would swallow me up is starting to become a regular thing now.

I'd almost forgotten that he'd seen *all* of it. But, clearly, Duke wouldn't want to do any of that with me. And he said he was offering to do the bucket list with me to help me feel better. Just a friend helping out another friend, right?

I'll take what I can get.

'Right, *obviously*.' I laugh, waving him off, while my mind desperately scrambles for something else to say so we can quickly move on from the sexual topic. 'Doesn't helping me with the bucket list go against what you said, though? Your whole old man spiel about small moments being better.'

Duke pokes his cheek with his tongue, eyes darkening slightly at me. 'I'm not *that* much older than you. Six years is nothing.'

'Stop calling me Baby Hensley then, if I'm not *that* much younger than you.' I cross my arms and tip my chin up.

'Never. You hate the name too much.' Duke leans lazily against the fence. 'Anyway, helping you does go against what I said, but that's why I'll only do it on one condition.'

Duke steps forward, eating up almost all the space between us. I might be tall for a girl, but Duke towers over me, his broad frame so close, I notice the distinction between his almost black irises and pupils, watching them expand the longer he stares at me, like they're feeding off being near me. 'For every big thing we do on your bucket list, you have to enjoy a small, little moment of my choosing. Something I think makes life worthwhile. So you don't forget that the slow life here ain't all that bad in Willow Ridge when you're living it up in the city.'

'Like what?' I breathe out.

'Like spending the evening surrounded by friends, laughing in your favourite bar. Which is where we're supposed to be right now.' Duke pushes off the fence with his foot, signalling for us to start walking. 'We probably shouldn't keep them waiting much longer.'

Right, he basically came over here to tell me to get my ass moving because it's time to leave. God, why is it suddenly so hot in here?

'So, do we have a deal? A big moment for a small one?' Duke checks over his shoulder at me as I catch up, a smirk dancing on his lips.

I grin, not even hesitating to say, 'It's a deal.'

Because when life gives you an opportunity like this, you don't think twice about taking the reins and jumping into the saddle.

7

Cherry

'And you're certain you don't have *any* others back there?' Duke asks the teenage boy behind the skate rink desk the following weekend, dark brows drawn in even as his tone remains gentle.

'Sorry, dude, we don't have as many in less popular sizes.' The boy barely offers a smile, completely oblivious as to why Duke would want a different pair of roller-skates to the *hot-pink* ones sitting on the desk.

I press a fist to my mouth to stifle the giggle bubbling up. Duke's dressed head to toe in black – black leather jacket, dark jeans, tight black T-shirt, not to mention the black tattoos covering his arms – which will just make the skates stand out even more. At least if I fall on my ass today, it still won't be as funny as Duke Bennett having to wear roller skates so pink they might blind someone.

'S'alright. Thanks, anyway.' Duke grimaces, then reluctantly swipes the garish skates from the desk with a quiet sigh of defeat. He holds them at arm's length, like he's scared if he brushes against them, he'll magically turn into a pink unicorn.

When he faces me and catches sight of my grin, he just shakes his head. He nods towards the seats, letting me go ahead, then waits until we're out of earshot before he lets the complaints flow.

'How is it that the only skates they have in my size are goddamn *pink*?' he grumbles, pulling his boots off and shoving a foot into one of the pink monstrosities. Black ink ripples as the muscles in his forearms shift, just like they do when he's mixing drinks at the bar or wiping down the tables. Duke continues, 'I'm all for flouting gender stereotypes, but wouldn't you expect them to at least have colours other than *hot-pink* for a size thirteen?'

'Hey, that's your fault for having big clown feet.' I bump my shoulder awkwardly his bicep. Quickly, I lean down to start lacing up my skates, which are a nice, unimposing off-white and perfectly complement my frayed denim shorts, cropped white T-shirt, and the light-blue flannel shirt tied around my waist.

'Yeah, well . . .' Duke lets out a breath of a laugh. 'You know what they say about big – actually, never mind.'

I immediately stop tying my laces, while he picks up the pace of his, like he suddenly can't wait to get out there and show off the colour. 'Oh my God, were you . . . about to make a *dick* joke?'

Duke's hands ball into fists as he sharply inhales. It takes him a second to respond, his voice more monotonous than before. 'Nope.'

'You totally were. You were gonna make a dick joke.' My gaze tumbles down to his skates, his large hands hovering over them, and I can't help but swallow at the thought. Because there's nothing *small* about Duke, he's six-foot-three—

'Cherry.' Duke closes his eyes, his tone on the edge of pleading now. 'Please stop saying the word . . . *dick*.'

His shoulders hunch in a wince, as though me saying *dick* puts him in physical pain. I'm not sure whether to laugh or be bothered that he seems so appalled.

'What? Why—'

'Move your asses and get over here!' Rory yells from the rink, her words descending into a squeal as Wyatt grabs her hands and starts spinning her around. Her ginger waves become a blur, melting into the strobe lighting that flashes around the rink.

For a moment, I forgot they were here. What I thought was an opportunity to spend some one-on-one time with Duke outside of the bar when he'd texted me suggesting we try ticking off roller-skating from my bucket list, turned into a *group outing*. When he picked me up today, I discovered Wyatt and Rory already in his truck.

'You don't mind that I invited the others, do you?' Duke had asked when I opened the door, then let me know that Fliss *and* Wolfman would also be meeting us at the roller rink.

'The more the merrier,' I'd replied with a measly attempt of a smile, my cheeks aching by the time we got here from trying to stop my face from dropping.

But it's fine. I'll get over it.

'Coming!' I shout back to Rory, finishing tying up my skates and reminding myself that today is about ticking an item off the list, *not* spending time with a guy.

Wobbling far more than I'd like to, I bring myself up to a stand, spotting where Wolfman and Fliss have just skated onto the rink. Fliss takes to the floor so easily, skating to the rhythm of the music as blissfully as a bird soaring along the breeze. With a too-cocky grin for someone who's only ever skated once before, Wolfman follows. He keeps relatively close to the edge with the rest of the people on the rink but manages to stay steady on his feet. He shouts, 'Show off!' at Fliss.

She throws him the middle finger as she rockets past, hair billowing behind her.

Rory, on the other hand, is pouting at Wyatt like a little kid, begging him to come rescue her from where he'd pushed her into the centre of the rink after spinning her around. His laugh rings out, almost as loud as the music, where Luke Bryan's 'Country Girl (Shake It For Me)' is currently playing. The sight warms my heart as I know Wyatt would never have been that bothered about coming roller-skating before meeting Rory. Yet now, I've never seen him do and smile so much.

'Ready to shake it, Baby Hensley?' Duke slides up beside me where I'm now at the opening to the rink, clutching the wall for dear life. I mentally prepare myself for the incredibly high likelihood that I'll be falling on my ass, or even face-planting, at some point today. In front of Duke, to make it worse.

But I'll survive. Besides, didn't Kelly Clarkson say that what doesn't kill you makes you stronger? And that's why I'm here. To make up for all those roller-skating parties I missed when my epilepsy started, which left both me and my parents with a silly fear of me falling.

I swallow down a reassuring breath, before nodding. 'Let's shake it.'

'For the catfish swimming down deep in the creek?' Duke asks with a stifled smile along with the chorus, pretending to detest this song, even though I've seen him tapping his foot to the beat plenty of times when it's been playing from the jukebox at the bar. He gestures ahead of him for me to step onto the rink first.

'Obviously,' I add with a chuckle, plonking my feet onto the rink and praying that I last at least thirty seconds before collapsing. I throw one last glance over my shoulder at Duke, and the tangle of nerves in my stomach is met with a shot of confidence at the way he's watching me. Maybe I can do this, knowing he's there behind me. 'Don't forget the crickets and the critters and the squirrels, too.'

'Of course,' he responds.

I turn back round and school my features into determination, waiting for that unexpected burst of motivation to start moving.

Except, it doesn't, but I do move forward – because Duke suddenly gives me a shove, rolling me further into the rink. I let out a rather loud *woah!* as I scramble to get my balance, probably looking like a spider on a hot plate.

I'm instantly in the middle of the flowing sea of people skating in a clockwise direction around the rink, denim and plaid whipping past as they try to dodge me. My heartrate skyrockets at the chaos.

But it forces me into unexpected action, and I have to start taking long strides to fall into pace with everyone so that I'm not holding people up or cutting them off.

I want to look behind me to shoot a daggered look at Duke but there's no way I can take my eyes off my path without toppling over right now. My legs are all wobbly like a little foal's first steps. My heart rattles behind my ribcage as I try to remind myself to keep putting one foot in front of the other to the beat of the music. But I'm still upright, and that's what matters.

Because I can do this.

I let out a chuckle of disbelief.

Warm pride bolsters me, straightening out my shoulders and giving me extra drive with each stride I take. Damn Duke, because as annoyed as I am at him for pushing me, I'm not sure I would've picked this up as quickly without it.

'*What the hell are those?!*' Somewhere in the background, Wyatt's and Wolfman's laughs bellow out, filtering through the music and skating crowds, presumably as they caught sight of Duke's flashy skates.

'Oh my God! I want a pair!' Rory's voice then rings out.

Fliss suddenly blasts past me, somehow already skating backwards, and hollers, 'Woo! You go, Cherry!'

She circles back, slowing down to skate leisurely by my side and hook an arm through mine. 'You're doing way better than I expected,' Fliss admits, her grin shining.

'Thanks for the belief,' I laugh through long breaths, half-focused on the direction I'm heading.

'I only say that because I fell flat on my ass the second I got on the rink during my first time.' She shrugs. 'But that's how you learn to get back up.'

Right. That's what this is all about. Getting back up from where I let myself drop to all those years ago.

'Hey, girls! Wait up!' Rory's voice rings behind us, and then she's suddenly latching onto Fliss's other arm, forming a chain. She's racked with giggles, joy radiating off her, cheeks all rosy. 'Let's go dance in the middle – I just asked the DJ to play one of Hunter's songs to piss Wyatt off.'

Ever since Rory found out about our famous, country singer middle brother, Hunter, she seems to have made it her personal mission to get his songs playing wherever we are. Mostly because she knows Wyatt is fed up with everyone squealing over our lovely, but annoying, sibling.

'Hold on and I'll help you towards the middle,' Fliss says, tightening her arm around mine and leading me away from the crowd. I catch Duke's eyes across the rink, where he, Wyatt, and Wolfman have already given up on the skating and are just leaning against the wall, chatting. *Crushing it*, he mouths to me. He then ticks the air like he's crossing off the item on my bucket list, before quickly returning his attention to the guys. Joy flushes through me, my cheeks heating.

Cheers and chatter ripple through the skating crowd as Hunter's song blares through the speakers, but not as loudly as Wyatt's groan and Rory's subsequent cackle. It's one of his livelier songs, guitar strings plucking quickly and adding a choppy beat to skate to. Strobe lights flicker around us, filling the rink with a cacophony of colour that pulses to the beat of the music.

Rory starts shaking her hips, and Fliss grabs my arm, twirling me around with her. An awfully high-pitched squeal leaves my lips as I'm too aware that if we disconnect I will most definitely go barrelling down to the floor. The lyrics and chords of the song blend with the rushing beat of my heart. But it's okay, because Fliss drags us over to Rory, who then immediately takes my hands so we can spin around together too. She's belting out the lyrics, and I give myself permission to just forget about how scary this all is and *revel* in it. Let the music and the laughter of my friends carry me away for however long we dance for—

But then Rory's letting go of my hands, and I'm hurtling straight towards the wall.

Where Duke is leaning, readying to push off to join Wyatt and Wolfman who have started skating ahead.

My frantic scream isn't a quick enough warning for him to move out of the way.

The last thing I see is the wild whites of Duke's eyes before my body slams into him, breath whooshing sharply out of my lungs.

Where I expected us both to tumble to the ground, I'm instead spun around in Duke's firm grip and pressed against the barrier.

My hair falls over my face as my back hits the barrier, then something solid and warm wedges between my thighs – the only thing stopping me from dropping to the floor. I swallow when I realise it's Duke's thigh. His *thick* thigh, where corded muscles strain against the dark denim, carrying all my weight. My rapid heart rate drops lower in my body, the heat radiating from Duke's thigh and settling deep within my core.

One strained, tattooed arm slams on the edge of the barrier beside me while the other snakes around my waist, caging me in and forcing my head up to meet Duke's frenzied gaze. I also suddenly realise that it's not just Duke's thigh keeping me up, but the way I'm fighting for purchase by fisting his T-shirt. His cypress scent invades my senses, churning up memories of being pressed against his chest and cradled in his arms all those years ago.

I need to get out of this situation. Any confidence I'd built this evening immediately flushed away. But when I shift to try to gain balance on my skates again, all it does is rub Duke's thigh between my legs, the friction of his solid muscles against me shooting a lick of heat up my spine. A whispered gasp leaves my lips before I can stop it.

Duke's eyes flash, shooting down once to where I'm straddling his thigh – his pupils instantly blown out – then back up to me. I swear he gulps.

One of us *needs* to move.

'I'm sorry—' I start.

Duke wriggles his arm away. 'No, I should—'

And then, just as we both push against each other at the same time, our skates gain a mind of their own and decide to shoot off in different directions.

I'm not sure who pulls who down, but our hands are suddenly latching onto the other again frantically as we flip and hurtle towards the ground. At one point I even see a hot-pink skate above me.

We're a tangle of limbs and skates and hair before we smack against the ground, me flopping diagonally across Duke, with one of my legs hooked around his.

Pain vibrates up through my arms as they take the brunt of my fall, stopping my head from walloping against the floor. Laughter echoes in the distance. My breath whooshes out of me as the room finally stops spinning, and just as I try to remove myself from where Duke and I are ravelled together, his hands clutch my waist, fingers digging in tight with a groan. A rumbling, guttural groan that sounds oddly . . . *sexual*.

Along with the way his large hands are splayed across my waist, the heat of his strong fingers imprinting into the slice of bare skin between my top and shorts, the groan has my cheeks heating even more. And when I go to clamber off him again, his fingers grip me tight, ensuring I cannot escape the press of his hard body below mine.

It's then that I turn to him and realise he's wincing, face creased and strained with agony.

'Are you okay?' I ask.

A strangled noise comes out first, but then he says, 'Your leg. You're squashing . . . *everything*.'

My eyes shoot down to—

'Oh. *Oh*.'

As carefully as I can, I roll myself off him, deliberately moving my leg *down* and away from his likely bruised junk. The long, sharp huff of a sigh he releases once we're detached practically screams *I am so done with this*, and I silently berate myself for ever thinking anything good could come out of Duke Bennett helping me with my bucket list.

8

Duke

'I'd rather chew through a jean jacket,' I deadpan at Montana as I pour the cocktail I'd just been whipping up into four tall glasses with precision.

'Oh, Duke, come on,' she whines, stamping her foot. 'The bar could use a bit of a shake up, get some new customers in here for once.'

My eyes roll by their own accord. I like the customers we already have, and they like the way I run the bar. Why change things when everyone's happy?

'I still don't think *speed dating* is the solution.' I reach for the cherries in a nearby tub and hang a couple over the rim of each glass, adding the finishing touch to my signature cherry-flavoured porn star martini. 'Everyone knows everyone in Willow Ridge already. An extra two minutes talking to the quarterback from high school ain't gonna magically make them more interesting.'

With a saccharine smile I place the cocktails on the tray in front of Montana and nod towards the table of four middle-aged women getting shockingly drunk for a Wednesday afternoon. Happy hour doesn't even start for another few hours. So far, they've toasted to the signing of a divorce, to sexual freedom, and to all of them finding *boy-toys*, the latter resulting in the lady dressed in nothing but leopard print winking at me as she gulped down her third cocktail. I might have offered a shy smile had she not been the mom of one of my football teammates in high school. Instead, I had to suppress a shiver.

But this just proves my point – we have plenty of interesting customers already.

'Ugh,' Montana huffs, rolling her eyes, before spinning around and stomping off. She mutters to herself, 'Sue me for trying to bring some excitement into our boring small town.'

My eyes suddenly catch on Cherry, who's cleaning one of the tables nearby and struggling to bite down on her grin, clearly having listened in on the whole conversation. I narrow my eyes at her when she glances up, her cheeks reddening. Not as dark as her lipstick though, the same deep purply-red as the cocktails Montana just carried away.

Making sure my gaze doesn't linger too long, I quickly turn to grab another bottle of beer for Billy, a sixty-something who always comes in after babysitting his grandkids on Wednesday mornings. Usually, he's chewing my ear off, telling me every little thing the troublesome twins do, but today, he seems far too interested in the divorce party across the room. He doesn't so much as give me a thanks as I slide his bottle across the bar to him.

Part of me is glad he's found something else to be

excited about, but I do kind of miss getting to hear his story. Listening to the locals is one of my favourite things about this job. It's how people know me – I'm the one they can always come to, that they can always count on to be around.

I'm not sure if I could ever give that up.

That's why I should turn down that offer that's been on my mind. The one I still need to reply to, but for some reason, can't quite seem to say no to yet. Or yes.

It's not long before Montana is marching back, determination hardening her features, and she hooks her arm around Cherry, dragging her over to the bar too. They exchange whispers as they approach. Taking a step back and leaning against the counter behind me, I cross my arms, awaiting the next round of arguments.

'Cherry *also* happens to think we should do the speed dating,' Montana explains, nudging Cherry with her hip.

I just wave my hand in a rolling motion to say, *go on then*.

'It *is* on my bucket list,' Cherry admits, nibbling her thumbnail.

Something shiny paints a glittery slice across the tops of her cheekbones – a new kind of makeup she's started wearing, I think. The neon signs and twinkling fairy lights keep reflecting off her cheekbones, making my fingers itch to grab a napkin and pen so I can draw her, emphasising the raised glow and delicate, shadowed hollow of her cheeks.

'Wait a second.' Montana leans an elbow against the bar. '*Duke* knows about the bucket list?'

'Um—' I start to explain.

'He's, uh, supposed to be helping me with it too,' Cherry confesses, tucking her hair behind her ears as she avoids my gaze.

Supposed to? I thought I'd already started with the roller-skating. Though, it's not like I didn't notice the way her face dropped when she discovered I'd cowardly invited the rest of our crew along, instead of being left alone with her beyond the realms of the bar. Man am I glad I had the others there as some sort of buffer though, especially when Cherry went flying into me and I had no option but to press my thigh between hers to keep us both from toppling to the ground after spinning her around. Feeling her roll her hips against me when we were so close, hot breath mingling in the little space between us, had me forgetting for a second that we weren't alone.

And then scolding myself for even thinking about these things. I'm sure it's just a symptom of loneliness, but still. My manhood got the brunt of the fall that happened seconds later, but I probably deserved it.

Even so, I don't like knowing I might have disappointed her.

'Well, why didn't you say so?' Montana smiles, shaking her head at Cherry. But then her eyes suddenly flash bright and wide. 'Woah, does that mean he's helping you with—'

'The first half!' Cherry shrieks, cutting her off as that rosy blush spreads further down her neck and chest. She explains again, nodding at me for further confirmation, '*Only* the first half.'

Wanting to reiterate such for everyone, *especially* Cherry, I repeat, 'Right, only the first half.'

Montana holds up her hands, eyes flicking between the

two of us with one brow slightly perked. 'Okay, well, in that case, Duke, you have to agree to the speed dating.'

'Not sure I do.'

'But it's on Cherry's bucket list.' Montana presses, then throws her arm around Cherry's shoulders. She pats Cherry on the cheek, making her giggle, the sound sending a zap of dopamine to my heart. 'Don't you want her to be happy?'

You have no fucking idea.

But speed-dating? Literally hosting an event for the girl I've been trying to protect for her older brother to go on *multiple* dates with *multiple* guys in one night? That's not what I had in mind.

'Sure,' I grit out, locking eyes with Cherry, who watches me coyly.

'Yay!' Montana claps.

'Wait.' I hold up a hand. 'That wasn't me agreeing—'

'Then it's settled. I'll start making some flyers in my break – shall we do next Thursday? Oh! This is gonna be so much fun.' Montana completely ignores me, having decided that despite being her boss, my opinion on the matter is irrelevant.

Just as Montana throws both her arms around Cherry to continue the unnecessary excitement, the bar door swings open and Sawyer struts in, head to toe in denim, along with a white T-shirt, brown boots, a faded cowboy hat that I swear he's had since high school, and the new moustache he's sporting.

His face immediately brightens when he sees us hanging at the bar, brown eyes becoming even more animated as he passes the middle-aged divorcees who greet him with flirtatious waves too. He tips his hat towards them, making them all giggle like they're forty years younger when he says, 'Ladies.'

For a second I think he might head over to their table first, knowing that his internal compass usually directs him to wherever he think he'll get the most attention, but he must decide the three of us are enough for now. Probably because Montana is here, and he's always trying his luck with her.

Sawyer slaps a hand on the bar as he almost stumbles towards it. 'Whoops. What are we celebrating?'

'Were you limping?' Cherry asks, raising a brow. I hadn't noticed, but it wouldn't surprise me if he's still busted up after that bull got him at the rodeo.

'Nice to see you too, little one.' Sawyer brushes off the question and gives Cherry a condescending pat on the head. She shoves him off, rolling her eyes, which makes the corners of my mouth twitch.

Sawyer turns to me. 'Alright, man?'

'All good. You staying long? Want a drink?'

Sawyer eyes the liquor bottles on the shelf behind me, mulling over his decision. Since his father was an alcoholic and he's eager to avoid going down the same road, we have a secret three drink rule – if he orders anything after his third drink, I'll make sure it's non-alcoholic, while everyone else is oblivious. Though, something tells me anything alcoholic might be off the table since the news his father is in hospital.

'Nah, better not. I'm off on the road soon. Just thought I'd pop in to say hello to my favourite bartender. Got a competition in Kansas this weekend.' He twists to face the girls, pumping his brows up when he shoots a grin at Montana. 'Now, what was all the fuss about?'

'We're organising a speed dating night,' Montana enlightens.

Sawyer barks out a laugh. 'You're joking?'

'Apparently not.' I shrug, giving him a hopeless smile.

'No joke.' Montana hooks her arm through Cherry's again. 'We're gonna find Cherry a hunky man to take care of her.' She then ducks her head to whisper into Cherry's ear, though I catch every word, '*And* to help you finish the second half of your bucket list.'

The words land sharp, unexpected blows to my stomach. I quickly grab one of the limes nearby and a knife to start cutting it up, giving my hands something else to do besides curling into fists at the thought, while I try to keep my mind focused on the lyrics of the Kashus Culpepper song playing in the background. Because, *fuck*, I hadn't really considered that just because *I* said I wouldn't help Cherry with all those sexual items on the list, doesn't mean she isn't going to find someone else to.

The list starts running through my mind again, each line making the roiling in my stomach more intense. The image of some random guy's hands running over her tanned skin flashes into my mind and the lime I'm cutting goes flying across the bar as I press the knife into it too harshly. Everyone shoots me a look, and I try to laugh it off.

It's not that I'm jealous. *Obviously.* It's just – I'm not sure that seems safe. What if the guys she chooses don't treat her well? Wyatt would be angry if he knew.

'Oh, but no man for you, Montana?' Sawyer adjusts his jacket and gives it a brush down, all the while keeping a cocky smirk plastered across his face. I'm grateful for the distraction even if it does make me roll my eyes at my friend. 'Got your sights set on a handsome, *champion* bull rider instead?'

'Oh, Sawyer, you wish.' Montana flicks her chestnut hair behind her shoulders. 'I'm actually seeing someone. Besides, Cherry made me pinky promise years ago I wouldn't sleep with you, and, as much as it pains me, I do have to honour that.'

Sawyer's jaw drops, and he covers his heart with a hand, feigning some sort of wound. 'Cherry, I can't believe you'd do that to me. You know how much I love brunettes as well.'

I snort, wondering how my friend gets away with some of the things he says sometimes.

Cherry full on groans, 'You're actually an idiot.'

Sawyer just sighs at Cherry. 'Well, it's on your conscience that she'll be missing out on the best night of her life.'

Montana giggles, fluttering her lashes at Sawyer while he shoots her a wink. Cherry turns to throw me a helpless, wide-eyed look that almost begs, *save me*. It's a struggle to keep my smile from unfurling.

Get a room, am I right? I mouth.

She rolls her lips together, tempering her responding smile. Her eyes brighten with the laughter she's holding back – but I know the melodic sound so well, it still rings in my mind. And it really makes me want to make things up to her.

* * *

'What do you, um, say to skipping all the cleaning tonight, just doing the basics to close up, and getting off early?' I ask Cherry over my shoulder as I finish locking up the front door of the bar now we're finally closed for the night. The plan to fashion the perfect small moment for Cherry while showing her I'm serious about this bucket list finally finishes formulating in my head. One that can maybe also keep her distracted from the second half of that list. If she's busy ticking all these big and small moments off with a friend, maybe she won't be too worried about the second half. You know, for Wyatt's sake – what kind of friend would I be otherwise? Protecting Cherry from any idiots is the least I can do for the family that protected me growing up.

Cherry furrows her brow as she collects up the last empty glasses from one of the booths. 'Close early? I mean, *obviously* I'm down to go home early.' She pauses for a second to lift the piled-up tray, then carefully begins heading for the bar. Her next question comes out more lightly. 'Why, have you got plans?'

'Uh . . .' I lean back against the door, taking advantage of the few seconds when her back is turned to me to take another deep breath. 'No, well, yes.' *Eloquently put, Duke*. 'I was hoping with you.'

The tray lands on the bar with a bang before some of the glasses topple over and Cherry scrambles to pick them back up, cursing under her breath. For a waitress at a bar, she sure is clumsy. Just like that time she knocked over a whole tray of drinks because one of Sawyer's bull-riding friends winked at her. Once she's got the glasses stabilised, she quickly pushes out an apologetic smile.

'Oh, um, really? How come?' she asks, running her teeth along her bottom lip, the cherry-red stain faded now after hours of talking and working. And biting her lip, she's always biting her goddamn lip.

I rub the back of my neck, staying put by the door. 'I just thought since we ticked one thing off your bucket list, then it was my turn to show you a small, slow moment.'

'Oh.' Cherry's shoulders immediately drop and a soft curve graces her lips. 'I suppose it's only fair.'

'Exactly.' I nod. Releasing the breath I'd been holding, I finally let myself walk over towards the bar, relief sweeping through me at the speed of her agreement. At the prospect of getting to spend a little more time with her tonight. Usually after closing time, it's back to my dark apartment, where I'm left with my thoughts.

She hovers by the bar. 'Can we still do our closing time argument on the drive over? I had a really good one for tonight.'

'Anything you want, Baby Hensley.' I take a chance and push myself closer to her, leaning an elbow on the bar top, as opposed to heading to the opposite end like usual. Her brown eyes watch the movement, trailing gradually back up my arm. My heart races suddenly being under her scrutiny, and I start to question whether I'm about to throw myself into a bucket load of trouble.

9

Cherry

'Put that pizza lid down or you're going to let all the heat out,' Duke grumbles at me from the driver's side of his truck.

I've been so distracted by the two boxes of hot pizza on my lap, keeping my legs all toasty, and the sizzling cheesy smell wafting through the air each time I take a peek at the top one, that I hadn't been paying attention to where we're driving.

We managed to catch Piper's Pizza Truck just as it was closing for the night – a food truck that sporadically pops up in Willow Ridge during the summer evenings when one of the chefs from Ruby's Diner isn't working – on the way to wherever we were going after I posed the closing time argument of *pepperoni vs ham and pineapple*. So, now we've got one of each, after deciding the only way to truly settle the debate would be to do a taste test.

And because I'm a fiend for pizza.

'Sorry, sorry,' I yelp, shutting the lid quickly, and

finally taking in our surroundings. We're in the middle of nowhere, that's for sure, racing along some dirt road track, with the twinkling lights of Willow Ridge behind us.

After the roller-skating incident the other day, I'd fully convinced myself that was the end of my bucket list with Duke. If anything, the speed-dating idea was a blessing really, a good distraction to help me focus on talking to the opposite sex, and, as Montana pointed out, ticking off some items on the second half of that bucket list. But then Duke brought up about still owing me a small moment and suddenly the deal is back on.

It's a few more minutes before we hit a slight incline, and the road climbs higher ahead of us, a nervous buzz filling my stomach.

'Don't worry, I'm not taking you too high up,' Duke assures me, pulling over to the side of the road and cutting the engine. It's so empty, the pastures below completely drenched in nothing but silence and moonlight as I scour our surroundings. 'I just wanted to get us a bit further away from the lights of the town.'

I furrow my brow at him while he unbuckles himself and climbs out of the truck. He rounds the front, when I'm distracted by his phone lighting up in the centre console. I chance a quick glance at the screen, only for my stomach to plummet when I notice several texts from a woman called Kelly. He's even got the setting turned on so he can see the latest text in the notification, the top one reading: *Last night's call was great. Excited about where this is heading.*

I can't think of a single woman called Kelly that would be age appropriate for Duke to be seeing in Willow Ridge. Everyone knows everyone in our small town, so

I'm aware of a few women Duke's been with, even if he does try to keep most of his escapades infrequent and quiet. Not that I should care. Now, or ever.

Although there was that girl he was talking to at the bar the other night who was visiting a friend from out of town. Anyone could see how beautiful she was with her deep brown skin and a waterfall of black curls down her back, I'm sure Duke was just as enraptured.

Duke opens my door and grabs the pizza boxes from me. I jump out afterwards, teasing, 'Getting me *away from the lights of the town* makes you sound a bit like a serial killer, not gonna lie.'

'If I was a serial killer, then this has been a very elaborate, twenty-one-years-in-the-making plan to murder you.'

'Well, joke's on you, because I took self-defence classes at college.' Duke shakes his head with a chuckle. Even though I tried to forget, I still find myself saying, 'Your phone kept going off, by the way.'

'Oh, thanks.' Duke tucks the pizzas under one arm and reaches to get his phone. When I chance a glance back, he's checking the screen, a small smile fighting to break out on his face. *How nice for Kelly.*

But then he pockets his phone, shuts the door, and gestures for me to follow him around the truck bed. It's then that I suddenly notice there's a bunch of blankets and pillows scattered in it, stopping me in my tracks. How did I miss those when we were leaving the bar earlier?

'What's all this for?' I ask, peeking over the edge of the truck to inspect the set-up further. This seems like something you'd see on a Pinterest board, all cosy and snuggly. Maybe even . . . romantic?

Nope. Just a friend helping a friend. Besides, he probably does more for this Kelly girl.

Duke runs his hand along the truck before pulling down the tailgate. 'I sometimes take my bike out here, when I just want to ride away from everything. From all the noise. And this is the best place to see the stars, in my opinion.'

My gaze travels up, finding a dark sea of glittering pinpricks above, their light raining down on us.

'On a clear day, you can always see the stars,' I'd told Duke years ago when I helped redecorate the bar. It's why I put fairy lights along the rafters. 'And when there's a whole vast universe up there, it really does make you feel like your worries needn't exist.'

It's one of the things I miss about living in a small town like Willow Ridge – none of the raw beauty of the world is as filtered out as it is in built up towns and cities. Wherever you are, you'll always hear the whispering breeze through the pastures or the whinnying of the horses grazing there. You'll always get to watch the sun setting behind the mountains, it's orange glow bleeding through the valleys and along the dirt tracks.

I can't believe he remembered.

Even just being able to gaze up at them now, their glow already invigorates me.

'Just reminding you of what you'll miss when you're gone,' Duke says from where he's climbed up into the truck bed, a flask in hand. I swallow as I take him in, because the sight zaps at my heart, making me wonder if it'll be more than just the stars that I'll miss.

I push out a smile. 'Okay, this is a pretty good small moment, I'll give you that.'

He bows at me. Trying to temper down my smile, I climb up into the truck bed before dropping into the blankets piled beneath me. I don't hold back from shovelling a piece of pizza down, going for ham and pineapple first because it's my favourite, even if most people screw their faces up when I say so. Duke follows suit and we chomp in a comfortable silence, occasionally tipping our heads up to watch the stars.

When I twist the cap off the flask to wash down my food, the smell immediately awakens me, because I'd know my favourite drink anywhere. 'You brought me Jack and Coke?'

'Diet Coke, actually – it's your favourite, right?' he checks.

'The whole drink is, yeah.' I'm a sucker for a Jack Daniel's and Diet Coke – its taste always reminds me of laughter and dancing at summer rodeos. But I usually stay away from stronger drinks like whiskey when I'm under the prying eyes of the town.

'Fuck, that's good,' I groan as I take my first sip.

Warmth immediately simmers through my limbs as the drink pours smoothly down my throat. The smoky taste sends calm flooding into my bloodstream. When I take another swig and let out a hum of pleasure, Duke shifts. I wipe away a drop of liquid that catches on my bottom lip with my thumb, and I swear his dark eyes follow the movement.

He clears his throat shortly after. 'Glad – uh, glad you like it.'

It's difficult to force my brain not to read into this all – the stargazing, the bringing my favourite drink. How it's so thoughtful, it feels borderline . . . intimate. But I remind myself that this is what Duke's like. He's not the guy who tells his friends how much he loves them; he's the guy who strives to help his friends whenever they need him.

He's the listener, the one who probably knows you better than you know yourself.

Before I know it, I've drunk about half of what's in the flask, sipping it down like it's juice, and already a warm fuzziness spreads out in my limbs.

'Yeah,' I sigh out, shuffling around so my back is against the side of the truck bed. Duke twists and copies me. 'Thank you. For all of this.' I'm back blinking up at the stars, seeing if I can pick out any of the constellations Mom taught me when I was younger.

'Like I said, we made a deal,' Duke replies with a shrug.

As he also tilts his head up to watch the stars, chewing on a mouthful of the pepperoni pizza, I let myself be reckless and admire him. The way his tattoos peek briefly out from his T-shirt, stretching with the column of his thick neck as he looks up. The breadth of his shoulders and chest, like a wide shield, ready to protect you from harm's way. The quiet smile that always plays on his lips, forcing the corners up in a faint curve, even when resting. The latter always gives him that approachable edge, one that makes you want to spill all your thoughts to him.

'In all honesty,' I admit, picking up another slice of pizza, 'I thought you might not want to help me again after I squashed your size-thirteen dick.' The words come out quicker than I can stop them.

Suddenly, Duke's choking, whacking his chest with his fist. He reaches his hand out for the flask and I quickly oblige, letting the Jack and Coke save him from the coughing fit. After a few more gulps, he lets out an exasperated sigh. 'Jesus, Cherry. Did you have to say it like *that*?'

'What?' I laugh at the way his eyes have gone comically

wide. 'You wouldn't care if Wyatt or Sawyer said it like that.'

'Yeah, because they're not—'

'A girl?' I cut in, angling my head at him. 'You guys don't exactly treat me like a girl.'

Duke's jaw drops as if he's going to protest, but he takes another long sip from the flask instead. After screwing the cap back on, he tosses it between us. 'Ah, it's just . . . easier that way, Cherry. You're Wyatt's little sister. It would be weird if we treated you like every other girl we know. Imagine the shit you'd have to put up with from Sawyer and Wolfman.'

'I already put up with shit from those two.' I chuckle, making Duke laugh too, his smile beaming even in the darkness of midnight. 'They're always doing and saying things in front of me to annoy Wyatt. It's only you who doesn't.'

With that, Duke's expression softens, tempering any brightness in his eyes. Slowly, his eyes trail over the pizza, and up my body to my face, leaving a fluttering in my heart and a heaviness settling deep in my stomach. He swallows, dark eyes locked with mine. 'I guess I'm just a really good friend.'

'Right.' I roll my lips together. 'And you were being a *really good friend* when you pushed me into that racing crowd of people at the roller rink.'

A warm rumble of laughter fills the air. Duke stretches out his legs, letting them lie beside me. 'It made you learn quickly though, didn't it? Plus, I think you got me back when you fell on me.'

Copying him, I bring my legs out from underneath me where they'd been crossed and stretch them out beside his.

I try to sneer at him, but my smile can't contain itself. 'Oh yeah, I mean the minor heart attack it gave me was totally on the same level as being kneed in the balls, I'm sure.'

'Whatever you say, Baby Hensley.' Duke rests his arms behind his head, leaning back so he can stare up at the starry sky. 'But it was worth it. The way your face lit up when you finally got a hold of things was the best part of the evening.'

My body jolts at the words, while Duke's completely stills. His eyes stay painfully trained on the sky above, but his Adam's apple bobs. And there I thought he wasn't watching me at that point.

After a long blink, Duke finally looks down at me. 'Let's just sit and watch the stars for a bit, yeah?'

I mimic zipping up my lips, eliciting a quick smile from Duke, before he's looking up again. But that smile never leaves his face. Not for the long moment I continue watching him until I finally follow suit and bask in the twinkling glow of the stars above.

Boldly, I let one of my sneakers drop to the side and rest against his leg gently, testing the waters I thought were always too dangerous for me to dip my foot into, to see if he'll move away. But to my surprise, he doesn't. Instead, he slides his own closer to me, letting the warmth of his calf diffuse into mine. It's the smallest touch, probably nothing compared to how he touches other girls, but it has my body lighting up brighter than all the stars speckling the dark sky.

10

Duke

Cherry looks bored. She's looked that way for the past five speed-dates she's been on, and the drawing I've been sketching of her on this napkin only reflects that back to me.

There's a smile playing on her red lips, yes, but it's barely there. And her eyes keep wandering – to the drink she's barely touched in front of her, to the other dates going on beside her, to the bar where I'm working. She idly plays with a lock of her hair, coloured light from all the neon signs cascading off the shiny strands as she twirls it around one finger. She nods and listens, adding the occasional input to whatever conversation she's having.

I try to pull my attention away and unclench my unexpectedly tight jaw as I screw up the napkin and throw it in the trash behind me. It's not like I'm qualified to assume I can decipher Cherry's mood easily anyway. But all I can think about right now is that she doesn't look *happy*. Not like the bright-eyed, red lips pulled into a soft smile Cherry I've grown accustomed to when she's working at the bar. When she's with me.

I'm jolted back to reality when Montana rings her bell to signal it's the end of the date. Though, as Montana then announces to the group, it's halfway through the night, meaning it's time for a drink break as opposed to making the guys move on to the next table. It also means the bar is about to get very crowded, which is a needed distraction.

I've got to give it to Montana and Cherry, though – as much as I bemoaned the idea of hosting this speed-dating event, it's gone better than I expected. Everything has run smoothly, no hiccups in sight with Montana handling the logistics like a pro, so that Cherry can focus on her dates. Given the small timeframe they had to pull this together, the turnout is much larger than I expected too – with a few familiar faces like two of Wyatt's ranch hands, Flynn and Josh. And now all those singles are flocking to the bar with their wallets, so I can't really complain.

Jeb – my number two who's worked here since before I took over from my grandfather and covers me anytime I'm not around – is behind the bar, working through all the orders with me. Shaking and stirring all kinds of drinks and creating new concoctions of flavours for people to try always gets my creative juices flowing and my mind calming.

Slowly, the crowd at the bar begins to disperse once they've been supplied with plenty of alcohol to calm their nerves, and they move off in clusters to mingle with each other amongst the wooden tables and bar stools.

Numbers are already being exchanged, along with hearty laughter and promising smiles. The last few people grab their drinks, leaving one person left to approach the bar – Cherry.

Maybe it's just the way the lights are angled in the rafters, but I swear all the light in the room seems to pool around her as she shuffles towards the bar. With a sigh, she leans her arms against the bar as she eyes up the liquor bottles behind me.

Jeb places a hand on my shoulder as he passes behind me. 'Gonna head out back for a break now the crowd's died down.'

'Sure thing, take your time,' I reply.

'Can I join him?' Cherry laughs, moving to rest her chin on her fist as she regards me. She hasn't ordered a drink yet, but I find myself starting on a cocktail for her.

I reach behind me to grab a bottle of vodka and measure out a small amount, trying to keep my hands busy. 'Not having a good time?'

Her sigh comes out more like a chuckle, but I don't miss the disappointment that briefly flashes across her face. She shrugs, the movement making her silky hair fall over her shoulder. 'I can't figure out if I'm terrible with guys, or guys are just terrible,' she contemplates. 'Is it normal for a guy to spend the whole three minutes talking about how they should take money away from creative college courses and put it into *more useful*—' she uses air quotes for the last two words '—degrees after I said I was studying interior design?'

My hands still, something oddly akin to rage flickering in my chest. Jesus, don't guys know how to treat a woman anymore? Don't they realise that Cherry is solely responsible for bringing this bar to life, for designing and decorating a place that not only pulls on the small town charm of Willow Ridge, but blends the retro with the modern, ensuring every patron of mine feels like they belong?

'No, Cherry. That is *not* normal. Who the hell said that?'

She waves it off like it's nothing. 'Ugh, Dale Callaway. He was a jerk in high school, so I don't know why I'm surprised. Oh, but he did soften the blow by making sure to tell me *well done* for getting hotter since high school.' She gives me two sarcastic thumbs up and the snarkiest of smiles, before rolling her eyes and slumping back against the bar.

That makes me snort. Even though thunder rumbles in the back of my mind at the idea someone would disrespect Cherry so brazenly like that, I can't help but notice the light already shimmering brighter in her eyes by the second since she's been at the bar with me. Like someone's finally added some extra kindling to the fire that was dimming inside of her.

'Yeah, well,' I begin, adding the remaining juice and flavourings to the shaker, 'Dale Callaway only says that shit because he's trying to make himself feel better after his dad handed his business over to his nephew instead of his incompetent son.'

One plus side of being the local bartender – you learn *everyone's* secrets.

Cherry's lips pop open and she covers her mouth as a laugh squeaks out of her. I flash her a grin and start shaking up her drink, suddenly revelling in the way she watches me with wonder as I work, the way she's glowing now, any hint of boredom vanished. I'm not normally one for theatrics, not in a small town bar like this, but my heart is suddenly beating faster under Cherry's shining gaze, so I grab a glass with one hand, giving it a small flip in the air, before pouring her cocktail into it from above me.

Her laugh rings out like silver bells, each peal sending a shot of dopamine through me. It's a high I feel oddly eager to chase.

A quick round of applause snatches our attention away and I realise a few of the singles were watching me make Cherry's drink, now clapping to appreciate the entertainment, even if the show wasn't meant for them. It makes me remember where we are. That this is a speed dating event basically created for Cherry to find someone.

I push out a quick smile of gratitude to the people who clapped, then shove Cherry's drink in front of her, adding on, 'Enjoy the rest of your dates, Baby Hensley.'

Maybe I was the one to put that light back in her eyes, but I've also stamped it out just as quickly.

* * *

I've relegated myself to my office to do God knows what, but anything other than watching Cherry on her dates. After sending her off with her drink to mingle with the others – exactly what she should have been doing, as opposed to hiding out at the bar with me – Cherry's expression dropped and stayed like that as she sat down for her next round of dates. If I thought she looked bored before, well . . . I wouldn't want to be the guy sat opposite her now.

I've just about tidied everything up in here that I can, the monotonous activity of cleaning and sorting out my office helping to calm my thoughts. Given that I've left Jeb behind the bar alone for a while, I should probably head back out to give him some company. Flickering neon signs greet me as I head back out, and once I reach the bar, I chance a glance at Cherry's table where she's now on a date with a guy that I used to play football with at high school – Reid Wells, who's also the son of Cherry's family doctor. He's a good man – probably one of the only people Wyatt knows in Willow Ridge who he'd be okay with dating his little sister. Though, if Cherry's attitude to any of her other dates is anything to go off, she's likely just as bored with this one.

Except . . . she's not.

She's laughing. Full on giggling like a schoolgirl as she talks with Reid. She's even biting her goddamn lip. I've only ever seen her do that around me.

I grip the edge of the bar tight, counting down the remaining minutes as I watch them, noticing how Cherry hasn't glanced away once. Every bit of her attention is focused on Reid, wonder sparking in her eyes like it was when she watched me.

The ring of the bell is fucking music to my ears.

Reid brushes his hand over Cherry's as they say goodbye, my jaw immediately tightening at the sight. Jesus, I need to get a grip.

Opportunity pings in my mind though when I see the

next person to sit down with Cherry is Flynn – Wyatt's ranch hand. I've barely even considered the idea before my legs are whisking me over to their table.

'Hey, man.' I place my hand on Flynn's shoulder, and he turns, shooting me a smile. 'I'm afraid I have strict instructions from Wyatt to make sure none of his ranchers go on a date with Cherry, so how do you fancy swapping? Jeb will teach you how to throw some drinks about.'

It's a long shot, given that I didn't intervene when Cherry sat down with Josh for her first date, but Flynn doesn't even consider that, his face lighting up as soon as I said the word *throw*. He's up and out of his seat with a *hell yeah,* racing over to the bar. I watch as he explains the situation to Jeb, who just rolls his eyes at me, but humours the kid, grabbing some shakers.

'What are you doing?' Cherry rears back in her seat as I settle into mine, trying to ignore the countless glances that have been thrown our way.

'Giving you a break. You looked a bit fed up. Can't I help a friend out?'

She sucks her teeth, eyes narrowing at me. Then, she announces, particularly loudly, as if to make sure Reid hears from the other table, 'I actually really enjoyed my last date.'

'That's good,' I grit out, a long silence following.

Cherry crosses her arms. 'Well, if you're going to interrupt one of my dates, you can at least make conversation. Dale Callaway might have insulted me, but he *tried* to talk to me.'

My bottom lip drops at her sudden attitude – a side of her I'm not used to. 'I can do that.'

'It'll probably require more than four words.'

'Wow.' I smother my laugh, rubbing my hand across my stubble. 'Clearly ticking these items off your bucket list has done wonders for your confidence already.'

I relish how hard she tries to bite back her emerging smile – *bingo*, that's what I'm here for. Within seconds, her straight shoulders have relaxed, and she leans towards me on the table. 'I think it's going to take a lot more than doing a few things to feel stronger, but . . . well, I did do a pole dancing class with Montana this week and that made me feel pretty good. So maybe it's helping a bit.'

Fuck. I *really* did not need to know that.

Wyatt's little sister, I remind myself over and over in my head, closing my eyes for a second to push any images out of my mind. I just nod, unsure if I can string any words together.

Oblivious to the effect that has had on me, Cherry continues, 'But it hasn't translated into dating yet. Like I said, I'm terrible with guys. I never know what to say or if I do talk I just babble. You know me.'

It makes no sense to me – because how hasn't she had guys throwing themselves at her when she looks the way she does with those dark, enchanting eyes and cherry-red, heart-shaped lips? When her laugh is a melody I'd happily listen to on repeat?

I furrow my brow. 'You talk easily to me.'

'Yeah, well . . .' A faint blush rises into Cherry's cheeks, as she glances down at the table. The silence that hovers between us when her eyes flick back up to catch mine is electrified. Her tongue darts out to wet her lips before she admits, 'This is by far the best date I've had all night, anyway. It's . . . easy.'

My mouth opens to reply, *this isn't a date*, on the tip of my tongue, but nothing comes out. Not when she's looking at me with hope glistening so intensely in her eyes—

I'm saved by the bell, literally. Montana lets it ring out to signal to switch dates, and there's suddenly someone hovering beside me. It's harder than I'd like to admit to rip my eyes away from Cherry, but I find the strength to get up. I give her a quick smile and head back to the bar, where I spend the rest of the night watching countless more men enjoy the chance to go on an *actual* date with Cherry. A chance I continue to remind myself I'll never be allowed to have even as I'm lying wide awake in bed at the end of the night.

11

Cherry

A rainbow of dazzling lights flash and flicker around me, while cheers and squeals echo along with the whoosh of rides, the distant music from the live band across the other side of the fair filtering through. Laughter floats on the air, along with bubbles blown by children as they pass by. The sweet and sugary scent of cotton candy wafts through the warm summer evening, mingling with the mouth-watering smell of freshly cooked corn dogs sizzling nearby.

This might be one of my favourite parts of summer in Willow Ridge – the town fair. Even Sawyer does whatever he can to make a trip back for one night, knowing how fun it is, usually bringing a date with him – tonight it's a beautiful woman called Cassidy who works in the feed store in town. Wolfman's babysitting for his twin sister, so he brought his four-year-old niece, Bonnie, along, and my heart melts watching him take her on the kids' rides, despite barely being able to fold his massive frame into them. The little girl has curly dark hair just like Wolfman, but the brightest blue eyes.

My head is spinning so much from being on the waltzers with Rory and Fliss that I accidentally bump into Duke as we clamber off the ride to join him and the rest of our group. His large hands fly out to steady me but retract as quickly as they caught me. He shoves them straight in his pockets afterwards.

Fliss grabs Rory by the shoulder for balance too. After catching her breath, she asks, 'Okay, so what's next?'

'I'm thinking Ferris wheel,' Rory suggests, pointing behind us to where the huge wheel currently sits idle, the evening sunshine glinting off its metal frame.

'Sounds good to me,' I add, trying to feign confidence in my tone, which only makes Wyatt's head whip round so he can perk a brow at me incredulously.

'*You* want to go on the Ferris wheel? Pretty sure the last time you went on any ride above six foot tall you bawled your eyes out.' Wyatt crosses his arms.

'That was years ago. I've grown up since college.' Fake it 'til you make it, right? He doesn't have to know that I've been close to peeing my pants every time I've thought about making myself go on one of the bigger rides today to try to tick facing my fear of heights off my bucket list.

'I just don't want you getting stressed, y'know?' Wyatt frowns, a divot appearing between his dark brows. 'Remember what happened when you went to that theme park when you were fifteen? The nearest hospital was ages away. Stress isn't good for your—'

'I'll be fine, Wyatt,' I rush out, trying to push the bleak

memory of ruining Montana's theme park birthday out of my mind. 'Chill out.'

The concern doesn't dissipate from Wyatt's face, but he does hold his hands up in surrender, mouthing, *okay*.

'Do *you* wanna go on the Ferris wheel, Bonbon?' Wolfman jiggles his niece in his arms. Her gorgeous little blue eyes light up with glee, and for a second I'm jealous of a four-year-old's lack of fear.

It's a low point, I know.

'Ferris wheel sounds fun,' Sawyer admits. 'As long as we get our own pod.' He shoots a saucy wink at Cassidy and the rest of us groan.

'Sign says the Ferris wheel isn't open for another ten minutes,' Fliss adds, covering her eyes from the early evening sun to squint and read the sign better.

'Oh, damn.' Rory throws her hands to her hips. 'Well . . .'

'Hey, isn't that Honey Goldman?' Wyatt interjects, nodding his head to our left, forcing all our gazes to follow.

'What?' Sawyer almost gasps, his eyes frantically scanning the surrounding fair.

'There.' Wyatt points through the crowds, somewhere towards a ring toss stand. There's a few people around the activity, including a woman with her long blonde hair pulled back into a ponytail, helping a young boy. 'Yeah, that's *definitely* her.'

'Oh yeah,' Wolfman chimes in. 'I forgot to tell you – guess who got a job at Willow Ridge High? I couldn't believe it when I heard.'

Rory taps Wyatt on the arm. 'Who's Honey Goldman?'

'Ask Sawyer, he's the one who used to spend so much

time with her,' Wyatt suggests, forcing everyone to turn to the bull rider.

There's a paleness to his face while his eyes are trained on where Honey must be in the distance. I wonder where he's gone, because there's no way his mind is still with us. But he's quick to blink away, pulling his brows together with a shake of his head. Sawyer tightens his arm around Cassidy's waist, throwing on a cocky smile.

'Bit of an exaggeration,' he scoffs. 'She was just some random choir girl who used to tutor me so I didn't get kicked off the football team.' He glances back once to where Honey was, a muscle feathering in his jaw. 'Anyway, wanna go get a drink, Cass? I'm kinda done with all these rides and games.'

'Sure thing.' Cassidy places a hand against his chest before Sawyer salutes us with a 'Catch you guys later,' and whisks her off towards the drink vendors.

'Well, that was weird,' Fliss snorts. 'Somehow I don't think she was *just some random choir girl*.'

'Uncle Miles.' Bonnie tugs on Wolfman's T-shirt from where he's holding her on his hip with one arm. 'Can we go on the carousel too?'

'I don't see why not, Bonbon.' Wolfman pokes her on the nose, making her giggle. Duke clears his throat beside me, but quickly looks away, flexing his arm as he scratches his head.

'Oh – yes, let's go on the carousel!' Rory suddenly squeals, far more excited than even Bonnie seems about the prospect. 'That'll be a great opportunity to take some fun pics too.'

'A second ago you wanted to go on the Ferris wheel.

Which one is it, princess?' Wyatt asks, wrapping his arm around her waist.

Rory rises onto her tiptoes to check out the sign for the Ferris wheel behind us. 'Fliss was right, they're not opening for another ten minutes. Why don't Duke and Cherry go wait by it so we can be first on while we go get some pictures?'

I open my mouth to speak – but before I know it, Rory's grabbing Fliss and Wyatt's hands, and dragging them off as she sings, 'Perfect, thanks, guys.'

Wolfman just shrugs at us. 'See you in a bit, I guess?' And with that he's carrying Bonnie off to the carousel.

That was a bit . . . random.

Duke offers me a hopeless smile, then gestures towards the Ferris wheel, its edges dotted with red and green lights, and we walk in silence until we reach it. No one else is hanging beside the ride, just the two of us.

'So, I guess we just wait now then,' I sigh, adjusting my white cowboy hat on my head as I scour the fair, toeing the ground with my boot.

Taking one glance up as we arrived at the wheel had my chest tightening instantly, even though I know my fear's irrational. In fact, according to Google there are less deaths by Ferris wheel than a lot of other rides, so the odds really are in my favour here.

And yes, I did Google *death by fairground rides statistics* before coming here. That doesn't stop me from anxiously shaking my leg, though.

But I can't chicken out now. I've made a good start with my bucket list – I feel like I'm on a winning streak, each item an extra building block to the woman I'm becoming.

Plus, it's fear that holds us back from what we want most in life – that's what Rory always tells me. If I can start tackling this fear, one that is literally based on zero grounding, then surely I can take on anything. Moving away from home, having to be a professional in a new job, and even trying to flirt with a man are far less deadly than sitting in a rickety box fifty feet in the air.

'Yeah . . .' Duke presses his lips together into a brief smile, rubbing the back of his neck before he knocks on the vendor booth below the Ferris wheel, which causes my brows to lower. 'Or we could tick off facing your fear of heights without the rest of the group around? Avoids Wyatt or Wolfman rocking the cabin to scare you.'

Before I can respond, a tall, brawny old man appears in the window of the booth, shoots a glare between the two of us, then cocks his head towards the wheel. Duke gives him a thumbs up, then proceeds to reach over the gate to unlock it, the old man disappearing back down into the booth like he was never there. My jaw is still hanging down when Duke turns back to me.

He explains, 'Waylon's an old friend of my grandfather.'

Well, that's an odd coincidence.

With a half-smile, Duke gestures for me to follow him up onto the platform below the wheel, but my feet stay glued firmly to the ground. And now my heart rate has kicked up, body suddenly aware that I *don't* have ten minutes anymore to prepare to climb into this massive death trap. I mean, these things might be tall and look sturdy, but they creak and sway in the wind. And even the slightest movement has the cabins swinging so violently, I don't know how more people don't fall out.

I'm not sure I trust those Google statistics anymore.

I've closed my fists so tight that my nails are digging into my palms. I shake them out as I babble, 'Maybe we should start somewhere a little . . .' My head tilts up to the highest point of the wheel. 'Lower.'

Duke holds his hand out to me. Tenderly, he says, 'Come on. You can do this.' When I'm still unconvinced and unmoving, he adds, 'I'll be right here with you.'

Each word wraps around my heart, giving it a gentle squeeze. I swallow thickly, letting my eyes drop to his outstretched palm, following the path of his tattoos. I start with that new mystery horseshoe, eagerness to discover its meaning still abundant. My gaze wanders along the barbed wire wrapped around his forearm, the trees above them, and each petal of the roses blooming across his bicep.

Each inked illustration reins in the loud adrenaline coursing through my veins, calming my hands into a lighter tremble. They're so familiar – a reminder that I'm safe in his arms. That even if I fall, he'll be there to help me back up, to keep me strong when I feel like shattering.

Because this is Duke. Warm, strong, gallant Duke. I'm safe with him. He's got me. Even when he doesn't realise that he does, he's *always* got me.

12

Cherry

Tentatively, I step towards the Ferris wheel. When my foot lands on the metal platform there's a quiet creak of metal, making me freeze. God, why can't Ferris wheels be made of something sturdier like goddamn *concrete*?

I'm motionless, one foot on the platform, the other on the grass, while Duke just watches me softly, hand still hovering in the air.

After a beat, he sighs – but it's not condescending, nor one of impatience; instead, there's something akin to understanding behind it. 'Look, if you don't want to, we don't have to. Having fears doesn't make you weak, Cherry. It makes you *normal*. Everyone is scared of something, but that doesn't make us less strong, no matter how irrational some fears might be. I'll still think you're amazing, regardless of whether you get on this ride or not.'

How does he know what to do and say to me like it's second nature?

'What's yours?' I find myself asking.

'Mine?'

'Fear.' I let my eyes wander around the metal contraption above me. 'You said everyone is scared of something.'

A small crease appears between his brows as his gaze drops to the floor. He contemplates for a second, Adam's apple bobbing before he admits, 'Losing anyone else. Not having the people I love around me anymore. I've lost too many. I'll do anything to make sure I don't risk that.'

Considering that I'm not sure Duke even tells Wyatt much about his mother or grandfather, I don't know what I've done to deserve his vulnerability. Regardless, he's given me his, so it's my turn to give him mine.

'Okay, let's do this.' I try to push all irrational thoughts from my mind as I march past Duke and clamber into the first pod.

My limbs tense up, spine curling, as the pod starts to wobble from my added weight, and again when Duke gets in. I force my eyes closed, focusing on my breathing and trusting Duke to lock up and secure us in. It's only when I feel his weight settle beside me that my eyes shoot open again, instantly examining the wheel.

'Shouldn't you sit on the other side to balance out the weight?' I ask, legs bobbing. Can't we have a count down or something so I know when it will start?

'Hey, look at me.' Suddenly, Duke's warm fingers are wrapping around mine where they were fidgeting in my lap, intertwining them until they're locked together in a bind that feels scarily permanent. Like even if we were freefalling, he'd never let me go. My eyes shoot open to find his. And then he says, with a squeeze of my hands, 'I've got you, Baby Hensley.'

His words knead out my taut muscles. My surroundings start to blur in my periphery as I focus in on Duke's dark, tender, *unyielding* stare. The same stare I kept catching landing on me at speed-dating last Thursday. I can't pretend that night, him sitting with me, hasn't been on my mind ever since. It hit me so hard, like slamming straight into a brick wall, how I've never enjoyed talking with a guy as much as I do with him. Or laughed as much. Or had my body flushed with as much heat as when I'm around him.

With Duke, everything I feel seems *magnetised*. And I'm wondering if I'll ever find that sensation in all these other places I'm searching.

Suddenly, a loud, metal clang vibrates through the wheel as it starts to move, rocking the cab in a way that has me scrunching my toes like I stupidly might be able to hold on tighter through my boots. Nausea bubbles in my stomach as we slowly climb into the air, my legs shaking faster.

'I'm okay, I'm okay,' I whisper to myself.

'What's a firework kiss?' Duke asks abruptly. His fingers pulse against mine, dragging my attention back to him.

I breathe out raggedly, 'What?'

'A firework kiss.' I swear his eyes dart down to my lips once, neon lights faintly reflecting in them. 'It was on your bucket list. I don't know what it is. Tell me.'

Oh, yes, the last item before the list descends into the most chaotic sexual inventory that only emphasises my lack of sexual experience. Which Duke has regrettably seen.

Why is he asking me about this now? Considering how put off he was when he read that list, and how adamant he was about ensuring I knew him helping me with the bucket list did *not* include anything sexual.

'It's, um . . . a kiss where you feel fireworks.'

Duke slides slightly closer, tugging on my hands that are still harboured within his. One of his thighs lightly brushes mine, his warmth seeping into my bones. He echoes, '*Feel fireworks?*'

I chuckle, a little exasperated at having to explain this to him. 'Yeah, like when you, uh, when you kiss them it feels like a thousand fireworks going off inside of you.'

Little does he know sometimes all I need is for him to smile at me to feel that. I can't imagine the kind of marvellous explosion that would come from the touch of his lips against mine…

'Hm,' Duke hums, gaze dropping to my lips again. An orange glow slowly lights up his side, shining against his cheekbones and dancing in his eyes. I'm mesmerised by the way it brings out all the shades of brown in his irises I don't normally get to see in the dark lighting of the bar. 'And how does one achieve that exactly?'

My laugh comes out high-pitched. Heat crawls over my skin and up my spine at the way Duke's still watching my mouth, as if he's trying to imagine the experience I've described. My cheeks flame as I admit, 'I—I wouldn't know. That's why it's on the bucket list.'

'You've never imagined having one?'

Only with you.

'Well, sure, but—'

A metal creak sounds and—

'Tell me what it would be like.' His rough command makes my back straighten. Fuck, that voice did more to me than I expected.

'I . . . I guess it would have to be a long time coming. Something you've both been wanting for ages.'

His responding noise of contemplation is more like a growl. I imagine that sound echoing in my ear, the hairs on the back of my neck standing at the sensation.

'So, it probably wouldn't be *soft*?'

'No . . .' I'm breathless at his words. Warm honey drips down my spine. 'I think it would be—' I stop to swallow, my mouth watering at the images flashing into my mind of Duke's lips crashing against mine '—hard. *Rough*.' The last word has his pupils completely blowing out, nothing but darkness filling his eyes. 'Like you'd grab each other and . . .'

Duke wets his lips; his voice laced with gravel. 'Hey, Cherry?'

'Yeah?'

There's a tightness to his jaw as he says, 'Look to your left.'

It takes longer than I'd care to admit to drag my eyes away from Duke's mouth but when I do, wonder flushes through my body, softening every muscle until I'm pliant and all-consumed by the scenery ahead of me.

The sky is a melting pot of pastel pinks, purples, and oranges, small wisps of cloud dappled across it all like drops of candyfloss. Inky mountains cut through the sugary skyline, a platform for the golden sun that's beginning to set behind them, raining deep orange rays between their peaks and flooding the valley below. Pinpricks of starlight break through the top of the sky where a faint stroke of darkness begins.

It's goddamn breathtaking. I want to take a photo, but I don't think anything could do this moment enough justice.

'Look at that, a big thing for a small one,' Duke whispers to me, squeezing my hand.

It's then that I realise we're still holding hands. That we've stopped moving. In fact, I think we might have stopped moving a while ago, but I just hadn't noticed because I was too entranced by thinking about kissing Duke. By his full, hypnotising lips. The kind that I know would bring my body to life with a single touch.

I think . . . all of that was on purpose. A distraction to keep me safe from the climb until we reached the reward.

But how could I have been so scared of *this*?

I don't care how high up we are if this is what I get – able to see the golden-drenched town of Willow Ridge from the heavens, as if I'm an emerging star, readying myself to gaze upon and watch over the beautiful world below. My skin tingles, limbs becoming lighter as I let my eyes trail over our surroundings. But it's not from fear, not the usual faintness that sweeps through me on rides like these. Instead, it's *power*. Aliveness. A strength that only comes from realising how great and vast the world is, how insignificant your worries and fears really are in comparison.

'How are you feeling?' Duke questions, his thumb running across my knuckles in a way that sparks through my body. He hasn't let go yet...

My response is on the tip of my tongue, so unfamiliar, the only word I can use to describe how I feel right now. Because it's a sensation I haven't experienced in years, one I almost don't dare to say through fear I've misunderstood what it truly is. But with the security of Duke's hold on me, the golden sunset dousing me in its radiant warmth, and the knowledge that I survived – I got on this Ferris wheel and rose to my fear's challenge, it feels only right to reply, 'Invincible.'

And I carry that feeling through the rest of the night. Through the climb down, and back up again in the Ferris wheel with the rest of the crew, proving to my brother exactly how strong I am. Through letting loose as we dance to the lively music played by the country music band, allowing my body just to be free and do what feels right, never thinking that it's too weak. And through the drive home, curled up in the backseat of Wyatt's truck with Rory and Fliss, relishing in every time I catch Duke glancing at me in the rear-view mirror.

13

Cherry

'Don't you look all lovely and grown up,' my mom gasps as I rush into the kitchen, checking I've got everything in my clutch bag before Levi picks me up to head into the city for Montana's birthday. If I'm going to make it until closing time like my bucket list expects – and not give in to the usual paranoia of overexerting myself – I've got to make sure I'm fully stocked on makeup to keep it topped up all night.

My mom's eyes zip up and down my outfit – a cute, tight black dress that cuts off high on my thighs so I'm showing off my long legs – my best asset, given that my boobs and ass are practically non-existent. I've paired it with some black strappy heels and a dark-red clutch bag to match my signature lipstick.

'Thanks, Mom.' I walk over to her and press a kiss to her cheek. 'Hope your shift tonight goes okay.'

'Thanks, sweetheart. Make sure you've got your meds with you. And you know your father can always pick you up at midnight, you don't have to stay out as late as everyone just to try and fit in—'

'Mom, I'll be fine. Please, stop worrying,' I beg as her lecture instantly has my shoulders hunching. Still, it comes out a little snappier than I planned, and Mom's eyes flash, probably because it's the first time I've reacted that way, as opposed to holding back the frustration. But for some reason, today I feel a little bolder.

Maybe that bucket list is working its magic already.

'I'm sorry. It's just—' I stop myself to sigh. 'I'm twenty-one, Mom. I go out clubbing all the time at college. I haven't had a fit for two years, despite doing a lot of the stuff you tell me not to, and it's only been *me* looking out for me there. I . . . I'm not a kid anymore.'

A weight lifts from my chest, even though my heart is rattling at the words.

'Oh, Cherry. Come here.' Mom holds her arms out for me. I step into her embrace, letting her squeeze me tight. When she finally releases me, she strokes my hair, long and silky just like hers.

Her eyes soften. 'I'm sorry. I'm afraid you'll always be my baby, and your father's, but . . .' She sighs, a shine taking residence in her eyes. 'I know you probably don't need us watching over you so much. Don't think we don't trust you to look after yourself, because we do. I think it's just ingrained into us to always be looking out for you, even if, like you said, you're not a kid anymore.'

She gives me another quick hug, then holds me out in front of her to admire my outfit again. 'Now, go break some hearts at that club.'

* * *

'I usually think long hair is kinda childish when you're older, but on you it just looks hot.' The guy I've been talking to at the bar of the club – Clay, I think is his name – throws me an innocent smile, as if he thinks that backhanded compliment will work. You know, tear a girl down enough that I'll be more likely to go home with him tonight.

I take a long sip of my drink – the one I've been trying to make last much longer than this – to stop me from telling Clay to *just fuck right off*. And to think, I'd agreed with Montana I'd try to tick something off the second half of my bucket list tonight too – her mom's away, so she said we could stay in her guest room if I wanted to bring someone back.

Fat chance that's happening now.

'There you are!' Montana bumbles into my shoulder, spinning me around clumsily to face her. Her cheeks are flushed from dancing, as opposed to her lips which show little trace of the lipstick she had on earlier. I can tell from the glassy sparkle in her eyes that she's drunk on love as well as alcohol tonight.

'I've been looking everywhere for you – oh.' Montana stops herself when she notices the guy behind us. She raises her brows at me with a silent question, to which I give a subtle shake of my head. Wrapping an arm around my waist, Montana drags me away, shouting behind to the guy, 'Sorry, I need to steal my friend!'

I don't even say goodbye, just down my drink as we head towards the restroom. Once we're inside, Montana heads to the sinks to start topping up her lipstick.

'Thanks for saving me,' I say, blowing out a breath.

'Always, girl. Anyway, I think I wanna finally go home with Austin tonight.' She lets out a giggle when she catches my eye in the mirror – and that confirms where all her lipstick has gone.

'Yeah you do, you little minx!' I squeal, coming behind her to wrap her in a hug, squeezing tight.

'I know, I know! Will you be okay getting back without me? You can obvs still crash at mine.' She spins in my grip. 'I don't think I'm gonna make it 'til close, but I know you wanted to stay . . .'

'Yeah, of course.' The usual excuse of *I'm getting tired and probably shouldn't overdo it* lingers in the back of my mind, waiting to be used, but I push it away with a shake of my head. 'I can still get a lift with Levi – he was pretty keen to stay 'til the end anyway, so I'll go find him.'

'You sure?' Montana checks once more, batting her long lashes at me. It beats her bringing Austin back with us and having to sit next to them in the car while they make out. Or trying to sleep in the guest room when all I can hear is her creaking bed.

'Positive, birthday girl. I've got your spare key anyway.' I pull her into a hug again. 'Now, go find your man, be safe, and promise you'll let me know when you get to his, yeah?'

'Promise! Tell me when you get home too!' Montana slaps a big kiss on my cheek before dashing out the restroom. Chuckling, I whip out my phone to locate Levi.

Cherry: Hey, Montana's going home with Austin. Where are ya?

Levi: Course she is. I'm outside smoking. Come find me.

I filter my way through the crowded club, ducking behind a few groups to avoid the man I was talking to earlier, as I head outside. When I finally spot Levi, smoking on his own and leaning against the wall, my chest falls slightly with relief. No sign of his friend, Tiller, who came with us tonight, though. There's a few other people outside, and a couple leave as I make my way over. I rest against the wall next to Levi, letting out a long exhale.

He chuckles, smoke cascading into the air. 'I'm impressed you've made it this long.'

Levi offers me his cigarette and I shake my head. He shrugs and takes another pull, blowing the smoke leisurely away from me.

I breathe down as much of the cool summer's night air as possible while attempting to ignore the faint aroma of smoke, letting it revitalise me enough to continue dancing for another couple of hours. 'I'm trying to make it 'til close for once. It's a cool club.'

The last remaining people smoking drop their cigarettes to the floor, then head back inside, leaving the two of us. City lights cast the midnight sky with a faint glow while the soft rumble of distant cars occasionally fills the air. I love nothing more than getting lost in the loud pulses of club music, but the few minutes of quiet is welcome.

Though, the lack of stars dappling the sky does make my heart ache a little for the serenity of Willow Ridge. And sitting in a truck bed to watch them with a certain bartender…

'Yeah, it's not a bad club at all,' Levi agrees. 'I like that they let people up on those platforms to dance. Haven't seen that before.'

I nod with a smile, letting my eyes close for a moment. 'Right? So cool. I wish I could dance like them. Must be fun being up there.' No cares whatsoever as you just let your mind and body meld with the melody of the music – I bet it's liberating.

'Ah, you're way hotter, though.' My eyes shoot open. 'Doubt any of them could give as good of a lap dance either.' Levi twists towards me, shuffling along the wall. His smoky breath fills up the air between us and trying not to grimace is a struggle, especially when he's grinning at me like I'm a prize.

Instead, I just let out trembling laugh, sliding a few inches away.

'Well, it was Montana who got the lap dance, and she's gone home with someone else, so couldn't have been that great,' I joke, checking once to the open door. We're still the only ones out here. My skin prickles, the night's chill no longer welcome.

I'm all too aware of the way my heartrate is climbing.

'Well, I wouldn't have gone home with someone else,' he shrugs and flicks his cigarette to the ground.

Suddenly, his hands are wrapping around my waist, caging me in, as his head ducks down towards me—

'What are you doing?' I press my hands against his chest, keeping his lips from reaching mine. My clutch bag crumples against him and his nails dig into me.

What the actual fuck?

My eyes keep flicking between him and the door as I struggle to push back at him.

But Levi doesn't even look shocked, he just regards me with heavy, bloodshot eyes, leaning into my hands.

'Oh, come on, Cherry. Let go for once, enjoy yourself – Montana's always talking about how you're trying to let loose this year.'

Is he kidding me?

'Not with you,' I croak.

I clench my jaw to stop my teeth from chattering. From revealing the fear coursing through me. My arms ache with how much strength I'm channelling into keeping as much distance as possible between us.

My body begins to shake.

Blood rushes in my ears.

I . . . I don't know what to do.

Levi angles his head at me, as if waiting for me to give in. To give up.

I try to think back to what I learnt in those self-defence classes but I'm so scared if I take my attention away from Levi for one second, he'll do something worse.

'Why not?' he drawls, still smiling. Like he's not even fighting to push back against me when I feel like my arms are about to give way. 'Come on, Cherry. I can teach you a few things.'

His grip is too hungry, borderline painful. He goes to press himself into me and—

'Ugh, get off me!' I shout, bringing my knee up between his legs. He grunts and stumbles backwards, even further when I shove him again, dashing straight for the door.

I don't look behind.

I just *run*.

The music inside the club pounds in my head, threatening to force the tears welling in my eyes to spill. Strobe lights flash, sporadically cutting through the club to illuminate a broken exit route. Hands slide across me as I push my way through the crowds and groups gathered along the sides of the dancefloor. Every touch reminds me of Levi's, my knees wanting to buckle.

But I don't stop.

My feet scream in agony, reminding me that my black strappy heels really weren't designed for running.

I don't care, though. Not until I've forced myself through the club and the cool air bites into me.

I'm not sure how long I've been running outside when I finally settle into a brisk walk, giving in to my protesting legs. The club is out of sight, nothing but midnight drenched city streets around. I'm suddenly incredibly aware that I'm a young woman out in the dark alone, with no way of getting home. And the only place and people I know around here aren't safe for me anymore.

Every street I look down is filled with either too many dumpsters, dampness, or the dark. I've walked away from the bustling nightlife. I clutch my bag closer to my chest for some futile semblance of warmth, hoping it might also help keep me from crumbling. I'm not sure how much longer I have before I fall to pieces.

Eventually, in the distance, a neon twenty-four-hour diner sign flickers like a beacon of hope. Pain splinters through my shins as I race towards it. Barrelling through the metal doors, I hate that I have to check around just to make sure Levi's not here, as if this was somehow his plan all along, knowing I'd run here. My heart almost trips over itself with the immense relief that he's nowhere to be seen – just a couple and an old man filling the countless empty booths.

When I brush my face, my fingers come away wet

115

and black from my mascara. I'm not sure when I started crying, but from the pitiful way the waitress behind the counter is looking at me, it was clearly for a while.

'Take a seat, honey,' she offers as I wipe under my eyes. 'I'll bring you something warm to drink.'

I barely manage a grateful smile, then make a beeline for the booth in the corner. The one that's slightly in the shadows, where I can hide.

There's only one person I want right now. Only one person who knows how to bring me out of the darkness. So, I pull out my phone and dial his number, a wave of calm washing through me when I hear his voice.

* * *

Metal doors blast open, hurried footsteps echoing through the deserted diner. My head shoots up from where it had been resting in my hands to find Duke scouring the diner frantically, looking like he'd raze down everything in his way until he found me.

My heart pumps faster again, completely undoing the effort I'd put in to finally calm it. Even more when I note the tension in his muscles, bulging and shifting under his black T-shirt as he continues his rigorous search of the diner. One fist is closed around his black leather biker jacket, veins popping underneath the tattooed sleeves of his arms.

And when his dark, unforgiving eyes land on me, everything else disappears. No diner, no noise, no relentless memories of Levi pressing against me continuously running through my head to the point of mental exhaustion.

116

Just Duke Bennett.

Safety.

Even from the other side of the diner I can see the way his throat bobs as he stares at me, fire still blazing in his eyes. Every long stride he takes towards me only brings the wildness of his stare more into focus. And once he reaches the edge of the table, his pupils are so blown out, I feel like I could fall straight into his soul.

Hot fury radiates off him, burying deep into my bones. I'm half expecting him to explode – not at me, but at whatever chain of events has put me in this corner booth, mascara smudged on the back of my hands.

Instead, he just holds out his jacket for me, waiting patiently and silently, as I shuffle out of the booth. Then, he gently wraps the jacket around my shoulders and uses it to tug me against his chest. His heavy arms encircle me, and I let myself melt into the safety of his warm embrace. The place where I know that if I fall, he'll always be there to pick me up and carry me home.

Whatever it takes.

Duke rests his chin on top of my head, tucking me tighter into his solid body. That woody, cypress scent fills my senses, slowly kneading out the tension in my body along with the way one of his hands strokes down the back of my hair. Softly, he whispers against my parting, 'I've got you, Baby Hensley.'

14

Duke

Cherry hasn't spoken a word since we got in my truck. Just sat there with my jacket tucked around her, fingers gripping tight like it's the only thing holding her together right now.

I wish I could just pull over and wrap her in my arms right now. Let her cry all her pain and fear into me – I'll take every last drop, no matter how much it hurts me. I also wish my Silverado wasn't such an old piece of shit and I had heated seats to warm her up a bit more, given that the strappy black dress she's wearing is doing a terrible job at covering her up. Those long legs of hers bare and hanging over the edge of the seat. I should've kept that blanket from the other week in the back just in case. Though, the last thing I ever expected to find myself doing in the early hours of a Sunday was rescuing Cherry from the city.

But here we are.

She called *me*.

As if she knew I'd burn the whole goddamn world for her.

'You don't have to tell me what happened, but . . . if you want to talk about it, you know I'm always here to listen,' I eventually say, even though I'm desperate to find out who did this to her. Who I need to make pay for hurting her.

Cherry shifts in her seat, some passing headlights momentarily lighting up her face – the exhaustion painting every line, and the glassiness of her dark, heavy-lidded eyes. All she does is nod, so I turn my attention back to the road. Although not knowing what happened is agonising, I'll happily be patient with her. Hell, I'd wait a thousand years for Cherry if it meant I got to see her smile again.

I free one hand from the wheel to rub it over my face. Where the locks I usually keep on my emotions have gone, I don't know. Tonight took me by surprise and now all these feelings, unspoken words, buzz inside of me, ready to pour out.

A couple more minutes of silence pass, nothing but the faint whirr of the odd car and the low hum of the truck's engine filling the air. Starlight begins to speckle the sky the further away from the city we drive, the orange-tinged hazy glow from the nightlife slowly fading.

Then her sharp sigh cuts through the quietness. 'Levi forced himself on me.'

The truck swerves abruptly as my body jolts, but I quickly get it back under control, hands clenching the steering wheel until my knuckles are practically bulging out of my skin. Red fills my vision, my muscles stiffening as I try to fight my rage.

'I need to turn around,' I croak out, looking frantically for signs of when I can turn off and head back to the city. For God's sake, why can't you do U-turns on the highway?

How fucking *dare* he touch her.

I'll make sure he never even gets to look at her again.

Sliding up in the seat, Cherry stiffens. 'What? Why?'

'I'm gonna kill him,' I push out, teeth gritted.

'No, you're not.' Cherry laughs as she shakes her head. The sound – the brilliant, heart-warming melody that is her laugh – tugs me out of my fury.

I glance at how she's sitting, arms crossed, and one dark brow perked up at me, not appreciating my murderous intentions, clearly.

'Right now, you're going to carry on driving back to Willow Ridge,' Cherry declares, waiting for my sigh and nod before turning to face forward again. 'Levi can wait.'

'Fine, but he's fired.'

'Good,' is her terse response.

'Are you hurt?' I ask, unable to stop myself from glancing over her to check.

'No, I'm . . .' Cherry unfolds her arms, sinking back into the seat and threading her arms into my jacket, fully wearing it now. I fight the smug grin that wants to break out knowing her scent will be all over it. 'I'm just shaken. He only grabbed me. It didn't go any further. But I feel, I don't know . . . so *stupid* for trusting him and—' a sob escapes from her, my chest cracking open at the sound and the silver brimming in her eyes '—for freezing. I—I should've fought back more, should've stood up for myself better, but I just ran and—'

'Hey.' I reach out for her, stroking her silky hair to cradle her head. I keep my thumb rubbing at the base of her skull, hoping I can caress away her tears. 'Look at me.'

Glistening eyes flutter up to meet mine. I keep flicking my gaze between her and the road ahead, but don't miss the way the moon highlights the long column of her throat working.

'You are *not* stupid. You're the smartest girl – no, person – I know, Cherry. You could move mountains, I'm telling you. And just because you're goddamn beautiful doesn't mean anyone is allowed to touch you without your consent. It is *never* your fault. You got that?'

She nods, lips popping open. 'You – you think I'm beautiful?'

'I . . .' *Ah fuck*. I thought I'd gotten away with that slipping out. I'm hoping the darkness filling my truck cab is enough to hide the heat tingling along my cheeks. I slowly retract my hand from her head, placing it on the wheel. 'Yes, yes I do.'

Out of the corner of my eye – because I couldn't possibly face her as I admitted such – I see her nibble on her thumbnail. She does that when she's nervous, I've learnt, or is thinking intently.

'To be fair, he's the one who got *hurt,* technically.' Tucking her legs up beneath her, Cherry snorts. 'I kneed him in the balls. Told you I knew self-defence.'

Chuckling, I'm all too grateful for the quick redirection of the conversation. 'You have a habit of doing that, don't you?'

'Oh, shut up.' She waves me off. 'That was half your fault anyway for being just as clumsy as me.'

'I blame the hot-pink skates.' I flash her a grin.

'Or your clown feet,' she counters.

Still, her smile lasts barely five seconds before she twists in her seat to rest her head against the window and stare out at the passing scenery. We finally zoom off the highway and make our way towards the familiar country roads filled with too many memories. Snow-tipped peaks of the shadowy mountains are faintly illuminated by the glowing moon in the distance, acting as Willow Ridge's north star.

'Please don't tell Wyatt,' Cherry pipes up again.

'Cherry, he's your brother. I can't lie to him. He's my best fr—'

'*Please*, Duke.' Her fingers land on my forearm. The hairs on my arm stand to attention as the tips of her long red nails faintly graze my skin. 'I don't want to make a big deal out of it. I'd also like my brother to not end up in jail. It's my story to tell once I've processed everything. At least then I can stop it from becoming the town's gossip.'

'Okay, okay,' I groan.

'Promise?' Her fingers pulse against my arm.

'Promise.' *Anything for you, Baby Hensley.* My eyes briefly leave the road to catch hers, which are finally glistening with a bit more hope. 'Now, let's get you home.'

'No.' Now her fingers wrap around my arm, reminding me of too many recent dreams of her slender fingers digging into my skin . . . 'I can't go home.'

'Why not?'

Cherry's gaze reaches beyond me, somewhere out of

the driver's side window where her thoughts must lie. She worries her lip and finally loosens her grip on my arm. Though, her fingers still rest there, hand moving with my arm as I shift and turn the wheel, like she's more stable when we're connected.

I know the feeling.

'I was supposed to be staying at Montana's. If I go home, my parents will wonder why I'm back and start asking questions and . . . I'm just not ready to talk about it yet.'

'Okay . . . So, should I take you to Montana's, then?'

'Um . . .'

'That's not an answer, Cherry.'

'I just . . .' Her breath shuttles out as her body deflates, fingers finally slipping away from my arm.

'Hey, you can tell me.' I release one hand from the wheel and fold it around hers. I'm being way too greedy with touches tonight.

Cherry's body stills, eyes locking onto where I'm harbouring her hand. The usual concern runs through my mind about whether I've pushed the boundaries between us, but then she twists her hand, soft skin sliding against my rough palms, and laces her fingers between mine. I've never noticed the gaps between my fingers before, yet suddenly, all the nerve endings in my hands are lit up, relishing how *right* it feels to be connected to Cherry. How the bumps in our knuckles line up so perfectly, fingertips slotting into the ridges effortlessly. I have to ignore the way my body whispers *meant for me*.

'I have a key to Montana's place but . . . I don't want

to be alone tonight.' As she admits this, Cherry's gaze remains locked on our intertwined fingers.

Tentatively, her thumb rubs over the edges of the tattoos across the top of my wrist, exploring. It's a tiny movement, inconsequential really, but to me, it's goddamn brazen. Not even trying to hide the way she's letting her searing touch wander, especially when she just told me she didn't want to be alone . . . The words brand my mind as deeply as the warm pad of her thumb against my hand.

Because when you've wanted someone secretly for so long, everything they do – whether it's just a glance, or a smile, or a quick touch – *burns*.

I shouldn't read into it.

I should just insist I take her back to her parents.

But we'd have to drive past my place anyway. Plus, I'm not sure I'll be able to sleep knowing she's been hurt tonight, and I've just left her alone. With no one there to make sure she's safe. To make sure she sleeps soundly.

Wyatt would want me to look after her, right?

That's why I drove all this way.

To protect her.

To keep Baby Hensley safe.

It takes me a few seconds to prepare mentally for what I'm about to suggest, all the while I give Cherry's hand a tender squeeze, to remind her I'm here. Then, I ask, 'Did you want to stay at mine?'

She doesn't hesitate one second before saying, 'Yes.'

15

Cherry

I've known Duke for almost all my life, and I've worked in the bar, which his apartment sits above, for over two years. Yet this is the first time I've ever been allowed up the stairs and through the front door.

For years I've tried to imagine what it was like inside. Which parts of his personality would manifest and where. Would it be full of smooth surfaces and muted colours, reserved and quiet like how he often presents himself to the world? Or would it be messy and collaged with colour, a testament to the true artist within him? A reflection of the emotion he never shares with us, perhaps.

The interior design student side of me would have a field day designing a home for Duke. Like how I'd make the apartment open-plan – modern and sleek like Duke's fashion sense, but also easy to move around, ensuring his living experience matches his calm energy. Or how I'd design the sitting area as the focus of the space because I know how important being with friends and family is to him, even if it's just to sit and listen to them talk.

And when I step inside, the realisation of just how deeply I know Duke hits me like a load of bricks, tumbling in my stomach.

Because his apartment is exactly as I would have designed.

A small kitchen lies at the other end of the open-plan apartment, one wooden-paned window behind it, moonlight shining through and reflecting off the sleek black countertops and breakfast bar. Slate-grey couches sit perpendicular to each other in the centre of the room, surrounding a dark wooden coffee table, and angled towards the large flat-screen television hanging on the wall. A lighter grey bean bag chair accompanies the couches, most likely the place Wolfman and Sawyer fight over to sit. Wooden flooring extends throughout the room, while retro art prints and paintings of motorcycles, mountains, and rodeos are strategically scattered across the cream walls. Canvases of complete and half-finished paintings are also wedged into any empty spaces, the talent and labour poured into them worthy of being far higher than where they're currently stowed away.

I've gone and thrown myself straight into the deep end without anything to help me float. Because I'm in Duke Bennett's goddamn apartment. A place that was once only ever a figment of my imagination.

I almost flinch when Duke decides to help me take his jacket off – I hadn't realised how tightly I'd been grasping it, relishing the way his cypress scent soothed my frayed nerves. Neither of us have said anything since we parked up, all the events of tonight whirring through my mind.

How fiercely Duke embraced me in the diner, how tenderly he held my hand in the car – and don't even get me started on the sincerity with which he called me *beautiful*. That's going to be etched into my memory forever. It's hard not to read into any of that. Especially when I've never seen Duke show that level of emotion before. It was so palpable, I could almost taste it.

'I'll grab you a hoodie, something a bit more comfortable,' Duke says as he finishes sliding his jacket off my shoulders. There's a sudden hoarseness to his voice, like he's been breathing heavily. 'Make yourself at home.'

I wait until he heads off into what I assume is his bedroom. Rubbing a hand up and down my arm, I wander around the apartment, admiring the art more closely, and snooping as much as I can into the paintings he's been working on. Usually, I only get a glimpse at his talent through napkin sketches.

What becomes glaringly obvious though as I saunter further inside is that Duke left in a *rush*. There's a half-full glass of something on the coffee table, a pizza box that's still got two slices and a crust in it sitting beside the drink, and papers scattered across the surface. Even through the gap in the door to his bedroom, I can see him rushing to close drawers that had been left open, and tidy clothes from the floor.

Because he came to rescue me.

A weight pulls down on my heart at the thought.

And then it tugs even harder when I filter through three smaller canvases with portraits of a woman I'm certain I recognise. In the first, the woman's smile is framed by her short black curly hair, while cerulean and cobalt strokes paint an aura around her, lighter shades used to give her brown skin an almost otherworldly glow. But as the paintings progress, the colours become darker, the paint strokes messier, and the portrait more abstract. Where the first portrayed clear features and minor details, like the swirls of browns in her irises, the others lose their sharpness and clarity. The third is mostly made of mottled shapes and heavy brush strokes that just about give off the impression of a person—

'My mom,' Duke's voice rumbles behind me.

Immediately, I whip round to find him leaning against his bedroom door frame, arms folded, the hoodie clutched in one hand. One corner of his mouth twitches as he glances between me and the paintings. When I decipher his softened stance and gaze as confirmation that he's comfortable with me looking at the paintings, I inspect them closer. To appreciate the jarring sensation of experiencing such joy from the first painting, only to have it shadowed by the growing melancholy of the others. 'They're beautiful – *she's* beautiful.'

'She was.' The pad of his footsteps get closer. I expected him to stay by his bedroom, keeping a distance between us like usual. But he's suddenly behind me, broad chest faintly touching my shoulder every time he inhales. His scent is everywhere, each breath a little rougher as I drink it down. 'A great artist too – my grandmother has a lot of her paintings up in the house. It's where I get my creative side from, I guess.'

'She taught at the high school, right?' I check. 'Art?'

'Yeah. My dad taught there too. History. That's how they met.' A brief, almost inaudible chuckle comes from him. 'You would've liked my mom, I think. Our house was full of colour growing up – must have had that same eye for interior design as you.'

Duke unexpectedly runs his fingers down my arm until it meets the painting I'm holding, fingers curling around mine over the canvas edge, making my breath hitch. A shiver ripples down my spine, my breath threatening to never release. He's touching me in so many new ways tonight . . .

But what shocks me the most, is that Duke doesn't put the canvas back as I expected. Instead, he swallows audibly before he explains, 'They're supposed to represent my memories of her. I used to be able to remember her face so vividly, but as the years go by, I've struggled to recall the smaller details. Like I know she had black hair, but I can't quite picture how the curls fell anymore. I'm pretty certain most of my memories now are actually constructed from photos. It was the same with my dad, but I was only one when he passed so I know nothing there is real memories.'

My knowledge of Duke's family is built from small town gossip. Not even from Wyatt, his closest friend, because I'm certain those two rarely talk about their feelings. To be given the privilege to hear the truth directly from Duke's mouth is . . . extraordinary.

'This first one—' I let him retrieve it from my grasp '—is actually based on a photograph my grandmother has in her house. The others are what my mind could conjure up with what's left of my memories.'

I'm all too aware of how rare this moment is, how I don't want it to end – just like that little snippet of his fear he shared with me before the Ferris wheel. Because how often does Duke have anyone just listen to him, like he does for everyone else?

'You should display them,' I suggest.

Duke shrugs as he slots the canvas back with the others. The slice of moonlight shining through the back window catches in his eyes, the deep umber suddenly sparkling with cracked memories and reminiscent joy. 'I don't know . . . I just do it because it makes me feel better to paint. I'm not really sure how to deal with my grief, otherwise. Never got taught beyond a therapist's office. But painting . . . it works for me.'

He lets out a breathy laugh as he turns to gesture to the rest of the paintings littered around his apartment. 'Hence the overflowing collection.'

A grin spreads across my face as I spin to face him properly, grateful for the small, vulnerable insight into his life I'm not sure I would have gotten had I never come here tonight. 'Thank you, for telling me.'

Duke nods softly, keeping his head tilted down at me as his eyes immediately flick to my mouth. His tongue slowly wets his bottom lip, only emphasising how full his lips are—

'Arms up,' he suddenly instructs, holding out the hoodie.

I obediently do as he says. The silence in the room swarms me. Carefully, Duke slides the sleeves of the hoodie over each of my hands, pulling my arms through with such care, it makes me feel invaluable. A reminder that the harsh hold Levi had on me earlier was nothing close to what I deserve.

You're the smartest girl – no, person – I know, Cherry. You could move mountains, I'm telling you.

There was always a part of me that feared Duke's gentleness with me, aside from the occasional teasing, only reflected how fragile he saw me. I've never been able to scorch the day of my fall from my mind, caught up on the safety I felt in his arms, while I always wondered if that day solidified how he'd always see me – a girl in need of saving.

But now I'm looking at the painting of our friendship from a different angle – there's no trace of pity, only strokes of respect and devotion. He offers me tenderness because that's what I deserve. Because even the strongest girl in the world is worthy of being cared for.

'There.' Duke slides the hoodie over my head, pulling my long hair out so it doesn't get caught. His eyes sweep over me once, lips rolling together then parting, a shaky breath escaping them.

'Can I hug you again?' he asks on a whisper, forcing my gaze up to lock with his. 'I . . . I've wanted to hold you since you told me what happened, but I was driving and—'

'Yes, please,' I say, and immediately wrap my arms around his waist.

He sighs into my hair, warm breath filtering through the strands and sending a satisfying shiver down my spine. Slowly, his thick arms wind around me, one along my lower back, the other across my shoulders, and he presses me closer into his warmth. My face falls flat against his chest, ear pushed up against the broad expanse, listening to the rushed beat of his heart, while mine stays unhurried in the sanctuary of his arms. When Duke's chin rests on top of my head, I'm completely and utterly encompassed by him – his scent, heat, and body wrapping me up until we're basically one. I let myself melt into him.

'Thank you for calling me,' he whispers against my parting, so quietly, I almost think I've made it up in my head. But when his fingers pulse against me, where they anchor me into his embrace, almost to punctuate his gratitude, I know I heard correctly. Louder this time, he adds, 'I know I can't take away what happened, but I meant it when I said I've got you. Whatever you need to feel better – I'm here. Always. I don't care what time it is or how far away you are. I've. Got. You.'

* * *

After Duke finally let me go, we battled over who was sleeping in his bed and who on the couch. Obviously, being the gentleman he is, he insisted I take his bed. The sweet, warm moment from before was immediately drowned with cold water when I suggested his bed was big enough for the two of us and his face screwed up further than I'd ever seen before. That was enough to shut me up and accept that I'd be spending my first night in Duke's apartment in his bed *alone*. Not quite how those dreams I pretend never happened have usually panned out.

Before saying goodnight, he sorted me with a towel so I could shower off the night, and a pair of old sweats that he thought might fit me to sleep in. The joke is, even when he was a teenager, Duke was always *broad*. So, the only thing that remotely fit was the T-shirt he left on the bed, with the hem just about hitting the tops of my thighs.

Once I'm showered, I leave the bathroom, raking my fingers through my incredibly knotted wet hair and—

There's a half-naked Duke Bennett searching through one of his drawers ahead of me, immediately halting me in my tracks. My bottom lip drops just as his head whips up, but I don't meet his gaze, eyes already wandering down. Moonlight filters through the blinds, devastatingly illuminating every hard line and ridge of his muscled torso, while shadows only emphasise the way his waist tapers into a deep V down towards his grey sweatpants. Two of my weaknesses hitting me at once.

I'm finally enlightened to all his hidden tattoos, my eyes frantically flick between the dark illustrations of mountainous landscapes, wolves, roses, and barbed wire, like they're desperate to soak up this image—

'Cherry.' Duke's voice snaps me back.

I tear my eyes up to meet his – his are wide and bulging, while the rest of his face strains, the lines sharper in the moonlight. I struggle to muster up a response, certain my mouth has dried out, any moisture in my body having gone straight to between my legs. Exactly where Duke's wild eyes keep glancing down to. Probably because I'm only wearing his T-shirt. I wasn't expecting him still to be out here.

Quickly, I sputter, 'The sweatpants were too big.'

His throat works once. 'Right.'

'I could always stick on some of your underwear as shorts—'

133

'No.' The word rushes out, his shoulders pitching higher. 'No, that's a bad idea. You're fine as you are. I'll get out of your way.' He abruptly faces the drawers again, chest rising with heaved breaths while he scrambles to find a top.

Tugging at the bottom of my T-shirt, trying to cover myself as much as possible, I lean against his desk to wait before getting into bed. Attempting to cut through the awkward silence, I chuckle as I admit, 'I forgot you wouldn't have conditioner because you shave your head. My hair's gonna be a knotty mess tomorrow morning, so no judging.'

Duke yanks his T-shirt over his head quickly, mumbling, 'You never look a mess.'

For some, Duke might seem like he doesn't say much, but tonight he's come in, all guns blazing with the compliments. I can't help but savour it.

I go to pull myself up to perch on the edge of his desk properly but accidentally knock his laptop in the process and the screen blares to life. Blood drains from my face when I catch sight of the email open, and the question leaves my lips before I can stop it, 'Are you leaving Willow Ridge?'

16

Duke

I really should have fought my own will harder in the car. Seeing Cherry in my apartment feels so wrong, but also *so goddamn right*. I'd be lying if I said I haven't dreamt of her here once or twice, wrapped up in my arms in bed, or lounging on the couch with me – even if I did berate myself for days afterwards. But the good thing is, it was always just a figment of my imagination, where no one knows what's going on. Where I can't hurt or upset anyone.

But now she's here, wearing the white T-shirt I put out for her, and *nothing else*. She's forgone the sweatpants, and miles of long, slender, smooth legs shoot out from beneath the top. I'm certain my brain has short-circuited and lost all memory of how to function. Even trying to pull a T-shirt over my head feels too overwhelming. And when I hear her say something about shampoo and looking a mess, I can't stop my thoughts from spilling out, 'You never look a mess.'

My body's drowning in adrenaline after having to pick her up at the diner and then learning what Levi did to her. Even more after cradling her sweet body against me, knowing that, even if it was for only a minute, I could be her solace.

I can't paint or go for a ride right now to process and push back down all the emotions swirling in my body, because I need to be here for Cherry. Which means I'm struggling to stop my thoughts from spilling out. Just like when I told her about the paintings of Mom. But that's not how we're raised here as men in small towns – even if I know it's toxic, it's hard to shrug out of that. Especially when it's served me – I found purpose amongst the storm of grief by being there for my grandparents after Mom died, and the same again when Grandfather passed, let alone in general for the town.

Though, I can't pretend that the way Cherry just held space for me to talk didn't feel refreshing. That it didn't crack a small light onto those shadows I try to keep at bay.

But worry spikes through that light again when Cherry suddenly asks, 'Wait, are you leaving Willow Ridge?'

My head shoots through the T-shirt with a scrambled pop. 'What? Where did you—'

'You're selling the bar.' Cherry leans against my desk, eyes flicking between me and the now lit-up laptop screen. Her fingers clasp the edge of the desk so tight, like she might fall. 'Sorry, I – it came up on your laptop. I didn't mean to pry—'

'Cherry.' I wasn't ready to get into this yet. I haven't even said yes.

'*Duke.*'

Slamming the drawers shut, I then run my hands over my head. 'No, it's – ah, fuck – it's just a valuation. To see what collateral I have.'

'Collateral?'

A heavy sigh rushes out of me, and the next thing I know, I'm walking back until my legs hit the edge of the bed and I take a seat. My head falls into my palms. 'I . . . an old friend of mine, Kelly, wants to partner up and open a bar in the city. Another Duke's, I guess. Somewhere that reminds him of home.'

'Oh . . . Kelly is a *guy*.' The last word comes out on a laugh.

'Yeah.' My brow furrows. 'Kip Kelly, remember? From the football team?'

Cherry nods, her expression softening.

'He owns a few bars in the city already and found a space for another which he wants to work on with me. We keep in contact every now and again, but he reached out at the start of the summer and . . .'

Cherry settles herself next to me on the in bed, the worry in her eyes moments ago now extinguished and replaced with something bright and hopeful. 'That's amazing. A good opportunity, right?'

Tension swarms my chest. 'I guess . . . Duke's does well since it's the only bar in town, but I'm nowhere near the richest guy in Willow Ridge. I can fuel my passion for motorcycles and keep my grandmother afloat so the opportunity to invest in and run a second bar could offer the extra cash that would make life just that little bit easier, while expanding my grandfather's name and legacy, but . . .' I roll my lips together, trying to push back down the fears crawling up my throat. 'It's complicated.'

'Right.' Cherry tilts her head with a chuckle, then starts shuffling up the bed until she's shifting herself under the covers. I was hoping to be out of the room before she got in, so I didn't have the image of her in my bed etched into my memory. 'If you don't want to talk about it, that's fine. You always respect my boundaries when it comes to how I feel, so I'll always give you the same grace. But I'm also always here to listen. I know you like to be the shoulder for others to lean on, but you're allowed to speak your mind too. I'm your friend, Duke. You can trust me.'

Would it be so bad to let her into my thoughts? To see that I'm not as stable as she might think. What if she doesn't want to lean on me anymore? I love being there for her.

'Besides . . .' Cherry's chest deflates on a sigh. 'I think I'm gonna struggle to sleep with everything running through my mind about tonight, so you'd be doing me a favour. Give me something else to focus on so I might manage to get some sleep in.'

When she puts it like that, it's hard to turn down – the opportunity to make her feel better.

She flips the bedsheet back beside her and pats the mattress. 'At least sit with me, though. Don't be weird and hang on the edge of the bed.'

A raspy laugh leaves my lips as I go to protest—

'Please?' Her big eyes blink at me, glistening in the moonlight like pure magic. The bewitching kind that has me forgoing all my rules until I'm sidling up next to her, my legs under the covers, accidentally brushing hers and me wishing I wasn't wearing sweatpants so I could feel the heat of her skin.

Cherry slinks down into the bed so she's lying on her side, one arm tucked under the pillow as she looks up at me through her dark lashes. Calm floods my bloodstream seeing her there – warm, happy, *safe*. In *my* bed.

'So . . .' She nudges my leg with hers, the small touch already sending sparks through my body. 'Why's it complicated?'

I pull down a long breath. 'Do you remember what I said on the Ferris wheel?'

Her brows shoot up. 'About the kiss?'

'No, I—' I've done a good deal to try to push that conversation about the firework kiss out of mind. But hearing that she hasn't forgotten, that it's her immediate association when I mention the Ferris wheel has my blood rushing quicker. Because, *fuck*, it sounded like she was talking about *us* when she described it. 'No. About being scared of losing people.'

'Oh . . .' Cherry bites down on her lip, making it harder to forget the memory of watching her mouth form the words *rough* and *hard*, as her voice cascaded along my skin like a whispering breeze. 'Right, yeah.'

I close my eyes and rest my head back against the wall, swallowing thickly. Each word starts off strangled but eventually becomes smoother the longer I speak. 'I'm . . . worried that if I pursue this opportunity, I'll have less time for people in Willow Ridge. The very people who propped me up after I lost my mom. I'll have to spend some time in the city and then I won't be around as much for my friends, or family, or the town, if I'm honest, and they'll hate me for that. That's what I'm useful for – I'm always there for my customers, my friends, the whole goddamn town.'

I think back to how the whole town pooled together resources to help keep Duke's afloat when my grandfather first fell ill and I had to take over, to how the Hensley's helped me organise a fundraiser – Hunter performing, Wyatt's mom baking – and then to how Wyatt came back from college for a few weekends even while he was in the midst of studying to lend a hand with busier shifts.

'What if I miss something that happens with Wyatt or Wolfman because I'm working away? Wyatt, especially, he's always been there for me, and what if I can't help him out with the ranch as much? I owe that to him. I can't lose anybody else—'

'Oh, Duke.' Cherry reaches over, filtering her fingers through one of my hands.

The bold, unexpected move makes me freeze. Alarms blare in my head – this is crossing a boundary, especially since we're in bed, and I know it's all my fault for being so lax and needy with the touches I took from her earlier. As if I've gone and brushed away the line between us in the sand.

But that doesn't mean I let go.

I'm transfixed by her innocent dark eyes, glistening like they've just discovered a hidden piece of my soul, as she says, 'You're not gonna lose anyone. If anything, I think people would encourage you to go – you're always looking out for everyone else, when was the last time you did something big just for you? When did you last let yourself have something you wanted without worrying how other people would feel?'

All I can do is shrug.

'Come on.' She squeezes my hand. 'Tell me – what's something you really want?'

You, you, you, my entire body sings, no matter how hard I try to fight it.

All I can do is level a look at her. Battle to keep my composure. A silence hovers between us as our eyes lock, Cherry's dancing between mine, as she swallows.

'I—' Her hand tightens around mine. 'I'm just saying you deserve to do this for yourself. Your friends and family – the whole of Willow Ridge – always want the best for you. You've done so much for everyone, you're always there for them, no matter who it is that turns up at the bar. And I know you do more than just listen for this town – you've fixed cars, given out free food and drink, found motels for people when they were too drunk to get themselves home.'

Cherry's gaze drops to our hands as she adds, 'Even carried people to hospital after they've fallen from their horse . . . Maybe it's your turn now, to be looked after by Duke. Besides,' she says with a grin. 'When you're not around, you'll be leaving Duke's bar in capable hands.'

The chuckle rings out of me, and I can't help but jest, 'If that lap dancing escapade is any indication, then no, I don't think I will be.'

'Oh my God,' Cherry squeals, pulling her hand from mine to hide herself under the sheets. 'I'd hoped you'd forgotten about that.'

'Believe me, I'm trying to,' I reply too quickly, the words rushing out before I can veil the desperation in my tone.

Slowly, Cherry brings down the covers again, teeth tugging on her bottom lip when her face comes into view. Fuck, how many times have I thought about being able to catch her lips between my teeth when she does that? Wondered if she'd moan or gasp? It's like it's all hitting me at once.

That's what all this vulnerability does to me.

I think that's a signal to call it a night.

Before I say or do anything more.

I shrug. 'Truth is, though, you'll be gone by then.'

And just like that, the light fizzles from her eyes, and all that distance builds back between us. She rolls onto her back, letting her hands rest over her stomach as she stares up at the ceiling. She whispers, 'I'll just be in the city where the bar is instead. Where you could be too.'

Oh.

I hadn't thought about it like that…

'Maybe we should make another deal,' she blurts out. When my response is merely an inquisitively raised brow, she elaborates, 'If you agree to the second bar, I'll do something in return.'

I know she doesn't mean it sexually, but *fuck*, that's how it sounded. That's how messed up my head is right now. That's what happens when you let Cherry Hensley walk around your apartment in just a T-shirt.

In the midst of all my racing, burning thoughts, a bright idea pings in my mind. 'If I move forward with the business deal, you have to take a horse-riding lesson.'

Her eyes flash, but she doesn't hesitate to nod and confirm, 'Okay. I can do that. Promise.'

'Good . . .' I really should leave now. 'Thank you, Cherry. For letting me talk. I'll give the bar some more thought.'

Given everything Cherry's just said, I decide to momentarily relent and get one more touch before I go. So, I take Cherry's hand, giving it what is meant to be a quick squeeze, but she clutches me tighter when I try to pull away.

Tired, shadow-lined eyes regard me with hope as she asks, 'Will you wait with me until I'm asleep? Just so I'm not alone with my thoughts.'

And of course, my response is, 'Anything you want, Baby Hensley.'

17

Cherry

A shift of solid warmth behind me wakes me up. I keep my heavy eyes closed, hoping to block out the sunlight for a little longer. Luxuriating in the toasty warmth of the sheets, I snuggle myself further into them.

It's then that I realise I'm not alone.

Because my attempt to shuffle about is stifled by two weighty arms folded around me, clinging onto the curves of my waist like there's no tomorrow. Like they're the glue holding all my broken pieces together. The scorching heat encompassing me, reminding me that I'm tucked up and safe from any of the previous night's distress, is actually radiating off Duke's broad, long body. His T-shirt I borrowed to sleep in has ridden up in the night, and now his hands are branding my bare skin.

It also means that my ass is pressed against his crotch. The feel of something hard against my ass cheeks only makes me swallow and my breath shudder.

Inch by inch, my body wakes up further, triggered by

every point of contact with Duke. His soft, rhythmic breaths against my neck filter through my hair, leaving goosebumps across my chest. One thigh has slipped between my legs, as if providing my tired body with support, alongside reminding me torturously of that time his solid thigh propped me up at the roller rink. How badly I wanted to grind against it.

My skin tingles, body coming alive under his touch. Sometimes all it needs is a glance from him, and I'm lit up like a thousand fireflies.

And last night made me far too aware of such. That I'm here, chasing highs and trying to feel as alive and wild as possible, when all I need to do to experience that is be in Duke's quiet presence – whether we're having silly debates whilst closing up the bar, or watching the sunset from the top of a Ferris wheel, hand in hand, or just stargazing from the comfort of a truck bed.

Even when I was spiralling into hopelessness last night, frightened and frustrated, all it took to lift me up was hearing his voice.

I've got you, Baby Hensley.

It's what makes me stop and relish this moment. It's not like I haven't dreamed of this before – waking up to the quiet of the morning, wrapped in Duke's arms.

He must have accidentally fallen asleep after talking with me last night. I probably should move but I can just imagine the panicked look on his face when he wakes up and sees what's happening right now.

Besides, I don't want him to let go just yet.

Because right now, it's like Duke's arms create this forcefield around me, all the thoughts swarming my mind instantly quietened in his presence. I know it's going to take a while to process and deal with what happened last night with Levi, but here in Duke's arms, I'm certain I could take on the world.

For the first time last night, I could've sworn I saw the same fight in his eyes that I recognise in myself when I'm around him, trying not to let my true feelings slip out—

Duke suddenly lets out a groan, one that sounds like he's still half asleep, suspended in that lazy morning bliss. It makes me wonder if he'd make the same noises if I pushed my ass back against his hard length.

But then I go instantly rigid when he nuzzles his face into the crook of my neck, squeezing me tighter and trying to tuck his hands around me further. My tenseness lasts barely more than a second when he inhales deeply, as if he's trying to drown himself in the scent of me. Instead, I melt into a goddamn puddle. Especially when he lets out another groan. Like he's addicted to breathing me in and finally got another dose.

God, this might be the best feeling in the world.

Except I'm proven wrong a second later when Duke tugs me in closer and sleepily grinds his erection against me, this time the groan that rumbles out borders on a growl. I can feel every steel-hard inch of his length, as well as the molten desire beginning to puddle in my core. He must be having a *wild* dream.

Now *this* is the best feeling in the world.

Heat licks up my spine as Duke refuses to let me go, keeping my ass pressed against his hardness, making my mind wander down too many filthy roads. Like how all he'd have to do is pull down his sweatpants, push my panties to the side, and slide straight in because I already know I'm soaking wet for him. Because that's how quickly my body is trained now to respond to thoughts about Duke Bennett. He wouldn't even need to feel guilty about fucking me if I stayed facing away from him, we could just pretend I was someone else.

Although, in all honesty, I'm slightly concerned whether the wetness pooling between my thighs would even be enough, because based on the hard length crushed against my ass, I'm not sure if something that large would even fit inside of me.

Fuck, I have to press my thighs together to try get a hold of myself—

Duke jolts behind me because I've just gone and squeezed his leg between mine like a vice. A frustratingly horny vice.

Just like that, Duke seizes up, the sound of his sharp inhale echoing through the room. I keep my body heavy and limp, my breaths even and laboured, as if I'm still deep in slumber and try not to react as Duke gently eases his arms out from around me, clearly attempting not to wake me. His leg slips from between mine and I'm suddenly aching to be encompassed by his warmth when his body finally slides away. He shuffles behind me, and the rasp of his hands over his stubble fills the silent bedroom. I wait, expecting him to flee from the scene.

Yet, he doesn't. I almost sense a strange heaviness on the back of my head, like that feeling you get that someone's staring at you.

Now could be a good time to pretend to wake up. It

would be less awkward. We could just laugh about him falling asleep beside me and—

The mattress dips and Duke leans in towards me. It takes every ounce of my self-control not to move when his fingers brush the shell of my ear, tucking my hair behind it. A soft sigh leaves his lips, and I fight back the whimper that wants to escape. Even more when Duke presses a light kiss to my head before hopping off the bed.

And once I hear the bedroom door close behind him as he leaves, I lie here, smiling silly and basking in the glorious realisation that Duke Bennett might be struggling to ride the line he's drawn between us as much as me.

After crawling out of bed to grab my purse and quickly apply some concealer and mascara, silently sending a *thank you* to last night's Cherry for putting makeup in my purse in case I needed to touch up my face in the club, I finally psych myself up enough to head out of the bedroom. The smell of waffles immediately hits me and I stop short at the heart-warming – and panty-melting – sight of Duke making breakfast. He's wearing those grey sweatpants still, which, even though he's clearly not hard right now, I can still see the outline of every single inch that was pressed up against me earlier.

I suppress a full-body shiver at the memory, heat coursing straight between my thighs again.

'Morning,' I squeak out, tugging on the hem of Duke's T-shirt that I'm still wearing as I take slow steps towards him.

Duke's head shoots up, making him pause from where he was cutting up strawberries, and his eyes instantly fall to my bare legs. Like they're naturally drawn to where I'm exposed, even if his strained features suggest he's fighting it. He takes a long blink, before meeting my gaze and he clears his throat. 'Morning. How did you sleep?'

'Better than I expected, thanks.' I settle onto one of the stools at the breakfast bar. It gives me a chance to fully take in what Duke has been whipping together – freshly made waffles, chocolate spread, and an assortment of berries. My mouth was already salivating from Duke in his sweatpants, but now it's working overtime. 'This looks amazing. You didn't have to do all of this.'

Duke scrapes the strawberries he was cutting into a bowl and gives a nonchalant shrug. 'I didn't think you'd be too pleased with cold pizza for breakfast, which was the only other option.'

'You underestimate me,' I jest, popping a slice of strawberry straight into my mouth. 'Cold pizza is one of my favourite foods.'

'You really do have strange taste.' Duke shakes his head at me.

I grin. 'Ah, you wouldn't say that if you knew what else I liked.'

His eyes flash at me and he swallows. 'Get eating, then.'

We quickly fill our plates with the waffles and all kinds of toppings. I can't stop the noises of enjoyment that vibrate in my throat as I scoff down my food, making Duke chuckle every time. Each mouthful tastes even more delicious with the added knowledge of the effort Duke has made to make all this for me, a warmth kindling in my chest.

'So,' Duke starts after finishing his last bite, 'I, uh, don't know whether you had any plans for today . . .'

He rubs a hand over his head, and I can't stop my eyes from flicking to his stretched triceps, following the shift of muscle as discreetly as I can.

'But I usually pick up my grandmother from church on a Sunday, then go to hers for lunch before opening the bar and wondered if you – you obviously don't have to – but maybe you might want to join? Might help to keep your mind off things.' Duke flashes me a soft smile, dark eyes searching mine. 'You do owe me a small moment for the speed dating still. But only if you want to.'

The rational part of me says I should go home. I'm likely running on a high despite how well I think I slept in Duke's embrace, and the exhaustion will hit me later. Yet, I also know if I go home, I'll end up sitting in my room, playing last night over and over in my head. So, would it really hurt to spend longer with Duke?

The person who wouldn't think twice about changing his plans to drive over an hour to come to pick me up without knowing the reason, talk me to sleep to help keep any nightmares at bay, and then cook me a huge breakfast the next morning.

The person who would do anything for me, it seems.

Smiling silly, I settle my cutlery down and flash my grin at Duke, immediately receiving a heart-warming, beaming smile back – the kind that sparks in his eyes too. 'I couldn't think of a better way to spend my day.'

18

Duke

'Gram, you can't put that word down!' I sputter with disbelief as I watch my eighty-year-old grandmother place her Scrabble tiles to spell out *dicking*. Cherry chokes on the sweet tea she's sipping.

'Why not?' My grandmother furrows her brow, then tuts at me. Her dark-grey curls hang in a loose bun while her gold-rimmed glasses sit perched on the end of her nose. 'Don't you try cheating now, Junior. Just because you're losing, and I've bagged myself forty-five points with a triple word score.'

'Yeah, *Junior*,' Cherry adds on with animated, glistening eyes now she's recovered from almost choking to death. I guess her using my grandmother's nickname for me – the main way Gram was able to distinguish who out of me and my grandfather she was telling off – is payback for all the years I've been calling Cherry *Baby Hensley*. 'Don't be a sore loser.'

I press my tongue to my cheek as I fiddle with the cross

dangling from the chain around my neck – the one my grandmother got me years ago and I always don whenever I pick her up from church. Being ganged up on by Cherry and my grandmother was not what I had planned for today. 'I'm just not sure that's really an appropriate word for Scrabble.'

'Why? What's wrong with it?' My grandmother exudes too much innocence as she picks her new tiles out of the bag. A painting of Jesus sits on the faded floral wall behind her. 'Isn't that what you kids get up to these days? A good dicking?'

'Gram, I swear to God.' I wipe a hand over my face.

Cherry cowers behind her glass of sweet tea, covering her mouth as she tries to stifle her laugh. Even if I am completely mortified at the number of times my grandmother has said the word *dicking*, it's worth it to see Cherry smile so much after everything that's happened to her in the last twenty-four hours. Plus, the adorable little skip she did when I dropped her home to change before we came over to my grandmother's was enough evidence that I'm keeping her mind out of the shadows for now. Though, I'm not sure how many more skin-crawling minutes of my grandmother misusing all kinds of rude words I can take.

Gram waves me off before organising her new letters on her rack. 'That's what Waylon always says when the fair is town – full of damn kids having a good dicking about.'

'Ah.' Cherry rolls her lips, barely managing to contain her grin. 'I think a *good dicking* and *dicking about* are slightly different things, Mary.'

And if this wasn't torture before, hearing that from Cherry's lips has now made it ten times worse. I pull at the neck of my T-shirt, its tightness suddenly imposing.

'Well,' Gram just shakes her head, 'whatever they mean, I hope you're doing both, Cherry. I sure did when I was your age.' She nudges Cherry with her elbow.

'Jesus Christ!' I throw my head back against the armchair and groan. Here I thought this would be a calm day for Cherry, but now my grandmother's telling her she should be sleeping around. I don't need her being encouraged anymore to finish off that second half of her bucket list.

'Don't be such a prude, Junior – and mind your language. You won't make me any grandbabies that way.' She shoots me a look, wrinkles deepening around her frown, while I pray for the ground to swallow me up. 'It's your turn, Cherry.'

Cherry's still biting her lip when she glances at me. Hesitantly, she runs her slender fingers along her tiles, red nails clicking against them as her eyes dart around the board. Her tongue slides along her bottom lip when she finally releases it from the grip of her teeth, and then she picks up three tiles and props them on the board. It takes me a second to pull my attention from her and realise she's spelled out the word *cock*, using the *k* from my grandmother's previous word.

'You're a bad influence,' I remark, raising a brow at Cherry.

She widens her eyes with feigned innocence, even going so far as to press a hand to her chest with bewilderment. 'It's what you call a male chicken, isn't it? Now who's got their head in the gutter, hey?' Cherry jests. 'This is a family game, *Junior*.'

There's a flash of challenge in her eyes, one that makes me grateful my grandmother's here, otherwise I'm not sure I'd be able to stop myself from trying to shut Cherry up with my mouth. Whatever happened last night left my self-control when it comes to Cherry as frayed as the rips in her jeans.

Once we've finished our game of Scrabble – and my grandmother inevitably wins – we help put together some lunch and eat outside on the back deck, buttery sunlight warming us the whole time. Conversation flows easily, reminding me of all the Thanksgivings and Christmases we've spent with the Hensleys – how they'd always invite us as an extension of their own family. Though, today Cherry's on a mission when it comes to discovering everything she can about my childhood, as opposed to making polite small talk like usual.

Like she got a taste of the true me last night and needs more.

Knowing how naturally Cherry can slot into this part of my life has my heart prancing. I have to rub a hand over my sternum to try to calm it. I know that every day I get with her, helping with this goddamn bucket list, is just borrowed time before she leaves. But even if it's only a month and a half, I'll do what I can to give her the joy and safety she had snatched away from her last night. I'll weather whatever storm comes her way, no matter how thunderous, if it means keeping her dry and warm. *Safe*.

We settle ourselves back inside on the couch with

glasses of sweet tea once we've finished clearing up lunch. The quiet hum of the radio filters through the room, while golden rays of sunshine cut across the space, sparkling against Cherry's hair. The memory of her hair, so soft and satin-like beneath my lips, has my fingers itching for another feel.

'Oh, Junior,' my grandmother suddenly pipes up. 'Put that nice one on from the other day, won't you?'

'Care to elaborate a little more there, Gram?' I respond, given that *nice one on from the other day* could easily be a song from last weekend, or five months ago.

'That love song by that handsome boy with the good voice.'

It's not much, but thankfully we are talking about a song I played her a couple of weeks ago, and I remember the way she gushed over how attractive he was, grabbing my cheek as she jokingly said, *he could give my grandson a run for his money*.

'You mean "Heaven" by Kane Brown?'

'That's what I said,' she confirms, eliciting a chuckle from Cherry.

'Sure.' I shake my head at Cherry, then head to the stereo to connect my phone.

Still, my thumb hesitates over the play button on my screen when it comes to it. I'm all too aware of the weight of Cherry's heavy stare on me, waiting. Usually, the post-lunch ritual on a Sunday of me and Gram dancing isn't witnessed by anyone else. Just a slice of our own healing process, so that she can feel that little bit closer to Grandfather again, so that *I* make the most of my time with her too.

155

Tightness lingers in my chest at the thought of sharing that moment, but it doesn't crawl any further, just hovers there . . . like something is keeping it at bay. And when I turn to catch Cherry's eyes, as soft as a whisper as she watches me, I know why. When I think back to last night and everything I confessed to Cherry, the way she so openly listened to this side of me, reminds me that maybe it is okay to be vulnerable. To let others see *me*, rather than always being the one to listen and be there for them.

Swallowing down a deep breath, I finally press play on the song and offer my hand to my grandmother. Her eyes light up, memories already sparking to life in them. She slips her weathered hand into mine, allowing me to help her to her feet before she lays her hand on my shoulder. We slowly sway to the soft music.

'It's kind of a ritual of ours on Sundays, sorry,' I explain to Cherry over Gram's shoulder, offering her a half-smile in apology.

Her grin gently spreads out, dark eyes never leaving me. 'It's a beautiful ritual.'

I swallow thickly at the way Cherry's watching me with such tenderness, it's – *fuck* – it's scary and brilliant all at once. I want her to look at me like that more. I want to be completely and utterly laid bare for her, so she might see every deep, dark corner of my soul, because being the subject of her gaze is a goddamn privilege.

'Oh dear.' Gram halts after a while and pulls her hand from mine, resting her other on my shoulder with more pressure. 'My darned hip is giving me grief again. Never mind, you'll just have to take over for me, Cherry.'

'What?' Cherry's lips pop open.

I sputter, 'Um—'

'You can't leave Junior on the dancefloor all alone,' my grandmother insists, already tugging Cherry up and giving her a nudge in my direction. 'Step in for me, love. It will be like I'm watching his grandfather and I when we were younger.'

Gram flops back onto the couch, humming with comfort. She widens her eyes at us as if to say *get on with it*. Both my and Cherry's jaws work when we turn to each other, and when neither of us move, my grandmother tuts. 'Take her hand, then, Junior.'

I feel like a goddamn teenager with his crush at prom, too nervous to slow dance. And I didn't even take a date to prom – unless you count going with Wolfman and Sawyer as a three-way date.

I tense my hands to stop them from shaking, but I still relish the way her soft skin slides against my palm as her fingers mould around mine. Carefully, I wrap my other hand around her waist, letting my fingers splay out, down across her hip, while pulling her closer to me. Her free hand trails up my chest, climbing over my shoulder where it settles. Sparkling brown eyes blink up at me, and I begin swaying us.

Right. This just feels so *right*.

Having Cherry in my hands. Feeling her slender curves beneath my palm, letting the shape of them imprint onto my mind. It was the exact same when I woke up to find her tucked into me this morning. I'm not sure how it even happened – I remember the first sound of her soft breaths once she fell asleep, my words trailing off, speechless at how beautiful she was even while sleeping. I must have fallen asleep right there myself too, resting back against the wall watching her.

Is it a testament to how much she draws me in that I woke up with her in my arms, my body needing to be close to her even unconsciously? All I knew was that waking up to the sweet smell of her, and the way her body slotted perfectly into every line of mine, might have been the best day of my life. Because it felt so goddamn right. Like all this fighting to keep that line between us had been a dream.

Kane Brown wasn't wrong when he said I don't know how heaven could be better than this.

'Don't stop for me, just going to grab something for the pain.' Gram suddenly stands and hobbles off out towards the kitchen, leaving us alone. So much for wanting to watch us because it brought back good memories. It's probably a good excuse to stop. Gram's not watching anymore, and she'll no doubt end up getting distracted by something in the kitchen and not returning for another ten minutes, knowing her memory.

'Thank you,' Cherry suddenly whispers, her pinky finger brushing up against my neck, grazing the tattoo there. Shivers rush down my spine even from the featherlight touch. 'For bringing me here today, showing me this. I know it's difficult for you to let people in.'

'Oh . . .' I tug her slightly more into me, trying to soak up every bit of her warmth before I inevitably have to let her go, and those walls return between us. She presses closer willingly, making me swallow. 'I just don't really know how – to let people in, that is.'

Her big brown eyes blink up at me, waiting.

For me to let her in again.

Maybe it was the quiet of the night that had me spilling my thoughts last night, thinking they'd just get lost in the darkness. And dancing here with Cherry, holding her in my embrace, maybe that's where anything I say today can stay. My secrets trapped within the small gaps between our bodies, never to resurface again from this one unrepeatable moment.

I suck down a shaky breath before admitting quietly, 'My grandparents were of that generation where you didn't really talk about your feelings. They did their best, and I love them, but they were also dealing with not just losing their daughter but having to suddenly raise a child again. Sitting down to talk about our feelings wasn't exactly a top priority.'

My grandfather's words ring loudly through my mind. *'Us Bennetts are tough, Junior. We don't let things like this knock us down. The best thing to do is to just keep moving.'*

Cherry's fingers pulse against my shoulder. 'I'm sorry, Duke. That sounds hard.'

I shrug. 'I guess I just never really learnt how to let people in. Therapy helped – still does – but it's not the same. In all honesty, Wyatt was my biggest saviour during that time – all of you Hensleys were. Immediately making me and my grandparents part of your family traditions. Letting me sleep over probably more than I should have. Inviting me along to any of your family activities knowing my grandparents probably were too old to always be taking me out. It helped remind me I wasn't totally alone, even if I couldn't say it.'

Cherry's eyes soften at me, along with her smile. 'This works, though. Letting me see you in small slices – your art, your passions, your family. It's like I get to slowly put the puzzle pieces of Duke Bennett together. It helps me to understand you better.'

My brows shoot up as my eyes search hers. 'That's something you want? To understand me?'

'Mhm.' She nods, mouth spreading out into a glorious smile that has my heart somersaulting. 'I feel closer to you in the last twenty-four hours than ever and it's been amazing.' Then she goes and rests her head against my shoulder, her warmth completely encompassing me. 'Last night, with Levi, I've never felt more defeated than I did then. But with you looking after me and bringing me here, I've never felt more alive.'

19

Cherry

Duke: Just letting you know – Levi won't be working at the bar again.
Duke: He's alive, FYI. I didn't kill him, just fired him.
Cherry: Wow, more than one text AND a joke from Duke Bennett? What did I do to be so lucky?
Duke: Funny.
Cherry: Thank you, though. Makes me feel a lot better.
Duke: I'm glad.
Cherry: Hey, Duke?
Duke: Yeah?
Cherry: I can't sleep again.

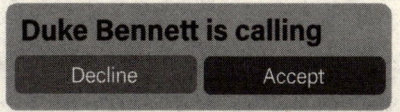

'Sorry I'm late!' I call out as I rush through the door of Sitting Pretty, the coffee shop on Main Street where I'm meeting Rory and Fliss the following day. I'm immediately greeted by the rich aromas of coffee and caramel, the buzz and steam of the coffee machines filtering amongst the light chatter from customers.

With the wellness retreat at Sunset Ranch heavily booked this summer, any day Rory and Fliss have time off together, we jump at the opportunity for a coffee or smoothie date. Luckily, Rory's family are visiting from England this week, so the retreat doesn't have any other guests, giving her more time to spare. They're the best kind of friends that pass no judgement – if I suddenly told them I wanted to quit college and run away with the circus to become a sword eater, I honestly think they'd hug me and start googling what the best circuses to join are. Plus, they introduced me to smutty romance books and that is something I can never thank them enough for.

'I was up late last night and overslept,' I babble my apologies as I drop into a chair. The reality being that I had such a deep, long sleep after being on the phone with Duke while he told me all about his grandfather, opening up another tiny kernel of his life to me.

'I think him getting me involved with the bar business was his way of showing love, like there was no doubt I'd be taking it over eventually,' Duke tells me. 'Even if it probably wasn't legal to have me helping out in my teens.

'You know, I remember one time at Thanksgiving I told him I was interested in studying interior design and he came up with a whole plan for me to start my own business.'

Duke chuckles on the other end. 'Yep, that sounds

162

just like him. An entrepreneur at heart.' He hums for a moment. *'Makes me proud though – growing up during such a difficult time, especially as one of only a few Black people in a small town – but he never gave up. Never let the world stop him from achieving what he wanted.*

'He'd be proud of you too, y'know?'

Rory chuckles, grabbing my hand and giving it a squeeze. 'Girl, you're like five minutes late, it's fine. We already told them to start your drink when you arrive, so it's all good.'

'You're the best, thank you.' My shoulders drop and I take in the coffee shop – the sunlight scattered across the mint walls, cutting through the large windows that look out onto Main Street.

'I'm personally more interested by the fact you were up late last night,' Fliss chimes in, quirking a brow at me over the brim of her coffee cup as she sips slowly. 'Anyone the cause of that?'

'Spill!' Rory demands, eyes wide with hope.

'Calm down.' I shake my head at them, chuckling. 'I just couldn't sleep, that's all.'

Duke was no doubt conflicted about letting me stay and, even if I'm reading into our time together too much, it felt intimate. It was *our* moment together, a chance to be closer than we ever have before and I kind of want that to stay just ours for now. There's something slightly exhilarating about keeping it a secret too. It makes me wonder what else Duke would do if he knew no one would ever find out…

'If you say so.' Fliss winks just as the barista sets my coffee on the table. The nutty, caramel scent of the drink wafts up and I inhale it down like it's a drug. Almost like how Duke breathed me in when his face was nuzzled into my neck yesterday morning.

'Oh, behave.' I narrow my eyes, sipping my coffee and welcoming its toasty heat. 'I actually have a favour to ask you.'

Fliss perks up. 'Oh yeah?'

'Will you give me some riding lessons? I used to ride when I was a teenager, but . . . well, then I had my first fit and I fell. My parents didn't want me to get back on, and honestly, I was a little too scared to as well, especially when at one point I was having seizures every month.' Rory suddenly brushes her foot against my leg. 'But God, do I miss it. I know Wyatt will probably have a heart attack if he finds out, but I'm kind of done with letting my epilepsy hold me back, you know?'

'I think it's a great idea.' Fliss beams at me. 'I'd be honoured to, Cherry. I'll have a look at when I can fit you in around the ranch and let you know, yeah? It will be so fun!'

My heart could burst with joy – at my friends, for being so supportive and kind, and at myself, for taking this first step towards riding again.

'This is exciting.' Rory grins, bouncing in her seat. 'What spurred this on?'

'Oh . . .' I drink down some of my coffee to avoid my nervous laughter from spilling. 'I've kinda been doing this bucket list Montana made me.'

'Um, I wanna see this list,' Fliss requests.

I chuckle at her demand and reach down into my bag, pulling out the folded list. You never know when you might be met with an opportunity to tick something off or come up with a new idea to add to it. The girls snatch it from my hands and lean into each other as they scour the crumpled paper, Rory letting out the odd *ooh* as certain items pique her interest. When they hit the more sexual activities at the bottom, their eyes widen, and they start pointing to each one with a giggle.

'Well,' Rory starts, 'I for one will always support girls having more orgasms, so this looks great.'

Shortly after, Fliss drops the list to the table. 'I'm not gonna lie though, shower sex is *so* overrated.'

'Sex in a bathroom, however,' Rory counters, raising a brow and flicking her gaze between us, a smirk tugging at her lips.

'Please don't say any more.' I internally shudder. 'That's my brother you're talking about.'

She chuckles, but then leans back in her chair as she takes a long sip of her smoothie. 'I never said it was with Wyatt.'

'Where was it? And who?' Fliss asks.

'At Duke's bar with Wyatt.'

'For God's sake!' I curse, making Rory and Fliss cackle. 'That's my place of work, you sex fiend! Now I won't be able to pee without wondering if you've been bent over whatever toilet I'm using.'

And then I'm descending into their fit of giggles, ribs aching from the laughter tumbling out of me. The kind that is so full of joy and elation that it becomes silent, and tears stream from my eyes. To a point that we look a little concerning, all flopped over the table, shoulders bobbing up and down. But it's goddamn glorious, and I've missed having friends that make you feel all warm and golden from the inside out. The kind of group I never found growing up.

When we finally manage to catch our breaths, Fliss

straightens the list back out on the table. 'You've been doing all this on your own?'

'Well, the roller-skating obviously we all did, and the rest, um, I've been doing with Montana.'

'Hmm,' Rory muses as she points to *face my fear of heights* on the list. 'Funny, I don't remember Montana being on the Ferris wheel with you . . .' She gradually drops her mouth to her straw and slurps slowly, lashes fluttering at me.

I narrow my eyes at her. 'Why do you say that?'

Rory straightens her shoulders and then relays with a grin, in the exact same manner she said it the other week, 'Why don't Duke and Cherry go wait by it so we can be first on while we go get some pictures?'

Oh. My. God.

That was . . . planned?

'I'm so confused right now,' I confess, all too aware of the way my heart is suddenly racing. That same adrenaline that coursed through my veins when the Ferris wheel cranked into action and our pod started ascending upwards seeps into my bloodstream again.

Fliss adds, 'Me too.'

Giving a little squeal, Rory wiggles in her seat, then bites down on her bottom lip to contain whatever excitement has her buzzing like a neon sign. 'Someone might have called in a favour so they could take you on the Ferris wheel in time for the sunset.'

A breathy laugh escapes my lips. I can't stop blinking as I take in what she's just admitted. I feel like I'm reliving the moment, my head spinning as we get further from the ground, surging up towards the wheel's summit, terrified about what this means.

My gaze darts everywhere while I try to pull the pieces of the puzzle that is Duke Bennett together. My heart begs me to dig as deep as I possibly can into all of this and uncover Duke's secret obsession with me, but my head, and the paper on the table, suggests that he's only done it to help with the list.

Except . . . maybe it does mean something. Now that we've paused at the top of the wheel, there's nothing but glorious, golden sunlight splattered across the cornflower sky, drenching me in the sweet warmth of Rory's revelation.

Maybe all these polarities in the way Duke acts towards me, the disorientating switches between hot and cold, aren't just part of his nature. Sure, I don't miss the way he's always looking to keep a barrier between us, or the way he never touches me first if he can help it, or how he always finds subtle ways to remind me that I'm Wyatt's little sister – I'm always Baby Hensley, for God's sake.

But I also didn't make up the fury in his eyes when I'd been hurt the other night, or how he kissed my head when he thought I was still asleep, or the way he watched me like I'd hung the moon as we swayed in his grandmother's living room.

Or the way he groaned with a primal kind of pleasure as he sleepily ground his hard length against my ass yesterday morning. No, I can still hear that loud and clear in my mind, and I'll probably be replaying the sound as I let my hand drift between my thighs tonight.

My smile threatens to explode.

'Just to confirm, we're talking about Duke, right?' Fliss checks.

Rory just rolls her lips and glances at me.

'He . . . might have been helping me too.'

Fliss's jaw drops as Rory jiggles again in her seat, clapping her hands together with too much glee in her eyes.

'As *friends*, obviously. I'm sure Sawyer or Wolfman would have offered to do the same,' I say, even though I'm not convincing anyone, including myself.

Fliss tuts. 'Cherry, haven't you read *any* of the romance books I've been recommending? We all know that anyone who has to persuade others that they're *just* friends, are never *just* friends.'

'She's right.' Rory folds her arms on the table. 'Just like when I snogged Wyatt that time to make his stupid ex jealous – told him I was helping him out as a friend. What a load of bullshit.'

'Seriously?' Fliss snorts. As do I, because I can remember that night vividly, the rest of our group watching them act as if they weren't besotted with each other as they shared one of the most passionate kisses I've ever seen.

'I was drunk, scorned, and jealous – not a good combination.' Rory tosses her copper waves behind her shoulders. 'Anyway, can we please return to Cherry and Duke?'

'Yeah, so what's next for you two?' Fliss squints at the list. 'Wild swimming or shower sex?'

'He's not helping me with the sexual stuff!' I shout, announcing to the whole café who don't even pretend not to hear me as people on the other tables turn to glare at us.

Rory holds up a hand and mouths *sorry*, then leans further into the table, Fliss following. She keeps her voice hushed and adds with a wink, 'Yet.'

168

My only response is to groan, hide my face under my hands and slide down in my chair. They're incorrigible. But I love it.

'Hey, look.' Rory reaches over to give me a nudge. 'We're only teasing you. *However*, I am serious about Duke asking me to distract the others. I'm not trying to betray his confidence, but I think if you guys enjoy spending time together, then you should do more of it. Regardless of what anyone – aka Wyatt – might think.'

I separate my fingers, allowing me to peek through. My gaze flicks between my two friends as I mull over Rory's words.

Sometimes it's like Duke and I are constantly in this game of push and pull. We can't help but gravitate towards the other, always in each other's orbit – like binary stars. Yet, when one gets too close, the other withdraws, as if the pull between us is too much. But maybe it's more like tug of war. There's a clear line between us that neither are ready to cross first, so we're always gently tugging the other closer, then retreating as they do, hoping they'll be first to fall.

All I know is that I've been slacking in this game. And I think it's time I finally become this strong woman I'm so obsessed with being and pull a little harder.

Because I'm going to make Duke cross that line.

20

Duke

'Duke, seriously, where the hell are we going?' Cherry asks for the hundredth time since we parked across the street from Willow Ridge High. She dubiously scans the football field as we race past, her hand wrapped firmly around mine as I lead her to where the next item on her bucket list awaits on a Thursday night.

I'd offered out a hand to help her get down from my truck – whatever I can do to touch her somehow, even if it is brief and swept off as just a bit of chivalry. The cool slide of her fingers across my palm sent shivers skittering across my skin, and then she just never let go. Her fingers shuffled about and eventually slipped between mine, pulsing as her grip tightened. I just wanted to pause and marvel at the way the gaps between my fingers seem so perfectly formed to fit hers.

'Patience, Baby Hensley, we're almost there.' I flash her an irksome grin, to which she rolls her eyes.

'Do you know what this reminds me of?' Cherry asks. Silvery moonlight rains down on the apple of her cheeks

'Mhm?'

'Your senior year prank.'

I bark out a laugh, a little too loud considering we're trespassing right now, but the brilliant memory rushes back to me too quickly.

Toilet paper dangling throughout the gym, wrapped around desks, and stuffed in lockers, all witnessed by a cunning little twelve year old who caught Wyatt and me sneaking out that night and demanded we take her with us in return for not telling.

'What a night.' I shake my head as we round the edge of the fence and head down the alleyway that leads to the outdoor pool. 'I can't believe you convinced us to let you come with.'

'*Blackmailed* is probably the right term,' Cherry giggles, and the sound vibrates through my very soul. It's so care-free and innocent, that I can't help but think back to last weekend when I picked her up from the diner, the contrast in her now.

Rage crackles beneath my skin even just thinking about it. The way Levi didn't even try to feign ignorance when I confronted him on Monday, acting as if it's what she wanted. The self-control it took just to fire him and not call a hunting-party on his ass afterwards is something I deserve a medal for.

I chuckle. 'You realise that means you've technically already broken in somewhere, though? That didn't even need to be on your list.'

'That was before my fall, though. It doesn't count.'

'If you say so. Did you ever tell your parents?'

Cherry crosses her heart with her free hand. 'Never.'

'You are a good girl, aren't you?'

'Only for you,' she admits, biting down on her lip, eyes locking shamelessly with mine.

It makes me stop and swallow.

Fuck, I bet she'd be such a good girl as well.

So eager to please.

I'm incredibly glad that we've finally reached the pool gate where I can turn my attention elsewhere, as opposed to the thoughts that are already making my cock twitch. Somewhat reluctantly, I slip my hand from Cherry's to whip out the key in my pocket, my energy immediately dulled from the loss of contact. Like she's the spark that brings me to life.

'Okay, so I know it technically doesn't count as breaking in if you have the key, but it is trespassing, which is close enough,' I tell Cherry as I slide the key into the lock, giving the handle a wiggle like Wolfman suggested. The lies I had to make up to convince him to give me the key were ridiculous. Eventually something clicks and the gate rattles open. 'And I thought we might as well double up with another item.'

Edging the rusty gate open, I gesture towards the pool ahead of us, midnight-blue water barely lit up by the pale orbs of light dotted along the pool's walls. The water is unbelievably still, the star-speckled sky reflecting along the surface, ready for us to dive into the liquid night.

'Again, it's probably not the kind of wild-water swimming you had in mind, but—'

'It's perfect,' Cherry gasps, immediately slapping a hand over her mouth when she realises how loud she was. She winces, but her grin still overpowers the expression. 'The swimsuit wearing makes a lot more sense now.'

Cherry glides in, letting me shut the gate behind us. I hesitate for a second, taking down a few slow, long breaths.

Because I think I've let myself go too far.

Having her fall asleep in my arms, being the reason she didn't break into pieces that night, gave me a high I'd never felt before. As does every night now, when she calls me up so I can help talk her to sleep, knowing I'm the last thing she thinks of before she drifts off.

So here I am, about to walk into what might be our most torturous situation yet.

Swimming together, at night.

Seeing Cherry in her bikini.

Half-naked.

I never saw myself as a masochist, but clearly I don't know myself as well as I thought.

I didn't have to do this. I could've avoided this item on her list. But when it comes to Cherry Hensley, nothing makes sense except for *her*.

Because Cherry's like a beautiful storm – one that I can't help but chase, even if I know the outcome could be catastrophic. But somewhere in the middle of all that danger I'd be risking could be a quiet moment of brilliance for just the two of us – the eye of the storm – while the world rages on around us. And for some reason, right now, driving into that tornado of temptation seems worth it, if only for that.

Cherry is already sitting on the pool's edge, sneakers beside her as she dips her long, slender legs into the water, swishing them about. So much uncharted territory that I'd give anything to run my hands over. Blue light ripples across her body, reflecting through the water, highlighting every beautiful inch of her tanned skin. It gives her silky hair a blue tinge too and I have to fight the urge to take a photo on my phone so I can paint her later.

Midnight Beauty, I'd caption it.

'Are you coming in?' she asks, fluttering her dark lashes at me. Her gaze drops to my jeans, then once to my T-shirt, and back to my face.

'Of course,' I respond, shrugging off my jacket and dropping it beside her.

Once I whip off my T-shirt, I look down to catch where Cherry's wide eyes are trained on my chest, cherry-red lips popped open. I clear my throat and her eyes shoot up to mine, a strong blush spreading over her cheeks. She cuts her gaze back to the water when my fingers start playing with my belt. It doesn't take me long to work my jeans off, leaving me in just my black trunks. I settle myself beside her, dropping my legs into the cool water, skin prickling in response. My puddled jacket acts as the barrier between us. The line I mustn't cross.

'Your turn,' I say.

Her eyes flash again, and I don't miss the way her chest lifts higher, pressing against her tight black halter neck. But then she's pulling her top over her head, revealing the flimsy bikini beneath that barely contains her breasts. It might as well be a couple of scraps of material strung together.

Now my eyes are the ones widening.

I force them toward the pool ahead as she also shimmies out of her shorts, tossing them behind us. I don't look at her properly yet, not when I'm unsure if I'll be able to stop my eyes from roving over every inch of her incredible body.

'It's gonna be so cold,' she says as she swirls a finger

in the water. She splays out a hand above the surface, watching the light reflect off it. The same one that was wrapped up in mine moments ago. I wonder how it would feel against the rest of my bare skin—

No, I'm in enough agony already, let's not go down that road.

I nod, pressing my lips together. 'Best thing to do is jump straight in, get your head completely under.'

'On three?' Cherry grins, teeth tugging on her bottom lip. Her legs bob in the water, anticipation vibrating off her.

'One,' I start. 'Two . . .'

'Three!' Cherry yells and throws herself in with a loud squeal.

I submerge myself quickly after, the cold instantly racketing through my body. The stark contrast makes me tense for a beat before the water's embrace eases it away. Nothing but silence floats beneath the surface, and it's a small moment of unbelievable calm that I force myself to bask in for one more second, before shooting back up.

Cherry whips her hair back as she breaks the surface, a long trail of water splashing me. Her innocent giggle echoes around us as I wipe the water from my eyes, scowling. But then the brightest smile I've seen from her yet spreads through her pink cheeks, reminding me again of why I'm here.

'Come on, then,' I say, nodding towards the other end of the pool. I start taking slow strokes through the water, lazily kicking my feet. 'It only counts as swimming at night if you actually swim.'

'I guess so,' Cherry hums, pushing off the wall to swim beside me. 'Shall we race?'

'How about we just . . . relax?' I suggest, twisting in the water so that I'm swimming on my back. The warm summer night air kisses my bare chest, creating a welcome contrast to the cool water beneath me. I can't remember the last time I went swimming. Cherry copies me, her long body stretching out under the moonlight.

'Okay, but I hope you're not trying to turn one of my bucket list items into one of your slow, little moments again like you did on the Ferris wheel,' she jests, the splashing water doing little to hide her playful tone.

'I would never dream of hijacking your big moment.'

'I'm rolling my eyes, by the way.'

The laugh that barrels out of me is pure joy.

We continue our swim in comfortable silence, up and down for several more lengths, just relishing the serenity of the moment. The soft waves of the water as we glide through, the distant calls of animals, filling the late night air, the inconceivable peace of just *being* with that one person who fills you with contentment.

Once we reach the pool's wall at the shallow end again, I lean my arms against it, legs stretching out behind me as I float on my stomach. Cherry copies, my eyes unable to resist from trailing along her body, until her ass pops out of the water, and I snap my attention back to my arms. I take in a deep breath, chlorine filling my senses.

Maybe if I breathe down enough of it, it'll dissolve this stupid obsession away.

Cherry's elbow nudges mine as she twists again, propping her arms up behind her, breasts lifting out of the water. My jaw clenches when I notice her peaked nipples, too obvious through the thin fabric of her bikini.

Does she wear things like this every time she swims? A hot rush of both desire and jealousy slices through me at the thought. I'd be silly to think she's just worn this for me, but surely she has other less revealing swimsuits—

'I'm having my first riding lesson with Fliss on Sunday,' Cherry suddenly states.

'Hey, that's great. I'm proud of you, Cherry.' My hands itch to touch her, even just a gentle squeeze of the shoulder, something to show her how much I care. But our bare, wet skin meeting is probably not ideal right now.

'Thanks, I'm excited. And for you to move forward with the other bar, too,' she adds with a wink. 'Thanks for helping me with the list, I . . . I don't know if I would've asked Fliss otherwise. But doing all of this,' she gestures out to the pool ahead, 'has made me feel better. More confident. You help me feel more alive, Duke.'

'I . . .' I pause to swallow back all the words that want to spill out. *You've made me feel more alive since the moment you walked through the door of my bar over two years ago. I live for the holidays, when my life is graced by your dazzling joy again. Because when you're not around, I'm like an old, crackling neon sign, struggling to keep alight, but you give me life, and I've never shone as bright as when I'm around you.* 'I'm glad.'

Cherry huffs out a little laugh.

'You know . . .' she starts but then worries her lip. She tucks a wet lock of her hair behind her ear. Something almost molten burns in her eyes. 'We could get three ticks tonight.'

I turn. 'Sorry?'

Cherry pushes off from the wall, wading through the

water until she's opposite me. Her dark hair spreads out around her like a blanket of midnight. The air becomes chillier. *Heavier*. 'You said earlier that this ticked two things off the list. But we could tick off a third.'

I try to remember what else I'd seen written on the list.

But Cherry elaborates before I can get there, 'Skinny-dipping.'

Gaze intertwined with mine, sparkling under the pool's reflection, Cherry starts fiddling with her bikini top beneath the water.

Alarms blare in my head.

This is too dangerous.

Wyatt would kill you if he knew about this.

But I can't move. I can't speak.

Even though my bottom lip drops, nothing comes out.

Not even when Cherry drags the straps of her bikini over her arms unbearably slowly, making sure to keep everything below her shoulders under the water. The top floats up to the surface with a soft pop, hanging between us, daring me to glance down through the dark water at her bare chest. But I keep my focus on her unrelenting stare, one that seems to have darkened even more.

'Cherry . . .' I grind out through my tight jaw, wishing my blood wasn't rushing down south as quickly as it is right now. My hands clench into fists by my side, heart clamouring against my chest.

It only takes a few seconds before her bikini bottoms join the top too. A daring curve of her mouth spreads out before her teeth tug on her bottom lip, exactly where I want to be biting right now.

I am in so much trouble.

'Your turn,' she purrs, a slight breathlessness to her voice.

'Cherry,' is all I can say again.

It's the same word thrumming in my veins.

Cherry, Cherry, Cherry.

All my body wants right now.

'I thought you wanted to help me. Don't you want to make me feel better? *This* would make me feel better.'

The little menace. I angle my jaw, narrowing my gaze at her. 'You are not as innocent as you pretend to be.'

She shrugs, the movement bringing the tops of her tightened breasts out of the water, the wet curves glistening under the moonlight.

Pure torture would be a better caption for her now.

Fine. If she wants to play this game, then let's do it. Still holding Cherry's stare, I tug down my trunks and throw them onto the poolside with a wet slap. She starts at the sound.

I exhale shakily. 'Does this make you feel better?'

Her eyes flash.

'It makes me feel . . . daring.' Cherry swishes her arms along the surface, creating gentle ripples. Neither of us have looked away from the other's eyes, almost like we're both waiting to catch the other first. Waiting for the other to cross that line. 'How does it make *you* feel?'

How does being naked in a pool with the girl I've had to fight against my own dreams about, who also happens to be my best friend's little sister, make me feel?

'Conflicted,' I grunt out.

'Because you think Wyatt would be annoyed?'

I nod.

'Do you think he'd be annoyed if . . .' Cherry wades forwards, forcing me back – except I can't move any further, because I'm already against the wall. She doesn't stop until there's barely a few inches between us, my body tightening in response. Up close, she looks even more radiant under the moonlight. Too angelic considering that she's just cornered me. *Naked*.

'If I did this,' she finishes and lifts her arms out of the water, settling them on top of my shoulders. My breath catches in my throat. All the wires in my brain are suddenly frazzled, burned by her touch. By her boldness.

All I can do is nod again.

Because I want this so badly.

I want to feel her wet skin on mine, every inch of her beautiful, bare body pressed against me. I want to flip us around, press her back against the wall, and take her right here. I want to hear the water crashing around us as our bodies slam together.

Cherry's eyes flick between mine, searching. 'And what about this?' Then, she shifts up and wraps her legs around my hips—

I reach out and grab her waist to stop her body from being flush against mine. From feeling how painfully hard I am. A small whimper leaves her lips as my hands splay across her ribs. My grip is tighter than I'd like, but it's only evidence of how hard I'm fighting myself on this.

Finally, I break our stare and close my eyes, begging for my body to gain some control over itself. Holding her like this, learning what the bare, *wet* skin of her waist feels like in my hands, is making me second-guess whether this is reality.

'Closing-time argument,' she whispers, her breath caressing my lips. Cherry leans her face closer to me, faintly – *so faintly* – brushing her lips against mine, as she ponders, 'Kissing your best friend's little sister. For or against?'

'Against,' I lie, but don't move my mouth away.

'Fine, I'll start.' Her cold fingers trace the tattoos over my shoulder, where my sleeve starts, every inch of my skin lighting up under her touch. Each word comes out as a breath. 'I think it would feel really, really good.'

My arms tremble, trying to keep her where she is. Any closer to my body and she'll feel exactly how much I agree with the idea that kissing her would feel *really, really good*.

I open my eyes just as I say, 'It would be wrong.'

Her nail drags up my neck, my cock throbbing in response. 'That makes it hotter.'

'Wyatt would kill me.'

'Wyatt?' Cherry angles her head, blinking big doe eyes at me with the most innocent of smiles. 'Who said I was talking about *us*?'

With that, she pushes off me, twisting around as she falls into a leisurely swim, giving me another flash of her ass. It's then I realise little Cherry Hensley knows *exactly* how much power she holds over me.

And I am completely and utterly fucked.

21

Cherry

'*You always were a natural in the saddle – I have no doubt you'll jump up onto that horse tomorrow and be galloping off with ease. You've got this, Baby Hensley.*'

Duke's parting words from our phone call last night run through my mind as I watch Fliss lead one of the horses into the corral. I'm leaning against the fence, readying myself for this riding lesson – eight years of fear bubbling to the surface, which I confessed all about to Duke on the phone too.

I know it's probably not healthy that I've been trusting him to help me get to sleep every night since last weekend – that I'm reliant on his soothing voice to keep my mind calm when soon I'll be without him completely . . . Except, the rational part of my brain that tells me to not get so attached just doesn't seem as convincing anymore. Because after the moment we had in the pool on Thursday, something tells me *he* wouldn't be so opposed to that idea either. I could practically hear the cracks in all the walls he's been building between us. They echoed along the dark water's surface, inviting me to slip between them. To *explore*.

It's safe to say I did *not* sleep much that night. Too many hot, wet thoughts swirling through my mind.

Watching Duke Bennett struggle to hold onto his self-control as I slipped my bikini straps over my shoulders and then see it almost shatter when I wrapped my legs around his solid waist – *that* gave me a heady sense of power I've never experienced before.

One I can't help but want to chase again.

So, I'm going to take the last remnants of that power still faintly buzzing under my skin and ride this goddamn horse.

After taking a cleansing breath, I walk into the corral to join Fliss. The size of the horse has my fists clenching, nails digging into my palms as my stomach roils. I'm far taller than I was when I last rode a horse, yet the height of this filly makes me gulp. Man, thirteen-year-old Cherry was goddamn brave. Jumping up onto massive horses, galloping through fields, and trotting along winding dirt roads without a tremble of fear – I don't know how she did it.

'I know you rode for a few years when you were younger, but I think we should go right back to the basics,' Fliss suggests. She gives the beautiful filly whose reins she's holding a gentle rub along the neck as she offers me a comforting smile. She fishes a small mint from her pocket, feeding it to the horse. 'Start with just some trotting on Moonshine. This is all about making you feel comfortable on a horse again, so we don't need to rush it. As far as I'm concerned, you're in charge here. We'll take everything at whatever pace you want. Sound okay?'

'That sounds great,' I admit shakily, reaching out to join Fliss in stroking Moonshine along her neck. I appreciate the approach Fliss is taking with this lesson – she knows what happened with my fall, but she's not going to baby me. She's giving me the control. A strange rush of strength flares in my chest knowing that, my shoulders straightening out.

With a nicker, Moonshine leans into my touch, her dark eyes seeking me out and flooding my veins with calm. Just feeling her soft coat under my palms, letting her mane run through my fingers, feels so *right*. It reminds me of that same feeling on my first horse riding lesson. Like I'd found my calling, that one place where the world quietened around me and just gave me a space to truly be me.

Funny how that same feeling springs up around Duke too.

It's a little full circle when his words from last night pop into my mind again, bolstering me. He was the one who found me when I fell – a stroke of luck that he was riding his bike along that dirt road at the same time – and now his words are giving me the final push to get back up.

'You wanna use the stool to help you up?' Fliss asks, nodding to where it's by the gate.

'Nah, I'll be fine without,' I decide, determination widening my smile.

'Sadly, not all of us are graced with super-model legs

like you,' she jests, likely because she's barely pushing five foot two. She nudges me with her elbow. 'You ready?'

I gulp down a final deep breath. 'Hell yeah.'

Fliss hands the reins over to me, and I relish the roughness of the worn leather as it scrapes softly against my palms. My fingers clasp tight, and I give a quick nod to Moonshine – a little silent promise that I trust her and that she can trust me. That we're a team. Then I'm slotting my foot into the stirrup and grabbing the pommel, before pushing up and throwing my leg over the saddle.

And I'm sitting. Up on the horse.

I didn't fall.

A laugh barrels out of me. Loud and free.

I freaking did it.

'Fliss, oh my God! Look at me,' I squeal.

'Yes, girl!' she cheers, grin widening by the second.

The instinct to squeeze my legs against Moonshine's haunches comes through naturally, just the automatic next action my body knows to take, even after eight years out of the saddle. With my hands wrapped firmly around the reins, Moonshine huffs and takes off, breaking into a steady, slow trot.

A small wobble forces me to engage my core, and with a deep breath, I'm letting the waves of Moonshine's movements flow through me. Like we're one. Like we were always meant to ride together. I guide Moonshine in the direction I want her to go, everything coming back to me as memories of galloping freely along emerald tree-lined dirt roads spring up in my mind.

'Well, I guess my job is done.' Fliss laughs, beaming at me.

Because I did it.

I got back up.

But I only glance at her quickly as I need to stay focused, to really make this lesson count. No being lazy now. No getting distracted. Though, after a few laps of trotting around the corral, not becoming distracted becomes slightly difficult when I spot movement in the distance. Two people heading towards us.

I pull back on the reins to slow Moonshine down, allowing me to better see the two men walking over – one with the widest smile, competing against the sun's brightness as he takes me in, while the other's face is screwed up.

Fliss grabs the side of the reins when I bring Moonshine to a halt, just as Wyatt calls out, 'What's going on?'

He huffs out a breath as he and Duke reach the fence, immediately jumping up and leaning against it. Duke rests beside him silently, but the admiration in his eyes speaks to me louder than any words could. I didn't realise he'd be at Sunset Ranch today, but *he* knew *I'd* be here...

I give Wyatt a shrug. 'I've decided to start riding again.'

'Since when?'

'Since the rodeo.' I make sure to catch Duke's eyes, almost to add in, *since you.* He smiles, ducking his head shyly.

Wyatt chews on the inside of his lip, his stern eyes flicking about the scene before him. Somehow, I think I might have rendered him speechless – like he can't quite believe I've done this. That I found some strength, and it has me lifting my chin higher, along with the way Duke's watching me again, a smirk dancing on his lips.

'I'm not sure I like this,' Wyatt finally admits, folding his arms, brows still pulled together. 'Doesn't feel safe.'

Duke snorts beside him and says, 'I don't think that really matters right now, man. You're a bit late – she's already on the horse.'

Fliss and I giggle in response, and I widen my smile at Duke, that he's willing to go against Wyatt, something up until the other night in the pool I was certain he'd never do. But clearly his resolve is weakening. What else might he go against Wyatt for now?

'Doesn't it worry you a bit?' Wyatt turns to Duke. 'You were the one who found her after her fall. Aren't you . . .' *Scared*. He doesn't have to say it, but I see it – in the way his muscles tense as he crosses his arms, the desperate shine to his eyes, the feathering of his jaw each time the horse shifts. An ache settles in my heart, and I realise that learning to ride again, even if it worries my family, is just as much for them as it is for me. If they can see me thriving, not cowering, maybe they'll finally stop seeing me as a frail little girl.

'I'll be okay, Wyatt,' I try to assure him, softening my determined expression. It's hard to talk about my fall, but still I push the words out. 'I didn't have any warning when I fell before. But I know my triggers now, and I know when I can and can't push myself. I've been looking after myself fine for the last few years and haven't had a seizure in ages. Because I know me better than anyone else. And I *know* I can do this.'

Huffing, Wyatt's mouth forms a stark line. But he doesn't argue back.

'Besides,' I start, my grin playing out. 'If you're so

187

worried about me falling again, you could always send Duke out with me when I ride. He was the one that saved me the first time after all. He's always looking out for me like a brother, right?'

The last question is a tease that has Duke's eyes widening and tattooed neck working as he swallows. Because it's only a matter of time before I break him, and we'll be riding past this line that I *know* he's struggling to stay behind.

22

Duke

'Do you remember that time I joked that you were a serial killer?' Cherry asks as she hops out of my truck the next week, eyes warily scouring the slightly dilapidated barn ahead. 'Yeah . . . you're really living up to that today.'

Levelling her a look, I shut the truck door once she's out of the way and snort. 'We're on Sawyer's land still. It's a short drive from the main ranch. Surely I'd be smarter than that.'

'Or maybe this is just a ruse to make me think you're not smart enough to be a serial killer, when really—'

'Shut up and get walking.' I give her a playful shove forward, not even overthinking the action for a few seconds before doing it like usual. Not excusing it as just a way to consolidate the idea that I'm her annoying friend. But just simply because it feels right.

To touch her.

I have no idea where the strong boundaries I'd put in place have disappeared to. Because today really has

189

nothing to do with Cherry's bucket list, nor does she owe me a small moment, yet I still got Jeb to cover me at the bar tonight so I could steal her away for the afternoon.

'What is this place, anyway?' Cherry questions, angling her head as she reaches the door. I give the tight, rusty lock a pull, the scrape of metal echoing through the surrounding fields, then haul the sliding door along. It rumbles until it comes to a thud.

'I like to call it my therapy barn,' I joke, gesturing for Cherry to enter.

I flick on the lights. Bulbs buzz in the rafters as they illuminate the stacks of canvases on tables – the ones I'd done of Cherry hidden elsewhere – paint pots scattered amongst them, circled around two larger canvases upright in the centre of the barn. There are sheets below them to catch any paint even though there's plenty of stains dotted around already. In the back of the barn, my two motorcycles sit, the light glinting off their black, shiny exteriors, emphasising every sleek curve and angle. I should probably cover them up but just seeing them calms my heart instantly.

'Duke, this is . . . incredible.' Cherry's last word comes out on a breath. Her sneakers scuff against the floor as she skips further into the barn, exploring the whole set-up.

'Sawyer offered it to me a few years back. They were gonna tear the place down – I can't even remember what for – but I said I could find use for it.' I press my lips together, trying to hold back the grin that really wants to explode at the way Cherry's regarding me with the brightest of expressions. 'I come here whenever I feel overwhelmed or . . . sad. It's my safe space, I guess.

Somewhere I can throw on my favourite music and paint out all my feelings.

Speaking of music, I fish my phone from my pocket and link it to the speaker on one of the tables, choosing Shaboozey's latest album to play.

'I, uh . . .' I rub the back of my neck, joining Cherry beside the two large canvases. 'I thought maybe after everything that's happened in the last couple of weeks – good and bad – you might want to paint it out. Have some time to just create.'

'I love that idea,' Cherry admits, running her delicate fingers across some of the half-finished canvases piled on the tables. 'College can kind of stifle my creativity sometimes. Don't get me wrong, I love all the interior design projects I get to work on, but sometimes when it's for an assignment, there's parameters to what you can do and it can feel a bit forced. Not like when I worked on Sunset Ranch for Rory and Wyatt – I could just let my creativity flow there.'

'I get that,' I respond, knowing how impressive the transformation she assisted on for Sunset Ranch was. Those redecorated guest houses have Cherry's keen eye for design written all over them.

'I hope I get to work on more ranches or retreats wherever I end up working next year,' she hums.

I perk a brow. 'Not a lot of ranches in the city.'

'More reason to come back then, I suppose.' She meets my teasing smile.

The old flickering lights might not provide the best illumination for painting, but they do everything to highlight Cherry's beauty, glistening against her silky hair and shimmering along her cheekbones. Even in her sweatpants and cropped tank top, she's more beautiful than any work of art I've created. Not even the painting of her floating in the water I made last week could capture anything close to the wonder that is Cherry Hensley.

A wonder I can't seem to tear my eyes from.

Like a moth to a flame, I'm enraptured, my resolve gone as she gets bolder by the days. Even just thinking about that moment in the pool, the ever so faint brush of her lips on mine, the slide of her wet skin, and the softness of her waist in my grip…

It has me *craving* another touch.

'Well, you've got two choices.' I join her where she's checking the different paint colours. 'We can just paint quietly for a bit, or—' I reach down to grab the bucket of balloons filled with paint beside the table and hold it up for her to see '—we can throw some paint balloons and make an absolute mess of those big canvases. Your choice.'

'Um, *obviously* I wanna throw paint balloons. What!' She grabs a red balloon from the bucket, tossing it between her hands. 'This is so cool. You're actually the best.'

I put the bucket down and give her a quick, nonchalant shrug, even though my heart races at the praise. 'Anything for you, Baby Hensley.'

'Yeah?' Cherry's tongue darts out to wet her lips, leaving them shining. 'Well, I don't know about you . . .' She bends down to grab another paint balloon and heads towards one of the larger canvases. 'But I have a *lot* of pent-up frustration that this might help me get out.'

'Frustration?'

'Oh yeah.' She perks a brow at me. 'I think you know the kind I'm talking about.' And the way she suggestively bites down on her lip afterward has my cock twitching. *Fuck, does she mean frustrated . . . sexually?*

'Right.' I clear my throat then join her at the big canvas, hefting the bucket of paint balloons with me. 'Ladies first.'

Cherry takes a deep breath before throwing her balloon with all her might, and it whooshes through the air, making a loud *splat* as it hits the canvas straight in the middle. Blue paint erupts across the canvas like a liquid firework, plenty scattering along the floor below too.

'Woo!' she hollers, giggling straight after. 'That felt so good.'

Cherry doesn't hesitate before launching another paint balloon at the canvas. Her bare shoulders move so loosely beneath her tank top, like any worries weighing on them have vanished. Swiftly, I pile a few balloons into my arms and begin hurling them at the canvas with all my strength, watching as the purple paint scatters across the green splatter below, colours running together as they drip down the canvas.

Cherry hums beside me as she grabs another couple of balloons, turning to me as she says, 'You know what, I think there's just one final thing that'll help to get all my frustration out.'

I notice the spark of mischief in her eyes a second too late—

Paint explodes in my vision, splattering across my face and arms as one of the balloons collides with my chest. I want to be annoyed, but when all I can hear is Cherry's silvery laugh bellowing through the barn, I find myself chuckling too as I wipe the paint from my face, revealing her bright, beaming smile completely aimed at me.

God, I love being with her.

The sight and sound of her smile and giggle unleashes my own grin, and I'm shaking my head at how fucking happy this girl makes me. How honoured I am to be the one making her laugh.

'Oh, you're dead,' I warn her, readying one of the balloons in my hand.

I pick up my foot but she's already dashing away, squealing mixing in with her laughter. Even though those long legs can carry her quickly, she's no match for me, and I catch up, launching the balloon at the back of her head. It breaks against her hair as she screams, green paint dripping all down her back. And when she turns around to shout at me, I toss another that splatters across her shoulder, drops sprinkling across her face and side too.

'Oh my God!' she yells, running her fingers through her paint-drenched hair, but her smile never leaves her face. 'That's gonna be a nightmare to get out.'

'You started it.' I flash her a smug grin.

Twisting on her heel, Cherry dashes towards me, raising her other balloon, unadulterated laughter ringing out—

The high-pitched squeak of sneakers slipping in paint screeches through the barn. Cherry's laugh morphs into a screech and suddenly she's tumbling towards me—

My hands shoot out to catch her but it's not quick enough and she collides into me, the air whooshing out of my lungs as the room tilts and the paint balloon bursts between us.

We twist awkwardly, legs ravelling around each other.

In the split second between falling and smacking against the hard ground, I manage to cradle her head and ensure I take the brunt of the fall.

'*Oof*,' she grunts, collapsing against me when we finally hit the floor.

Her legs bracket my thigh, and her knee slides up and squashes all my goods in the impact. The gut-punching pain rips all the breath from my lungs, the ache wedging deep in the bottom of my stomach – for the *second time* this summer, goddamnit. It takes me a good few seconds to finally gulp some air down.

'I'm so sorry.' Her body trembles with laughter in my grasp as she braces her hands either side of me to lift herself up. The paint-soaked slice of skin between her top and sweatpants slides against my palms. 'I kneed you in the balls again, didn't I?'

'Just a little bit,' I croak out, eyes closed.

But the cloud of warm breath that lands against my lips immediately distracts me. My eyes shoot open to find two wild, umber pools glistening down at me.

Black, paint-matted hair falls around us like curtains, creating a barrier against all the rational reasons why we shouldn't be lying here, her straddling my thigh, my fingers now trailing over her hips almost instinctively. My fingers splay out possessively, giving in to that impulse that screams *mine, mine, mine* when I'm holding her.

Better to give in to that impulse than the one that wants to start grinding my hips against her.

Cherry's gaze flicks between my eyes and lips once. Twice. The long column of her throat working on the third glance. I dare myself to let my gaze wander to her lips too, tracing the heart shape, smiling at the blue paint bisecting her full bottom lip. Then, I dip down to the rest of her body straddling me, noting once again how every inch of her seems so perfectly crafted. Especially those goddamn long legs that I could happily die between. With the paint dappling her skin, it only reminds me further that I'm holding a masterpiece of a life in my hands, a woman who deserves to be idolised.

When Cherry's mouth parts, a soft breath shuddering out and cutting through the electrified silence, I'm suddenly all too aware of my heart rattling against my chest. The pulse point on her neck fluttering. My cock throbbing in my pants, like it's completely forgotten that it got squashed not thirty seconds ago.

Her teeth graze her bottom lip. And then she goes and asks, 'Kissing your best friend's little sister. For or against?'

I wait for the alarms to start blaring in my mind . . . but only my need sounds. To feel her, to taste her, to be all-consumed by her.

Wild eyes flick between mine, searching.

When was the last time you did something big just for you? When did you last let yourself have something you wanted without worrying how other people would feel?

Her words echo in my mind, and for the first time in what has felt like forever, they make me want to say *fuck it.*

My voice is ragged as I admit, 'For, Cherry. I've always been for.'

And with that, I surge upwards and capture her lips with mine. One hand sifts through her hair, the other gripping tight to her hips to keep her flush against me as I bring us into a seated position, her gasp filtering into my mouth as I do. But she doesn't pull back, and the tenseness of her body lasts barely even a second before she's grabbing onto my shoulders for dear life. She uses their solid expanse as leverage to rock herself further into me, returning the kiss with an unexpected, wild fervour.

Fireworks explode throughout my body, sparkling along every inch, awakening me to a point of aliveness I didn't think possible.

Firework kiss – tick.

Her eager kiss hits me like a strong mouthful of whiskey – the sweet taste of her sears through my body, awakening every one of my nerves, while the warm flavour floods me with calm. With every inch I give her, Cherry takes a mile, increasing the pressure and speed of our kiss like she's been starved. Like if she doesn't drink me up now, she'll lose me forever. Like she has no idea that I'd happily give her all of me until the day I die. It only makes me want to prove that with my mouth.

A tentative brush of my tongue against the seam of her lips has her opening her mouth immediately, her nails digging into my shoulders when our tongues collide. The breathy moan that escapes her lips in response is music to my ears, making all the hairs on my body stand. It urges me to slide my fingers through her glossy, albeit slightly knotted hair, and wrap it around my palm so I can use it to help angle her head back further.

'Is this okay?' I quickly break our kiss to check, and she nods, lips crashing back into mine. 'I need words, Cherry,' I murmur against her mouth.

197

'Ugh, yes,' she groans, all bratty, like I'm so terrible for keeping her from kissing me properly because I want confirmation that she's happy with how I'm touching her. It only makes me tug her hair harder, allowing me to take her mouth deeper, that moan bubbling up from her throat again and going straight to my already painfully hard dick. The one that's turned my sweatpants into a goddamn tent.

Hands now fisting my T-shirt, Cherry tries to pull herself closer, the heat of her radiating into me. With her breasts pressed against my chest, fire sparking at every point of contact between us, I take her bottom lip between my teeth. Her hips buck against me in reaction, legs squeezing around my thigh. Every thought I've ever had about trying to keep a barrier between us goes flying out the window and I want nothing more than to rip our pants off and feel her sweet pussy grind against my thigh.

I swipe her silky hair to the side, and drop my lips to her neck.

'You should tell me to stop,' I whisper against her skin.

'Please don't stop,' she moans back.

Savouring the taste of her, not even caring about the paint splattered over her skin, I run my tongue along the column of her throat, feeling out her quickening pulse. Cherry rewards me with a breathy moan, grinding against me once more. Her eyes flash as I bring my lips away to catch her gaze. Like she's shocked at the pleasure she gets from the friction between our bodies, and her need for me.

Desperate to hear more of those delicious sounds, I plant kisses up her neck again until I get to the sensitive skin beneath her ear. Then, I give her earlobe a soft nip. To my delight, with another sweet whimper, Cherry rocks herself against my thigh again. I want to tattoo every sound she makes on my body so that I never forget them. So that I can replay each one over and over and *over* again in my head, drowning myself in the ecstasy of her pleasure.

Cherry angles her head to start kissing my neck too, the touch of her lips against my skin sending fire coursing through my veins.

But then she sputters and rears back to wipe the thick smudge of paint away from her lips. It only drags it across her face, her mouth still painted blue, along with her cheek now.

'Sorry,' she giggles innocently, licking her lips – which are full and puffy from such rough kissing – and then winces. 'I have so much paint in my mouth.' Cherry sticks her tongue out, and it's covered in blue. A grimace takes over her face as my laugh rumbles in my chest.

I wipe away the paint covering her bottom lip with my thumb, savouring the feel of her soft mouth. The mouth that tasted like fucking *heaven*. With a sigh – because the last thing I want right now is to stop kissing her – I suggest, 'I think maybe we should get cleaned up.'

I've spent the last couple of years adhering to all these boundaries keeping me away from Cherry, but now, I'm done with them. I don't want *anything* to get in the way of giving her the pleasure she deserves. So, if that means stopping to clean away all this goddamn paint, so my mouth can run freely over her body, then that's what we'll do. It *can't* end here.

Cherry's grip on me loosens suddenly, and she blinks, looking around the barn as if she forgot where we were. Hell, I know I did. 'Right.' A titter trickles out of her. 'Probably a good idea.'

We both sit there for a moment, wrapped up in each other, unmoving, until I finally shift and say, 'Come on. Let's go get you in the shower.'

23

Cherry

Duke's hardly said anything since we got in his truck and drove back to his apartment, despite his tone being *incredibly* suggestive when he mentioned having a shower. I know technically I was the one who cut off the kiss – darned paint getting in my mouth – but what if that's the end of it? A quick moment of weakness from the both of us, where we could indulge in it because no one was watching for once, and now he's dropping back into his usual caretaking mode, where I'm just Wyatt's little sister.

I rub at my sternum to try to loosen the tightness there, even as my heart threatens to beat out of my ribcage as we climb the stairs to Duke's apartment. I can't bring myself to talk, to fill the silence. What's wrong with me? Where has bold, confident, *strong* Cherry that basically propositioned him in the first place gone? I literally just had my dream kiss – a goddamn firework kiss, exactly like I described to him – with the one guy I've wanted for years.

Quietly, he unlocks the door and gestures for me to enter first, placing a hand on the small of my back as I walk through – the touch immediately sparking heat within my core as I'm still so worked up from that kiss. I shuffle inside, standing in the middle of the room so not to get paint anywhere as I wait.

'I'll go get the shower running,' Duke says, moving towards the bathroom. It makes sense for him, dropping back into our usual routine, saving him from admitting his feelings. And I almost – *almost* – let him get away with it.

'Duke, wait,' I blurt out. Even if all this time working on my bucket list together hasn't meant anything to Duke, it has to me. It's made me realise that I'm strong enough to do whatever I put my mind to – including putting my feelings on the line. And I'd rather attempt to get back into the saddle, even if only to fall, than regret having never tried.

He turns to me, his face immediately creasing when he notices my concern. Wildness sets ablaze in his eyes, like he's readying to fight whatever I'm battling. 'Everything okay?'

My breath shudders out. 'Is . . . is that it?'

'Is what it?'

'Because I need to know.' I can't stop the thoughts from spilling out, whatever dam I had holding back this crush destroyed from that kiss. From the way I felt stars shooting through the skies of my soul. Even if nothing else happens, that kiss will be branded in my memory forever. 'What this means to you. I'm sorry, I know it sounds silly because all we did was kiss but . . .' I step away from Duke and rub my hand along my forehead, my fingers trembling.

'Hey, hey. It's okay.' Duke follows me instantly. He reaches for my hands, harbouring them in his own, soothing my racing heart.

'I don't wanna scare you,' I admit, the prick of tears surfacing.

His large hand comes up to cradle my jaw and I let myself lean into his touch – where he always manages to anchor me to safety. 'Cherry, you can tell me anything. I've got you, remember?'

I swallow, trying to muster up that unexpected bravery that has been around the past weeks. 'Duke, I've . . . I've liked you for years. And when I say years, I mean since I was a *teenager*.'

There's a widening of his eyes as they flick between mine. I've ridden this rocky journey he's had us on for years, weathered every push and pull, holding on to the reins with hope that something might be at the end of it all.

But what if Duke hasn't done the same? He's six years older than me – he probably barely sees me as an adult. He's likely not even thinking beyond today, when I'm *miles* ahead in our future, ignoring all the times he's insinuated nothing could happen between us.

'I know it was just a kiss, but that – that means a lot to me. And it's okay if it doesn't to you, but I need to know that. You went so quiet on the way back that I just freaked out. Maybe you're regretting it because of Wyatt, I don't know.' My laugh trembles out. 'Either way, I need you to *talk* to me. I don't want to build up this idea of us in my head. I don't want to let myself start falling if you're not going to be there with me.'

The few seconds of silence that follow are deafening. Duke doesn't move, the weight of his gaze unbearably heavy. I wonder if this is my last moment in his hold, the last opportunity to feel his soothing touch, but then he whispers, 'I'm right here, Cherry. Falling with you.'

Each word breathes bright hope into my heart.

Duke pulls my hands to his chest, and his heart pounds beneath. His eyes dip between us. 'I've been falling since the day you started working at the bar. And I've spent all that time fighting against it because I didn't want to do the wrong thing. Because I was scared. I *am* scared. That's why I went quiet, I think . . .' His lip drops, hesitating. It's my turn to caress his face, my hands trailing up his neck until I'm brushing my thumbs against his cheeks, gazing into those umber eyes of his. 'Because I've wanted this for so long too, and now I'm here, I'm almost overwhelmed. That, and I was really struggling to keep my hands off you while we were still covered in paint.'

He wets his lips as his smile plays out, mine following quickly.

'But I'm not sure this is so wrong anymore, because that kiss – *fuck*, Cherry.' Duke laughs, shaking his head. He grabs my waist, tugging me into him. 'That was fucking heavenly. *You're* fucking heavenly. I don't see how something that feels so right could possibly be wrong . . . I'm not sure how this is all gonna pan out, but whatever happens, I promise I'll be right here with you. Even if it terrifies me.'

'Because you've got me, right?' I ask.

Duke presses his forehead to mine. 'Because I've got you, Baby Hensley. Always.'

I don't give him a second before I launch myself at him, my arms circling his neck. Duke's reflexes are quick enough that he grabs my waist, pulling me up and into him so he can kiss me back. Fireworks sparkle along my skin again at the taste of him, exploding deeper inside my core with each stroke of his tongue. Tightness winds in my stomach. But I need *more*.

My hands drop to the waistband of his sweatpants and—

Duke's hands shoot out to bracket my wrists as he breaks our kiss, halting me. I let out a little groan at the loss of his lips.

'We need to shower,' he demands, dark eyes enflamed.

When he finally lets go of my wrists, I try to run my fingers through my hair, only to find it knotted and crusty with dried paint. That's going to be a pain to wash out. But God, was it worth it. Making out with Duke Bennett dripping in paint should've been on the bucket list, because I don't think anything has made me feel so exhilarated before.

I bite my lip, grinning when his darkened gaze snaps straight to the movement. 'And when you say *we* . . . does that mean you'll be joining me?'

Duke drags his eyes slowly up to meet mine with heavy lids, his nostrils flaring. 'Is that what you want?'

Tentatively, I filter my fingers under the hem of his T-shirt, feeling the burn of his gaze. 'Yes.'

'Okay, but I'm not going to fuck you in the shower, Cherry.'

The word *fuck* jolts me, warmth puddling deep in my stomach. Because that is exactly how I imagine it would be with Duke. It wouldn't be sex, or making love, it would be a good, hard *fuck*. All those years of pent-up attraction spilling out. He's built for it too – I bet those thick arms could hold me up against the wall for hours. And he might act all gentle and caring around me, but when we were kissing earlier in the paint, I saw his control snap. I *felt* how badly he wanted me.

'If you say so.' I shrug and start lifting, revealing inch by inch of dark, chiselled muscle. My mouth dries, and when Duke doesn't stop me, even going as far as to finish removing the top when my arms can't reach over his, I'm speechless. My heart clamours in my chest.

Because he's a goddamn work of art.

I have an unbelievable need to trace the hard lines of his body with my tongue. I don't know why the sight of him is hitting me so deeply. It's not like this is the first time I've seen him shirtless – we were literally skinny-dipping the other week. But now, this is all *mine*. No boundaries or lines or rules to stop me.

A goddamn miracle.

'My turn,' Duke hums, the low, promising timbre of his voice making the hairs on my body stand. The ache between my legs becomes almost unbearable.

With a featherlight touch, Duke's fingers skim my stomach before he hooks them under my crop top. I raise my arms, letting him peel the top off. I can't help but gulp, especially when my eyes flick down to where his sweatpants are barely hiding how hard he is. Duke's hands splay over my waist, pausing for a moment to let his thumbs stroke my curves before he starts backing me up. He walks me backwards until we're into his bedroom and I'm pressed against a door. He reaches for the handle, letting us into the bathroom. Even though his hold on me is gentle, wildness swarms his eyes, his muscles strained.

Fingers trail up my back, leaving a searing heat in their wake. They reach my bra, and it's unhooked with one quick flick. Duke draws the straps down my arms, letting it fall to the ground. The cool air kisses my breasts and his sharp inhale echoes through the bathroom.

'Fuck, Cherry.' The column of his throat works as his eyes devour me. 'You're a masterpiece.'

I'm buzzing with need, agonised by the fact that his hands are back by his side, flexing, instead of touching me. Like they should be.

'Me again,' I practically breathe out with the way my breath is racing right now.

Duke's eyes shutter closed for a beat, then shoot open as my fingers curl around his waistband. The intensity of his stare weighs on me as I tug his sweatpants down, letting them drop to the floor. Fuck, even his thighs are mouth-watering. Which is just made worse now that I can see how goddamn huge he is, straining hard against his underwear.

Duke begins loosening the tied up strings of my sweatpants, brows knitted together, and head dipped as he does. He steps out of his own pants, and runs a finger along the inside of my waistband, far too close to where I need him. Then he drops to his knees and presses a kiss to my navel, sending a jolt of electricity through me. He rests his forehead against me, fingers curling around my waistband.

'Cherry,' he whispers against my skin.

One name, too many unspoken meanings.

I cup his jaw, lifting his gaze to mine. Fire ignites in his eyes, pupils enlarging. Two pools of pure desire that I want to dive into.

Duke doesn't break eye contact as he finally pulls down my sweatpants, knuckles skimming my legs as he does, the tingling sensation they leave going straight to my core. Carefully, he helps each of my feet out of the legs, brushing his hands up the back of my thighs as he stands again. It only makes me want him to touch me more, causing me to let out a small, breathy whimper.

The faint smirk on his face tells me that he knows exactly that.

That he's purposefully prolonging this.

As if I – no, *we* – haven't waited so long already.

When Duke's back towering over me, I'm all too aware of how close he is, how if I move even the slightest bit, my stomach will brush up against his hard cock.

Staring down, I can't help but swallow again.

But before I can go to remove his underwear, Duke moves towards the shower and turns it on. The sound of the water rushing snaps me back to reality. Holding his hand under the shower for a few seconds to test the temperature, Duke eventually nods and turns to me. 'You first.'

His eyes flick down to the black thong I'm still wearing. He's not going to take it off . . . Even if he's joining me, he's still genuinely going to make sure I have a shower.

If that doesn't sum up Duke Bennett, then I don't know what does.

Fine. I drop my thong and step into the shower, submerging myself under the water. The hot water doesn't come close to the heat searing inside my core. But it's a welcome sensation, the soothing water sliding over my body, paint slowly dissolving off my skin and landing into the multicoloured pool swirling on the shower floor. I run my hands over my hair, letting the water soak it. When I wipe the water from eyes, Duke is still standing at the door, bottom lip dropped as he watches.

He looks at me like I'm the eighth wonder of the world, and it washes away any lingering insecurity with the water.

'I'm waiting,' I say, glancing once to his underwear, making sure to rub a hand over my breasts just to tease him. His frame tenses in response, eyes closing for a beat before reopening with a deep exhale.

'You—' Duke grabs the waistband of his underwear '—are the bane of my life, Cherry Hensley.' Then he pushes them down, releasing every deliciously thick, hard inch of him. I can't stop my eyes from widening, or my lips from popping open.

Jesus, I'm in trouble.

'There's no way that's going to fit,' I admit, realising a second too late that I've said it out loud.

Duke steps into the shower, shoulders bouncing as he chuckles. I back up as he eats up the space between us, a solid wall of dark, shifting muscle. His head hangs out of the shower's spray, peering down at me as the water rushes over his back. And his impressive length brushes my stomach, only highlighting the enormity of it. I've only been with two guys before and it's safe to say neither of them had *anything* on Duke.

'Firstly,' he starts, placing his hands on the wall either side of my shoulders, 'we'll make it fit, don't worry.'

Oh my God.

Who is this man and what did he do with shy Duke Bennett?

'And secondly, when did I say I was going to let you have it? Don't be greedy. I told you – I'm not fucking you yet. We're just having a shower.' He perks a brow, letting his smirk fully spread out. The ache between my thighs is torturous at the sight of that smug smile. I don't want a shower, I want *him*. 'Now,' he purrs, 'be a good girl and turn around so I can wash your hair.'

Gulping down the whimper that wants to escape, I obey, unable to do anything with the way he's just spoken to me. As I turn, my ass brushes against his cock and I can't help but arch my back a little, pressing back into him more. Duke grabs my hips, fingers pulsing as a silent command to stop.

Probably a good thing, seeing as I feel like I might combust.

'Careful,' he whispers in my ear, reaching to the shelf beside us to grab some shampoo.

And then his fingers are in my hair, gently massaging the shampoo into my scalp. My whole body loosens under his tender touch, breathing finally steadying, even as the flames inside me still kindle. This whole moment feels so sensuous, yet so safe. Like this is a promise, that whatever happens, he'll always take care of me.

I've got you, Baby Hensley.

He could be fucking me against the wall if he wanted to. But instead, he's washing me. Making sure I'm clean and happy and warm. Not because he thinks he needs to either – no, not the way others try to help me out because they think I can't – but because he *wants* to, even if he knows I can take care of myself.

His hands briefly leave my hair to grab another bottle. 'You got conditioner?' I check over my shoulder as he pours it into his palms. It's not like he knew I'd ever be here again.

His eyes catch mine, softening even if just for a second. 'Anything for you, Baby Hensley. I picked some up just in case.' He carefully caresses the conditioner into my hair. 'This,' Duke murmurs, raking his fingers through my hair, his breath hot against me, 'is one of my favourite things. Like fucking silk.'

'Really?' I ask, then turn around, letting his hands slip through my hair. I place my hands on his chest to edge him back so I can wash the conditioner out of my hair under the water. He begins lathering up some body wash in his hands next. 'What else?'

Eyes darkening, Duke takes my face and leans in to skim his lips against mine. 'These too. Especially when you bite down on them.'

He starts washing my body, hands sliding over my wet skin. Duke slows down to caress my breasts, meticulously exploring their curves, before rolling one of my nipples between his thumb and finger. My body bucks in response, making his eyes widen. He does it again with a grin, catching on to how sensitive they are. I close my

211

eyes to try to ignore the throbbing between my legs that's as fast as my heart.

Heavy hands continue to roam my body, trailing and worshipping, like he's trying to commit every inch of me to his memory. They slide over my stomach, round to cup my ass, his head leaning against my shoulder.

'I don't think there was any paint on my ass,' I giggle when he seems unable to draw his hands away. His hot breath rumbles out in a laugh against my shoulder.

'What about here?' he asks, then slips his hand once – *only once* – between my legs, cupping me for the shortest second ever. The friction is everything, but also nothing.

I'm furious.

Pushing his hands off me, I wipe my own along my body to get some of the soap on my palms. I let myself explore the ridges of his muscles, learning all the edges and lines that I've always had to admire from afar. His solid body begins to soften until I say, 'I think you had some paint here as well,' and wrap my fingers around his cock, giving it one long, slow pump. That's going need at least two hands later.

Duke's eyes widen and he growls, 'Cherry.'

I rub my thumb over the tip once too, just to add to his frustration. I don't miss the way his legs tremble.

'Cherry,' he grinds out once more. 'Dry yourself off and get on the bed, *now*.'

212

24

Duke

Walking out of the bathroom to find Cherry on my bed, wrapped in a towel, wet hair trailing over one shoulder, has me stopping in my tracks. The sunset pours through the window, dousing her skin in an otherworldly golden glow. Against the canvas of my white sheets, she's the subject of the most glorious painting I've ever seen.

I lean for a second in the door frame – something to hold me up – and make sure I'm not dreaming.

This is *Cherry goddamn Hensley*.

The beautiful, strong, *cunning* woman who sets my body alight, and is goddamn torturing me with her slender body and soft curves. The mischievous twinkle in her eyes when she bites down on those lips. The way her delicate fingers wrapped around my cock in the shower—

'Duke?' Cherry asks, pulling her legs up onto the bed.

I adjust the towel slung loosely around my hips, though it does nothing to hide the raging boner I'm still sporting.

The way Cherry glances down to it, pressing her lips together, says enough.

There's no way that's going to fit.

Fuck.

Slow. This *has* to be slow.

For both me and her. I've waited too long for this, I can't rush it, can't get too caught up and not savour every moment with her like she deserves – especially now I know how much this means to her too. Now's the time to prove to her how much I care, to devote myself entirely to her pleasure.

Besides, she's younger, she's . . . possibly less experienced than I originally thought given the bucket list.

Have a guy give me an orgasm.

I'll give her every orgasm she needs, along with the fucking world. But we'll take it slow. No rushing to try to tick things off some silly bucket list, and then burning out.

'Mhm?' I reply, stalking towards her. Letting her gaze devour me as I get closer, like I'm her last meal. And, God, I cannot wait to taste her again.

'You were staring.' Her big brown eyes watching me with something like wonder. They glance down once to where my hard cock is caged behind the towel, and she swallows. Then she licks her goddamn lips, like she's getting ready to take me.

Nope. Can't have her eye-level with my cock any longer.

'I'm always staring at you.' I press my knee into the bed beside her and begin climbing on. She edges back when I nod towards the head of the bed, lying herself down until

I'm hovering over her. 'And even when you're not around, I'm still thinking of you. How goddamn breath-taking you are.'

'Yeah?' Cherry breathes out.

'Can I?' I run a finger along the top of the towel, awaiting her nod before I unfold it from her body, laying her bare for me.

Dusky pink nipples point up at me, begging to be played with. I want – no, *need* – to make her body quiver again like I did in the shower.

'I thought you said I was the *bane of your life*?' Cherry quips.

I press a kiss to her neck and her body instantly arches up into mine with a soft moan, like I'm the hit she needs to come alive. 'Oh, you're that too. This,' I trail a finger down her body as I continue to brush my lips along her collarbone, relishing the way her breath begins to race, 'is fucking torturous. Always on my mind. Why do you think I'm always so quiet? It's because I can't stop thinking about you.'

And with that Cherry wraps her arms around my neck and tugs me into a kiss. She's frantic, opening her mouth to me immediately, those years of pent-up desire spilling out like a waterfall again. But I only give her gradual, relaxed strokes of my tongue until she calms and matches my slower pace. Her hand brushes over my head, fingers trailing about the patterns shaved into my hair. A small moan escapes her mouth as I sink my teeth into her bottom lip, tugging, just like I've been dreaming of doing for years.

And it was worth the wait.

Nails rake up my back, my skin exploding into goosebumps, the sensation shooting straight down to my already aching cock. I trail my lips along her jaw and down her neck, sucking and kissing at her tender skin, revelling in the way her body jolts below me. It's almost enough to distract me from her hands sliding down to the edge of my towel and—

I catch her wrists with one hand and pin them above her head. Cherry gasps and presses her chest up towards me, those perky breasts just grazing my chest. Fuck, she looks damn edible laid out for me like this.

'Not tonight,' I say, pressing kisses slowly down towards her breasts.

Cherry lets out a needy whine. 'But – oh, *fuck*—' I take one of her nipples in my mouth, rolling my tongue around it '—but why not?'

'Because.' I pause to do the same with her other nipple, giving this one a quick nip and getting far too much satisfaction at the way a tremble rushes through her body. 'I want to take this slow. I've been waiting so long to get to taste you, to *feel* you. I can't rush this.' I press a kiss to her sternum, her body lifting as my lips leave her skin. 'And . . . I want to prove to you how much I want this. How much I *need* this. I'm not good with words, and I'll work on that, for you, but until then, let me *show* you instead, Cherry.'

Cherry's eyes soften at me, a devastatingly beautiful smile following – one that deserves to be in a gallery.

'So,' I begin, dropping my lips back to her chest, 'let's start with you telling me how you like to make yourself come.'

'What?' The word is barely more than a breath as I make my way up to her neck, kissing her just below her ear, whilst I keep her hands locked above her head.

'I want you to tell me how you make yourself come.' When I pull back to look into her sparkling eyes, lids heavy with desire, she swallows. Watching her slender throat work forces me to kiss it again. I could stay here for hours just worshipping every inch of her beautiful body with my mouth. 'If I let go,' my fingers pulse against her trapped wrists, 'are you going to be a good girl and tell me how you like to play with yourself?'

She nods, still trying to bite back her smile. I release her hands and she admits, 'I normally use a vibrator.'

'Okay, noted for next time,' I say, making sure that ordering a vibrator is the first thing I do tomorrow.

Lazily, I trail a finger down the centre of her chest, over her stomach, and down one of her thighs, avoiding the spot that's already glistening for me. 'And when you don't have a vibrator?'

Cherry's gaze is trained intensely on where I'm stroking her. She swallows again, her body tensing as my finger traces circles up her thigh.

'Then I . . . use my fingers.'

There we go.

'Like this?' I ask, finally swiping my fingers through her slick centre, a growl vibrating in my throat at how wet she is. My cock throbs, knowing how hot and wet she's going to feel when I can *finally* sink into her.

Cherry's arousal coats my fingers, and I spread it over her clit, then start circling lightly. She lets out a breathy moan, gripping for purchase in my sheets. She tries to nod and make a noise of agreement, but it's basically a whimper, so I press a little harder just to tease.

'Duke . . .' Cherry begins, one hand coming up to massage her own breasts, as if she's acting out how she'd feel herself when she's alone. It's so fucking hot.

'Yes, baby?' It's taking every ounce of my self-control not to bury my face between her legs right now, to lap up all that need pooling in her centre. I just know the taste of her will be divine.

'I . . . I also put my fingers inside of me.'

'At the same time?'

Another little nod and whimper. She wets her lips and I settle onto my knees.

'Then spread your legs wider for me, baby.'

Shuddering breaths race out of her pretty mouth as she carefully lets her thighs fall further apart. I don't think I've ever been as hard as I am right now, staring straight at her glistening pussy. I'm in heaven.

Quickly, I switch to rubbing her clit with my thumb, keeping up the rhythm, as I slide one finger into her, my cock twitching at the feel of her slick heat, at how tight she is even just around a single digit. I could finish right now just from the sensation of her like this. Cherry's back arches as I curl my finger inside of her, finding where she needs me, and I start increasing my pace with each thrust.

'How many fingers do you like?' I ask.

'T-two.' Cherry gasps and I immediately slide another in, stretching her further. Even just from my fingers I can feel the way her body has to accommodate for me, and the way she's already fluttering around me. I can't help but groan again.

'Do you like being full, baby?' I ask, my gaze flicking between her pussy and her rolling eyes. 'Do you like the way my fingers are stretching you right now?'

'Yes, yes, yes,' she chants out in time with each pump, coming completely undone.

It's a side to her I've never seen before – the way she almost drops into a trance, when usually she has so much on her mind. Even when she was grinding against my thigh earlier, I could see the thread starting to unravel, the chase of her pleasure taking over like she was starving. 'What else do you like? Tell me, Baby Hensley.'

Using that nickname in this setting feels unbelievably *wicked*. A heady rush coming from the thrill of knowing how wrong it is, but also how goddamn right it feels.

'I like to . . . imagine things. It stops me from getting distracted from other thoughts when I'm trying to make myself come.'

What I would give to spend a night inside her imagination, watching whatever delicious scenarios she conjures up. 'Oh yeah? Tell me what you think of when you play with yourself, baby.'

I've barely even finished my question when she says, 'You.'

'Fuck,' I rasp out and drop my head between her legs, licking straight up her centre, before plunging my fingers back inside of her and sucking her clit. Cherry cries out and her hips buck. I press one arm over her stomach to pin her down, making sure she goes *nowhere*. Because divine doesn't even come close to how fucking good she tastes, and I want to stay between these sweet thighs for hours.

219

'Tell me what you imagine us doing,' I breathe against her, barely managing to get the words out as I'm too addicted to devouring her pussy. My fingers are sliding in and out of her so easily now, coated with her wetness.

'Kissing me,' Cherry breathes out.

I press a soft kiss to her clit. 'What else?'

Cherry's fingers grip the sheets. 'You going down on me.'

'Yeah? Am I doing it how you like it?'

'Better. It's – *God* – it's better than I could've ever imagined.'

'Keep telling me, baby. Don't stop.'

'I . . . God, I think about you fucking me. In the bar. In your office.'

Jesus Christ, I'm gonna explode. I can't stop myself from grinding against the bed, everything is driving me wild – these fantasies she's telling me, the sweet taste of her, the warm feel of her fluttering around my fingers. Blood rushes in my ears, and I just want to dive into this moment and never stop falling.

'You bend me over your desk and grab my hair and – oh God, Duke, please don't stop.' Cherry's hand caresses my head, gently pushing me further into her glorious pussy. Her body starts to tense beneath me as my fingers wind her tighter and tighter with each stroke. Knowing that she feels confident enough to ask for more, for what she wants, with me has my heart tripping over itself.

'Attagirl, grind against my face while you think of me fucking you over that desk. Use my tongue until you're coming all over it.' My words are mumbled as I flick my tongue harder against her, meeting the force in which she rolls her hips. I haven't stopped grinding against the bed either, getting off purely from the sweet taste of her, but added with all these dirty thoughts she's admitting to – I'm on the verge of barrelling into release myself.

'Oh God, I think—' she cuts herself off, her thighs tensing and beginning to tremble around my head as she lifts her hips. She reaches down to grab my shoulder, a punishing grip of sharp nails that sends a hot, rushing thrill down my spine, adding to the pressure building there.

I'm trying so hard to hold off, not to finish myself until I've got her there first. But it's not a second later that Cherry cries out, thighs shaking as her body arches up with the orgasm that waves through her. The masterpiece that is Cherry Hensley coming has me finishing only a moment later in my towel, heat sparking through my body as I groan against her now dripping pussy. Her sweet body tightened, dark eyes rolling back, and a melody of a cry leaving those pretty lips is all I need.

As we both come down from our highs, I give her a few more lazy licks, lapping up what's left of her orgasm. Then, unable to let go of her just yet, I trail kisses up her body while my hands roam over her soft curves. Relishing the feel of something that was once just a hazy, distant dream. A wicked fantasy that kept me up at night. An impossibility, that now feels so real in my heart, like the puzzling wisps of my soul have finally been rearranged to fit together. All I needed was Cherry Hensley.

Heart stammering at the way she gazes up at me with glossy, blissful eyes, I lean down to press a chaste kiss to her lips.

'Was that okay? How do you feel?' I check in, aware of how much I'm overwhelmed by everything, and that, even if Cherry's not a virgin, I still want to make sure that wasn't too much for her. I need her to know that we're a team, and that I always look out for my teammates.

A soft, beautiful smile tugs at her lips. 'It was perfect. Thank you.' She pulls me in for another kiss, this time letting her tongue lazily stroke against mine.

'Your face is soaked.' Cherry giggles, wiping her mouth as I settle myself beside her on the bed. Stretching one arm out, I let her cuddle into me, her head against my shoulder as I tuck my arms around her. Her warm body melts into me, a leg coming up over my hip, so that we're flush against each other, every inch of our bodies touching. Like they should've been all these years.

'As is my towel,' I admit.

Cherry's eyes flash, lips popping open. 'Did you…?'

'That fantasy of yours in my office, fuck, it really did it for me. And the taste of you . . . God, you don't realise how long I've been craving that. How long I've been craving *you*.'

I tilt her chin up, catching those glistening umber eyes which are still so wide as they blink up at me. Her teeth skim her bottom lip.

She then adds, 'Too long,' before snuggling back into me, her arm draping over me and squeezing tight, body slotting perfectly against mine. 'Can I sleep here tonight?'

You can sleep here for the rest of your life.

'You better, because I'm not finished with you yet. We've got a lot of orgasms to make up for. I want a hundred ticks next to that item on your bucket list,' I say, holding up a hand to draw a tick in the air, emphasising my point.

Cherry chuckles against my chest, mirth bubbling there in response. Something tugs on my heart, but its rhythm stays calm – calmer than I think it's been in a long time. I've always thought of life to be a little like an ocean – sometimes it's serene and flows, other times you're swept up by crashing waves. Some days you have to swim harder than others. But with Cherry in my arms, I feel like I'm finally anchored, able to weather whatever storm is coming.

A feeling I probably shouldn't let myself get used to when we've only got six weeks left of the summer. I sigh against her hair, my fingers sifting absentmindedly through the silky strands. 'And, honestly, I don't think I can let you go just yet. Not now I can finally hold you. I know we probably have a lot to figure out, but tonight, I'd like to pretend that you're all mine.'

25

Cherry

I'm having the best déjà vu when I wake up, encircled once again by the thick, tattooed arms of the man I've dreamt about being with for years. His safe warmth dissipates into me, wrapping me up in what feels like the equivalent of heaven.

This time, I don't feign being asleep. I don't feel guilty about pressing my ass back into his morning wood, especially after he got me off twice more throughout the night – he wasn't joking about putting multiple ticks next to that item on the bucket list. Half of me wants to run to the top of the mountains and just scream – because for God's sake, we could've been doing this years ago. But the other half appreciates that I'm here now, when I'm strong enough to be honest about what I want, like yesterday, and when he's ready to be vulnerable with me too. Even if there's the lingering thought of how will we tell Wyatt . . .

But maybe no one has to know about this right now.

I've spent the last eight years with the whole goddamn town getting involved in my life, let alone just my family, but this – me and Duke – is out of their reach. No one can interfere with what they don't know.

There's just *us*.

And it's perfect.

Plus, spending time with Duke in secret was already hot, but knowing what we did last night without anyone realising, just makes it ten times sexier.

Duke's groan rumbles behind me when I rub my ass against him again, his warm breath filtering through my hair. 'Tease,' he whispers, then plants a kiss against my neck.

'Morning.' I giggle as his hands lazily roam my body, exploring my curves, brushing underneath my breasts, trailing over my stomach and hips, almost as if he's searching for something. His gentle touch lights up the nerves under every inch of skin he passes.

And then, just as he nuzzles his head into the crook of my neck again, pulling me tighter to him so our bare skin is flush, he sleepily sighs out, 'You're really here. You're not a dream.'

My heart trembles. Even more when his fingers clutch at me tighter, like he's worried I'll slip away, unaware of how strongly I'm tethered to him. A tether that's been *years* in the making. Something like that doesn't break easily – and I would know, because I've laboured over the years to reduce the power it's had on me. But no matter how hard I've tried since the day he found me after my fall, no matter how far I've run away, there's always been that tug in the back of my mind, pulling me back to Duke Bennett.

'I'm here,' I reassure him, melting further into his hold. I slide my hand along his arm until I reach his fingers, slipping mine between them. He immediately curls them tightly into his palm. 'Can we just stay like this forever?'

'I wish.' He lets out a warm chuckle, but I don't miss the way a rigidness sets into his body behind me. 'But sadly, you're going to have to go home at some point so your parents don't wonder where you are. And we both have to work later today.'

I let out a groan, wondering if maybe I can avoid reality for a little longer. No wonder Duke wasn't sure if I was real – yesterday feels like a distant dream now. Uninterrupted time together, no prying eyes, all our cares and woes burst along with the paint balloons when they hit the canvas.

'What a terrible boss I am, making you work.' Duke peppers my neck with more kisses. The hot press of his lips sends heat licking up my spine.

'So terrible,' I jest, and turn in his grasp under the sheets until I'm facing him, catching his heavy-lidded eyes. Glittering morning light filters through the blinds, a slice of sunshine highlighting the carved angles of his muscles so beautifully that I run my hand along his bicep to appreciate his strong body. To just relish the fact that I can touch him whenever I want. A soft smile breaks through his cheeks while his dark lashes flutter at my touch.

Then, I hook a leg up onto his hip, pulling myself towards him so we're still as close as possible. His eyes flash when the tip of his cock accidentally grazes my centre, and even the faintest of touches makes me whimper.

'Cherry,' he warns me, grip tightening against my skin, which only has warmth puddling deeper in my core from his searing touch.

'What?' I breathe out, feigning ignorance.

'Please don't torture me like that.'

But that only makes me want to more. I think trying to unravel Duke's resolve is my new favourite hobby.

'Like this?' I buck my hips again, sliding along his cock and situating the tip right at my entrance. Despite trying to remain calm in his embrace, my body screams for him to thrust into me.

God, how the hell am I going to survive my shift tonight knowing I can't touch him for hours, when I'm struggling to do anything but right now?

'This bucket list has made you too bold,' Duke jokes, raising a brow at me.

I grin, biting down on my lip, already anticipating the way his wild gaze darts down to catch the movement. 'This is going to be difficult, isn't it? Keeping our hands off each other, so no one knows. We're on shifts together every day for the next week.'

Duke presses a soft kiss to my lips. 'We'll take it day by day. Our shifts will just work like they always have, I guess. I'll spend mine stealing glances at you whenever I can, wishing I could touch you, and you'll spend yours tormenting me with your beautiful laugh and torturously long legs, and everyone will be none the wiser.' One of his hands drops between us, my body jolting when his thumb starts working lazy circles over my clit. 'And maybe I can give you something to keep you satisfied until closing time.'

* * *

Turns out, Duke Bennett is a massive liar. Yes, I have spent ninety-nine percent of my shifts longing after him, stealing glances at his quiet beauty whenever he's not looking, and drooling over the way the muscles in his arms shift when he's shaking up a cocktail.

But I never knew before what it was like to feel the strength of those thick arms encircling me as he kissed me like there was no tomorrow and now I do. Which is goddamn torturous when you've got to make it through a seven-hour shift on a busy Friday night pretending you're not constantly thinking about your boss's wicked tongue.

I've finally had a taste of what I've been starved of for so many years, and I need *more*. I'm already addicted to his kisses, his touch, my body weary without it.

Which I must try even harder to conceal since Wyatt, Rory, Fliss, *and* Wolfman are all here in our usual booth. Looking my brother in the eyes has definitely been more difficult than usual – I can't imagine how Duke is feeling.

I collect some empty glasses from a table that has just left, leaning over to grab the last one from the corner. I stand back up and carry the tray to the bar where Duke has just finished pouring some drinks for Montana to take to another table. She flashes me a smile before heading off, and then Duke's walking behind me, brushing his fingers against my hips. He dips his head quickly to ask, 'Mind helping me grab something in the back?'

'Mhm.' I nod, absentmindedly depositing the tray of empties on the bar and follow him round the back, expecting him to head into the stock room.

Except, he doesn't – he takes one quick look along the empty corridor and hauls me into his office. I barely have time to register what's happened before Duke's hands are suddenly clutching my hips, spinning me around and pressing me back against the door. I'm left breathless as his broad frame crowds me, his pupils already so blown out I can't fathom how his eyes still manage to darken further when they catch mine. My heartbeat drops between my thighs when he reaches to lock the door.

'Are you trying to torture me?' he asks, but it's more of a plea.

When he angles himself closer to me, the impressive bulge straining against his jeans brushing my stomach, I'm immediately enlightened as to just how close to the edge he already is. My mouth starts to dry out, breath quickening. I can't help my teeth from tugging on my bottom lip as I consider what would happen if I pushed him a little further.

But now, with the way he's staring at me, gaze wild and agonised, his grip pulsing against me, I think he might be about to fall to his knees. And the idea that I could cause that when our friends – *my brother* – are on the other side of this door, has my body suddenly more alive under his touch. I watch him for a moment, letting my eyes dip to where his throat works, his tattoos shifting.

'I have no idea what you're talking about,' I respond back, lacing each word with a sweet innocence, despite pressing my body closer to him and arching my back so my breasts lightly graze his chest.

A raspy breath close enough to a growl vibrates in his throat. One hand drops to the hem of my short black strappy dress, toying with the material between his fingers. The touch of his knuckles is featherlight against my bare thigh, yet it causes my core to flare.

'This dress, Cherry,' Duke says croakily.

'What about it?' I shrug, causing one of the loose straps to tumble off my shoulder. Duke's eyes instantly flash to it, then his other hand is following to trace the bones of my shoulder, fingers leaving fire in their wake. The rest of my skin craves the heat of his touch, my hips screaming to be cradled by him again. To feel the desperation in his clutch, like holding *me* was the only thing holding *him* together.

Duke's fingers run up my neck to cup my jaw, while his other hand still plays with the hem of my dress. Slowly, his thumb drags across my bottom lip, eliciting a whisper of a gasp from me. Duke's voice drops thunderously lower. 'It's incredibly short, Cherry.'

'My panties match,' I add, his thumb still hovering against my lips.

A muscle in his jaw feathers. 'I know. I saw every time you brazenly leant over one of the tables in front of me earlier.' Duke brings his lips dangerously close to mine. I gasp again, staring up at him with a trembling brow. The heat of his breath tingles across my mouth as he whispers, 'You did that on purpose, didn't you? Trying to tease me when you knew I couldn't do anything about it? Making me want that pretty little pussy of yours?'

The ache between my legs begins to throb, heavy and hot. I consider shaking my head, continuing this role of innocence, but that feels like it would be shying away from how I truly feel – being with him makes me feel unapologetic and alive – exactly what I'm supposed to be chasing, and he's not holding back either, not thinking over what to do or say for once. So, I just nod, letting the corners of my mouth tip up and relishing in the way he mirrors me with a smirk of his own.

Abruptly he spins us until I'm facing his desk, the edge pressing into my thighs.

'But who said I couldn't do anything about it?' Duke whispers, pulling my hair away from my shoulder so he can plant a kiss there. The meeting of his lips against my sensitive skin has goosebumps breaking out across my neck and chest. 'I could fuck you right here, you know?'

Oh God. Yes. Do it.

Duke continues to press hard kisses to my neck, each one sending shivers shooting across my skin. 'I could bend you over my desk, flip this torturous little dress up, and fuck you like you've been craving. I'll do it exactly like you've imagined.' The hand holding my hair out of the way moves to between my shoulder blades and presses down, whilst the other drags my hips back, so his hard cock pushes into me again. My body happily follows his command, bending until I'm flush against the cool desktop. 'Would you like that, Baby Hensley?'

'Mhm,' whimpers out of me with my racing breath.

'Words, Cherry. You know the rules, don't misbehave.' Duke gives me a light slap of the ass, making me jolt against the desk. It sends a zing of pleasure straight through me, while a heady satisfaction underlines it, knowing that I bring this side out of Duke. Two weeks ago, he'd barely touch me.

'Yes, Duke. I want you to fuck me over your desk.'

He hums with satisfaction, but the sound is gravelly with need. Duke lifts up the skirt of my dress and strokes his fingers up my inner thigh, making my legs shake with anticipation. 'Even with everyone just behind that door?'

'Yes. I don't care.' Now I'm the one sounding desperate. But when he brushes his fingertips so lightly across my panties, just grazing my clit, I don't care. All my mind and body knows is that I need him. *Everywhere*.

His touch explores the edges of my panties, fingers hooking one by one beneath the elastic to gradually pull it to the side, baring me to him.

'It would have to be quick, otherwise people will wonder where we were. And—' Duke hisses, then lets out a long exhale as his fingers swipe through my wetness. 'Fuck me, you're already soaking. I could slide into you right now. I bet you'd feel so good as you stretch for me.'

He doesn't wait another second to plunge his fingers into me. I throw a hand over my mouth in time to capture my moan, my other hand gripping the edge of the desk as fire blazes to life in my core.

'Shh, baby.' Duke keeps one hand pressing me down against the desk as I squirm from the pleasure – the way he strokes me inside slowly, curling his fingers each time to hit that perfect spot, and the crude, wet noises coming from me, a testament to how much he's turned me on in the matter of minutes.

My hips buck and roll, needing *more*. Needing the friction against my clit that he's starving me of. It's all I can think about, everything else crumbling away. I don't care where we are, who's outside – I just need Duke.

'Lift your hips, sweetheart.' Duke curls his arm around me as I bring my hips up for him. His fingers slip between my thighs and press against my clit. The first touch sends sparks dancing behind my eyes and pressure building between my hips. He starts slowly circling my clit. 'Don't worry, I've got you.'

I'm biting down on my own hand to stop the moans from escaping, my eyes rolling back. Pleasure swirls in my core, my muscles tightening as it gets heavier, but Duke doesn't pick up his pace at all, continuing at a leisurely rhythm that feels at odds to the urgency of this situation.

And then he stops.

He pulls his fingers from me, and I turn my head to see him suck my arousal clean off them, my lips popping open. I press up onto my arms, still bent over the desk as I watch Duke round the desk to come before me. He brushes a hand tenderly over my hair, tucking the loose locks on one side behind my ear.

'Why did you stop?' I ask, wide eyes blinking at him.

A faint smirk dances on Duke's lips. His thumb strokes my cheek, reminding me too much of the feel of his fingers against my clit mere seconds ago. 'That was just a taste of what I'll give you later if you're good for the rest of your shift.'

'So, you're not going to fuck me?' I ask, realising that by trying to push Duke over the edge, I only sent myself over with him.

He puts a hand either side of me on the desk, dipping his head until we're eye level, the wildness of his dark eyes just begging me to get lost in him again. 'Not yet. When I finally fuck you, I'm going to have you coming all over my cock until the only thing you remember is how to scream my name. And I can't do that with the whole town in the next room.' His lips capture mine just as a whimper leaves them, and he swallows the sound. The urgency of his kiss – the hot, hard press of his lips against mine – only seals his promise. 'Now, let's go grab some bottles from the stock room before people wonder what we're up to.'

26

Duke

The golden rays of the late evening sunset filter between the city buildings cutting into the darkening skyline made up of strokes of deep fuchsia and amber. The sunlight catches the strands of Cherry's black hair next to me, glittering. I wish I could run my fingers through her hair like I can in the confines of my apartment. Part of me wants to tuck her into my side, stow her away in my Silverado, and speed back to Willow Ridge, where I can savour her touch. Where I can make up for all the lost time.

But I owe Cherry this meeting about the bar – she did get back on a horse after all.

'This is a bad idea,' I admit, rubbing the back of my neck as I wait outside the empty building to meet Kip. There's not even an emerging star in the sky to be seen yet, but the bars around us are already beginning to fill, lines forming outside the doors, chatter filling the streets with people ready to dance and drink away the working day.

'The bar or bringing me with you?' Cherry smiles blissfully beside me.

Even though I know it was a risk her being here, having Cherry beside me soothes my frayed nerves. Like she's my lucky charm. I'd almost forgotten what it's like to have someone by your side, what it's like to let someone in. And it's even better when it's the most beautiful girl in the world. Besides, I struggled with saying no to her before, but I must have left all my self-control behind when I crossed the line kissing her, because trying to fight her coming with me was futile. As was stopping myself from whisking her into my office to touch her like last week, while her brother was the other side of the door.

Fuck, what have I gotten myself into?

Can't say there isn't a small, protective part of me that relishes the fact that we can make a better memory of her time in the city. This time, I'm here to keep her safe, to watch over her.

'Firstly, you won't know if this is a bad idea until you try it, and based on your track record recently of indulging in potential bad ideas—' Cherry stops to point at herself and grin '—I'd say the odds are in your favour of it working out pretty well.' I level her a look, making her giggle. 'And secondly, the chances of anyone from Willow Ridge being in the city right now is so tiny, it's pointless worrying about it.'

If all bad ideas ended with Cherry Hensley's thighs shaking around my head, I'd *definitely* engage in a lot more of them.

'Duke!' Kip's voice rings out as he heads up the

236

sidewalk towards us, weaving through groups of people walking by. 'So glad you could make it.'

He thrusts his hand towards me, and we shake, only for him to pull me into a hug and pat my back. Once we've gotten through our exchange, he turns to Cherry, eyes flashing. 'Wait, aren't you Hensley's little sister?'

'Yep – and Duke's interior designer.' Cherry beams and shakes Kip's hand too.

'Is that so?' I ask, perking a brow.

'Mhm.' She bites down on her bottom lip, and I force my eyes closed to regain the composure that instantly slipped at the sight of such. All the memories of her doing that as she moaned for me flashing in my mind. Cherry chuckles, likely too aware of the effect she has on me.

'That's great,' Kip says, none the wiser. He fishes some keys out his pocket to unlock the bar doors. He tugs open one and gestures for us to go inside. 'Can't wait to hear what you think we could do with the place. Bring some of that Willow Ridge charm to the city.'

'Exactly my thoughts,' Cherry agrees and follows Kip inside.

Heading in behind them, I'm greeted by the empty bar that is only one signature away from being partially mine, my mind already pinging with hundreds of thoughts and questions. Cherry's explaining to Kip how she helped redecorate the bar back home, giving a good backstory as to why she's here – not just because I'm falling for her. I should probably join them, but my legs and eyes want to wander.

It's bigger than the bar back home, as I knew from the specs I already had, but I'm happily surprised to learn that the extra space isn't too imposing. This is still a bar, as opposed to the more nightclub-esque haunts Kip owns around the city. But Duke's is supposed to be cosy, the place where you know you'll bump into friends, and can share a drink along with memories and laughter. A kind of sanctuary, I suppose – maybe sometimes more for me than the customers.

I know the vibe will be different here in the city, but I don't want to lose that completely, and I can already see how we can bring that warmer energy to this place – plenty of corners for booths, beams along the ceiling, a small dancefloor that ensures an abundance of embraces and arms cheerily slung around shoulders. I run my hands along the smooth wooden surface of the bar, my gaze flicking to each corner, noting how I can keep an eye on everyone from here, and that's what matters most – being there for my customers.

It's that knowledge that has my muscles loosening, and I lean my elbows on the bar to admire my new venture. A gentle buzz hovers under my skin as possibilities fill my mind.

Cherry joins me, leaning down against the bar too. A lock of her silky hair tumbles over her cheek as she angles her head at me. God, she's beautiful. 'You look happy.'

'Yeah . . . I think this could work.'

'I can definitely see you here.' Her glistening eyes roam the bar. She starts pointing around the place, Kip sauntering over and nodding. 'You've got plenty of space for booths – I definitely think you wanna keep the same red and dark wooden vibe from Duke's, tie it all in with neon signs. You could even have them surrounding the shelves behind the bar, really add that old school country vibe.' Everything she describes comes to life in my imagination, fitting perfectly with my own visions. Cherry continues, 'Standing tables in the middle, throw a jukebox by the dancefloor, and – oh! That larger space over there, definitely big enough for a mechanical bull.'

My brows shoot up. 'A mechanical bull?'

Cherry giggles, then bats those long dark lashes at me. 'Oh, come on. We gotta be a little cliché with it. I've always wanted you to put one in Duke's, but there was never any space.' And man, am I glad there was never any space, because I don't think I would've survived seeing Cherry ride that bull all summer.

I sigh out a laugh and look over to Kip. 'I guess we gotta get a mechanical bull, then.'

'I'll look into it.' He grins and pulls out his phone to write down a note. 'So, what do we think? We gonna do this? All that's left is to just run through some paperwork, sign some dotted lines, and then Duke's can find its home in the city.'

My gaze drops to the bar, second-guesses and what-ifs clawing their way up my throat. The most important question tumbles out as a whisper when I turn to Cherry, 'You think the guys would like it?'

Her eyes soften at me, a faint smile gracing her lips. 'Hell yeah. They'd love it. That'll be their booth, over there, whenever they come and visit.' She points to the nearest corner, which would edge the dancefloor. And I see it too – no doubt Rory, Fliss, and Sawyer shuffling their boots on the dancefloor, laughter pouring out of them and smiles brightening up the night, while Wyatt and Wolfman shake their heads and grin at their friends, nursing their beers together.

Still here with me.

Just like Cherry is.

My smile spreads out, mirroring Cherry's now full-on grin. I turn to Kip and hold out my hand. 'Let's do this.'

It takes a good couple of hours to run through everything, and Cherry sits happily at the bar with her iPad, sketching out ideas she had for the bar earlier and curating mood boards. Her soft voice from that night a couple of weeks ago keeps running through my mind every time I start to second-guess my self – *when was the last time you did something big just for you?* The memory of her fingers slipping between mine reminds me that I can do this. That, even if what we have ends when the summer does, there's no way I can go back to my life before without her now – I need an excuse to be near her somehow. And this bar will do that.

Because Cherry Hensley has imprinted herself on my very soul. She's rewritten everything I knew about myself and shone light into the darkest corners of my mind, helping me see that I don't have to hide. Even before I got the privilege of touching her, *tasting* her, she was pulling apart my seams and sewing me back together, weaving her love and laughter into my very being.

That's what gives me the strength to sign on the final dotted line. It's nowhere near the final step, with all the work that will need to be done on the bar before opening, but it's a step in a new direction. It's letting myself ride past the line I'm always avoiding.

'This is going to be great, Duke. I promise you.' Kip's eyes brighten. 'You know what? You guys should come check out Haze. See the vibe of another bar here, get a feel for city life. I'll get you a private booth too, some drinks on the house. As a celebration.'

Cherry chimes in before I can even consider saying no, 'That sounds perfect.'

* * *

Music thumps in my bones as we sit in our booth at Kip's bar, Haze. Cherry happily sips on her third Jack and Diet Coke beside me, my arm stretched behind her. Dance melodies melt into each other, deep-blue mood lighting lining the glass shelves of the two bars either side of the room gives the impression of being submerged underwater, away from the chaos of the world, and heat from Cherry's body pressed against me all floods my veins with calm. As well as the joy radiating off her as she wiggles in the seat to the music.

It's not enough – any touch from Cherry is never enough, not when there's still so much more I want to give to her – but I'm conscious of taking too many risks today. I'm trying my best to let the music drown out the voice in the back of my mind wondering if it's all a trap – the calm before the storm, when I then lose everything.

Maybe one more drink out in the open together, before I drive us back.

Except, Cherry leans into me, warm breath sending shivers across my skin as she suggests into my ear, 'We should go dance.'

I shake my head, hand clasping tighter around my non-alcoholic beer. 'I don't know . . . There's a lot of people here. Someone could know us.'

'Don't make me turn this into a closing-time argument.' She quirks a brow at me, teeth sinking into her bottom lip teasingly. 'Because you know I'll win.'

My laugh barrels out and I place my bottle on the table. 'Will you now?'

'I got you to kiss me, didn't I?'

The ease of which she speaks of us kissing out in the open has my body tightening – though it's mostly because the flash of that memory, our first kiss with her straddling my thigh, fills my mind.

'Duke,' Cherry laughs my name, shaking her head at me. She deposits her glass clumsily back on the table, enlightening me to how quickly the few drinks she's had have gone to her head. And made her bolder than usual, it seems.

Positioning herself in front of me, she throws her hands on her hips and levels her dark eyes at me. The blue lighting filling the bar glows around her, and I realise how easily I could get used to looking up at her like this, shining brightly above me. Slowly, she bends towards me, sliding her smooth palms against my stubble until she's cradling my face.

'Nobody knows us here – I'm sure of that. It's dark and crowded. No one will care if you touch me. *Where* you touch me.' A wicked grin spreads out those tempting dark red lips of hers, and I feel suddenly compelled to get down on my knees, completely under her spell, ready to fulfil her every command. 'Please just come and dance with me. When will we get another chance to get lost in the music together?'

'Cherry . . .'

'Last time I was in the city, at the club, all I could think about when we were dancing was how badly I wanted to be with you. How badly I wanted to feel your body behind me, your hands on my hips.'

A groan rumbles in my throat because, *fuck*, if I haven't dreamed of being able to do that too. And here she is, dangling said dream in front of me with such ease. My eyes cut beyond her, to the people flooding the dancefloor in the centre of the bar. Bodies flow in a rhythm under the strobe lighting, pressed tightly together as they feel the waves of the music, barely any cracks amongst the throng of people for secrets to be spilled. To be noticed.

Would it be so bad? To let my hands wander freely in the darkness and have a taste of what it'd be like to be together in public? Not to have to hide?

'And,' she adds, 'I never got to tick off staying at a club 'til close from my bucket list. I know it's not a proper nightclub, but I think it would still count.'

Cherry must sense my defences slowly breaking down because she moves her hands from my jaw and holds one out in front of me instead. I close my eyes before sighing out the rest of my self-control and slide my fingers between hers. The happiness that lights up her eyes is reward enough.

Cherry leads us out of the booth towards the dancefloor, fingers pulsing against mine as we get closer. We weave through the tightly packed, swaying crowd, bodies pressing and waving against us as we move into the centre. The further we submerge ourselves into the dancing throng, surrounded by movement and hidden from the world, the deeper I drop into the depths of liberation, the voices in my head quietening.

Freedom flows in my veins, and I slip my hands around Cherry's waist, stopping her and tugging her towards me. Her back presses against my chest, the heat of her body melting into mine as her hips start to sway, giving me a rhythm to move to as my hands drop to her hips. Nails raking against my skin, she trails her hands up around my neck, brushing her fingers up the back of my head as she pushes her ass back against me, gliding her body side to side with the beat of the music. I drop my lips to her neck, relishing the way her body arches instantly.

We stay like that until the lights end the night – my hot breath against her neck, our cheeks pressed together, as I grip her hips, letting them guide our movements, while a rainbow of flashing lights rain down on us.

There's a heady rush of power that comes with holding her here, surrounded by so many people, being able to show off that she's mine. That I'm the lucky man that gets to embrace her, to be the one to listen to her worries and talk her to sleep, to make her smile, to hear the melody of her laugh *and* her sweet moans.

That I get to worship this masterpiece of a woman, no one else.

Even if this is the only time I get to experience this, to be with Cherry without any cares in the world weighing me down, it'll be worth it.

Cherry Hensley.

The best bad decision I've ever made.

27

Cherry

'Okay, I wasn't sure what you needed so I got one of everything and I also ordered pizza,' Duke explains as he bustles into his bedroom after coming back from the grocery store. Under each arm is a brown paper bag, filled to the brim.

I'm curled up in the foetal position in his bed, but just about manage to lift my head to watch as he drops the bags on the bed, one of them toppling over so that God knows how many different boxes of tampons and sanitary towels tumble out, along with several bars of chocolate.

Even though I feel about as strong as an overcooked piece of spaghetti – the cramps that unexpectedly started this morning having sucked all my energy away – I manage to wriggle up until I'm leaning on my elbows, giving me a better look. It also lets me admire him, standing at the end of the bed, the late morning sunlight accentuating his edges with a golden glow – the portrait of a saviour.

But despite the way the sunshine also emphasises how delicious he looks in his tight white T-shirt and grey sweatpants, I can't help but wince at the sympathy in his gaze. I'm momentarily transported back to that day on his office floor, humiliated to my core. My period coming a few days earlier has really put a dampener on the whole sexy running around in secret thing we had going on. And made the lacy underwear I packed to wear for our day off together completely obsolete.

The whole plan of *let's stay in bed together all day* has taken an unfortunate turn. As well as postponing the opportunity to *finally* get to sleep with Duke, which I'm certain was what a day in bed translated to. Not that I'm desperate or anything . . . but I have wanted this for years, so cut me some slack.

Still, sex isn't exactly at the top of my priorities when I feel like a sweaty potato.

I croak out, 'I thought you were only getting me something for the pain. You didn't have to get all of this . . . Though, the pizza I very much appreciate.' I could've sorted the rest out once I was dosed up – it's not like I haven't been dealing with this for years, and nor does he need this burden on him either.

It's mine to carry. Mine to deal with.

'Ham and pineapple, obviously.' Duke offers me a gentle smile and shrugs before packing the boxes back into the bag. 'Besides, I was worried you might have felt embarrassed about asking me to get this stuff – which you don't need to be. I'm a grown man, I can handle a period. And Jessie at the grocery store didn't bat an eyelid because I buy these for the restrooms at the bar anyway.' He laughs, then draws his features together, his movements halting for a second. 'And, um . . . well, whatever you don't need I could – maybe I could keep here for the future.'

The unexpected suggestion has me lifting myself up higher on my elbows to stare at Duke with widening eyes, my heart suddenly fluttering – even more than my emerging fever was causing. The last couple of weeks have been – well, honestly, I don't think there's enough words to do the dream that is being with Duke Bennett justice. I've had the privilege of experiencing even the deepest corners of his softer side, as well as the hard, rough edges that bring more passion into my life than I thought fathomable.

The only thing that hovers silently between us is that word – *future*. I've got just under four weeks left before I'm supposed to go back to college, and I'm not ready to let this go. We might have spent the best part of the summer together so far, but that whole time I was teetering on the edge of my feelings, and I've only had a couple of weeks to experience the joy of letting myself fall.

Floating might be a better way to describe how it feels, actually.

All I know is that I don't want it to stop.

I want to bask in it without anyone trying to stop me for once. I want to relish the rush of ecstasy each time I'm secretly the subject of his smile.

But asking Duke for a future isn't just asking for him to manage a long distance relationship with me – it's also asking him to put his friendship on the line with Wyatt.

And if the years of him holding back from me proves anything, it's that *that* isn't going to be an easy step for him to take.

Yet what he just said—

A torturously sharp cramp slices through my lower abdomen. I groan and scrunch my face up, trying my best to ride out the pain.

Jesus Christ, I hate being a woman. Don't we deal with enough already?

I don't think Duke realises what he's getting into with my never-ending menstrual cycle of agony. Surely he can't want this.

'Shit, hold on, let me get you some water.' Duke drops the bag back on the bed and dashes out the room. With what seems like superhuman speed, he returns, sitting on the edge of the bed beside me, and handing me a glass of water and the painkillers just in time for my long-ass cramp to end. 'Here, take these.'

I pull myself up to a seated position with the little strength I have and obey, taking the glass with shaky hands and popping two painkillers into my mouth. The whole time Duke strokes my hair, fingers slipping through the strands. I sigh back into the pillows, resting my head against his shoulder. He shifts so he can put his arm around me, tucking me in closer to his solid chest, letting his warmth cradle me.

'That looked nasty. You know,' Duke starts, using his free hand to rub my leg slowly. 'I heard that orgasms are a great way to relieve cramps too . . .'

I let out a breathy laugh. 'Believe me, you do *not* want to touch me right now, Duke.'

He angles his head down at me, brows knitted together. 'Why not?'

I scoff, rolling my eyes, but already there's a sting at the back of them. I have to look away to blink it away, silently cursing my goddamn hormones for letting my insecurities get to me so quickly. 'Because I'm a sweaty, bloated mess. I feel, and probably look, disgusting right now.' Not to mention it's goddamn embarrassing that even if I did want to do anything sexual with Duke, I probably don't have the energy even to muster up a moan.

Duke shakes his head, a frown marring his face. 'You're kidding me, right?'

'No . . .'

'Cherry, you're beautiful. *All* the time.'

Shutting my eyes tightly, I slide back down in the bed, hiding myself further under the sheets. 'You don't have to lie to me to make me feel better. I'm used to feeling this way.'

But there's an unexpected adamance in his voice as he says, 'But you shouldn't have to feel that way.' Hardness takes over his features, sharpening their edges, treading dangerously close to the ferocity in his expression I witnessed that time when he rescued me from the diner.

Then Duke's jumping to his feet and storming out the bedroom. Clattering and scraping sounds from the other room as I lie in bed, waiting. I wonder if for a second maybe I've just really annoyed him with all my whining and he's not coming back. But then he's marching into the bedroom again, a canvas tucked under one arm, and a small box with paintbrushes sticking out of it under the other. He deposits everything he's gathered onto his desk, jogging back out only to return with another glass of water.

The grocery bags are moved to the floor, and Duke swivels his desk chair around, before he approaches the bed again.

'May I?' he asks, beginning to drag the sheets away from my body once I nod, revealing the T-shirt of his I'm wearing, which has bunched up around my waist, and my massive panties that say *Sunday* on them, even though it's Wednesday. Duke chuckles to himself when he spots them and I just about muster up the energy to grin back.

'What are you doing?' I enquire, my smile faltering at the way Duke's admiring my body, something like wonder shining in his eyes as I lay there on my side. It's so at odds to the thoughts in my mind.

His eyes flick back up to me, keeping hold of my gaze as he lowers himself into his desk chair and picks up the canvas and a pencil. 'I can't understand how you could possibly think you're not beautiful right now, because you are quite literally the most exquisite thing I have ever seen in my life. Even the finest painting in the world wouldn't come close to rivalling your beauty, Cherry. In fact—' Duke crosses one of his legs over the other, giving himself somewhere to rest his canvas '—your beauty is so compelling that it's my favourite thing to paint. Have I ever told you how many times I've painted you since you came back this summer?'

My lips pop open. 'You – you painted me?'

'Like I said – painting's my favourite kind of therapy. And I had a *lot* of feelings about you to work through.' He shoots me a grin, and it goes straight to my heart. Warmth kindles in my chest at how easily these admissions are coming from his lips – at how lucky I am to be the one to witness such from the man who rarely gives anything away. 'Are you comfortable? I'm gonna need you to stay like that for a while.'

Nodding, completely at a loss for words for what is happening right now, I snuggle further into the mattress and pillows, watching Duke's deft hands get to work on the canvas.

All those times I found one of his napkin sketches of me in the bar, I wished I could truly be his muse, not just something to draw to pass the time. If only I'd known the true reverence behind each of those pen strokes, the sheer power that comes from being marvelled at by Duke as the subject of his art.

'I know you struggle to like this side of yourself that you think is weak, but you gotta remember that no one is strong all the time. This pain you feel, it's not your choice, it's not your fault, so you don't have to deal with it alone. You're allowed to let others take care of you, to give you the love you need on the days when you can't find enough for yourself. It doesn't make you weak – it just makes you human.'

'You're always strong,' I respond, trying to ignore the tears welling again already. Especially as another cramp burns between my hips, this time slightly less intense, hopefully owing to the painkillers starting to kick in.

Duke laughs – despair underlining the sound. 'No,' he shakes his head, 'I'm not. Believe me.'

I know there's parts of him he hides away, that he plays the shoulder for everyone else in Willow Ridge, because it's easier. But he's slowly letting me see between the cracks of that façade, and somewhere behind them lay the Duke that's willing to take a risk on us.

'When do you ever need taking care of?'

He's silent for a long stretch of time, forehead creased as his gaze flicks between me and the canvas. A few pencil strokes later and the hardness in his face dissolves. 'There's three days in the year when I usually need someone the most. December eighth – the anniversary of my father's death, May twentieth – Mom's death, and July thirtieth – Grandfather's. It's not like grief doesn't hit me on other days but those are the hardest. The ones where I can't help but count up the years that have gone by, wondering who's next. Wondering how I've kept going without them. Wondering if I'll ever stop worrying.'

My brows shoot up. 'Duke, tomorrow's July thirtieth.'

An unexpectedly beatific smile dances on his lips as he swaps his pencil for a paintbrush, dipping it in the water and then into the first colour. 'Mhm. And I've got you with me for my whole shift.'

'But you organised our shifts before we even started—' I nod to him, unsure what word to use '—*this*.'

'I know.' This time he looks up, eyes softening as they drift over me for a long moment—like I'm too enchanting to rip his gaze away – before dropping back to the canvas. 'You . . . soothe me, Cherry. Distract me, I guess. When you're around, my mind likes to focus on you, instead of all the worries swirling about. Like at Sawyer's rodeos. I always need a bit of someone else's strength at those too.'

He gently the paintbrush across the canvas, wetting his lips as he concentrates. 'I'm scared that he'll get hurt, and we'll lose him. That I'll lose someone else. Every time he climbs into that chute my heart stops and my mind can't help but flash reminders of sitting with my mom in hospital, knowing I was about to lose her and feeling totally on my own. But having you there . . . I don't know, it reminds me that I'm never completely alone.'

There I was lamenting the way Duke always ended up saving me, trapped in this constant cycle of always having to rely on others, when really, he was just giving back the same care I unknowingly gave to him. Holding me up when he had the strength, knowing I'd shine a light for him on his darker days too.

Hope flares in my chest, coercing out my smile. 'I guess I have no choice but to keep coming back from college to watch them with you then.'

He flashes me a quick smile back, a silent promise in his brightening eyes. 'I guess so.'

If I hadn't been falling for Duke Bennett all these years, then there was no doubt that I was now.

We settle into a comfortable silence as Duke continues to paint me. Eventually, the painkillers work their magic, and my cramps turn into dull aches, though still never completely gone. The pizza arrives and I lazily chomp on slices while trying not to move too much. For once, I let myself just lie there, allowing that today I might need to share my strength with him, and give my body the rest it needs, not berate it for how it works differently to everyone else's. And when Duke's gaze is filled with nothing but awe and reverence as he admires me, accepting myself comes a little easier.

Being stuffed full of pizza sends me to sleep at some

point, my body jolting awake what must be at least an hour later when Duke's fingers softly graze my legs to wake me up. My eyes flutter open, and Duke's sitting there, displaying his finished piece to me, pride lighting up his face. I practically scramble over to the end of the bed to take it from his hands and look at it closer.

'Careful, it's still wet,' he scolds me with a smirk.

My eyes roam over the canvas, exploring the paint strokes that softly outline my silhouette, even under the baggy T-shirt, a faint desire underlining the effort gone into capturing my shape. I'm brighter than all my surroundings, golden hues used to highlight the muscles of my legs, the rise of my cheekbones, the sunshine glittering against the strands of my hair, in a way that almost appears like I was divinely created. Celestial. *Powerful*.

'Duke, this is incredible.' This time I don't fight back my tears, letting them spill softly. 'You've made me look so . . . so *beautiful*.'

A faint blush rises in his cheeks – something I don't think I've ever seen before. He shakes his head, though, reaching out to wipe away my tears with his thumb, my head falling into his hand. 'All I did was paint what beauty was already there, Baby Hensley. It's all you. It's *always* been you.'

28

Cherry

'You're staring,' Montana whispers teasingly as she passes by where I'm clearing some empties from a table that's just left the bar.

Except, I only got as far as putting my tray down because I got distracted by watching Duke shake up a cocktail while chatting with some of the locals perched at the bar. He looks so natural behind the bar, smile brighter than any of the neon signs above him as he laughs with customers. It's not even that late on a Friday evening yet, but the bar is already buzzing, first rounds turning into seconds, songs queued on the jukebox.

'Huh?' I say, feigning ignorance to my friend, and actually getting to clearing the table.

Montana stops, and rests her empty tray against her hip. Her expression is too knowing, and I can already feel the heat rising in my cheeks. 'You're both as bad as each other, y'know?'

'What do you mean?'

'Staring at each other. You *always* do it when the other isn't looking.' She perks her brow at me, chestnut hair slipping to the side as she angles her head. 'I'm guessing it has something to do with him helping you with the bucket list?'

'*You're* also helping me with the bucket list, remember,' I remind her, thinking back to last Saturday when I dosed myself up with plenty of painkillers and caffeine and managed to go out to karaoke with her and a couple of Austin's friends. I stack the glasses on my tray.

'I suppose,' Montana considers. 'But whatever ones Duke's helping you with has him gazing at you like you hung the moon, girl.'

My smile practically explodes across my face. You'd think I've only just been told Duke might have feelings for me, but even a month after we kissed, it still hits me just as powerfully each time I'm reminded. Even if I can't scream about it with my best friend.

Montana reaches out to squeeze my upper arm. 'I'm sorry I haven't been around as much to help you this summer, but I'm glad you guys are having fun.'

Guilt whirrs in my chest. I'd be lying if I said I hadn't enjoyed the thrill of sneaking around, the slight torture of having to keep our hands off each other at work while knowing he'll be making up for the lost touches later at night. But since that night at Kip's bar, when we were able to unlock all the constraints on our relationship and actually *be* with each other, *touch* each other without caring who saw, has left me wanting more.

Because everyone else gets to show off what they have, but me. I want more than my best friend catching Duke staring at me, I want her to see us together, to see how happy we are.

Because this hasn't just been something in the making only this summer. It's been *years*.

I'm pretty certain that's why those three words keep accidentally finding their way to the tip of my tongue…

But before I can muster up a lie to tell Montana, the bar door flies open and Rory runs in, screaming, 'We're engaged!'

Wyatt bustles in quickly after, eyes flashing at the sudden attention when everyone in the bar stands from their seats and cheers, raising glasses and bottles. Rory throws her left hand up in the air, letting the sparkling engagement ring glint under the red neon and twinkling fairy lights.

With a squeal, I drop my tray and run over, wrapping my arms around them both and pulling them into a three-way hug. Rory ends up getting sandwiched between me and Wyatt, her giggles bouncing between our chests. Joy radiates from them in waves.

'Congratulations!' I shriek, squeezing them both tighter.

Two of my favourite people in the whole world, getting married.

The first Hensley sibling wedding!

'Thank you,' Wyatt replies, kissing my cheek, which only makes my eyes well more as I try to fight back the tears.

Rory shimmies out from between us and slaps a massive, sloppy kiss on my other cheek. Then, she's reaching behind me, puckered lips ready for her next victim. I turn to find Duke already there, the bright joy in his eyes for his best friend and Rory makes my heart melt. Damn, I wish I could hug him too.

'Don't even think about it, Rory,' Duke cautions her, holding a finger up. Rory rolls her eyes but throws herself at him, wrapping her arms around his middle tightly as they laugh together in their embrace.

When they finally let go, Duke moves over to hug Wyatt, patting him on the back. 'About time,' Duke jokes. 'Congratulations, though, man. I kept the usual booth free for you.'

Wyatt just shakes his head, unable to rid the huge smile plastered across his face.

'Come on.' Rory grabs my hand and practically skips the entire way to the booth, dragging me with her, as if deciding my shift has ended. 'Fliss will be here soon, and I need to celebrate with my bridesmaids!'

* * *

'And I just want to say—' Rory interrupts her fourth speech of the night to hiccup, because I'm pretty certain she's had more glasses of champagne than anyone else here who's now gathered at the bar to celebrate.

Fliss, Wolfman, Sawyer – with a girl he managed to pick up at the bar within five minutes of being here – as well as my parents, and some other close friends and family made it over as the evening stretched on. The bar is electrified with life and laughter, achingly sweet smiles stuck on everyone's faces, and more hugs than I can count have been shared in the past couple of hours.

'Oops – sorry! I just want to say a massive thank you to Duke and this bar.' Standing in one of the booths, with Wyatt blinking lovestruck eyes up at her, Rory raises her glass towards Duke, who's leaning against a table beside me, a noticeable gap between us. 'Because it was here that a great friend of ours made me realise how much I loved Wyatt. He stopped me from listening to the voices in my head, and not only showed me how loyal a friend he is, but how much Wyatt cared for me. And for that, I'll forever be grateful. So, to Duke!'

'To Duke,' everyone cheers in unison – Wolfman obviously decides to howl instead – and we raise our glasses, taking long gulps afterwards, before breaking back into conversations laced with laughter and warmth. Duke lingers beside me with an unexpected silence.

Rory goes to pour herself another glass of champagne once she's flopped back into the booth, snuggling into Wyatt. Only a few drips come out, which makes her pout.

Duke chuckles, rubbing a hand over his head. 'Guess I better go find some more champagne. Gotta keep our bride-to-be happy.'

'Such a *loyal* friend,' I joke, reusing Rory's words, only for Duke to stiffen. His eyes cut to mine, then quickly away, a muscle in his jaw feathering.

'Right,' is all he says before he walks off.

Coldness sweeps over me as Duke disappears between the crowded tables of the bar, and I try to pretend it's because someone's left the door open, not because I'm worried I've just upset Duke . . .

But when I do finally glance over to the door, which is actually partially open as a group of people filters through, I'm illuminated to a whole new reason why my skin has prickled – *Levi*.

My heart lurches into my throat, blood rushing in my ears suddenly, as Levi strides into the bar, completely unbothered, talking to the friends surrounding him. I'm like a deer caught in the headlights, unsure what to do, my head yelling at me to *run*. I can't believe I was naïve enough to think I could avoid him now he isn't working at the bar. But instead of running *away*, my legs decide to kick into action and I find myself rushing towards him.

Before I can reach him, Duke's broad frame slides in front of Levi, blocking both my view and Levi's path. Levi's friends have all grabbed a table – most of them I remember from high school – and they all whisper and watch as Duke's voice rumbles, saying something I'm not close enough to make out yet. My steps falter when their voices become audible, and I lean back against the nearest empty table, clutching the edge for support.

'Dude, come on,' Levi begs, exasperation widening his eyes. He throws his hands in the air. 'What am I supposed to do? All my friends are here. It's the *only* bar in town.'

Duke just crosses his arms, unyielding. 'Yeah, well you should've thought about that before you hurt her.'

It's at that moment that Levi's eyes catch me around Duke's shoulder. They narrow at me while he shakes his head, a sourness taking over his expression. Duke follows his stare to find me, darkness swarming his eyes as they flare, moments before he turns back to Levi and steps closer, crowding Levi towards the wall.

'Don't you dare even look at her,' Duke practically growls.

Levi's eyes flick between the two of us, and then he laughs – a smug, snarky grin appearing. 'Oh, I get it now . . . Well, I just hope she's not as frigid with you.'

I don't get a second to let that cruel blow land because Duke suddenly crowds Levi, forcing him back up against the wall. Duke's thick, tattooed forearms slam to the wall either side of Levi, caging him in. Much like how Levi had me back at the club. He brings his face intimidatingly close.

'Get the fuck away from me!' Levi grunts.

I don't hear what Duke whispers to Levi over the subsequent gasps and muttering from people on the nearby tables, but I still see the colour drain from Levi's face.

A heady rush comes from the sight of it all. From witnessing this protective side of Duke that ripped out of the quiet, reserved version of him we're all accustomed to. In front of everyone as well. Even if they don't know what's truly behind all this, I can't deny the way my body tightens at Duke's broad, strained muscles trapping Levi so easily, or the way my shoulders straighten, emboldened by Duke's defence of me.

His eyes are wilder than the night he found me in the diner, fiercer than the day he carried me to the hospital after my fall because the ambulance was taking too long. All those years struggling under the weight of never feeling strong enough, lamenting over the way everyone always seems to be second-guessing me, thinking that no one would ever stand up for me and just let me make decisions and mistakes myself blows away. Because if there's one thing I know now, it's that Duke Bennett has *always* been in my corner. He fights for me quietly *and*

loudly, and it's the sight before me that finally confirms –
I love him.

'Woah, what's going on?' Wyatt asks from behind me,
making me start. He rushes over, rolling up the sleeves of
the flannel he's wearing as he joins Duke's side.

'We got a problem that needs taking care of?' Sawyer
sidles up next, much more casually, clicking his neck to
either side. There's a mischievous smirk playing on his
lips, as if he's excited by the prospect of a fight.

Wolfman follows quickly after, swallowing the last
dregs of his beer before whacking the bottle down on the
nearest table. He grins. 'Okay. Whose ass am I kicking
tonight?'

As tough as they all like to act, they're the sweetest
guys I know, and experiencing them all joining Duke in
this heated exchange only emphasises such – how they're
always there for each other. No matter what.

Between the gaps in their shoulders I just about catch
Levi shrinking from the four men now towering over him.
Montana comes up beside me and wraps her arm around
my shoulder – since she's spent time with Levi outside of
the bar too, I had to tell her and make sure he didn't lay
a finger on her either, even if I left out the details of what
happened with Duke afterwards.

'It's your call, Cherry,' Duke suddenly says, checking
over his shoulder to me.

Everyone's attention turns to me then, and my lip drops.
He's letting me make the decision here. Trusting me, not
anyone else, to decide the path of my story. I stand up
from where I was leaning, straightening my spine, and
announce, 'Throw him out.'

'Attagirl,' is all Duke replies with a wolffish grin before he grabs Levi by the scruff of the neck and drags him outside.

The guys surround Duke once he shuts the door and inundate him with questions – *what was that all about? What did he do? Are you okay?* As the chatter in the bar slowly begins to increase, the music finally melding with the buzz of conversation again, the roiling in my stomach and rushing in my ears slowly dials down.

And then it all disappears when Duke's dark, stormy eyes find mine, anchoring me back down.

'Just looking out for Baby Hensley,' he says, making the guys turn to me, brows furrowed. Duke checks, 'You alright?'

I nod, my eyes stinging, but I try to blink it away.

I've got you, he mouths, without anyone seeing now they're all facing me, and my heart trembles.

Then Duke is waving the guys off and shouting out to the rest of the bar as he heads off to grab some more champagne, 'Alright, show's over, guys. Let's get back to drinking. We've got an engagement to celebrate.'

29

Duke

The extra champagne bottles I bring out go down a treat. Enough to quickly pull the attention from me – and more importantly, Cherry – after the debacle with Levi, and back to celebrating.

Everyone's now surpassed the excited and loud stage of intoxication, and instead the booth is filled with heavy eyes, heads resting against shoulders, and glasses of water to try to combat the hangovers for the next morning.

With the night bleeding into the early hours of the morning, and the majority of the people who came for Wyatt and Rory having left about a half hour ago, the main gang are the last stragglers in the bar as they wait for their ride home. I imagine Luke, one of the only two cab drivers in Willow Ridge, will be picking them up, probably piling them all into one car despite the lack of seats.

Even though I should be listening to Rory's drunken slurs as she wraps her arms around my waist, hugging me with gratitude for the night, I can't help my eyes from wandering over to Cherry. I've had to return to the solace of the bar multiple times since throwing Levi out, anxious to be able to watch over her as much as possible.

I've never felt anger as hot and raging as I did when I saw him saunter in like he'd done nothing wrong. Or when I saw how shaken Cherry looked at his presence. The need to make him pay for what he did was practically trying to tear itself out of my skin, crackling in my veins like lightning.

No one hurts my girl.

I thought I would've restrained myself better than caging him in like that. And throwing him to the ground outside which no one luckily saw . . . I've dealt with enough anger from plenty of grief and discrimination over the years that I thought I'd learnt to manage it better. But there was more than just anger playing a role in my reaction tonight. Something I haven't felt in – well, I don't know if I've ever felt it like this before. And it *burns*, brighter and deeper than I thought imaginable.

So much so that all I can think about is how badly I want to hold Cherry, how desperately I need to show her how I feel, to remind her that I'm always here to keep her safe.

But I have to shake it off for now. Because if there's something else this night has reminded me, it's how much my friends mean to me. I've hit a peak level of happiness, surrounded by the warmth of my best friends' joy and support, knowing I get to bask in that with them – it's almost perfect, and I know how vital it is not to ruin that right now. Even if that means keeping the truth of whatever I have going on with Cherry in the shadows for now.

Rory's words of *how loyal a friend* I am really emphasised such.

'And you're sure you don't want us to stay and help clean up?' Rory asks. She's not let go of me for the past few minutes, and while I'm sure she is super thankful for tonight's celebrations, I think it's mostly because she's struggling to stay upright given how much of the champagne she drank.

'Positive,' I reply, walking her over to where Wyatt, Wolfman and Cherry are hanging by one of the booths. 'All you two should be doing today is celebrating, no chores.'

'Cab's outside,' Wolfman announces to the group.

'Oh, don't you worry.' Rory loosens her grip on me and tilts her head up, her eyelids heavy as she then proceeds to *boop* me on the nose. 'I'll be celebrating *all* night long with Wyatt.' A long string of giggles erupts from her, ginger waves bouncing – I don't think I've ever seen her this drunk before.

'Did you hear that, Hensley?' Sawyer chimes in as he joins us and the others, an arm around Jessie's waist – a girl he picked up earlier in the night. 'Apparently you and Red are gonna be celebrating *all night long.*'

'Delightful,' Cherry comments sarcastically. She shoots me a quick look, and I raise my brows, almost to say, *as will you be*, forcing a blush into her cheeks. Fuck am I glad I'll have her to myself soon.

'Oh, really? Well then, what are we waiting for?' Wyatt booms, marching over to us. I peel Rory from me and guide her into his arms, where he then makes her squeal by tossing her over his shoulder. He gives me a pat on the back with his free hand. 'Thanks for tonight, man. You're the best. Seriously. Couldn't ask for a better friend. Or best man.' He adds the last bit with a wink, and the suggestion hits me straight in the heart.

'Always, Hensley. Congrats, again. I'm so happy for you.' I give him a squeeze on the arm. 'Now get out of here. Bye, Rory.' She's still giggling where she's hanging over Wyatt's shoulder but manages to lift herself slightly to wave before Wyatt carts her off.

Cherry and I say our goodbyes to Wolfman, Sawyer, and Jessie, watching them all get in the cab with Wyatt and Rory. Once we've waved them off, Cherry heads back inside first, leaving me to lock the door.

'That was . . . a long night.' Cherry teases her bottom lip with her teeth as she starts to take slow steps backwards, only reminding me how badly I've wanted to feel her mouth again.

I've always thought Cherry was beautiful, but there's something goddamn bewitching about her right now – tanned skin all flushed, shining under the mood lighting with a desire-filled glow, so empty of my touch. She's lit up like a warning sign, ablaze from the red lights, and I want nothing more than to get burned.

I realise a second later I've started prowling towards her, like my body couldn't resist the opportunity to be close to her now everyone has gone. That magnetic pull between us suddenly heightened.

'Too long,' I agree, loosening one of my shirt buttons. Cherry's back hits the bar with a gasp and it's not a moment longer that I'm in front of her, hands splaying across her waist. I love looking down as those big umber eyes blink up at me. But before I can crash my lips against hers, I have to ask, 'Are you okay? After Levi turning up?'

'Yeah.' The darkness in her eyes softens, and she runs her hands up my arms. 'I'm always okay when I've got you looking out for me. Thank you, Duke, really. You have no idea what it means to have someone willing to fight for me.'

'Always.' I bring my forehead down to hers, taking a second to breathe in her scent. 'I'll always fight for you, Cherry.'

Because I love you.

My lips barrel towards hers not a second sooner – to take them with all the hunger I've built up over the night, to say the words I'm scared to admit with kisses instead. Cherry moans into my mouth, wasting no time before she unbuttons the rest of my shirt, letting her fingers roam my body, tracing the lines of my muscles. She runs her nails down over my chest as she opens her mouth for my tongue, sending a shot of desire straight to my thickening cock.

'Fuck, I've been waiting all evening to taste you. I can't wait any longer.' I pull my lips away and hoist her up to settle her on the bar top, and she lets out a sweet chuckle.

Carefully, I press my palms to her knees and spread her legs apart, revealing some dark-red lacy panties that match the colour of her lips under her black dress. I have to close my eyes to steel myself – to keep that last thread of my self-control intact. I rest my head against one of her thighs, whispering, 'My favourite goddamn colour, Cherry. You're killing me.'

My hands reach higher up her leg, pushing back her dress until I can hook my fingers under the waistband of her panties. Cherry watches me with glossy eyes, shining and wild with overflowing desire. Two dark pools that I just want to dive into and never surface. I hold her stare the whole time I talk to her.

'Here's how this is going to go,' I start, lazily dragging her panties down her hips. She lifts her ass up for me automatically so I can slip them over like the good girl she is. 'I'm going to lie you back on this bar and devour your sweet pussy until you've soaked my face.' I slide her panties down her legs and remove each of her sneakers and socks. I lift her dress up over her next, and remove her bra, pressing a kiss to her sternum. 'Then, you're going to get on your knees and get my cock nice and wet and covered in that goddamn lipstick you're always wearing.'

She swallows thickly, nodding. 'And then?'

'And then . . .' Pausing, I trail my fingers back up the inside of her legs, my other hand coming round to cup the back of her neck to ease Cherry down along the bar top. Seeing her laid out bare like this has my heart stammering – I've dreamt of this scenario too many times, part of me is slightly concerned I'm just in another dream. But when my fingers meet her pussy, no dream could ever create the delicious sensation of Cherry's slickness against my skin, or the heat of her beneath my touch.

Or the way my heart pulses *mine, mine, mine* when we're connected.

Revelling in the reminder that this is in fact my reality, I gently press a finger into her and curl it to stroke her inner wall. Leaning over her body, I trail kisses over her stomach, her hip bones, the dip of her thighs.

I tip my head up to meet her eyes, her black hair spread out around her, and I think my heart actually trips over itself. Because Cherry Hensley is a godsend. A beacon of life in the darkness.

She whispers, 'What next?'

'Then . . . I'm going to take you upstairs and finally fuck you on every surface possible. In every place I've ever dreamt of fucking you when I've had my hand fisted around my cock, imagining it was your tight little cunt bringing me to release.' Her eyes flare and it makes me feral. 'I'm going to show you how well you deserve to have been fucked all these years.'

And I mean it. My blood boils thinking about how many beautiful moments of Cherry Hensley coming undone have been missed. The world has been starved of how heavenly her whimpers sound as I unravel her with my fingers, how the sight of her body writhing is something that should be saved for salvation, enough to force you to your knees.

'God, Duke. Please, *now*,' she breathes out, but furrows her brow when I pull my finger out from her.

I hold it up before she can complain, suggesting, 'How about we invite Jack to play with us too?'

Cherry watches as I round the bar and reach for a bottle of Jack Daniel's, her lips popping open as I unscrew the cap and hover the bottle over her naked body. A wicked smile appears as she nods, and I don't hesitate to pour a line of whiskey over her body, dropping my lips to lick it off her skin quickly. With a gasp, Cherry's body arches up to meet my mouth, her breathing quickening the longer my tongue trails over her stomach and chest, lapping up every last drop. I flick my tongue across one of her nipples, making her shiver.

'Fuck, Duke,' she moans when I pour more onto her.

This time, I drag my lips down her body, sucking up the whiskey until my mouth reaches her clit, and I drop the bottle to the bar so I can thrust two fingers into her.

'Oh my God!' she cries out.

The mix of whiskey and Cherry's arousal in my mouth is even better than every time I've dreamed of this scenario.

I might have said I was going to take my time with Cherry when I fucked her, but that never meant I was going to be slow and lazy with it. It meant I was going to take all night. It meant I was going to devour her over and over, keep her coming until she can't take any more, no matter how long that takes. The one thing I won't be doing, is wasting my time with her.

So, I pump my fingers into her, keeping up a quick pace as I flick my tongue across her clit, sucking every now and again because I love the way her hips buck up into me when I do. Every sweet whimper that leaves her lips only makes me harder, a melody of moans and gasps that I want to play on repeat. The taste of her has me grinding myself against the bar, just to relieve the ache from how much I want her.

Cherry's nails clamber at my shoulders as she tries to anchor herself amidst the pleasure, and I pray to God that they leave a mark, so I can get the scratches tattooed on me, never letting me forget this glorious moment.

'Duke, I . . .' Cherry breathes out, face scrunching in concentration. Her teeth clamp down hard on her lip, but it doesn't stop the whimpering breaths racing out of her.

Feeling her muscles begin to tense around me, her nails digging into my shoulders, I press my arm over her lower stomach, adding more pressure as I increase the speed of my fingers and tongue.

She gasps as her legs begin to shake. 'Yes—oh, God, Duke—'

And then she's arching up into me, pussy fluttering around my fingers to the sound of her calling out my name. I hold her against the bar top to allow me to lap up the remains of her orgasm, getting my fill of the taste of her while she comes down from the high.

Cherry's pants echo through the bar as I help her up, cradling her flushed, shining face in my hands while I whisper to her between kisses, 'You're so fucking beautiful when you come, Cherry.'

Lips popping, Cherry pushes me back and hops off the bar, her fingers going straight to my belt buckle. 'You know, I always imagined that one night I'd just admit how I felt and get on my knees for you and—'

'Cherry.' I filter my fingers through her hair, cradling the back of her neck. 'Get on the floor now and show me.' When I let her go, I swipe one of the towels off the side to lay down on the floor. I tell her, 'For your knees.'

'A gentleman *and* a freak. I love it.' She giggles, licking her lips afterwards. The word *love* hovers in my mind again, my heart stuttering for a beat, but then I'm quickly distracted by Cherry's hands pushing my shirt off my shoulders and her lips connecting with my chest. My shirt drops to the floor, letting her explore my tattoos, peppering them with kisses, and occasionally running her tongue along my skin.

'Don't waste all your lipstick, baby,' I whisper, the words already slightly mumbled as the hot press of her lips electrifies my body, the blood beginning to rush in my ears, drowning out the sound of the music playing. Everything becomes just me and Cherry. Exactly how it should be.

Cherry slowly falls to her knees, dragging her nails down my stomach, leaving fire in their wake, until she reaches my belt. She makes quick work of unbuckling it, pressing her palm against my length as she does. I stagger back with a groan, holding myself up with my arms against the bar behind me.

But what happens next is what might just kill me. Cherry pushes my jeans and underwear down in one move, my hard cock springing free right in front of her beautiful face. Her eyes widen, mouth dropping open. Gaze locked on my cock, Cherry licks her lips, then tentatively wraps her slender fingers around the shaft, bringing the head to her lips so she can lick off the bead of moisture already gathered there. My eyes roll back with a groan.

'Jesus, Duke. I forgot how massive you are.'

Fuck, this actually might be the death of me.

R.I.P. Duke Bennett – died doing what he loved, watching Cherry Hensley lick his cock.

'If you keep saying things like that I'm gonna finish before it's even in your mouth.' I cup her jaw shakily, angling her head up to me. 'Just take it slow.'

'Yes, boss.' She giggles. I'm about to tell her off for calling me *boss*, but then I'm inhaling sharply as she licks a stripe up the shaft of my cock and swirls her tongue around the head. My muscles tighten, pressure already building at the base of my spine.

'Fuck,' I groan out when she proceeds to wrap her red lips around the tip, taking a couple of inches into her mouth slowly as she sucks, her tongue running up the shaft when she pulls back. My hand sifts through her hair, twisting it around my palm to keep it out of the way, following the bob of her head as she continues sucking me leisurely.

When she pulls back, there's a smearing of her red lipstick along my shaft, as well as around her lips, and the sight has me ready to blow. I think I'm going to have to accept this isn't going to last long.

'Is that good?' she asks, big eyes blinking up at me.

'Fucking perfect,' I admit. '*You're* fucking perfect. Keep going. And keep those pretty eyes on me, baby.'

Cherry obeys, staring up at me as she gives my cock another lick up its length, before taking it in her mouth again. My legs twitch each time she reaches the tip, flicking her tongue against it. Picking up her pace, Cherry begins taking more and more of my cock, humming as she does, like she's enjoying this as much as me. The vibrations of it skitter through my body, lighting up every nerve. I'm overwhelmed with pleasure, with the fucking wondrous sight of Cherry Hensley staring up at me, eyes watering a little as she takes my cock far enough to hit the back of her throat, making her choke a little.

'Fuck, baby, you're doing so well. Taking as much of my cock as you can into that pretty mouth of yours. Getting it nice and wet and ready for me to fuck you with it. Such a good girl.'

I can't help but groan out again, not holding back as she continues to take my cock deeper and deeper each time, now adding the pump of her hand to the mix. I'm lost in the sound of it all – her satisfied humming, the occasional choke, the wet noises from her saliva coating my cock, and my own moaning.

It's just about enough to cover the sound of the locks clicking, but not enough for when Sawyer's voice interrupts us, shouting, 'What the hell are you doing?'

30

Cherry

'Oh *damn*, are you getting a blowjob behind the bar?'
Sawyer's laugh of disbelief echoes through the bar as
Duke's eyes widen down at me. Colour drains from his face,
his body going taut. From the way Sawyer's footsteps are
closing in, I'm seconds away from being discovered with
my lips around Duke's cock, lipstick covering every inch.

Without a moment more to hesitate, Duke tugs my
head back and quickly tucks himself away. He holds a
hand out – a silent command to *stay down* – as he pivots,
scrambling to buckle his belt.

'Please don't come any closer,' Duke begs Sawyer, his
voice hoarse – possibly from groaning so loudly mere
seconds ago.

Champagne bubbles mix with the dopamine in my
bloodstream from my orgasm, forcing me to clamp a hand
over my mouth to stop any nervous giggles escaping. It
shouldn't be funny – we're moments away from being
caught – but for some reason, the pure bad luck and

poor timing of it all makes me want to howl. The close call is somewhat exhilarating too, just like when Duke had me bent over his desk weeks ago, strumming me so close to the edge while my family and friends were a few metres away.

Oblivious to the implications of what he might find, Sawyer just laughs again. 'Oh, come on, man. I ain't judgin'. You've got lipstick all over you, by the way.'

The muscles in Duke's back bunch together, straining under his tattooed skin. He wipes desperately at his mouth with the back of his hand. 'I'm serious, Sawyer. There's nothing to see.'

'Okay, okay.' I hear the brief scrape of a table leg against the floor, presumably where Sawyer has perched himself. 'I don't know why you're makin' a big deal out of this. Anyone would think you've got little Hensley behind there or somethin'.'

My breath catches in my throat, the words hitting me differently all of sudden when they're coming from Sawyer's mouth. There's just something in the way he says it, like it's so unbelievably impossible. His joke clearly grates on Duke even more as his hands clench the edge of the bar tighter, almost threatening to leave dents.

It's just a joke, though – hell, I was literally having to bite back my own chuckle a second ago – but hearing Sawyer actually say it, insinuating how terrible that would be, and seeing Duke's evident discomfort . . . it's somewhat jarring.

That the idea of Duke – *any* of Wyatt's friends – trying to get with me is *laughable*. I try to remind myself that it's only because they think it would be wrong, what Duke has been suggesting all these times, but I can't deny the slight twinge of shame coiling in my gut, as if it would be embarrassing to be seen with me. I'm just little, weak Baby Hensley, after all.

And when I'm cowering down here *naked*, pretending I don't exist, and Duke's so affected by the comment, not even looking at me, it's hard to ignore. The way that shame bites at my cheeks. The way I have to pick my nails just to distract myself.

The last thing I've ever felt with Duke is shame. But is he ashamed to be with me? It's not like I've been pushing him to be open about us, but I'm not sure I've ever cowered away from the idea either. It's always been Duke who's insisted on keeping this quiet – maybe he has more to risk from being honest about us, but wouldn't Wyatt be just as annoyed at me for being with his best friend?

I reach for Duke's shirt across the floor to wrap it around me.

Duke grits out, 'Sawyer, what are you doing here?'

'Sorry, I left my phone. I know you said to use the spare key in emergencies, but . . . well, can't say I expected to be walkin' in on this. Honestly, I'm happy for you, man.' The tone of Sawyer's voice gives away his smirk. 'Glad you're puttin' the bar to good use.'

Duke wipes a hand down his face, a gravelly sigh following. I wonder how quickly I could scurry out from behind here, maybe go hide in Duke's office or the staff room. Just so I don't have to stay down here, hiding.

'Hey, look, don't worry. Just gimme a second to find the damn thing and I'll let you get back to your fun night.' Sawyer's voice quietens with distance and Duke's shoulders visibly loosen, his muscles shifting down.

I want him to reach out to me or something, even if briefly.

But he doesn't. Instead, he sidles out from the bar still with his shirt off. 'I'll help you – it might be quicker.'

Sounds of shuffling and chairs scraping fill the empty haunt as I try to keep my breathing quiet.

'Wait,' Sawyer gasps. 'There's a dress and *panties* by the bar. You rascal, Duke Bennett.'

'Sawyer, no—'

The sudden thumping of a few running footfalls and Sawyer's laugh doesn't give me enough time to react before he's at the bar, leaning straight over to discover me, still on my knees. His bottom lip drops, wide brown eyes scanning me from head to toe frantically. He rubs a hand over his eyes. *'Cherry?'*

My heart races up in my throat, words failing me.

'Hi . . .' I say cautiously, finally bringing myself to a stand, making sure to hold the shirt as tightly to my naked body as possible. I flash him a smile, but he just continues staring at me, mouth agape. It's actually quite surreal – Sawyer being quiet for once.

'Duke.' He whips his head round to face Duke, whose hands are clutching his head, muscles strained as his arms lift. 'What. The. Fuck.'

'You don't have to make a big deal out of this,' I blurt, moving around the bar. I hold my hand up, like I'm trying to calm down a skittish horse, or in this case, a bewildered bull rider.

'My *ass* I don't have to make a big deal out of this, Cherry Hensley.' Sawyer crosses his arms, urging his eyes at me. 'You're Wyatt's little sister. This . . . *Please* tell me

279

this isn't real. That I passed out when I got home, and this is just some weird nightmare where my friends go behind each other's backs—'

'Hey,' Duke calls out. 'That's not fair.'

'Isn't it?' Sawyer throws his hands in the air. 'Duke, you had his little sister on her knees behind your bar giving you a goddamn *blowjob* on the night of his engagement. Are you telling me Wyatt knows about all that and gave you the green light?'

'It's . . . it's not like that,' Duke mutters weakly, shaking his head and dropping his gaze to the floor. There's a slight hunch to his shoulders now, and he leans back against the edge of the table behind him for support.

'Wyatt's *little sister* is standing right here and has an opinion on this you know.' I huff, folding my arms too. 'You're blowing this all out of proportion.'

Sawyer sighs, pinching the bridge of his nose. 'Cherry, I know you might not get it but . . . all we've ever tried to do is protect you, and then for one of us to slide in when Wyatt's not looking, it just—'

'Yeah, well, Wyatt doesn't control me. I'm an adult, okay? I can make my own decisions,' I say fiercely. Because if this summer has proved anything, it's that. My decisions are just as worthy as everyone else's. 'There's nothing wrong with me wanting to be with Duke, or him wanting to be with me.'

'Wanting to *be* with Duke? As in—' Sawyer's head volleys between the two of us '—you're *together*?'

His glare finally settles on Duke, and I drag my stare up too. But nothing comes. Duke's own gaze just flitters off as he rubs his hand across his stubbled jaw. The fact that he doesn't say has my heart squeezing painfully tight. Why does it feel like I'm the one fighting harder here?

I guess we haven't actually defined what is going on between us, we haven't been able to, really. And Duke's been there for me so many times maybe this is just his moment of weakness, and this time, I'll be strong for him. For the both of us.

'Yes,' I confirm, quickly dropping to grab my clothes from the floor. 'We're together.'

Sawyer barks out a strained laugh. 'Wyatt's gonna flip.'

'No, he's not, because you're not going to tell him.' I raise my brows.

There's a wince of pain that flashes across Sawyer's face. 'I don't know, Cherry. Wyatt's our best friend. How long has this even been going on?'

Again, Duke says nothing when Sawyer turns to him once more searching for answers.

I shrug. 'Like a month or so.'

'*A month or so?!*' A string of incomprehensible sounds follow from Sawyer's mouth, his jaw working up and down like a fish until he eventually slides out a chair and slumps into it. He throws his head into his hands and groans.

I'm almost surprised at how worked up he's getting himself, especially when there's no one here to rile up or impress. If anything, out of all our group, Sawyer was the one I'd expected to laugh this off and probably just use it as an opportunity to make awkward comments to annoy us. Sawyer mumbles to himself, 'Why did I have to be the one to walk in on this? Haven't I had enough to deal with this summer with Dad and the ranch and *her*?'

I move towards the table, but Duke walks quicker, finally piping up to say, 'Sawyer, I promise, it's nothing.'

His words slap me straight in the face. My heart lurches up into my throat, a painful lump wedged there as I struggle to convince myself that he's only saying that to calm Sawyer down. But something makes me not want to believe myself, that cowering version of me suddenly rearing its head and beginning to tear my heart into pieces. 'We're *nothing*?'

'Cherry.' Duke turns to me, brows drawn together. 'I think maybe I should talk to Sawyer about this on my own.'

'What?' My head jolts back.

'Can you – can you just go upstairs? I'll talk to Sawyer and help him find his phone and then . . . Then I'll come find you.'

'But why? I—'

'*Please*, Hensley.'

Each breath I take down gets heavier. I have to clamp my teeth together to compose myself for a second. To contain the fiery rage that's searing through my bloodstream.

'Fine.'

The click of a key in the lock forces me up from the couch. I only just managed to make myself sit down a minute ago, having paced around Duke's apartment since I got here, mind all jumbled with everything that went down tonight. One minute I'm hit with memories of Duke's lips on me, his dark skin lit up with a sheen of red neon, reflecting the burning desire inside of me. But then that heat turns white hot, making my skin crawl, thinking about how Duke didn't so much as admit to wanting to be with me to Sawyer, then demanded I come up here.

Why? Because I'm just Baby Hensley, right? I'm young and immature and don't know how to handle these things. I should just get out of the room and let the grown-ups talk.

No, that's not true. That's not what he thinks of you. Right?

Because what could he possibly have needed to talk to Sawyer about without me there? He probably thinks he can calm Sawyer down better than me – he is Duke, after all, always the shoulder for his friends, the one they can count on. God knows he's eased me through moments of anxiety and worry plenty of times, like he's been graced with some kind of otherworldly ability to soothe.

Except it doesn't work tonight. Not when Duke's broad body slides through the gap in the door and he shuts it behind him. The sight of him has my chest rising quicker and quicker so that my clothes start to feel too constricting. Duke presses a hand to the door as it shuts, leaning there for a beat before finally turning weary eyes to me. Even through the haze of night filling the apartment, I notice the shadows that have crept into his eyes, the lumbered shift of his muscles, like they've got nothing left to give.

He swallows thickly when his eyes land on me. 'Hey.'

'Hey.'

A heavy silence settles between us. I'm not entirely sure what I was expecting from him, but it wasn't this. Not this awkward hesitation, gaze flicking between me and the floor, too reminiscent of when Duke would actively avoid getting too close to me. That's the last place I'd *ever* want to go back to, so the sudden trembling of my breath isn't completely unexpected.

'Are you okay?' I push off from the couch, taking

tentative steps towards him. Dark, tired eyes watch me, full of storm clouds – the quieter kind that slowly roll in, dragging nothing but gloom with them.

'Yeah.' He lets out a long sigh. 'I – I should walk you home.'

'Walk me home?' I stop my path abruptly. My brows pinch together, an ache forming behind my nose from the sting of his unexpected dismissal. 'But I was going to stay here tonight. With you.'

A second ago my clothes were almost suffocating but now I feel totally exposed. I'm vastly aware of the chilled air biting at my bare skin, how I never even put back on my underwear, only my dress, and my panties are just sitting on the coffee table. Some small part of me probably thought Duke would just end up sliding them off again, anyway, and before we knew it, we'd be tangled up in his sheets.

How stupid of me.

Duke winces. 'I'm sorry, I know I said that I'd have sex with you and—'

'I don't care about whether you fuck me or not, Duke.' Even if I did hope that we'd just pick up where we left off, truthfully, all I want is the privilege of spending another night with him, wrapped in his arms, where he might talk with me until we pass out, where I get to discover tiny, exciting, new parts of him I'd never have known when there was a line drawn between us. 'I just – I want to *be* with you.'

'I think maybe it would be better if . . .' His lashes falter, fists flexing by his sides, the only movement in his otherwise stoic demeanour.

My ragged breaths fill the apartment.

'If what?' We should talk about it, not just give up when something gets difficult. 'What else did Sawyer say?'

'Nothing we don't already know.'

That makes me scoff. A hoarse laugh spills out of my throat as I throw my hands to my head, letting my fingers massage my temples. 'Well, I don't know about that. Because as far as I see it, all that mattered to me down there was defending what *we*—' I point between us '—have, but *clearly* something else was on your mind that I'm unaware of—'

'Cherry—' Fire flickers momentarily behind Duke's eyes.

'—so, I'd appreciate it if you told me what was said. It's the least you could do after basically *banishing* me up here.' Raising my chin a little, I pin Duke with my stare, crossing my arms to punctuate my point. I don't care if I seem callow or immature now. I'm saying my truth.

He gives me a rumbling sigh in response. Every one of his muscles is strained, like they're trying to break through the layer of tattoos covering them. 'I don't – *fuck* – I don't want to talk about it yet . . . My head is all over the place, and I just need some time to think things through.'

'Think *what* through, Duke?' *Us? Whether he still wants to be with me?* 'Why does it matter what Sawyer thinks? He's not going to tell Wyatt. I know he won't. And . . .' The edges of my vision blur into silver. 'Would it really be so bad if he did?'

Duke's stare drops to the ground. Defeat is written all over him, only emphasised when the next words leave his lips. 'I can't lose anybody else.'

Each word cuts through me, twisting in my gut. I'm scared to look anywhere else but him, afraid of the darkness closing in around me each time my head throbs. A lone tear finally trickles down my cheek. I let out another laugh, a gurgled one that mixes with the sob that also lurches from my throat. 'But if you had to lose someone, better the summer fling who'll be gone soon than your best friend, right?'

Duke's wide eyes shoot up to catch mine. 'Woah, baby, no.' Clumsily, he stumbles towards me, but I move out of his reach, wrapping my arms around me as the dam breaks and tears begin to stream. 'That's not at all what I'm saying. You know you mean more to me than that. *So* much more. I just – this is hard for me, and I only want some time to clear my head before we talk about it.'

'Time . . .' I shake my head. Time for what? To figure out how best to let me down? After he swore to me in this very apartment that it was safe to let myself love him, that whatever happened, however hard I fell, he'd catch me. Just like he always has.

Heart rattling against my ribcage, I suck down a sharp breath. 'You *promised* me, Duke. You promised me that if I let myself fall, you'd be there with me the whole time, falling too. But . . . but now it feels like I've jumped, and you're standing on the edge, just watching me. And it's too late for me.' My fingers scrape over my scalp. 'Because I can't go back. Not now I'm in love with you.'

The words leave my mouth before I can stop them.

Every part of him *drops*. Face, shoulders, hands.

'Cherry, *please*—'

'Oh my God . . .' I can't believe the first time I tell him I'm in love with him is with tears streaking my face and my heart cracking like someone's taken a hammer to glass.

'You know what?' Sniffing, I straighten up and wipe

away my tears. I can't stay here anymore. I can't look at this place, knowing the love that was nurtured and bloomed and allowed to flourish here was all for nothing. 'You're right. I should go home. I don't want to talk about this anymore, either. We should both take some . . . space.'

Not waiting for a reply, I grab my panties and stuff them in my bag that I left beside the couch earlier, then I haul it onto my shoulder.

Quietly, Duke says, 'Let me get my keys.'

Still not fighting. Still doesn't love me.

I pace right up to him, where he's blocking the door, but keep my eyes trained on his chest, knowing that if I meet his eyes now – the ones I've dreamt about being able to gaze into for so many years – I'll crumble. 'No, thank you. I'll walk alone.'

Duke doesn't budge. 'Cherry, it's the middle of the night, there's no way I'm letting you walk home alone.'

I can't stop my eyes from rolling, but I know he won't let this go. If I leave without him, he'll probably just follow me anyway.

'Fine.' I move around him and open the door. Over my shoulder I say, 'You can call me a cab. Luke should've dropped the others off by now. But you're not coming with me.'

'Are you serious?'

I think I make myself, and my whole feelings for how this night has ended, clear with my final word. 'Deadly.'

31

Duke

Exhaustion lies heavy on my shoulders from another sleepless night. Sunlight rains down on the ranch ahead as I climb out of my truck and shield my eyes from the brightness. The serene golden fields and landscape surrounding me contrasts so starkly with the storm clouds darkening my mind, a contradiction that leaves an uncomfortable sensation settling in my chest as I trudge up the steps to the main house at Sunset Ranch.

Not even hours riding my motorcycle or trying to paint out my emotions can pull me from this pit I've let myself fall into. My place is so scattered with drawings and paintings of Cherry now that the thought of spending any more time there feels unbearable. Having lunch with my grandmother also didn't help as much as I expected given that my supposed *moping around* was much too irritating for her, except for when it meant I wasn't paying enough attention during Scrabble and she won by a mile.

So here I am, knocking on the front door of Willow Ridge's resident positivity and wellness influencer, with the hopes she might help. I'm grateful to see Wyatt's truck already gone, no doubt somewhere else on the ranch where he's already working. I knock on the door several times, anxiously walking about the porch until the door swings open.

Rory's eyes flash at me with surprise. She's still in her pyjamas, waves twisted into a bun, and a smoothie in her hand. 'Hey! Well, isn't this a nice surprise!'

'Hey . . . Um, Wyatt's not in, right?' I check into the house behind her.

'Uh, no, he's working out on the ranch. We didn't get a lot done yesterday after Friday night – as you can imagine – so he's gotta make up for it today.' Rory chuckles, but quickly angles her head at my evident lack of returned laughter. 'Everything okay?'

I worry my lip. 'You remember that time you came into my bar after you and Wyatt had that argument?'

'Of course. I meant what I said the other night – we probably owe half of the reason we're still together to you.' Her smile plays out again, but it's short-lived. 'Oh, why don't we go sit round the back. The swing's great for DMCs.'

I raise a brow as I follow her, but she elaborates before I can ask, 'Deep and meaningful conversations. Does no one know about DMCs anymore?'

I shake my head at Rory as we head to the back deck, settling ourselves on the swing. The comfort of the pillows and blanket do little to soothe me. Especially when I notice movement in the distance that looks an awful lot like two girls on horses, trotting along the dirt road bisecting the ranch.

Rory chimes in, 'Oh, yeah, Cherry's having one of her lessons with Fliss. She's amazing at it, you know? Like she was born to be on the back of a horse.'

I just nod, mesmerised by how natural she looks, even from a distance. Despite being far away, I swear I can feel the joy radiating off her. The kind of joy *I* was making her feel only a few days ago. It makes my confession barrel out of me. 'I'm so fucking in love with her, Rory.'

'Oh, shit.' She props her smoothie on the floor. 'I didn't realise your feelings for her had got so strong.' Rory sighs, then throws her arm around my shoulders. 'I'm sorry, Duke, it must be tough having to be around her so much when you feel that way.'

Right, because Rory has no idea what's been going on for the last couple of months. She figured out weirdly quickly that I liked Cherry, and even if I denied it, I think Rory's always had a way of reading me. I might have let her in on the little secret that I was helping Cherry with a few things this summer, being as vague as possible when I asked for a favour at the fair so I could get Cherry on the Ferris wheel alone, but that's the last she would've heard.

'Yeah, it was . . . until we kissed.'

Rory rears back. 'You kissed? *When?*'

'Ah,' I stall, pretending that I'm trying to work out when it was in my head, even though I've had the date and time etched into my mind since the second Cherry's lips met mine. The day she walked into my bar looking for a job was the day my world started turning, but the moment we kissed was when my world found something worth turning for, eager to be forever in her glorious orbit. 'About a month ago?'

'Oh my God! I can't believe neither of you told me.' Rory huffs and crosses her arms. 'After everything I did to help you at the fair, as well. I'm not angry, I'm just disappointed.'

I raise a brow at her. 'This is supposed to be about my problems, not yours.'

She waves me off with a grin. 'Fine, fine. But I don't see what the problem is if you kissed. She obviously likes you back.'

Actually, she loves me, and I threw it back in her face.

Taking a deep swallow first, I then admit, 'I – I hurt her.'

'Oh, how?'

'Sawyer walked in on us . . . *doing stuff* at the bar and I freaked out.' I drop my head into my hands, hating having to relive that night again. I was a fucking coward. 'He didn't even really say anything I didn't already know – that Wyatt wouldn't be happy and all that, the whole reason I've tried so hard all these years to stay away from Cherry. And he promised he wouldn't say anything, but I had to tell Wyatt as soon as possible. That's what a good friend would do and – fuck, Rory, I couldn't think straight. I just felt like I was drowning all of a sudden.'

Rory rubs circles on my back.

'Before he turned up, all I could think about was how in love with Cherry I was. She makes me so happy – she makes me less afraid to be *me*, to honour the parts of me that maybe I don't always like to shine a light on. She makes me feel brave and has me doing things I'd never thought I'd do. Telling her all my deepest secrets.' I glance up at where Cherry's riding in the distance, a spotlight of sunshine breaking through some wispy clouds onto her. 'But when Sawyer caught us, it all hit me. Just *how* deeply in love with her I was, and how easily that could all come crashing down. Just like it had before, with Mom and my grandfather. How I could lose so much in one go because I got fed up riding the line and decided to break the rules. I'm not sure I can take it.'

'Oh, Duke . . .'

I finally lean back in the swing. 'She told me she loved me, Rory. And I said *nothing*.'

'But why? You just said you loved her?'

'I don't know.' I rub a hand along my stubble. Silence hovers around us, the only sound infiltrating it being the soft, barely noticeable echo of Cherry's laughter and voice, carried along the breeze. It's a melody to my ears, hearing that my fear hasn't brought her down completely. Because all I've ever wanted is to build her up. I would've sacrificed every brick in the walls I've built around me to keep her at bay, if I knew it would brighten her days even by a fraction.

Rory just watches me, giving me the space to think and confess, like I did a year ago for her. The longest sigh – one I've been holding in for maybe years – rolls out of me.

'Maybe there was a small part of me that thought there was a chance the summer would end, and Cherry would go back to college, leaving us in the past now she felt stronger and more experienced. It would be easier that way . . . knowing that it wasn't really a loss, because Cherry was always going to leave. I've liked her for years, so I'm used to saying goodbye.'

Weight lifts from my chest as each word of my admission slips out. The storm clouding my head starts to ease. 'But when it hit me how much I love her, and then she told me she loved me . . . there was no easy way out anymore. The line was gone. Everything had changed. There was either forever or nothing. And in both of those scenarios, I'm going to lose something. For the first time in my life, the only option was change, when I've tried to fight that for so long. There was nowhere to hide this time.'

Rory chuckles. 'Well, I honestly think you've just said more to me in one go than you've said to me in the whole year I've known you. Feel better?'

I blow out a breath, laughing too. 'Yeah. This is what she's done to me, Rory.'

'Look,' Rory starts. 'Love is scary as fuck.'

'Next self-help book title?' I joke.

Rory gives me a pointed look, but the corners of her mouth still twitch. 'And being with someone, loving another, does often mean we have to give up certain things. That we have to change. But a lot of the time those things we have to change were only holding us back. And love might be scary, but it's also fucking beautiful.'

Hazel eyes twinkling, Rory grins at her diamond-clad finger, engagement ring glittering as it catches the sun.

'I know you're scared about losing Wyatt, but he's your best friend. You've been there for each other through so much, I think it would take a lot more than you loving his sister to ruin that. If anything, leaving it like this with Cherry now, knowing she's hurt, is going to do more damage.' Gently, Rory takes my hand, giving it a reassuring squeeze. 'But you do need to tell him, otherwise it'll only make things worse. Wyatt's a reasonable guy, and all he truly cares about is knowing that Cherry is safe and happy. If you can show him that you'll provide that for her, then even if it's difficult for him to accept at first, he'll come around. Plus,' she adds with a light chuckle, 'out of you, Wolfman, and Sawyer, I think we can all agree he'd rather it was you dating his sister.'

That makes me snort. I nod, letting my laugh eventually peter out as I watch Cherry in the distance again.

I'm never going to commit myself fully to anything if I'm always afraid of what I might lose. It's the same with the bar – Cherry was right that it's a great opportunity, one that could mean when she graduates we could be closer sometimes – and isn't that what I want? Do I really want to hold back in fear that Willow Ridge will resent me? That I'll miss out on things at home when I could finally get the chance to be with the one person I've wanted forever, while building up my business so I can share that success with Gram, with my friends?

I think it might be my time to get on my own metaphorical Ferris wheel.

'I've got some grovelling to do, haven't I?'

Rory snickers, biting her lip as she nods. 'A *lot* of grovelling, more like. But it's okay, I'm here to help you. Besides, if you get Cherry back, and then get married one day, we'll be sort of related, and that would be so cool.'

'Okay, okay!' I hold up my hands. 'One step at a time, please. Let's just start with figuring out how I'm gonna tell my girl I love her.'

32

Cherry

It's not like Rory to be late, if anything she's normally early, yet I've been here in Sitting Pretty for fifteen minutes now. I keep checking my phone, hoping a text will come through letting me know she's just running late but she's on her way. It was Rory who text me a couple of hours ago inviting me for a quick drink in town.

Despite trying my best not to let what happened with Duke get to me when I was at Sunset Ranch for one of my riding sessions with Fliss, I know her and Rory could tell something was up. It sucked not being able to spill everything to my girls, especially since Rory was the one who insinuated that Duke might have had feelings for me in the first place. I realise that revealing our relationship – or whatever the hell it is – that's a decision for both of us to make together. Even if that means deciding to keep quiet and pretend nothing ever happened. Fuck, I really hope that's not what he wants. How is it possible to be so annoyed at someone yet miss them so goddamn much at the same time?

Ugh, I really need this chat with Rory.

This time, when I lift my phone for what feels like the one-hundredth time, a message finally pops up from her.

Rory: Hey, girl! Sorry, I'm not gonna be able to make it anymore – got caught up with retreat stuff! But don't worry, I've sent someone else to keep you company!! Don't hate me x

Don't hate her? Who could she have possibly sent—

The tinkling bell above the door of the café rings as a customer enters. My gaze momentarily flicks up to catch sight of him – black leather jacket shining under the lights, dark Wranglers hugging solid, corded thighs, and a motorcycle helmet snug in the crook of his arm. I fight the urge to let my eyes drift upwards, to catch those eyes that have the power to shatter my heart all over again. Because even just knowing he's here has my heart pounding like racing hoofbeats.

Surely this is just a coincidence.

My thumbs thunder across my phone screen, violently tapping out my message back to Rory.

Cherry: Please tell me you didn't send Duke?!

My table sits far at the back of the café, but I still sink down in my seat, hoping Duke won't notice me. My hair falls across my face, and I try to peek around it to catch a glimpse of him. He's joined the short queue at the counter, already in conversation with one of the baristas, smiling as if Friday night isn't weighing down on him like it has been for me, aside from the brief reprieve while riding – my new therapy, it seems.

My phone pings again and I scramble to put it on silent. Though, I doubt he can hear amongst the buzzing chatter and steaming machines in the café.

Rory: Oops . . .

Oh, for fuck's sake. She knows. But then that means . . . he must have spoken to her.

Cherry: OMG!! What did he tell you?

Rory: Everything, babe. Which means we're technically even because you kept a secret and so did I, soooo please hear him out!! I want to go on double dates!

Cherry: I hate you

Rory: love you too xx

I can't bring myself to look away from my phone, particularly as I can already sense someone moving closer to my table. It takes me a few deep breaths before I can muster up the courage to look up at him. When I do, our gazes catch and he halts a few inches from the table, two coffee cups in his hands, a bag hanging off his arm, and his helmet tucked under the other.

His eyes glisten under the twinkling café lights with so

many unspoken words. With memories of how I told him I loved him yet spent the night alone. The first person I've ever loved, letting me walk away.

'Hi,' he says, holding up one of the cups to me.

Tightness already clogs my throat as memories of the other night slam into the forefront of my mind. I nudge the chair opposite me out from under the table with my foot, the legs scraping against the floor. Duke's gaze struggles to leave me before he nods and takes a seat, placing his helmet on the table, and his bag on the floor.

'Thanks,' he rasps, before sliding the coffee cup along to me, 'for letting me sit.'

His eyes flick between mine, searching. Evidence that my heart is still open for him? Evidence that I'll be okay if his isn't for me?

'I know you're probably – and rightfully – angry at me, but I was hoping you might . . .' Duke pauses, blinking away once and taking a deep breath through his nose. 'I hoped you might give me a chance to apologise. To make it up to you.'

I purse my lips, regarding him for a second – as if to pretend that my heart didn't just do a little flip with relief that there's still hope kindling between us. 'Okay.'

Duke dips his head, a soft curve of his lips following.

'You didn't have to do this,' I say, bringing the coffee to my lips as I wait in his contemplative silence.

'No, I did. I really did.' Duke fiddles with his fingers against the table, my own itching to grab his hands, to feel that safety of his hold on me again. But I know that's expecting a lot when we're in public. 'I'm so sorry, Cherry. The last thing I ever wanted to do was hurt you. I just – I freaked out. But I know it's not an excuse for how I acted the other night. You were right, I should've stood up for our relationship, and the last thing I should've done was push you away like I did. So, I truly am sorry. The truth is . . .'

Duke's eyes flash, then he heaves down a deep breath and reaches across the table for my hands, wrapping his around them. I freeze from the contact, my lips popping open as I stare at where our hands are linked, out and open for *anyone* to see.

'I am so goddamn in love with you, Cherry. I'm pretty certain I've been in love with you for years, if I'm being honest.' Duke laughs nervously, a shake of his head following. 'You said you felt like you were falling without me, that I wasn't by your side, but that's only because I'm already so far down, so deeply, madly, *irrevocably* in love with you. And I promise you that I'm here, waiting to catch you in my arms. I've got you, Baby Hensley. Always.'

I bite the inside of my bottom lip to stop it from wobbling. All his words – the ones I'd needed from him that night – hit me in my very core, the deepest part of my soul, branding me there in a way that means I'll never be able to turn back from this moment. Because he's right, I've been falling for so long, there's no way I can ever claw my way back out of this love I have for him. This love we have for each other.

Duke rubs his thumbs over my knuckles. 'But that's also why I froze when everything went down with Sawyer. Because there's no going back for me, not now. And it all hit me then – that I've been so afraid of upsetting Wyatt *if* he found out about us, but there's no *if* anymore, it's only *when*. This,' Duke squeezes my hands, 'isn't just for the summer to me, which means one day we're gonna have to tell Wyatt. So, when that realisation struck me, I – I got scared. I pushed you away, if only to give myself some respite from the fear.

'But I'm ready, Cherry. If you want to tell everyone about us, then . . . then let's do that. I'm serious about being in a relationship with you – I *love* you, and that's all that matters. Wyatt will see that, I'm sure. So, hopefully we'll be able to figure things out. And to prove it, I got this done yesterday.'

Carefully slipping his hands from mine, the loss of his heat an unwelcome feeling, Duke shrugs his jacket off, then holds out one of his wrists to me, upturned. When I catch sight of the tattoo lying on the inside of his wrist, I grab his arm, dragging him closer so I can inspect the drawing – a small, intricate image of two cherries.

My eyes flick up to his. 'You got cherries tattooed on you? Duke . . .'

'Did I ever tell you what this one meant?' He lines his other wrist up, bringing the cherries side by side with the horseshoe tattoo I'd noticed at the beginning of the summer. 'I got the horseshoe to represent the bar – something that gives me life, that keeps me going every day.'

My thumb runs over the transparent sticker that covers the cherries so the tattoo can heal. I can't stop my bottom lip from trembling, even as I try to speak. 'You – you didn't have to do that.'

Duke harbours my hands again, bringing them to his lips to plant a kiss on either one. 'Yes, I did. Because *you* give me life, Cherry. You bring so much joy into my world. Every summer, I feel like I'm revived again, because *you* are home. Back with me. Where you're meant to be.'

My heart stammers, beating faster than I've ever known, and the song it sings is a continuous *mine, mine, mine*.

Duke Bennett is all mine.

'I love you too.' I push out a wobbly smile. 'I know I said it before, accidentally . . . but can we pretend this is the first time I'm saying it?'

Even Duke's eyes look shinier than before, his smile seeming to require more effort to keep calm. 'Definitely. I'd rather pretend the other night didn't happen at all.'

'Deal,' I confirm, tangling my feet with his under the table, just to be able to touch more of him. To weave myself into him, where I know I'll be steady. Where I'll be strong.

'Oh, I almost forgot.' Duke leans over to grab the bag sitting beside him. 'I think we got a little bit side-tracked with some of the, um, more *adult* parts of your bucket list . . .' I bite my lip as he perks a brow at me, his darkening eyes sending a zap of need straight to my core. 'But I think it's time we finally tick this one off.'

And with that, Duke pulls out a glossy, sleek black helmet. When he angles it around to show me the back, I almost fall off my chair as I read the cursive writing that spells out, *Baby Hensley*.

With a knowing smirk, and the darkest of eyes, gaze sending shivers skittering across my skin, Duke asks, 'Are you ready for the ride of your life?'

33

Cherry

I marvel at the freshly inked outline of a horse now permanently on the inside of my wrist, unable to contain my smile.

'Here you go.' Duke comes up behind me, reaching for my wrist gently so he can wrap up the tattoo, ensuring it keeps clean and heals well, even if it is only small. I'm sure the tattoo artist is supposed to do this, but since Duke seems to know the artist well from the countless tattoos peppering his own body, I imagine he doesn't mind letting Duke do so instead.

As he tends to my tattoo, I let myself lean back into his chest, basking in the harmony of being with him again.

'All done.' Duke punctuates his care with a kiss to my parting. 'Time to go.'

I'm still trying to adjust to these new public displays of affection over the last few days. Knowing we don't have to hide anymore – even if we are out of Willow Ridge today, so it's less likely people we know will be around.

We're still keeping things unaffectionate at work and around friends until we work out the best time to tell Wyatt, but when it's just the two of us, out and about, we let the odd touch slip out.

I bite down on my lip as I turn to Duke, watching him grab our helmets off the side of the counter where we left them – they fit perfectly into the dark, metal décor of the tattoo studio. We thank the studio as we leave, and when we reach Duke's bike, he plops my helmet on my head, flipping up the visor to flash a grin at me.

'Has anyone ever told you how hot you look in a helmet?' he asks, winding his arm around my waist to pull me into him again. God, Duke Bennett is a needy man when he's letting himself show his feelings. But I love it. I love *him*.

'Treat me right, and maybe I'll keep it on tonight,' I joke, filtering my hand under his T-shirt to relish in the feel of his muscles. And to teasingly skim my nails across his skin.

Duke groans. 'Bane of my life, Baby Hensley. I mean it.' He pulls away as I giggle, and adjusts his own helmet, climbing onto the motorcycle so I can jump on after him.

Luckily, after a few rides this week, I'm finally getting used to the way I need to move and lean with him on the bike. We take a longer route home, driving down deserted backroads with shadowy mountains for backdrops, and nothing but the roar of Duke's bike echoing through the emerald trees. By the time we're closer to Willow Ridge, the sun is almost set, dipping behind the mountains, amber rays streaming down them like rivers of gold. Duke brings us to a stop in the same place we watched the stars two months ago, their light breaking through the darkening cornflower sky above.

We climb off the bike where Duke stops beside the trees, remove our helmets, then walk to the other edge of the road to admire the view ahead. To behold the small, simple town below that brought us together.

'You know, the stars are actually my second favourite thing about Willow Ridge,' I admit, leaning my head against Duke's shoulder.

'Oh yeah?' he asks, running his hand up my arm and squeezing me closer.

I turn to him, staying in his embrace as his arm slides around me, and tilt my face up to catch his dark gaze. 'You're number one.'

'Likewise.' Duke doesn't hesitate to drop his mouth to mine, capturing my lips in a tender kiss. The fullness of his mouth against mine still sets off fireworks, sparkles fluttering in my stomach until they descend into a burning desire.

Duke's fingers trail down my arms until they find my hips, digging into the soft flesh to drag me closer to him. I can feel the impatience in his touch, the growing need in the heavier strokes of his tongue as it dances with mine. Then, Duke rips his lips away to kiss my neck. The hot press of his lips against where my pulse flutters sends an urgent shot of need straight to my core. One that won't be easily quelled. My fingers clutch at his back, a greedy whimper leaving my lips when his hardness grows against my stomach, too far away from where I need him. Where I'm aching with desire.

'I want you,' I breathe out, fingers digging into his muscles.

'Soon,' Duke whispers against my neck between kisses, drawing his lips back up to mine to take them again.

'Now,' I counter, and catch his bottom lip between my teeth. Tightening his grip on my waist, Duke groans, capturing my mouth again with a crash of lips and teeth. He takes and takes, tongue colliding with mine and exploring every inch of my mouth.

My fingers drop to his belt, hooking around the buckle to try to loosen it—

'Baby.' Duke pulls away and grabs my hands. I catch his eyes, pupils so blown out they could blend into the emerging night sky. 'Slow down. There ain't anywhere to do anything here. Let me get you home and I'll give you whatever you want.' He gestures to the vastness around us, the empty, silent dirt road, with nothing but us and his black motorcycle filling the quiet space.

I worry my lip as my gaze snags on the bike's leather seat. 'What about your bike?'

Duke's brow furrows. 'What about my—' He stops himself, eyes darkening as he angles his head at me. A smirk slowly plays out on his lips. The silence of the valley around us begins to close in, a shiver of anticipation whispering down my spine when Duke's hands reach my face. One cups my jaw, a thumb running tenderly over my bottom lip, as the other hand weaves through my hair, fingers tightening. Gravel laces his voice as he asks, 'Do you want me to fuck you on my bike, Cherry?'

He angles my head up to him more. A gasp rushes from my lips. 'Do you need me *that* badly that you want me to bend you over my bike and fuck you out in the open, where anyone could drive by and see? Would you like that?'

Oh fuck. Just the thought makes my thighs tremble.

'Yes.' I nod, letting my teeth sink into my lip. My chest heaves with a shuddering breath. 'So badly.'

The words have barely left my lips before Duke is walking us back across the road, his hands never leaving my quaking body, nor do his wild eyes. We bump against the end of his bike, and he twists me in his grasp, calloused hands scraping against the gap between my top and jeans, the sensation making my body beg to feel more of his skin.

Duke lines me up with the motorcycle, pressing his solid frame into my back, letting me feel every hard inch of how much he wants this too. Deft hands make quick work of the button and zipper of my jeans, before he carefully slides them over my ass, hooking his fingers under my thong to take it with him. He's on a mission – any hint of the man who wanted to take things *slow* vanished.

The summer evening breeze caresses my bare lower half, the nerves of being so on show starting to flutter in my stomach. But the whole time we've been here, no one's driven past. We're covered by the shadows of the trees and mountains, as well as the darkening night.

Duke sweeps my hair over one shoulder and trails hard kisses against my neck, then whispers against the shell of my ear, 'Hold on tight, baby.'

My hips hinge forward automatically, and my hands grab at the side of the seat. Every inch of me is shaking with need.

Once I'm fully bent over, everything bared to Duke, I hear him hiss. 'Fuck, Cherry. Look at you.' He swipes a finger through my wetness, making my hips buck when he gives my clit a light circle. After a few more featherlight touches, he slowly slides a finger into me, my body screaming *finally* at the sensation of him filling me. With slow, lazy strokes of his finger, Duke rasps, 'So wet for me. Are you ready to take me, baby?'

'Yes,' I breathe out, pushing my hips back against him so his finger thrusts deeper.

'Greedy,' he chuckles wickedly, and gives my ass a slap, before pulling his finger out. The sound of his belt and zipper has my body tensing with anticipation. But then he curses and groans, 'Fuck. A condom, Cherry. I thought I had one in my wallet.'

I look over my shoulder at him. 'We don't need one. I've been tested and I'm on birth control.'

'I've been tested too,' Duke confirms, swallowing.

'I want you to fuck me bare,' I whimper. His eyes flash and nostrils flare in response. 'Don't hold back. Give me everything you have, Duke Bennett.'

And with that, Duke filters his fingers through my hair, slowly wrapping it around his hand until he has a tight grip on me. He angles my head back, then leans over my body to give my earlobe a nip and whisper, 'Anything for you, Baby Hensley.'

My body jolts at the feel of his hard cock suddenly nudging my entrance. It's barely even touching me, but I can already feel myself having to stretch. A whimper escapes my lips as he begins to push, stars sparking in my vision, in my core – the pleasure already overwhelming me so much that my breath catches in my throat.

'You're gonna have to be a good girl for me, Cherry,

and breathe,' Duke talks me through it as he slowly begins to move, sheathing himself deeper and deeper, pleasure rippling through me with each gentle thrust. I try to focus on my breathing as my body struggles to accommodate his size, screaming at both the stretch and the deliciousness of it.

'That's it, baby. That's my girl.' Duke runs a hand down my back, then trails his fingers around my stomach until he finally reaches my clit. With each of his thrusts he circles my clit, pressing down to add even more pressure, speeding up the movement as he drives into me quicker. Harder. *Deeper.*

'Fuck, Duke,' I moan, not even caring that it echoes down the valley.

His only response is to fuck me harder, his thrusts becoming even more punishing, so much so that my legs turn to Jell-O, giving out and letting the bike take all my weight.

'God, Cherry, you feel so fucking good,' he groans, using his grip on my hair to pull me further back into each of his thrusts, the harsh slap of my ass against him ringing out. It's lewd and dirty and it turns me on even more – this rough, uncontrolled version of Duke behind me. 'You know what you look like, baby? Bent over my bike, taking my cock so well? You look like *mine*.'

He emphasises such with a slap of my ass, the pain sending a jolt straight to my clit. I scream out, suddenly feeling myself tipping over the edge as he continues to strum my clit, still pounding into me with rough, hard strokes.

'Duke, I—'

'Yes, baby? Are you gonna be a good girl and come for me?' His rumbling voice sending shivers across my skin with his filthy words is all I need to fall. Stars explode in my vision as my body tenses, a rush of ecstasy waving through me, my thighs trembling with pleasure.

I think I just died and went to heaven.

'Jesus, Cherry, that was so hot.'

I've barely registered Duke's voice when I feel him pulling my jeans down further, helping me out of them one foot at a time. Then he's picking me up, my legs instinctively circling his hips as he hooks both hands under my thighs. Throwing a leg over, Duke settles himself onto the seat of the bike, bringing me down onto his lap. His cock slides against me, jolting a spark of pleasure through my still-sensitive clit.

My arousal coats his shaft, every brutal inch of him glistening so temptingly. How can I still want more of him when he's just absolutely ruined me? When I've just seen more stars in my vision from that orgasm than all the night skies I've ever witnessed?

Duke takes my chin between his finger and thumb, guiding my gaze back up to his eyes. They're glassy and heavy-lidded with desire, while his full lips are swollen. 'Ready to give me another one?'

'*Another* one?' The words shudder out with my breath. My whirs – I can't even fathom the idea of being able to come again.

Duke chuckles, all deep and promising plenty more pleasure. 'I told you I was going to make up for all the orgasms you've missed out on.' His large hands settle on my hips, splaying out and gripping onto my flesh. Slowly, his thick thighs bulging as he balances us on the bike, Duke lifts my hips and angles his own so that his cock lines up with my entrance. The contact of him against my core makes every one of my muscles tighten, heat licking up my spine. 'And I think this pretty little pussy deserves more than just one, don't you?'

I swallow thickly as the head of his cock presses lightly into me, Duke still taking my weight as he holds me over him. It might have taken a while for my body to stretch for his size earlier, but I know I'm so wet right now, that there's no way he won't slide straight into me, giving me every punishing inch at once.

'Yes, I – I want more,' I admit, brows drawing together as my body screams to feel him inside of me again, trembling from the teasing of his cock beneath me.

'Attagirl.' Duke catches my mouth just as he drops my hips, impaling me. Pleasure rips through me, tearing away my sanity as he fills me instantly, as if that orgasm only doubled the sensations I can feel. I'm so overwhelmingly full – Duke's cock twitches inside of me while his tongue lashes at mine.

I struggle to return his kisses, needing respite from being so full.

'Rock your hips for me, baby.' Duke guides my hips forward, pulling me towards him so that his cock slides inside of me, pressing against my G-spot, a high-pitched moan spilling from my lips as a result. I continue with the rhythm he set, rolling my hips as his hands settle on my ass, gripping my cheeks to give me more momentum.

'Fuck!' I call out when Duke pulls me down so that I'm even more flush against him, the pleasure of him filling me bursting with intensity. And when he lifts a hand to start playing with my clit again, I know I'm a goner. The sensation is overwhelming as we rock on his bike, every time I grind my hips his cock glides inside of me, and I'm barrelling closer and closer to release.

'Can I please come inside of you, baby?' he asks breathlessly, still circling my clit with one hand as his other grips my hip, fingers tightening in my flesh.

'Yes, yes, yes,' I chant, like it's the only thing I've ever wanted, to have him marking me both inside and out. 'I'm so close.'

He picks up the pace, swiping my clit faster, while that bubble of pleasure grows and grows inside of me, so close to bursting—

'Oh my God, Duke!' I scream out as it explodes, and Duke has to catch me to stop me from falling back. I'm shuddering from the pleasure in Duke's grip as he groans, hard muscles tensing and cock jerking inside of me as he finishes too.

Our foreheads rest against each other as we try to catch our breaths, hot air mingling in the inches between our lips.

'My God, you're incredible,' he breathes out, elongating each word as his eyes rake over me, where we're still joined. His fingers pulse against my hips. 'I know sex on a motorcycle wasn't on your bucket list, but fuck me, it definitely should've been because that was the best sex of my life.'

I tick the air in front of him, my grin lazy and satisfied.

34

Cherry

'Cherry, this is gorgeous,' Rory breathes out as she flicks through the images on my iPad, eyes devouring all the designs I've created for a possible barn conversion wedding venue at Sunset Ranch. 'You came up with all of this?'

I chew my bottom lip as my smile threatens to overtake me, a strange rush of pride at my designs coaxing it out. A light rain patters at the windows of the main ranch house where we're spending the afternoon, waiting smugly while Wyatt and the ranchers have the unfortunate job of moving cattle soon. The unexpected storm that had the town at a standstill from power cuts and blistering wind yesterday wreaked havoc on some of the fences. Obviously, Duke ran at the opportunity to be an extra pair of helping hands when Wyatt called this morning for a favour – my brother oblivious to the fact that Duke was answering while I was naked in bed next to him – so I thought I'd keep Rory company meanwhile.

'Yeah,' I explain, leaning over on the couch to swipe

back to the original mood board I put together when my idea first bloomed. 'I had the idea a little while back – once the retreat at Sunset Ranch really picked up – and thought it might be a nice addition sometime in the future. It was just an idea to start with, more for my portfolio if anything, but now you guys are engaged and, well, I thought you might want to use it.'

'Aw, Cherry. Thank you.' Rory juts out her bottom lip, her hazel eyes adopting a shine. Not a second later she's dropping the iPad to her lap and pulling me into her arms. The couch gives a creak as our weight tumbles to one side, making us both giggle.

Once we're finished with our embrace, Rory sinks back into the cushions and picks up the iPad again, glancing through all the pictures and sketches – long wooden tables with vases of wildflowers dotted along them, the hay store floor above removed to leave large beams where twinkling lights can be twirled around, sheer material draped from the rafters. A romantic haven wrapped up in the rusticity of the very place the two of them met.

'I can't believe I didn't even think about having a wedding venue here. It would be so beautiful . . .' Rory's gaze whisks off out the window, towards the sunshine barely bleeding through the puffy grey clouds crowning the mountains ahead. Even on a dull day like today, there's still something magical about Sunset Ranch – golden light breaking through the clouds wherever it can while shadowy mountains stand proud. A testament, perhaps, to the dreams that are never given up on here, just like Rory and Wyatt's wellness retreat.

Rory toys with her engagement ring. 'It sure would be

sweet to get married on the ranch that brought Wyatt and me together. The place we've built our lives around.'

I reach over to squeeze her arm. 'Well, the designs and plans are all yours. And I'll help any way I can if you decide you want to do it. It will take a while to complete, and some money, obviously, but if you're happy to wait a bit before getting married, I don't see why you guys couldn't do it in time for your own wedding.'

'I can't wait to run it by Wyatt.' Rory wiggles in her seat, beaming. 'I bet he'll love it. He's always going on about how proud he is of your designs.'

I roll my lips to temper my smile. 'See it as my early wedding gift for the two of you.'

A feline smirk overtakes Rory then as she gives me a nudge. 'And just think, maybe you and Duke could use it one day too.'

'Woah there,' I caution her, slipping the iPad back out of her hands. Even if the suggestion did have my heart fluttering. 'Let's not get ahead of ourselves. I'm only twenty-one and it's super early days.'

'And you should probably tell Wyatt first too,' Rory mumbles, reaching for her Diet Coke on the coffee table. I try to fight the way my shoulders instantly pitch higher. Tighter.

'Well, obviously,' I laugh out, though her perked brow suggests my tone didn't quite match my expression.

'When, um, are you thinking of doing that, by the way?' Rory asks, spinning her drink can in her hands while her eyes flick between mine and the floor. She nibbles her bottom lip when I don't have an immediate answer, my jaw hanging open, the only sound filling the air the faint whistling of the breeze and the smattering of light raindrops against the windows.

'Sorry,' she then rushes out. 'I'm not trying to pry or tell you what to do but don't you think it's time? When you and Duke were exploring what was going on between you, I get the secrecy, but I don't think there's any reason to hide it now. You're together and happy.' Gentleness touches her smile. 'I think Wyatt should know that.'

With a sigh, I slump back into the couch and stare up at the ceiling, letting the memories of the summer with Duke sweep through my mind. 'Yeah, I know you're right. We said we were going to – before I go back to college, anyway, but I just haven't pushed it.' Pressing my lips together, I rub a hand over my forehead, before turning back to Rory. 'I guess I've just been enjoying the secrecy of it. There's not a lot of things in my life that my family – or the whole town for that matter – aren't involved in, and as soon as we tell Wyatt, as soon as we tell anyone, it's just another bunch of people's opinions on my life I don't need.'

'I'm sorry, Cherry. I guess I've just become one of those people.' Rory scoots across the couch, cosying into me until she's practically moulded to my shape, then she threads her fingers through mine. She gives my hand a squeeze, which I return, knowing she means well. 'But I'm just trying to be a good friend. I totally understand what you're saying, and I know I said Wyatt will be fine, but I just think it would be better to tell him sooner than later. If he doesn't handle it well, you don't want to be leaving for college on a bad note.'

'Yeah, I guess so.' I nod, soaking up her words.

Rory's brows draw in. 'Maybe it's a good way of showing him that he doesn't need to be involved all the time. You're not asking for his permission to date his best friend, you're showing him that's what's happening, and he has to deal with it.' A grin springs across her face. 'Show everyone who's really the boss in the Hensley family.'

A chuckle chirps out of both of us, and I lean my head against her shoulder as I consider such. Because maybe she's right – whether Wyatt is happy with me and Duke dating isn't going to change the fact that we are. He'll have to come to terms with it eventually, and he'll have to realise, along with the rest of my family, that they can't control every aspect of my life, even if they do it with good meaning. Besides, what better person for me to be with than the man who not only loves me, but my family too?

'You know what,' Rory perks up. 'Why don't you guys come over tomorrow for dinner? We can have a nice, relaxing evening and you can tell Wyatt then. Plus, I'll be there as a mediator because he can never be angry at me.' She bats her lashes, and I can't help but snort, knowing just how easily my brother caves to her. A wellness retreat was never his plans for Sunset Ranch until she turned up last year.

'Okay, yeah, let's do that.' I take a deep breath in, one of finality – that tonight is the last night Duke and I remain a secret. That tonight is the last night I hold back from what I truly want. 'I'll talk to Duke tonight and hopefully he'll be fine.'

Rory chuckles, patting me on the arm. 'Girl, that man is obsessed with you. He'd do anything for you.'

35

Duke

'You've got that look on your face like you're about to change your mind.' Cherry throws her hands to her hips, motorcycle helmet tucked under her arm. 'Wyatt will be fine. And if he isn't, he'll just throw a little temper tantrum for a day and then he'll get over it.'

She levels a look at me, standing next to my motorcycle outside the barn on the Nash family ranch where I usually keep them.

'Surprisingly, that's not what I'm the most worried about right now.' Even if it meant my sleep last night was more restless than usual. Good job I had Cherry beside me to keep my mind occupied when I was awake. I wave my hand through the heavy humidity in the air. 'It feels like it's gonna rain again.'

Full grey clouds crowd the sky, lighter than they were yesterday, but still carrying the threat of rain. And the last thing I need is letting Cherry drive us to Wyatt's on my motorcycle to become any more dangerous with poor weather. It's not quite the storm that had the town at a standstill from power cuts and blistering wind a couple of days ago, but the drizzly and dull aftermath still isn't promising.

If I had it my way, we'd still be holed up in my apartment, spending another day in sweats on the couch, Cherry's head resting against my chest, never leaving my embrace. Soaking up every last minute together before she goes back to college. Before Wyatt might decide I'm not worthy of his sister, or his friendship . . .

But I'm not the only one in this relationship, and I promised after a few sessions teaching her how to ride my motorcycle that she could take us on a longer journey, like her bucket list intended. At least I could dictate which roads we took – there wasn't a chance in hell I'd have her driving through the middle of town. Regardless of whether it's countless trucks or too many onlookers, the dirt roads between Lucky Star Ranch and Sunset Ranch are much safer.

Besides, as much as I love looking after Cherry, I understand that I have to let her try things, to trust that she'll figure things out instead of holding her back like she's used to everyone else doing. I want nothing more than for her to feel as strong and beautiful as I see her, and if that means giving her a chance to ride my properly – one chance – then I'll do it.

Anything for Baby Hensley.

I've taken some pretty damn big risks this summer and look where they got me – with the girl of my dreams.

'Duke.' Cherry sighs at me, yet there's a smile there – albeit an exasperated one, but still a smile.

In fact, I can't remember the last time I haven't seen her smile. Especially when I'm telling her how much I love her. It's become worryingly addictive – watching the way her eyes light up, deep umber and chestnut brown swirling in her irises, while her grin spreads out each time I say it. Plus, the way her skin prickles each time I whisper it in her ear when we're tangled in the sheets together also gives me as much of a high. I'm basically drowning in dopamine by this point, which is probably also why she convinced me so easily to let her ride my motorcycle over to Wyatt and Rory's this afternoon.

'It's been a whole forty-eight hours since the storm passed. It'll be fine. If we don't do this now, I might not get a chance before I go back to college, and you promised. Besides, I need all the adrenaline I can before facing Wyatt.'

'Yeah, you and me both,' I concede, deciding it's worth it when Cherry grins and practically leaps onto the motorcycle, popping her helmet over her head, *Baby Hensley* printed on the back.

Maybe I should've got *mine* written on there instead . . . either way, she looks too damn good on my bike. Long legs straddling the seat, poured into a pair of tight Wranglers that emphasise the soft curve of her hips and waist, and that torturously shiny black hair flowing from beneath her helmet.

Fuck, if I don't get on this bike we're going to end up with a repeat of the other evening, and I'm not sure if our luck runs as far as not getting caught having sex outside *twice*. Nor would Wyatt appreciate us being late to dinner for that . . .

I throw my own helmet on and settle on the motorcycle behind her, winding my arms around her waist and tugging her into me. Just giving myself a second to relish the privilege of getting to hold such a beautiful life in my hands. I run her through all the controls that we've gone over previously – clutch, gears, throttle, brakes – and get her to relay back all the other safety points I've explained before.

Once I'm happy that she remembers everything she needs to, Cherry settles into the seat, getting as comfortable as possible and giggling when she wiggles her ass a little too much against me. I give her waist a quick squeeze in response for teasing me.

But before I know it, she's started the engine, letting it warm up. Carefully, she shifts into gear and lets up on the clutch, pulling back on the throttle and we're moving. The pure joy in her laugh as we start riding, albeit slowly, pushes away all my worries about today, leaving me with nothing but love and admiration for this beautiful woman riding my bike.

As Cherry gets more comfortable, she starts to pick up speed, and her movements as we turn become more natural, no longer relying on me so much to help. The emptiness of the roads, rolling fields surrounding us, has calm washing over me as the breeze whistles past – and being here with Cherry, the woman I love, multiplies that tenfold. Even if the clouds leftover from the storm have blocked out the sun, I've still got the glorious light that Cherry brings into my life keeping away any shadows that might crawl into my mind.

And I hope tonight Wyatt will see that – the joy she

brings me, the safety I hope I give her. That we're meant to be. That we could ride back tonight knowing nothing stands in our way. No more fear of losing anyone.

Soon, the country roads begin to narrow as we get closer to Sunset Ranch, barely a couple of minutes away. As we approach a tight corner, Cherry slows down like she should but then gives it a bit too much throttle just as we finish rounding it and looks down at the gears—

I must see the fallen tree before she does.

'Cherry – brake!' My hands fly forward to press down on the brakes over hers, but she's already lost control of the bike, the wheels slipping beneath us—

Time slows as our world tips.

I hit the ground first and force every bit of strength into keeping hold of Cherry tightly against me.

We skid along the ground with the bike, stones and gravel tearing at my legs, until we descend into a roll, slowing as my bike crashes into the trees lining the road. Dust and gravel fills my vision, and my arms tremble from the might it's taking to keep Cherry close to me. Not to let her go. Never.

When we finally come to a stop, pain creeps into my limbs, spreading hot through my shoulder, which takes my weight as I lie on my side, Cherry clutched to me. My first few breaths feel like daggers in my lungs, but it doesn't stop me from moving, from releasing my tight hold on Cherry so I can flip up my visor and check her over.

'Cherry? Are you okay?' I ask, voice hoarse.

My head thumps with each second.

She mumbles something to me as I lay her out on the

ground, using the gentlest of touches in case she's hurting. Each movement sends my shoulder into agony, pain shooting across my chest.

'What was that, baby?' I question again, lifting her visor too – I'm cautious not to remove her helmet in case she's got a head or neck injury. I try to reassure her, 'I'm here. I've got you.'

But I'm met with fluttering, unfocused eyes. This time, she doesn't answer me. And when her body seizes up under my touch and begins to shake, I know exactly why.

36

Duke

'Sir, you're going to have to calm down,' the nurse at the desk cautions me, crossing her arms to signal she is *not* going to put up with any more of my bullshit today. The deep frown marring her face and shadows beneath her eyes suggests I'm not the only visitor that's had her exasperated either. 'Unless you're family, we can't let you in while she's not awake. I've told you twice already.'

My fingers clutch at the edge of the desk, begging for stability as the images of paramedics wheeling Cherry down a different corridor to me as she started having a second seizure once we arrived at the hospital torment my mind. My heart jumps into my throat knowing I wasn't by her side as medical staff pulled me away for my own injuries. How they didn't let me hold her hand. I barely managed a few minutes with the doctor before I was storming out to find out where they'd taken her. If she was going to be okay.

'Please, you don't understand—'

'Now,' the nurse raises her voice this time, throwing a hand to her hip. I immediately shrink back, recognising that I'm being offered my last chance here. 'If you know any family we can contact, then we can call them and could let you in with them. If they allow it.'

Family.

Wyatt.

But he'll know. He'll know what I've done. I'll have to tell him that his sister is in hospital because of me.

That she's battered and bruised because of me.

That she's just had two seizures because of me.

That she'll have to give up her driver's licence again for a while because of me.

That she could've *died* because of me.

Every dream I let myself have for the future, Cherry gracing each one, shattered the moment I saw that fallen tree. It wasn't my past life that flashed before my eyes in the moments prior to crashing, but the future I'd never get, because I was stupid enough to give into temptation. And now it's all gone. Slipping out of my fingers as I held Cherry, as I carried her from the wreckage, watching her consciousness slip from her too.

I'd been here before.

Marching down a dirt road, Cherry in my arms, as I try to catch up with the ambulance on its way. I don't care that I've left my bike behind. All that matters is her.

Each step has agony biting at every one of my limbs. Blood rushes in my ears, my heart racing so fast it might beat out of my chest. Even as my legs tremble, my arms quake, love powers me on.

'I'm sorry. I've got you,' I repeat to Cherry, over and

over, as she lay unconscious against my chest, cradled in my hold. I need her to know she's okay, that I'll always protect her. I know I didn't do a good job of it today, but I'll make it up to her. I'll walk as far and as long as it takes to get her to safety.

Even as the rain begins to pour.

All this pain because instead of staying behind that line that I drew all those years ago, out of respect for my best friend, I rode past it, so far that it's invisible now.

I finally push away from the desk with a sharp sigh that has the muscles in my chest spasming in agony.

My surroundings start to blur again, the ringing in my ears picking up. Rain lashes at the windows around the waiting area, like my fears are trying to claw in to take me away. Roiling nerves fill my stomach, and my legs are already starting to take me towards the exit.

To run.

But . . . I can't. Not this time.

I almost lost Cherry when I let my fear get the best of me before. Even if it means upsetting Wyatt – hell, even if it upsets the whole of Willow Ridge – it's the right thing to do. To show Cherry that I'm always here for her. That I won't push her away this time. That she's worth losing everything for.

Even if it means having to let her go too.

I drop down into one of the plastic seats of the waiting area behind me. The jolting action sends red-hot pain slicing through my shoulder, and the nurse just tuts at me when I groan. I swear there's a brief curve to her lips, no doubt thinking, *maybe that will shut you up.* God knows I deserve it.

With trembling hands, I fish my phone out of my pocket, still surprised the screen only suffered a few cracks considering Cherry's was ruined. The torn skin of my hands sting as I swipe through all the missed calls and numerous text messages from both Rory and Wyatt already. I swallow thickly as I pull up Wyatt's number, my thumb hovering over the call button.

How the fuck do I explain this?

With another ragged breath, I scrape a hand over my head.

It doesn't matter how I explain it, all that matters is that I have to. I owe it to Wyatt and Cherry. To be honest.

Finally, I press call.

Wyatt answers almost instantly. 'Dude, where the hell are you? Have you heard from Cherry? We've been trying to get a hold of both of you.' The faint panic already lacing his words forces me to blow out another deep breath. When I don't respond immediately, his voice hardens. *'Duke?'*

'I'm at the hospital,' I explain.

'What – are you okay? Is Cherry okay?'

Keep breathing, Duke. You can handle this.

'We're fine. But we got in an accident. On my bike.' Each word comes out laboured, the hand not holding my phone scrunched into a tight fist.

'Rory, grab my keys!' Wyatt suddenly shouts, the scuff of footsteps across the wooden floor already audible as he hurries around the house.

'What's happened?' Rory's voice rings out distantly on the end of the line.

'We need to go,' Wyatt insists.

'Neither of us are seriously hurt,' I try to reassure him, knowing that despite her seizures, as far as the paramedics were aware, Cherry's injuries weren't serious. 'But Cherry . . . she – she had a fit after the crash and—'

'Why the hell was she on your bike, Duke?' There's a gravelly edge to his voice now, like subdued thunder, the same kind I listened to only a couple of days ago with Cherry in my arms. 'Duke?'

'She'd been wanting to learn to ride for a while—'

'Why does that matter to you?' Exasperation makes his voice rougher.

'Hey,' it's Rory's voice again in the background, 'let me drive.'

The jingle of keys sounds before a front door thuds. Pounding rain fills the phoneline, rushing sounds and heavy footfalls, until Rory and Wyatt must reach the safety of their truck. The distant rumble of an engine cuts in.

'Jesus, Duke.' Wyatt breathes out on a sharp, shaky exhale. 'You know I wouldn't want Cherry putting herself in danger like that.'

'I know, I'm sorry. I thought the roads would be fine. We were coming over together, to talk to you—'

'Talk to me about what?' Wyatt asks.

My throat is too tight, too blocked up to push the words out.

He presses again, 'About *what*, Duke?'

'About . . . us.'

Wyatt's only response is to whisper back, repeating the word *us,* as if it's a foreign word he's trying to decipher, when in truth it's a reality he never expected. Perhaps even never wanted.

I push on, 'Look, I can explain better when you get here, just – they won't let me see her unless there's family and—'

'You're supposed to be my best friend,' is all he says, his voice stripped bare of all the previous anger, leaving it hoarse and drowning with disappointment. 'What have you done?'

Then the phone line goes dead and my heart drops.

All those years worrying about Wyatt finding out I liked Cherry crumble away as if they were nothing. Insignificant in the present moment while his little sister lies unconscious in a hospital bed because of me. Especially when he storms into the hospital, taking one look at me, my bloodied clothes, and walks straight to the desk without a word. Rory mouths to me, *I'm sorry*, as the nurse directs Wyatt to Cherry's room, but she doesn't get a chance to say more as her hand is interlinked with Wyatt's and he whisks her off, leaving me alone in the waiting room with nothing but my world shattering around me.

37

Cherry

It sounds like someone's poured thousands of pebbles over the roof. Their tumbling is thunderous, rattling down the walls around me. Each second of clattering causes the dull ache behind my brow to intensify, the throbbing falling in sync with the rhythmic beeping. I want to open my eyes, but even forcing my chest to lift with each breath seems too large a feat. My limbs are lifeless, my bones as heavy as stone.

Maybe I should just go back to sleep.

Except that goddamn beeping sound won't stop.

If I can just force my eyes open then—

Too bright.

Taking in a sharp breath, I squeeze my eyes shut again. Trying again, I gradually ease my eyes open, taking in the brightness around me. After a few seconds and blinks, everything turns to a dull grey. Through the window opposite me, nothing but marbled storm clouds fill the sky, casting gloomy shadows through the room. Like all the colour in the world has been sucked away. Rain pummels relentlessly against the glass panes, the occasional large drop smacking the window.

I gulp down a painful breath of air and push past the exhaustion enough to let my eyes drift down. That's when I see them and my heart jolts.

Wyatt and Rory.

Slumped against each other in the two chairs opposite, hands entangled. Rory's head rests on Wyatt's shoulder, his arm around her, while his leg bobs. Storm clouds fill Wyatt's eyes too, wild and rough, overshadowed by the lines creasing his forehead.

One further glance down and the white sheets offer a blank canvas below my bandaged hands. Wiggling my fingers only sends shooting pain through my bones, whatever grazes and torn skin lie beneath the bandages stinging. A shiver runs through me at the sensation of the cannula stuck in the back of my hand, and I force my gaze away.

Back to my brother. And my best friend.

'Hey,' I croak out.

Both of their heads shoot up, bloodshot eyes widening as they behold me. Tears prick behind my eyes at the deep exhaustion and relief that paints their faces. It takes no more than a couple of seconds before they're both at either side of the bed.

'Hey.' Rory perches on the edge. 'How are you feeling?'

My gaze strains to flick between them, hoping some semblance of a memory of what put me here will surface. 'What . . .'

'You were in a motorcycle crash,' Rory explains, her

intonation on the last word seeking clarification. 'Other than the cuts on your hands and probably a few bruises, you came out of it relatively unscathed, but you had a seizure afterwards.'

'*Two* seizures,' Wyatt corrects, his tone brisk.

That explains the hospital and lack of memory. And energy.

'What the hell were you doing on a motorcycle, Cherry? You don't know how to drive them. Do you realise how dangerous that is?' Wyatt asks. He doesn't sit on the bed like Rory, just stands there instead, arms crossed, a deep frown still marring his face, no softness in his concern for me. His broad frame is so tense, I'm certain he's shaking from the strain of it.

'I think—' Rory reaches across to place a hand on Wyatt's arm and shoots him a wide-eyed look '—Cherry is probably pretty tired and confused right now. I'm sure she'll explain later. When she's feeling up to it.'

A sudden flash of thick arms circling my waist lances through my mind.

Then his voice, *Cherry – brake!*

Panic spears through me, forcing me to shoot upright in the bed. 'Where is he?'

Rory almost falls off the bed at my abrupt movement.

'Oh my God.' My hands tremble as I bring one to my rattling chest. 'Is he hurt?'

'He's fine,' Wyatt grits out.

'How do you know? Where is he?' My voice is hoarse, scratching at my throat. Rory carefully places a hand on my shoulder, a tender, comforting touch as she eases me back against the pillows. She furrows her brow, messy copper waves bouncing as she nods. 'Cherry, I promise, he's okay.'

My chest heaves while my eyes shoot around at the wires on me, the machines I'm linked up to, ruining a quick escape to find him. 'But he took the brunt of the crash—'

'I told you he's fine.' Wyatt's jaw clenches, arms knotting tighter over his chest. 'What I wanna know is why the hell you were on Duke's motorcycle in the first place.'

I don't miss the accusation in his tone.

Does he think this is Duke's fault?

'Wyatt,' Rory scolds him, cutting him a quick glare. There's fire in that look that rarely touches her eyes given she's usually the most positive one out of us all. 'We said we'd talk about it later. Cherry's *just* woken up.'

Wyatt drills his gaze back at Rory, and they stay there in a silent stand-off for a few seconds, before I blurt out, 'He was just helping me. It's not his fault.'

With a furrowed brow, Wyatt scoffs, returning his attention back to me. 'Helping you with what, though, Cherry? That's what I don't get. Why are you guys spending time together suddenly? You never have before.'

I rub a shaky hand over my forehead, the throbbing intensifying again. 'With a bucket list Montana made me. It's just a silly thing I was doing for the summer to make me feel stronger and—'

'Not the one that was in your jacket,' Wyatt practically begs, eyes splaying open to emphasise his plea.

My mouth dries out. 'What do you mean?'

Wyatt clutches at his head as all the hardness in his expression washes away. The moving storm clouds outside the window cast him in further shadows as he mumbles, 'The doctors gave us your belongings . . . Your phone was smashed but there was a list in your pocket with it . . .'

'Wyatt,' Rory tries again, angling her head this time as she bulges her eyes at him.

Groaning, Wyatt pinches the bridge of his nose and turns away, several sharp exhales coming from him. My eyes flick to Rory's, and she tries to push a soft, reassuring smile through her freckled cheeks, but it does little to quell the trembling in my chest.

Finally, Wyatt faces me again. An eerie kind of calm appears to have washed over him, his face devoid of expression. It only makes him seem angrier. '*Please* tell me Duke hasn't been helping you with *that* list.'

'Wyatt,' I beg. 'Don't make this a big deal.'

'Don't make this a big deal?' He barks out a laugh of disbelief. 'You're my *little sister*, Cherry, and he's my best friend. I – *Fuck*. So what? All the helping me protect my little sister was just so he could take her for himself?' He wipes a hand down his face, voice pitching higher as it cracks. 'Jesus Christ, the stuff on that list. I can't believe he'd do this.'

My heart lurches into my throat, at how his words undermine the pureness of Duke's soul. Of every intention he's ever had with me. 'It wasn't like that. You know he wouldn't do that. And you're making it sound like I had no say in this.'

Wyatt scoffs, throwing his hands in the air. 'You're *six* years younger than him, Cherry. He's known you since you were a kid.'

'But I'm not a kid anymore.' My voice is croaky as I raise it, determined not to cower today, no matter how exhausted I feel. Sitting up in bed again, I imbue my backbone with determination and harden my voice. 'I'm twenty-one. I'm graduating college next year. I can make my own decisions. *I'm* the one who started it all, anyway, not him.'

'She's right, Wyatt,' Rory adds on, rounding the bed to be by his side. She runs her hand up his arm, his attention instantly falling to her face, expression and dark eyes slowly softening. 'This is *Duke* we're talking about. You know how much he cares about you. He wouldn't do anything to try and hurt you *or* Cherry.'

Wyatt pokes the inside of his cheek with his tongue, volleying glances between me and Rory. 'So you *both* kept this from me.' Then he whispers to himself, 'I can't believe *he* kept this from me.'

'That's because I don't have to run everything by you, Wyatt. I know you're looking out for me, I know it's because you love me, but I . . .' My throat tightens, eyes stinging. I tilt my head back for a brief moment, a shaky breath filtering from my lips. 'Sometimes it makes me feel like everyone just sees me as this weak little girl that can't handle things for herself. Whether you like it or not, I've liked Duke for years, and he's really been there for me this summer. He helps me feel strong. *Alive.* Like I shouldn't have to hide away from what I want, from who I am, no matter what others think. He lets me be unapologetically myself and worships me for it.'

'Jesus.' Wyatt sighs. He takes several steps back to lean against the wall. 'I mean . . . I could tell you had a bit of a crush on him when you were younger, but I thought that was just a phase.'

'Wyatt, I don't have a *crush* on Duke. I love him.' There's not even a hint of hesitance as I admit such. Because if there's one constant in this world, it's my love for Duke Bennett.

That makes Wyatt blanch. 'You *love* him?'

Unconditionally. Irrevocably. There's no going back now.

Softly, I nod. Rory beams at me, bright eyes twinkling. Yet Wyatt's face only hardens into something stone-cold. Those storm clouds creep into his dark eyes again, swirling with thunderous emotion. He takes a long blink, pressing his lips together, before he says, 'I need a minute.'

And with that, Wyatt disappears out the room, door swinging closed behind him with a thump.

38

Duke

Every smack of rain against the waiting room windows makes my muscles flinch. I pick at the blood crusted around the holes in my jeans from the road burn, my other leg bobbing, while trying to ignore the agonising throb in my shoulder.

It's been an hour since Wyatt and Rory turned up. Since he blatantly ignored me. Maybe that was my sign to leave, but I couldn't, not without knowing Cherry was awake and okay—

'Bennett,' Wyatt's voice rings out across the waiting room, forcing my head to shoot up. He stands in the corridor opposite me, cold, hard eyes locked on where I sit. The ferocity of his glare is enough to make me cower in my seat, but I force myself to stand even as my weary body protests. To meet him and whatever he's planning to throw at me. And if he's here, then Cherry must be awake, and that thought gives me the strength to rise to him.

I just hope she knows I'm out here, waiting. That I wasn't a coward this time.

He marches over, jaw dropping to no doubt volley all his anger at me, but the nurse behind the desk gets there before him, demanding with hands on her hips, 'If you two are planning on having some alpha male stand-off in my hospital, you better think twice and take your asses outside.'

Wyatt's steps screech to a halt as he considers the nurse, seemingly deciding that her wrath is not worth it, then he pivots his direction, breezing straight past me and nodding towards the exit in a silent suggestion.

'Sorry, ma'am,' I throw over my shoulder to the nurse as I follow him. It's the least I can do considering the grief I gave her earlier. She only rolls her eyes at me, though there's a sparkle to them that hadn't been there before.

The covered entrance of the hospital does little to shroud us from the blistering weather outside. The whistling wind has the rain lashing down in slants, still catching the bottom of mine and Wyatt's legs, soaking our jeans. Nonetheless, Wyatt stands there in the shadows, with his broad frame strained and a stubborn fold of his arms. The distant rumble of a summer storm filters through the sound of the pouring rain, while Wyatt remains silent, just piercing me with his daggered stare – the kind he usually saves for the guys checking out his sister.

It makes me swallow thickly.

I realise then that he's waiting for me to speak. To explain myself, I suppose, but there's something more important on my mind— 'How's Cherry doing?'

'She's awake. She's fine,' Wyatt pushes out, then cuts his gaze to the ground beside us, as if he can't stand to look at me for longer than a few seconds. His nostrils flare as he pulls down a breath, releasing it on a weighty exhale when he finally deems me worthy of his glare again. He just shakes his head as he says, 'She's my baby sister, Duke.'

'I know, I'm sorry—'

'And you're supposed to be my best friend.'

My heart drops to my stomach.

'I *am* your best friend.'

He doesn't deign me an immediate response, just a silent glower as a muscle beats in his jaw. I take it as a small victory, that he has no defence to contest me on that. Because I've always been his best friend. That's the whole reason we're here in the first place, in this pointless stand-off, because I was so terrified of upsetting him. Of losing him. After all the years we've stood by each other's sides.

That's why I have to keep fighting back. Why I can't let him push me away.

'I saw the list,' Wyatt says next through gritted teeth.

'The list?'

'Her bucket list, Duke.' He saws out on a humourless laugh, my face dropping as the reality of such kicks in. An eerie chill crawls across my skin and I try to control my breathing, so as not to reveal the trembling in my chest. Wyatt adds, 'I saw everything you've done with her. Even the motorcycle bit added on the end in *your* handwriting.'

Admittedly, even if we hadn't done all the sexual items on her list yet, that last one is too damning. Holding my hands up in surrender, I end up wincing from the way it makes the something in my shoulder grind together unnaturally, pain lancing through my chest. 'Look it didn't start off like that, I promise. We began with the roller-skating – and I invited you guys so it wouldn't give off the wrong impression to her. I was just trying to be her friend when she was in need.'

'Right, because that's what friends do – offer to fuck each other.'

The accusation slaps me across the face, my head rearing back. A string of incomprehensible sounds come out as I realise how Wyatt sees me in this moment – just like Sawyer did when he caught us – I'm a friend that's gone behind his back to sleep with his little sister. Except, that's nowhere near the truth. The opportunity to run my hands over Cherry's bare skin and curves, of getting to coax out her sweet whimpers and give her the pleasure she so rightly deserves is a privilege she's bestowed upon me, but it was never the endgame for helping her. In fact, I'd started this summer trying to encourage the opposite.

No, spending this summer with Cherry was about doing what I could to build her up before she left, to give her the boost she needed to flourish before I lost my chance. Yes, I've put Cherry in danger and got her hurt, and I'll accept his anger for that, but otherwise, we're on the same team here. All I've ever wanted was to make her happy – exactly as does Wyatt. I welcome the chill of the stormy air now as I inhale down a fortifying breath.

Wyatt tears his arms from his chest so he can run a hand through his hair. 'She's only twenty-one, Duke. That doesn't sit right with me.'

'You say that like twenty-one is so young, like I'm taking advantage, when doing the bucket list was Cherry's idea in the first place. What's happened between us was two consenting adults doing what made them happy. She's more than capable of making her own decisions.

She has been for a long time, regardless of whether you've wanted to admit that.'

Something like shock flickers across Wyatt's face, breaking his stone-cold demeanour momentarily. 'What's that supposed to mean?'

I take a step forward, grateful that Wyatt doesn't move back. 'Look, I'm just as guilty of trying to keep Cherry in a cocoon of bubble wrap, to make sure nothing bad happens to her given how much she's dealt with since her fall. But now I realise that doing that, it's only holding her back. She doesn't need all this fussing from us.'

Wyatt scoffs. 'Because you suddenly know her so well.'

'Yeah, I think I do.' I shouldn't be smiling, not in the middle of an argument, but one still creeps into my cheeks faintly, my love for Cherry eager to let itself shine.

'She says she's in love with you, Duke. That's why this is a problem – here you are saying you're helping her out as a friend, doing these sexual things with her as, what? A favour? And now she's gone and fallen in love with you only to get her heart broken.'

She told him she loved me. She wasn't afraid, and neither will I be.

Now my smile swings free, pride rippling in my chest. Wyatt's brow only creases further at my evident joy. 'She's not going to get her heart broken, because I love her too.'

Wyatt's jaw drops. 'You—'

'What are you two doing out here?' Beau Hensley's voice suddenly creeps through the rain, forcing both Wyatt and me to turn towards the entrance where his mom and dad wait, Malia shaking off the umbrella they'd been using.

My smile eviscerates as I'm reminded that it's not just

one Hensley I've let down, but Malia and Beau too – the very people who stepped up and welcomed me into their family whenever I wanted when I was just a lost, grieving ten year old. And this is how I repay them – putting their daughter in the hospital. Still, when they divert their path towards us, their eyes widen with concern rather than anger and then frantically scan me when I fully face them.

'Duke, honey, you're covered in blood,' Malia says, pressing a hand to her chest as she struggles to rip her gaze from my bloodied clothes. 'We need to get you inside and cleaned up.'

'I'm fine, honestly,' I try to brush her off.

'You're not fine, son. You've been in an accident too,' Beau replies, thick brows pulling together. The endearment of *son* doesn't go unmissed, lodging uncomfortably in my heart as the man I've always seen as a brother to me is currently avoiding my eyes while he hovers beside his father.

'Is everything okay?' Malia asks, eyes flicking between me and Wyatt. When neither of us reply, she huffs and folds her arms, pressing us with her stare.

Finally, Wyatt clears his throat and turns to me. His face is too blank to get a read on him. 'You should get your shoulder checked. I saw the way you winced. I don't want you in pain too.'

And then he's trudging back towards the hospital entrance. I take that small suggestion as evidence he still cares, but my heart races at the sight of him walking away from me again.

'Wyatt,' I call out, unable to stop myself.

His shoulders tense as he halts at the entrance but doesn't look around. 'Just . . . give me some time, Duke. I can't deal with all this right now. It's too much.'

39

Duke

'She'll be home soon,' Gram assures me from the armchair where she's reading, glasses having slipped all the way to the end of her nose. 'You're doing the right thing, giving them some space.'

My only response as I lay out on her couch the following morning from the accident, my arm now in a sling thanks to the broken collarbone I suffered from the crash, is to nod, hoping her words might finally settle the pattering mess that is my heart. The long conversation we had yesterday after I turned up at her doorstep, unable to sit alone in my apartment as I waited on news about Cherry, and whether Wyatt had forgiven me yet, eased it somewhat. Connecting with my grandmother over concerns I'd never have dared share before added a whole deeper level to our relationship that I hadn't expected. That I wished I'd have known about before, when I could've been sharing more with her.

But today's a fresh new day with fresh new worries and knowing I can't even call Cherry because of her battered phone and her need to rest, relying on Rory texting me updates instead and to relay any messages I want to send, has written over whatever ease I found yesterday, leaving me with a whirring mind.

The mid-morning sun glints off the edges of Gram's book, illuminating the clinch cover that I hadn't paid any attention to before. It looks scarily like a spicy book I know Cherry and Rory love to talk about, and I'm not sure how I feel about that.

Luckily, I don't have much of chance to dwell on the fact that my girlfriend and friend may have roped my grandmother into their spicy romance book club because the doorbell goes.

'Oh, will you get that, Junior? I've just got to the juicy bit,' Gram says, waving her book at me. The possibility that *the juicy bit* might mean my grandmother is about to read a sex scene with me in the same room has me flying up from the couch and out of the room alone, regardless of whether there's someone at the door. No wonder she comes up with all these filthy words for Scrabble.

The last thing I expect when I open the door is to find Wyatt hovering on the porch. Shadows line his eyes as his gaze stays downcast on the wooden floor for a beat before he offers me a weary smile – one that doesn't quite reach his cheeks.

'Hey,' he says, rubbing the back of his neck. 'Do you have a minute? To talk?'

'Sure.' I cock my head towards the bench on the porch, stepping out and closing the door firmly, even though I'm sure Gram will have her ear pressed up against it the whole time. I drop myself onto the bench, and Wyatt takes a second before he joins, a heavy sigh coming out as he does. Once again, the moment drowns in silence, but I sit in it, waiting for Wyatt to speak first this time since he sought me out.

'What was it in the end?' he asks first, investigating my sling.

'Broken collarbone.'

'Shit.' He scrapes his palm across his stubble. 'Is there anything I can do?'

'Not really. Just gotta rest, keep it in this sling for a while, and I guess I won't be throwing drinks about in the air for a while.'

'Any help you need at the bar, just call me, yeah?' He offers me a brief smile, and relief rushes through my veins just like when the sunshine finally broke through the slate-grey clouds this morning. Because the storm is finally over.

I've not lost him.

'Yeah, thanks, man.'

'So,' he continues, 'you love my sister.' Each word seems pushed out, like the notion doesn't sit right on his tongue. A sentence he probably never expected to say – hell, I never expected anyone to be saying such out loud, not when it was once just a fantasy to me. It still has my head rearing back, has my heart stuttering like I've been caught out, forgetting that it's all laid out in the open now. Nowhere to run. No *need* to run.

'Yeah. A lot, actually,' I laugh out, wincing. 'How's she doing?'

Eventually, a softness takes residence in his eyes. 'She's doing better – we just got her home. She's tired still, but honestly she seems more concerned about *you* than herself.'

My chest falls, muscles finally surrendering, knowing

she's safe, even if I'm not the one to provide her with refuge this time. My next breath might be my easiest yet.

Wyatt lets out a drained laugh, his leg now bobbing, heel of his foot tapping against the wooden boards below. 'Look, I know we don't always do this *talking* thing very well – not about our feelings, anyway. Toxic masculinity or whatever Rory calls it. We should probably work on it – Wolfman and Sawyer too.' He waves the idea off with a snort. Then he turns to me properly – any hints of ire vanished from his stony expression, just a need to understand remaining. It keeps the last sparks of hope in me burning. 'So let me start by apologising for how I acted yesterday – I'm sorry. I'm not gonna pretend I'm not still angry at you for letting her on your bike – I'd be mad at anyone for that.'

I shrug. 'I deserve that – and for what it's worth, I'm angry with myself too.'

'Still . . . I probably could have handled my reaction better, and I am sorry about that. I was overwhelmed, what with the panic of her *and* you being hurt, and then suddenly discovering you two were sleeping together which some people already knew about, but not me, your best friend? None of it made sense to me.' He chews on his lip, gaze floating off into the distance for a moment before returning to me on a sigh. 'So, I'm here to understand, and I need you to talk to me, properly. To tell me what's happening.'

'I can do that.' If it wasn't for Cherry, for how she's teased me open one small part of my life at a time, I'm not sure I'd have the gall. The strength to let him in. But like she said, the more I share, the closer I can get to people. I'm so afraid of losing the ones I love, but if I never let them in, how can I expect them to stay?

Wyatt regards me for a beat, then asks, 'How long has this been going on?'

I let out a long breath, running a hand over my head. 'It's been like this since she started working at the bar.'

Wyatt's eyes flash. 'You've been dating for *years*?'

'No!' I hold my hand up, Wyatt's chest immediately deflating with a relieved laugh. 'No, I've liked – *loved* her, maybe – for years. We've only been seeing each other this summer. I meant it when I said it started just as friends, I promise. I didn't expect this to ever happen.' A laugh teeters out of me as I shake my head. 'I honestly tried to not let this happen.'

'But you always wanted more?' he asks.

I concede, nodding.

'Why didn't you tell me?'

'She's your little sister. It felt wrong. I . . . *Fuck*. You're right, we really do need to get better at talking to each other, because it's hard to explain.'

'That's why we should start now,' Wyatt says, his stare unyielding.

My mouth begins to dry, the truth trying to crawl away, but I force the confession out, knowing I owe it to him. To myself. To Cherry. 'I'm terrified of losing *you*, Wyatt. You're the only one who knows how much I struggled losing my mom, and my grandfather, even if I still never really told you how much. You've always been there for me, and even though I've never cared for someone like I do for Cherry, I didn't want to risk losing you. I love *you* too, Wyatt. I don't have a lot of family left, and you're not just my best friend, you're my brother. I didn't want to ruin that and lose anyone else.'

Wyatt glances to the floor for a second, swallowing, before facing me again. He presses his lips together, then admits, 'I – I love you too, Duke. You're my brother too, and you always will be. It's gonna need a lot more to take you from me, you got that?' He nudges my leg with his, and my heart feels so fucking full, even from the smallest action.

'And I won't pretend I haven't noticed that Cherry seems a lot happier in herself this summer. More confident, definitely. She really put me in my place in that hospital room, and as much as it shocked me, I'm not gonna pretend I wasn't a bit proud of her. I know we as a family don't exactly give her a lot of room to be free – like you said. But . . .' He lets out a long sigh, slumping back in his seat. 'Well, I'm glad she has you to make her feel stronger. Someone who cares for her but doesn't clip her wings.'

'We're always happier when we're flying free, not caged,' I tease, remembering Wyatt's favourite phrase – the one that helped him through all his own difficult decisions and was the inspiration behind the eagle tattoo he got with me once.

'Hey, don't use my tattoo against me,' Wyatt chuckles, the first smile finally spreading out on his face. 'We just gotta promise that we'll talk to each other more, okay? Can't have my best man keeping secrets from me now, can I?'

Best man. My grin is irrepressible.

'Promise.'

Wyatt stands, holding out a hand to help me up – but also a silent confirmation that we're okay. I haven't lost him. He asks, 'You're gonna look after her, right?'

My throat tightens as I slap my hand against his and

let him take some of my weight to pull me up. 'Of course. I'll do anything for her. It's . . . crazy how badly I want to make her happy.'

He snorts. 'Yeah, love will do that to you. One minute I'm living my quiet life on my ranch and the next thing I know I'm planning to convert a barn into a wedding venue for this British wellness influencer I met last year because all I care about is making her smile.'

'You're down bad, you know that?'

'And proud.' He grins lazily. 'So, do you want a ride to my parents' house so you can see her?'

* * *

'I'm assuming the lack of a black eye on either of you guys means you've worked everything out?' Rory jokes when Wyatt and I filter into Cherry's bedroom once we arrive at the Hensleys' house. She's sitting on the bed, snuggled up to Cherry, a laptop resting on her legs.

But I don't get a second to respond because right then, when my eyes land on Cherry properly, exhaustion shadowing under her eyes, everything in the room disappears as my senses tunnel in on only her. My beacon of light in the storm. Cherry straightens up in bed, eyes flicking over me, over the sling that my arm is wrapped up in. Guilt strikes me knowing she's concerned about me when *she's* the one who's only just been moved from a hospital bed.

Still, after her assessment clearly determines I'm okay, she returns those beautiful deep brown eyes to my face, gaze entwining with mine as mirth soaks up her expression, the brightest of grins springing free. And my world finally feels like it can start spinning again, now I'm back with her.

'Yeah, we're good,' Wyatt says, giving me a pat on my uninjured shoulder. Then, he dips his head and clears his throat, bringing his gaze back up to find Cherry. 'Look, I won't lie – this is gonna take some time for me to get used to. You two being together and all that. But you're also two of my favourite people in the world, and hell, I guess in a way that's kinda cool – two of my favourite people, always together.'

'We can double date!' Rory squeals, clapping.

'Yeah, okay, princess.' He perks a brow at Rory and rolls his eyes, but a smile still dances on his lips. 'Anyway, I guess what I want to say is that I trust you both. I really do, Cherry, and I'm sorry if the family hasn't made you feel that way. All I want is for you to be happy, and . . . well, I get the feeling Duke does exactly that for you. He's got a lot of love to give, and you deserve that.' He flashes me a kind look. 'You both do.'

'Thank you, Wyatt,' Cherry replies, mirroring his gentle expression. She pins her shoulders back further, bolstered. 'It means a lot, really.'

'I think, um, maybe we should give you guys some privacy. To talk.' Wyatt cocks his head, and Rory quickly jumps off the bed, rushing over to him.

'We can finish playing *The Sims* tomorrow,' she tells Cherry, before she gives my good arm a quick squeeze and heads out the door with Wyatt, leaving me all alone with Cherry.

Where I belong.

'Hey, you,' she croaks out, silver already rimming her eyes.

'Hey, Baby Hensley,' I say back, pressing my lips into a smile, trying to hide how wobbly it is. 'May I?' I ask, gesturing to the bed.

Cherry nods, shuffling slightly over to make room for me. I place myself beside her legs, letting my hand fall to them, where I can rub reassuring circles against her thigh. She doesn't even blink at the contact – if anything, she relaxes further into the pillows behind her.

She reaches for me, fingers pulsing against my arm. My weary, aching bones calm at the sensation of just being close to her. Brow furrowed, she asks, 'Are you okay? I've been so worried about you.'

'Cherry, I'm fine. It's *you* who anyone should be worrying about. I'm so sorry I wasn't there when you woke up. They wouldn't let me in, and then Wyatt was angry, and I just thought I'd be better going home until you were ready—'

'Duke, stop.' Her brows pull together as a glossiness lingers in her gaze. 'I'm fine, just a bit tired and achy, but that's it. I just know you're beating yourself up right now about what happened, but it wasn't your fault.'

'You had two seizures, Cherry. That wouldn't have happened had I never let you ride my bike.'

She unexpectedly laughs, the sound all silver bells and glorious. 'Maybe you're right. But then maybe I would've had a seizure another time. Maybe I'd forget to take my meds one morning, or drink a little too much alcohol, or get too tired from my period, or do nothing at all and one would still happen sooner or later. That's just life for me, I'm afraid. And you're just going to have to accept that. My life isn't your responsibility, it's *mine*.' Wyatt was right, confidence shines off her like sunbeams. Even in her old pyjamas, she's so bold and beautiful. 'All I need from you is to stay by my side, to stand up for me, just like you did yesterday.'

Gently, I take her hands, trying not to wince too much at the bandages covering them. 'Always, Cherry. I promise you. I was so afraid that I'd lost you for good. That this was the world's way of punishing me for crossing that line with you. By hurting you.' The last words come out strangled, tears surging into my eyes and threatening to fall – a foreign sensation given how I usually strive to lock my emotions away. But no more – for her. For me. 'All I've ever wanted is to be one of the reasons that you smile. Even if I was just there on the sidelines, a brief moment of happiness you might easily forget.'

'It's okay. I'm still here,' she whispers to me, leaning forward to press her forehead against mine, giving me the solace that is feeling her warm skin on mine.

'I told Wyatt everything,' I admit, keeping my gaze entwined with hers. Just staring so deeply into those eyes I would sell my soul to wake up to every goddamn day. 'About how much I love you, how long I've loved you. I even told him how I afraid I was of losing him. I'm done hiding behind these walls I've built. I'm ready to bare the deepest depths of my soul, no matter how dark and fear-ridden, if it means I get the privilege of loving you even for one more second.'

Cherry cups my jaw, pressing a soft kiss to my lips. Despite the gentleness, there's a raging sea of emotions behind the brush of her mouth, unspoken promises waving through me. She whispers against my lips, 'You've got me for far longer than that, believe me. I've waited *years* for you, Duke Bennett. Do you really think I'd give up that easily?'

I kiss her back, this time with more fervour – with the kind of unrelenting need that I'd been holding back all these years. There's a strange rush that comes from being completely honest with your feelings. Hunger overtakes us, Cherry's hands clawing back the bedsheets to free herself as I drag her towards me with my good arm. Her thighs land either side of mine, soft body moulding against me as her tongue dances with mine. As our kisses seal every promise I've ever made to her. All the ones I plan to make to her in the future too.

'I love you so much,' I mumble between kisses.

'I love you so much too,' she responds.

I give her a lazy grin when I break away. 'I hope you're ready for countless Sundays playing dirty Scrabble with my grandmother.'

Cherry giggles, the sound a fucking melody I could listen to on repeat. 'I can't wait.' She mirrors my grin, but her eyelids flutter as she slumps in my grip. 'Lie with me for a bit, will you?'

I nod, twisting us on the bed so we can lie out and I can tuck her into my arms, blissfully unaware of the pain in my shoulder now my body is so overcome with love. Cherry settles her head against me, a hand covering my chest, above where my heart can't help but trip over itself for her. I press one more kiss to her head, stroking my fingers through her silky hair, as I admit, 'I've got you, Baby Hensley.'

Epilogue

Cherry

Two years later

The bar is almost full by the time I get here after work, and it's not even six o'clock yet. With a massive grin on my face – as always whenever I see the red neon bar sign that spells out *Cherry's* above the door – I walk inside and am immediately greeted by a wave of hearty laughter, sparkling conversation, and country music blasting from the jukebox.

Bulbs hang from the rafters above each of the high tables where customers lean, drinking and laughing away the long week. Their smiles are lit up by the rainbow of neon signs buzzing along the walls, interspersed with old licence plates from Colorado and photos from rodeos. Including one of me at my most recent amateur barrel racing competition that sits right behind the bar. *That* I try to pretend isn't there, but the rest of Cherry's I happily soak up, feeling the familiar energy seep into my veins. It's like a little slice of home – exactly how I designed it. My heart is so full the minute my feet hit the wooden floor, transported back to where I grew up, even if I always knew it could never contain me forever.

And of course, home wouldn't be complete without the tall, broad-framed man standing behind the dark wooden bar, the tattoos on his arms shifting as he pours out a cocktail, pure bliss and joy painting his face. He throws his head back with laughter, the biggest grin spreading out while he chats with the customers at the bar, completely in his element. Duke Bennett is as happy and handsome as ever, living the best of both worlds in Willow Ridge and the city – though he still doesn't appreciate it when I call him Hannah Montana because of that, but we'll get him there.

I can't believe there was a time when he actually considered turning down this bar. But I guess there was also a time when I never thought I'd get back on a horse *or* get to fall in love with Duke Bennett. The latter I still don't think has fully hit me even two years later.

I think it's been good for him, though – to branch out and not feel so tied to Willow Ridge all the time. He's still the caring, reserved Duke I've always known him as, but that quiet confidence shines a little brighter these days, a daring side to him waiting for opportunities to arise, as opposed to letting them pass by. Which my college friends loved trying to encourage out every time he'd come visit me during my senior year.

Duke's eyes find me through the crowds before I've even taken three steps inside, and my heart still does a little flip at the sight of him. At the reminder that I don't have to hold back my love for him. That he spends half the week with me in my apartment in the city when I'm working at the interior design firm that hired me straight out of college, and that I get to live with him back in Willow Ridge whenever I'm freelancing and slowly building up that business idea his grandfather laid out for me all those years ago.

It's funny that two years ago, I thought that would be my last summer ever with Duke, and now I couldn't imagine riding off into the sunset with anyone else.

With his eyes never leaving me, I make my way over to the bar, jumping up onto the stool in front of him. He greets me with the brightest of smiles and leans over the bar to kiss me.

'I've missed you,' he whispers against my lips, pressing another kiss to them afterwards. That delicious cypress and leather scent of his fills my senses, and I really wish it was closing time already, because the urge to climb up onto this bar and wrap my legs around him is *strong* tonight. Being adult Cherry is hard work, and this girl needs some relief.

'Missed you too,' I say back breathlessly when he eventually pulls away.

Duke gets straight to pouring me a Jack and Diet Coke. We don't have our closing-time ritual anymore, not now I'm girl-bossing in the interior design world as opposed to clearing up empty glasses with him, but I rather like our new routine of after-work drinks and chats whenever he's up in the city. And the occasional night of being laid out on the bar for him after all the patrons have gone...

'How was your day?' he asks, sliding my drink over

to me. I glance down the bar, noticing how many of his signature cherry-flavoured porn star martinis fill the hands of customers. Another little homage to me, alongside the name and the neon signs shaped like cherries that are dotted throughout the bar.

I take my first sip, and admit, 'Better now I'm with you.' That gets me a bashful smile. 'Oh, I actually got an email today from a ranch a half hour from Willow Ridge that wants help converting a few guest houses. They were inspired by all the stuff I put on my socials about Sunset Ranch and the other retreats I've been working on, it seems.'

'That's amazing. I'm so proud of you.' He reaches over the bar and squeezes my hand, his warmth wrapping around my heart.

When he lets go, he fishes a bottle of beer from the fridges below the bar. Giving a thumbs up to the other bartenders working with him, Duke rounds the bar to meet me, holding out his free hand to help me off the stool. 'The others are already here.'

My gaze follows to where he nods, finding my friends already cosied up in our usual booth beside the dancefloor which Duke keeps free when he knows the gang are coming up for the evening. Wyatt and Rory are snuggled up on one side, glowing from both the honeymoon they just got back from and the post-wedding bliss that has us all convinced there'll be another announcement from them soon. Wolfman's nursing a beer, his laughter howling out and echoing through the bar as he jokes around with Fliss. Even Sawyer made it tonight, his arm tucked around Honey, while her hands rest over her slightly swollen belly. The flickering neon signs lighting up the bar are no match to the bright joy radiating off all my friends.

And it's been like this since the first day Cherry's opened – Wyatt, Wolfman, Sawyer, Rory, and Fliss taking any chance they can to spend the Friday nights Duke has to work up in the city here with him. Showing him that no matter where he goes, they'll always support him, and our relationship – the number of double dates we've been forced on over the last two years is excessive. Still, it has my heart warming, being able to share so much happiness with them.

I grin, turning to Duke. 'Thank God. I'm dying to hear how well Wyatt survived Bali.'

Duke chuckles, shaking his head. 'I still can't believe Rory convinced him to go there on their honeymoon. But I'd put money on him loving every second of it.'

'He did look surprisingly happy in all those pictures Rory put on Instagram.' Pictures I'm sure he had no idea would be shared, anyway. 'Where would you wanna go on your honeymoon?' I ask Duke, musing on the thought myself as I twirl my hair around my finger.

'I don't know.' He shrugs, bunching his lips to the side as he considers. 'Probably somewhere secluded. Where you can just enjoy all the alone time together. Maybe some deserted roads where you can go on rides, and no one will pass by if you decide to stop for a quick break.'

He adds a wink on the end, running a hand down my back until he reaches my hips and gives me a squeeze. Involuntary shivers rush through my body at his touch. Too many memories of all the times he's bent me over his motorcycle in the past two years flash into the forefront of my mind, especially since it became a pretty good way of getting over the fear of riding again after our crash.

Clearly aware of the torturous thoughts he just put in my head, Duke stifles a laugh. 'Besides, I need to get you a ring and a wedding before we can start thinking about a honeymoon.'

'*We?*' I perk a brow at him, pretending that my heart isn't fluttering at the suggestion that just came out of his mouth. The future he's envisioning. 'Who said I was talking about us?'

Duke just levels a look at me while I try my very best – yet still fail – to bite back my grin. He places his hands either side of me on the bar, caging me in his broadness, and I can't help but swallow – at the darkening eyes drinking me in, the way they dip to my lips, making his tongue dart out and wet his own, like he's ready to take a bite. God, I still love how I bring out this uncontrolled version of him.

'Hilarious,' he grumbles, then brushes a featherlight kiss to my lips. His warm breath tingles against my mouth as my own shudders out. Lips still a hairsbreadth from mine, he questions, 'Have I ever told you that you're the bane of my life?'

I grin, fisting his T-shirt to tug him just that little bit closer. 'Maybe, but you still love me.'

He presses his forehead to mine, staring into my soul with those same umber eyes that saved me all those years ago. That have anchored me while I've strived to find my strength again. 'Always, Baby Hensley.'

Author's Note

When I set out writing Cherry's story, I was determined to bring more light and awareness to the health conditions she faces – endometriosis and epilepsy – as these are two conditions that have affected myself and ones that I love. However, I understand that no two people's experiences of these conditions are always the same, and therefore I want to acknowledge that Cherry's experiences are just one example of how these conditions may present and affect one's life, based on my own and my loved one's experiences. Therefore, the representation of her health conditions may not resonate with everyone who also suffers from them.

Cherry's struggles with endometriosis reflect the lack of understanding of women's pain, and the negative impact such can have on our lives. While my own experiences with endometriosis are by no means severe in comparison to some of my friends, there is a burden that comes with having to plan your life around the pain and exhaustion that comes with such a condition. I hope that if more awareness is brought to such, perhaps one day our medical systems will be able to better support women for their pain.

Acknowledgements

Duke and Cherry's story was already flourishing in my mind the second I introduced them in *Live, Ranch, Love*. To me, *Riding the Line* is a story of becoming the author of your own life, no matter the narrative others have set for you, and deciding that your struggles needn't define you. Working on this book came at both one of the best times of my life, and one of the hardest. But it is through working on stories like Cherry and Duke's that I found solace and comfort – and for that, I'll be forever grateful to be an author and working with such amazing people.

So, firstly, I want to thank my stepfather, Martin – for all the laughs and hugs you filled my life with, and for supporting me throughout all my writing endeavours. I'm sorry you never got to see my books published, but you'll always be in my heart.

To Mum, for always being there for me whenever I've needed you and for encouraging me to grow. To Dad and Judith, for your enduring enthusiasm for my writing and shouting about my books from the rooftops. To Hannah, for being the most thoughtful sister in the world and always sharing my weird humour – God knows we've needed it this year!

To Dave, I called you a real-life example of a book boyfriend in my last acknowledgements but every day you set the bar higher. Thank you for taking care of me, for being the best listener, and for bringing so much joy to my life. To my best friends – Izzy, Gina, Jenny, and Clare – thanks for always being by my side and inspiring all the beautiful friendships I get to write about.

To my agent, Maddy, for championing me as an author and always being there for all my random worries. To my wonderful editors, Belinda and Tessa, for your incredible support and expertise which has helped me grow so much as a writer, and for your unceasing love for the *Willow Ridge* series. To the rest of the teams at HarperFiction and Avon, especially Emily, Angelica, DJ, and Madelyn, for your hard work on *Riding the Line*, and the rest of the *Willow Ridge* series – thank you so much.

Another major thank you to Sam and Mel at Ink and Velvet Designs for their talented work on the beautiful UK cover for *Riding the Line* and bringing Duke and Cherry to life so perfectly – you have outdone yourself with this one! To my sensitivity consultants, Kat and Alexia, for helping me create Duke's story and background with authenticity and care. To Andrea, for all your feedback in helping me shape this book.

To the author group chat for all your advice, laughs, and support, and to the bookish friends I've made along the way. Lastly, to the amazing readers who make my days by sharing their love for the *Willow Ridge* series, and continue to support me, even from my indie days. I'm so grateful for you all!